WATCH YOUR MOUTH

KINGS OF THE ICE 2

WATCH YOUR MOUTH

KINGS OF THE ICE 2

KANDI STEINER

Published by Kandi Steiner, LLC
Edited by Elaine York/Allusion Publishing, www.allusionpublishing.com
Cover Photography by Cadwallader Photography/Utterly Unashamed, LLC
Cover Design by Kandi Steiner
Formatting by Elaine York/Allusion Publishing, www.allusionpublishing.com

To the weirdos.

Keep that shit up.

CHAPTER 1

WE RIDE AT DUSK

Jaxson

My whole life, I'd been walking in a fog, in a dense and heavy cloud that I thought would stay with me forever.

But one night with her had brought in the sun.

From the time I was *born*, I knew the plan for my life. That plan revolved around hockey. I had a stick in my hands at the age of three. I was playing on a team by the time I was five. My parents sacrificed family vacations for hockey camps, Christmas presents for hockey gear, and board game or puzzle nights for evenings watching video of every team we could study.

I was meant to live out the dream my father had. The dream that was stolen from him.

And that's what I did.

Don't get me wrong — hockey was *my* dream, too. Nothing filled my soul the way being on the ice did.

But no matter how I performed, I had a lashing waiting at the end of every game from the man whose approval I desired most.

It was impossible for that not to chip away at someone's spirit.

Before I even realized what was happening, I woke up in the middle of a life that felt like it was being lived by someone else. I was a professional hockey player — a defensemen who made my father passively okay with my performance twenty percent of the time and angry as hell the other eighty. He always felt I could do better. He was always pushing me to do *more*.

I survived the pressure through numbing myself with whatever substance I had available — mostly, alcohol and women. Fortunately, I'd also found a family in my teammates, especially in the last year.

Most days, they were the only thing keeping my head above water. They gave me a reason to play — not just for my dad, or for me, but for them.

One of my teammates who was like a brother was Vince Tanev, our new winger who'd stepped in like the leader he was born to be.

Which was exactly why I was trying to ignore the fact that I hadn't thought of much other than his sister since the night he won NHL rookie of the year.

I was at his house now, waiting on our goalie to meet up with us so we could play a round of golf. I hadn't seen them since our weekend out in Austin two weeks ago, everyone settling into the off-season. But now that I was in Vince's space, I couldn't help but think about his sister.

Which was a real fucking problem.

I'd spent the better half of the last fourteen days doing my level best to erase her and that night from my mind. Because it didn't matter how easily the conversation came, how heartily she'd made me laugh, or how my body had hummed to life with her hips in my hands as we danced in a crowded club.

Grace Tanev was off limits.

She was in a relationship. She was eight years younger than me.

She was my *teammate's little sister*.

That was a hurdle not even I could jump.

I didn't understand *why* I even wanted to jump it, but she had done something to me. If my life were going according to plan, then she was the nuclear bomb that blew it all to bits.

It was like she'd shaken me from a deep slumber, and now I was wide awake, looking around with a new perspective on life and absolutely zero desire to go back to bed.

I'd done a somewhat decent job of letting the idea of her go. I had resisted the urge to look her up on social media, had ignored the fact that she'd given me her number, that she'd put it in my phone before we said our goodbye.

Because that was exactly what it was — a goodbye.

Until it wasn't.

"You really want to lose your money *that* badly, Fabio?" Vince asked Carter with a whistle, shaking his head. We were at his new place on the beach, half of it still littered with boxes, waiting for Will Perry to show up so we could hit our tee time. "You know my game puts yours to shame."

Carter Fabbri, or *Fabio* as we called him, had been a rookie this past season, too. Unfortunately, he'd also been sent down to the AHL in March to help them during playoffs. That happened sometimes, if the NHL team could spare a player and the AHL team needed some help. But it always stung like a bitch when you were called down, because it meant one thing was clear: you were expendable.

Still, everything reset after playoffs. Carter had moved to Tampa to show his dedication to the team, and he'd be at camp with the rest of us come September. I wasn't sure where he'd end up after that, but I hoped he'd be with us.

The kid needed to clean up his performance if he wanted a permanent place as a center in the NHL.

"I've been practicing," Carter defended. "Besides, you've been so busy crawling up Maven's ass, my bet is you'll be too distracted to play."

"Hey, leave my ass out of this," Maven called from the kitchen where she was organizing glassware in the cabinets.

"But it's the best one I've ever seen," Carter said with a pout, which earned him a slug on the arm from Vince.

"Gotta say I agree on that one," I piped in, ducking before Vince had the chance to pull me into a chokehold. "I still dream about that yellow dress..."

I smirked with the tease, one I knew would piss Vince off. Maven was his fiancée now, but she'd been in all our lives throughout the season as a reporter tasked with covering Tanev's first year in the NHL. We all knew she was off limits, and we loved her more like a sister now than anything.

But I wouldn't miss out on a chance to give Tanny Boy a hard time.

Vince shoved Carter out of the way and started chasing me, and I dodged the coffee table and hopped over the couch, staying just out of reach. Carter started humming the "Benny Hill Theme Song," clapping his thighs in time with the bazooka sounds he was making with his mouth like we were Tom & Jerry.

I was sliding on my socks around the kitchen island, half-hiding behind a laughing, red-faced Maven, when a figure appeared in the foyer. I thought it was Will at first, so I kept up the charade. But when a suitcase was dropped to the marble floor and a soft cry followed behind it, we all stopped, our heads snapping in that direction.

And there she was.

Staring right at me.

The girl who was impossible to forget.

Those green eyes I'd fallen so easily into that night in Austin were glossy and red, her button-nose the same rosy shade. The bags under her eyes were a terrible hue of purple and gray, her shoulders slumped, bottom lip trembling the longer she stood there without anyone saying a word. She was petite even in heels, but standing there in flip flops, she was so slight, so small, like a little mouse.

Grace Tanev.

Her long, straight blonde hair that had blurred my vision the night I twirled her around on the dance floor in Austin was a tangled mess, dirty and greasy and dull. She'd covered it with a ripped-up ballcap that said *Asshole* on it.

But even with her lips in a flat line, I could remember her smile.

I could remember her laugh, her ridiculous dance moves, her even more ridiculous questions.

I remembered everything.

As put out as she looked, her bronze skin still blazed against the white t-shirt she wore, against the tiny denim shorts she wore with it, like she had been at the beach for weeks. Her shirt had a cartoon of an opossum wielding a gun like a cowboy and the text under it said *we ride at dusk*.

I would have laughed if the sight of her didn't make my chest spark with something possessive and feral.

She looked like hell, like she'd been *through* hell, and yet she was still the most beautiful thing I'd ever seen.

Before I could think better of it, I started toward her — at the very same time Vince did. He gave me a strange look before I stopped in my tracks and he continued on, rushing to his sister and wrapping her in a fierce hug.

Maven turned back to unpacking, giving them privacy, and Carter pretended to be on his phone.

I, on the other hand, couldn't look away.

What the fuck is wrong with me?

A flash of that night with her danced in my vision, and I knew the answer to my question. I thought I'd never see her again. I thought I was strong, resisting the urge to text her or to attempt to keep the connection we had so easily when I knew it was a bad idea.

But now she was here, in the same room with me, and I felt her pulling me in like a goddamn magnet.

Vince stepped back after a moment, holding Grace's shoulders in his hands as he spoke in a hushed voice to her. She said something back, and then Vince hugged her again and grabbed her suitcase. They walked down the hall and up the stairs, and when they were gone, Maven blew out a breath.

"That didn't look good," she said.

Carter's mouth pulled to the side as he looked up the stairs and then back at me. His eyes narrowed a bit then, but before he could say a word, Vince was back, running a hand over his head.

"She okay?" Maven asked.

"No," he said. "But she will be. I told her she could stay here with us."

"Of course," Maven said, rounding the kitchen island until she was slipping her arms around Vince's waist. "For as long as she needs."

Vince nodded, blowing out a breath and kissing Maven's forehead. He seemed to relax with her embracing him, but my muscles were coiled tight.

Carter tried to lighten the mood with a joke, and then our goalie walked in, breaking the tension of the moment as he grumped about it being too hot to play golf.

He was always grumping about something.

I mumbled a quiet lie about needing to use the bathroom before we left, excusing myself down the hall.

Then, I glanced over my shoulder to make sure no one was watching, and I made my way up the stairs two at a time.

You are an idiot.

Turn around.

She doesn't want to see anyone right now, least of all you.

She's fucking crying, bro.

Leave. Her. Alone.

I heard every word my common sense was trying to scream at me, but it was like I had plugs stuffed into both my ears, like I had no choice. My body moved without me wanting it to, mind powerless to stop me.

Vince's new place was massive, with so many rooms I wasn't sure which one he would have put Grace in. But I heard her sniffling through a cracked door toward the middle, and I paused just outside it, rapping my knuckles lightly on the wood.

"Come in," she said softly, pathetically, her voice hoarse.

I pushed the door open just enough to see her, for her to see me, and then we both froze.

I wasn't sure what I expected. Maybe it was for her to tell me to fuck off and leave her alone, because when she lit up with a smile, it twisted my gut — like I didn't deserve that, like it was dangerous for me to want every smile she ever had to give. Her cheeks lifted, eyes crinkling, and two more tears slid down in perfect unison, like the smile had set them free.

"Hey," she said, and it was just one word, just a greeting. But that smile, the way she watched me, it made me feel like I had the power to make everything okay.

"Who do I have to kill?"

She choked on something between a sob and a laugh, wiping her nose with a bunched-up tissue in her hands. She swiped the tears away next. "He's not worth the jail time."

My chest ignited then, the spark turning to flame.

He.

That confirmed my suspicion.

That night in Austin, she'd told me in the most adorable, but firm way that she was taken, dating some guy she'd met camping. Even then, I had a feeling he was a fuck boy. In fact, I was pretty sure she knew it, too.

Judging by her tear-stained face now, the guy had blown it.

Idiot.

"You okay?"

Her smile waned. "Yeah, yeah," she said quickly, waving her hand in the air like she was swatting a gnat away. "It's his loss, right?" She shook her head, her voice fading, and I had a feeling she was just repeating something a friend had said to try to make her feel better. "Nothing a little sunshine and saltwater can't fix."

She forced another smile, and I frowned, stepping more fully into the room.

"You don't have to do that."

"Do what?"

"Pretend to be fine. Pretend like you're not hurting. Pretend like the bright side is all you're thinking of."

Her eyebrows slid together, but then she looked down at where her hands still clutched the balled-up tissue, and she shrugged.

"It's easier than admitting the truth."

Carter called my name from downstairs, and I cursed, stepping out of the room and down the hall a bit before yelling, "Be right there!"

Then, I slid back into the doorway, chest aching at the sight of Grace so small on that large, four-post bed. It was pretty much the only thing in the room so far, other than an empty bookshelf, a few pieces of art on the floor leaning against the wall, a half-dozen plants, and a TV mounted but not hooked up yet.

"Go," she said with a weak smile. "I'm fine."

But her eyes said differently.

"What are you doing now?"

The question blurted out of my stupid mouth before I even thought about it — which was obvious, considering if I *had* thought about it, I would have kept my mouth shut. I would have listened to her when she told me to go. No — I wouldn't have come up here *at all*. I would still be downstairs, pretending like I didn't care that my teammate's sister had swung back into my orbit.

Grace arched a brow, and then sat up straighter, painting on another fake smile. "Hosting a ball. Isn't it obvious?" She splayed her hands, waving them out over herself and the room.

The corner of my mouth twitched up. This girl was heartbroken, and yet she was making jokes.

Two could play at that.

"Okay. So tomorrow, after your ball is over, of course," I looked up at her with a smirk on my face. "What are you doing then?"

"I really haven't gotten that far," she whispered sadly, thoughtfully.

"What if we went for a drive?"

Again — what the fuck, Jaxson?

"A drive?"

I nodded, even as my subconscious told me to shake my head and say *never mind, I'm an idiot, excuse me while I fuck off and leave you alone like I should have in the first place.*

"Where?" she asked.

"Anywhere."

She folded her arms. "And my brother?"

A warning flared in my gut, but I ignored it. "Do you tell your brother everything?"

What. Is. Wrong. With me?

This was a girl with a broken heart, fresh out of a relationship that clearly hurt her. She was twenty-two — far too young for me.

This was Grace Tanev, my teammate and one of my best friend's little sister.

Walk away, logic begged me. *This is not your place.*

But I stood tall, rooted in place against my will, watching her and waiting for her to be the stronger one because apparently, I couldn't be.

Mischief bloomed to life in her sea green eyes, the first real smile I'd seen since Austin curling on her light pink lips. Then, she popped off the bed.

"Road trip?"

My eyebrows shot up.

I had more of a drive along the beach in mind, or maybe a long winding road in the country. But that didn't stop me from opening my stupid mouth and replying, "If that's what you need."

If that's what you need, Jax?

This was absolutely insane.

Again, I felt like a prisoner in my own body, like no matter how loudly my common sense raged inside my head, I couldn't obey it even if I wanted to.

Because clearly, I *didn't* want to.

Just being back in this girl's presence had scrambled my fucking brain.

Her eyes narrowed a bit, like she didn't quite believe I was serious.

That made two of us.

"What about practice?"

"Off-season," I explained. And at that point, whatever was left of my common sense turned its back on me.

Grace's eyes sparkled like diamonds.

"Anywhere?" she asked, echoing my earlier sentiment.

"Anywhere."

Her smile climbed even more, and she crossed the room in two strides, holding out her hand for mine.

"We ride at dusk," she said, referencing her shirt.

I ignored the sirens in my mind when I took her hand, and she shook it like we'd just done a multi-million-dollar business deal. Then, she backed away in a moonwalk, making finger guns and a *pew pew* sound that made me snort out a laugh through my nose.

I was pretty sure I'd just taken a wrong turn and steered myself right toward Disasterville.

But I couldn't find it in me to change course.

CHAPTER 2

DON'T YOU FUCKERS EVEN THINK ABOUT IT

Two Weeks Earlier
Grace

I was used to cheering for my brother from the sidelines.

I'd been doing it my entire life.

From the time I was a baby strapped to my mom's chest and watching him learn how to hold a stick, my eyes had been cast up to my older brother. I'd watched him learn to play hockey as an awkward kid, watched him get a little better as a hormonal teenager, and watched him absolutely dominate as he transitioned from a boy to a man.

I looked up to him.

Perhaps because I never had a choice in the matter.

So, when I got to be there to see him accept the Calder Memorial Trophy at the NHL awards, essentially declaring him the rookie of the year — I wasn't the least bit surprised. I stood and clapped and screamed so loud the tables of athletes and their families around us stared at me like I was a wild child. I think even my parents — who were also screaming — were a little embarrassed by me.

Of course, I was used to that, too.

But regardless of living in Vince's shadow, I was still bursting with pride for him. That was my brother. He was a leader, a damn good hockey player, and an even better man.

I was honored to be his little sister.

The award ceremony was in Austin, Texas, this year, and I'd flown down from Michigan alongside my parents without a second thought. There was no way they'd miss anything when it came to Vince.

It was already unbearably hot in the city, something most of the attendees were complaining about. Me, on the other hand? I loved the heat. I'd take a simmering day in the city over a winter day in Michigan anytime.

Mom and Dad bowed out once the award ceremony wrapped up, knowing the debauchery that would take place soon after wasn't something they wanted to take part in. They doted on Vince for a half hour before finally hugging him goodnight, and then me by proxy.

I breathed easier once they were gone.

"Are you ready for this?" Maven asked me, threading her arm through mine as we followed the rest of the Tampa Bay Ospreys team toward the party bus waiting to take us out on the town. Maven was my brother's new girlfriend — which had shocked us all, considering he'd never been the relationship type. Maven was a catch, though — smart as hell, quick-witted, and absolutely gorgeous. She was watching me with her warm honey eyes now, her smile wide and bright.

"Are you kidding? I was *born* for this," I told her with a grin, shimmying my hips with a little twerk against her.

She barked out a laugh. "You're just like your brother."

I wish.

The thought was sudden, like a bolt of lightning, but it burned out just as quickly.

We boarded the party bus to the roar of two-dozen rowdy teammates, all of them chanting Vince's name as he hoisted the Calder Trophy high over his head in victory. He propped his foot on the first bus seat and did a ridiculous body roll celly dance with the trophy, making the bus full of hockey players cheer louder.

I'd seen it a million times, my brother celebrating. He was just the kind of person who excelled at everything he put his mind to. The fact that he was currently holding the trophy for NHL rookie of the year, *and* he could also craft beautiful vases out of clay, was proof of that.

"It's so loud!" I screamed over the noise.

Maven laughed, squeezing my arm. We paused by the driver at the front of the bus as my brother held his trophy up proudly.

"I've dreamed about this moment since I was in high school," he said, and by some miracle, the guys on the bus calmed enough so they could hear him. "Back then, I saw it as a solo award..."

He continued on, but I only half listened as I scanned the bus full of men watching him with rapt attention.

The Tampa Bay Ospreys.

I'd seen these guys clown around, heard them chirp each other enough that I knew they were like family. But in this moment, they were all focused on Vince, respect shining through their expressions.

He was already a leader to them after just one year on the team, and that made my chest swell with pride again.

As I scanned their faces, my eyes locked with a pair of twilight blue ones in the very back.

Jaxson Brittain.

He was a defenseman for the team, that much I knew because whatever team Vince was on, I made it my mission to know everything about them. I was my brother's biggest cheerleader — other than our parents.

I also particularly remembered Jaxson because of how those bright blue eyes had trailed the length of me on the tarmac in December when my parents and I had surprised Vince for Christmas.

That was *before* he knew I was his teammate's little sister, back when there wasn't a giant red flag protruding from my forehead.

And in that moment, his eyes had devoured me, had seared my skin and sparkled with dark, delicious promises.

I'd basked in the glow of his attention — however brief it was.

The memory of it now sent goosebumps parading down my spine.

Jaxson blinked, and I tore my gaze away and back to my brother just in time to see him pour a beer into his new trophy before chugging it to the wild approval from all his teammates.

"I hope you're ready for a long night out," Maven said to me.

In the next instant, she was tugged into my brother's lap, and I cleared my throat and looked away uncomfortably so I wouldn't have nightmares from watching him maul her. I was looking up at the ceiling when my brother acknowledged I was still there.

"Oh, shit, here, Gracie," he said, moving the trophy and scooting over so I could sit next to where Maven was still in his lap.

I scoffed, pulling my hair behind one shoulder. "Please. I'll pass on the third wheel." I turned to the bus full of Ospreys next. "Who's got an open seat next to them?"

It was silent for two seconds.

And then the bus erupted into chatter, every guy yelling for my attention while they shoved teammates out of seats to make room.

Maven laughed when I waggled my brows at her, a shit-eating grin on my face. I loved to fuck with my over-protective brother, and flirting with his teammates was the easiest way to do it.

Vince's jaw was tight as he stood up and pointed a death finger at every single one of them.

"Don't you fuckers even think about it." He glowered at everyone before focusing on Jaxson at the very back, and with a snap of his fingers, the sergeant gave his order. "Jax, let her sit next to you. You're the only one I can trust."

Those blue eyes slid to me again, only this time, they were wide open.

I thought I saw him swallow, which made me grin.

Nothing like making my brother's friends uncomfortable. I'd been doing *that* most my life, too, since he'd threatened every friend he'd had to stay far away from me.

Vince pointed at me next. "If any of them lay a hand on you—"

"Oh, my God. *Relax*," I said, and then I skipped to the back of the bus, smiling at every player as I passed.

I sank into the seat next to Jaxson, beaming at him with a mischievous smile.

"Hi," I said.

And this time I was close enough to see him gulp. "Hi."

God, that voice.

He spoke in a baritone, one I felt like an earthquake in the very foundation of who I was. That one word had rumbled through his chest, deep and smooth and subtly confident. If hockey ever failed him, he'd have a career in commercial voiceover.

I'd buy anything he was selling if he told me I was a good girl afterward.

One of the players tapped me on the shoulder, handing me a beer, which I chugged in one of my favorite party tricks to the roar of the back half of the bus.

I'd made it my mission in college to learn how to shotgun a beer better than any guy who challenged me. To be honest, that was about my *only* mission in college. I'd never been the academic type. But the frat parties and long nights on the town with my fake ID in hand had turned out useful.

It was fun to surprise people when they saw you as just a petite little thing.

I wiped the suds from my lips with the back of my arm when I turned back to Jaxson, and my smile climbed as his eyes raked slowly over me. He didn't do it as unabashedly as he had that first time on the tarmac, though.

This time, it was like it was against his own will, like I was something he shouldn't look at but couldn't help himself.

Kind of like a car wreck.

Which was what I felt like most of the time, if I was being honest.

"You shouldn't look at me like that," I said.

A muscle in his jaw tightened, his eyes flicking up to meet mine.

"I have a boyfriend. Well," I amended, tapping my chin as I took another beer from someone who offered it. I cracked the top and sipped from this one rather than downing it, sitting back in the seat and crossing my legs.

"Technically, we haven't put a label on anything, but we do very boyfriend-girlfriend things."

The truth behind that vague and awkward statement was that I'd met Trent while sharing a joint around a campfire in May, and then we'd hooked up in his van. I'd kind of just followed him around like a puppy dog since, mostly because I didn't exactly know what else to do.

But he didn't seem to mind having me around, and even though he told me he wasn't looking for any kind of relationship, he got jealous when he saw other guys try to talk to me. He also showed me public displays of affection, bought me gifts, texted me all day every day, and made plans that included both of us.

Felt very *relationship-y* to me, but what did I know.

"Trust me — you having a boyfriend is the least of my concerns when it comes to looking at you," Jaxson said.

I smiled at his honesty. "Ah, scared of my brother, huh?"

"I respect him."

"Same thing."

He chuckled, leaning back against the window as he took a pull from his own beer. "This is one of your favorite games to play, isn't it?" he asked. "Making your brother's friends fear for their lives."

"Top five favorite for sure," I confirmed. "But don't worry, I think he's preoccupied enough tonight that he won't watch you too closely."

I nodded toward where Vince and Maven were making out at the front of the bus, her straddling his lap, and him doing a piss-poor job of hiding the fact that he had a hand up her dress.

Jaxson laughed a little through his nose before his attention was on me again.

Fuck, he was hot.

Not the kind of hot I was used to, either. I'd been around hockey players my entire life. I *knew* the kind of hot they were, the swagger they walked with, the long, messy hair and crooked grins and scars in all the right places that made them look *just* bad enough to get you into trouble.

But Jaxson Brittain was a breed all his own.

His dark brown hair wasn't long and unruly, but medium length, tamed enough to look like he tried while also being just messy enough to make you want to curl your fingers in the strands and tug.

Every angle of his face was sharp — the slope of his nose, the cut of his jawline, the angle of his cheekbones. He had a face that was almost too pretty for hockey, with scruff lining his upper lip and the span of his jaw.

I wanted to touch that scruff, to feel it under my fingertips and against my neck.

Add in the fact that he had a mouth that did things to you — whether he ever touched you with it or not — and it was maddening. His bottom lip was plump and inviting, the curl of his smirk promising he knew *just* how to use that mouth, too.

He was built only the way a defenseman could be, with muscles that coiled his arms and back and abdomen and legs. I didn't need to see him without his clothes off to know that, either. You could see the bulges, lines, and cuts through his button down, could spy how his thick thighs stretched the seams of his slacks.

My bet was that he had an ass of stone, too.

I'd make that my number one mission to find out when we stood up to get off this bus.

As if the fact that he had a body cut by years of playing one of the most brutal sports wasn't hot enough, he'd also covered half that body with tattoos.

Long, sweeping lines of blue and black ink wrapped around his right arm, covering him from wrist to shoulder. I couldn't see those tattoos now, not in the suit he was wearing, but I'd marveled at them that first day I'd seen him on the tarmac.

I wondered if it was just his arm that was inked, or if there was more to discover under those expensive threads he wore.

And the icing on the Jaxson Brittain cake?

His eyes.

Diamond blue, somehow icy cold and searing hot at the same time. His dark brows were almost always folded over them, even when he smirked, but those blue pools shone regardless. They were the kind of eyes that saw right through you, that made you want to back down and look away for fear of having every dirty little secret you'd ever kept hidden discovered.

Those eyes were fixed on me at the moment, narrowed a bit, like he was trying to figure out the answer to a question I hadn't asked him.

"You're going to get me into trouble tonight, aren't you?" he asked as the bus carried us toward 6th Street.

I smiled, my hair falling over my face a little as I took a sip of my beer. I peeked up at him with a smile that would have made my *not-boyfriend Trent* grit his teeth in jealousy. My high heel dragged against the outer seam of his dress slacks as I crossed my legs the other way, leaning in a bit closer, and his eyes followed that movement with one eyebrow slowly arching into his hairline.

"I have a feeling you can find trouble all on your own."

It was a dare, one I could make with faux confidence because I knew none of my brother's teammates would ever take it.

But when Jaxson slicked his bottom lip, his blue eyes sparking with mischief...

I prayed he'd be the first.

CHAPTER 3

ONE-TWO PUNCH TO THE GUT

Jaxson

She wasn't wrong.

I was perfectly capable of finding trouble all on my own, and with her in the seat next to me, I didn't have to look far.

The first time I'd laid eyes on Grace Tanev on the tarmac at the Tampa Airport, I hadn't *known* she had that last name attached to her. I hadn't known those toned, tanned legs under the sundress she wore were off limits, or that the curious smile she'd thrown at me was her laughing in her head at my expense.

She'd known I was observing her with intent, that I wanted her.

And she'd had a grand ol' time watching me put the pieces together once I realized she was Vince's little sister.

That was months ago now, and I'd dropped the thought of her easily with us being in the heat of a winning season.

But when she'd walked onto this bus tonight, I'd felt that same spark in my chest, the one that made me want to grab her by the waist, sit her in my lap, and bark at any one of my fucking teammates that dared get too close.

That fire had been doused, however, when Vince told her to sit with me — tacking on that I was the only one he could trust.

Fuck me.

Now, her leg was brushing mine, bare and smooth under the little black dress she had on for the night's occasion. She also had a delicate pair of crystal-studded heels strapped around her ankles — one of which she not-so-subtly dragged along my leg when she switched positions.

She knew exactly what she was doing.

And if I didn't show restraint, my teammate would have my ass.

"Why are you so tense?"

Her question snapped my eyes back to hers.

I hadn't realized I'd been trailing her again, but it was a habit I was hard-pressed to break when I had a fucking knockout right in front of me.

She was the kind of beautiful that socked the breath out of you, a one-two punch to the gut every time she flashed her bright smile in your direction. Long blonde hair, plump pink lips, emerald green eyes laced with fire — all wrapped up in a sweet little package that made me want to toss her onto the nearest bed just because I knew I could do so easily.

"That's a blunt assumption," I said, regaining my composure.

"It's a fact. Look at you," she said, waving her hand

over me. "Your shoulders are up by your ears, and there's a vein popping out of your neck."

I had to bite down my laugh, along with the urge to tell her that my *tension* came mostly from keeping my hands to myself right now.

"You read body language, I take it."

"I do," she said with a smug smile, admiring her nails before she took another sip of her beer. I noted that her nails were cut short and void of polish, which made me even more amused by the gesture. "Palms, too."

"You read palms?"

"And tarot cards."

My eyebrow ticked up. "How very witchy."

"Careful, or I just might put you under my spell."

She wiggled her fingers with her eyes all big and bug-eyed in an attempt to rattle me, but I kept my gaze fixed on hers, taking a lazy swig from my beer.

She dropped her hand against her thigh with a smack, her lips flattening at my lack of response. "See? You're ramrod stiff."

The corner of my mouth quirked up.

If only she knew how *ramrod stiff* she could make me.

The party bus rolled to a stop at the edge of 6th Street, and my teammates spilled out into the rowdy Austin night one after the other. I sucked down the last of my beer, ready to join them, and as soon as my hand was free — Grace grabbed it.

It was so small in mine, so smooth where mine was rough, warm where mine was cold. And I felt it, from that very first touch — a jolt of electricity like Zeus himself had cast down a bolt of lightning. It was a warning sign and an invitation to the brave all at once.

I took the bait like a fucking sunfish.

"Come on," she said, tugging me down the aisle.

She let go only long enough to throw herself at the stripper pole in the middle of the bus, looking more like a primate swinging from a tree than anything close to sexy, before she snagged me again and pulled me behind her.

"Let's dance."

"I don't dance."

She sucked her teeth, glaring at me over her shoulder. "You're not allowed to be a fuddy duddy tonight. Not on my watch. So, drop your ego at the door, *Brittzy*."

She smiled auspiciously when I laughed at her using the nickname only my teammates called me by. Then, she stopped her forward movement, turning around until she was pressing up onto her toes with that smile right in my face.

"Tonight? You dance."

I tongued my cheek, shaking my head at her before she was skipping into the first bar with me having no choice but to let her pull me with her. I half-expected Vince to stop me with a hard fist to the chest when she hauled me right past him, but he was completely oblivious — already tangled up in Maven at the edge of the long bar.

Grace weaved us through the thickening crowd, pushing farther and farther until we were damn near crushed between those dancing in the back and those swarming the DJ booth at the front.

When she found the spot she liked, she twisted so quickly I practically ran into her. Her arms threaded around my neck as much as they could with me being so much taller than she was, and I had no choice but to find her hips with my hands — more to stop us from toppling over than anything else.

She beamed up at me, mischief and a dare sparkling in her eyes.

Then, she swayed her hips where I held them, side to side in a slow, teasing rhythm as she leaned in even closer.

"Don't look so scared," she said over the music, and then she turned, her back against my chest.

I removed my hands, holding them up like I was surrendering as she backed up even more, until her ass was slowly rubbing against the zipper of my slacks.

Fucking Christ.

She leaned her head back against my chest, smirking at the expression on my face before she grabbed my hands and moved them to her hips again.

"Relax," she said, the word drowning in the bass thumping from the speaker. "It's just dancing."

My nostrils flared when she slowed her tempo even more, one hand gripping me by the back of the neck while the other covered one of my hands on her waist. She wound her tight little body against me, and from this angle, I had a perfect view of the two modest swells hidden under her thin-strapped black dress.

She wasn't wearing a bra.

I groaned, biting my lip and looking up at the ceiling. I was halfway through naming all the Canadian provinces and territories when Grace dragged one finger along my jaw line.

It was slow and methodic, that fingertip taking my chin down with it until I was looking at her. The amusement in her green eyes died a little when mine found hers, something hotter slipping in on its heels.

And I was a stupid sonofabitch with a death sentence apparently, because I muttered a *fuck it* under my breath and gripped her hips against me even tighter before fitting us together.

The corner of her lips quirked up in victory, but she didn't tear her eyes away. She just watched me as my hands gripped the fabric of her dress, bunching it a little the more we moved. The beat was heavy and bass-driven, the crowd like a heartbeat around us. And just when I had the hang of it, Grace switched her tempo from side to side to just leaning against me and *barely* rolling her body.

I watched the wave-like movement of her chest, stomach, and pelvis, all while feeling every inch of the dance against me. The bottom of that body roll had her ass rubbing against me in a way that left me no fucking choice but to pop a boner.

I felt like a goddamn high schooler instead of a thirty-year-old man.

Snapping out of my daze, I matched her movement again, and when I did, it was enough to have me cursing under my breath.

We were practically fucking on that dance floor.

It didn't matter that we were fully clothed. She pressed against me just as hard as I gripped her to me, and all my restraint was obliterated with her ass rubbing against my cock.

Grace closed her eyes, leaning her head against my chest, and then she wrapped her hands over mine and started dragging them over her body. It was slow and subtle, so much so that anyone around us wouldn't have noticed.

But the second she ran my hand up her rib cage, I stopped breathing.

Grace had the decency to pause, but then she laced her fingers over mine and, together, we cupped her breast.

I was toast.

"Fuck," I ground out, and chills erupted over her shoulder where I'd muttered the curse. I tested the weight of her, palming her more confidently and feeling the fabric of her dress with my thumb until I struck gold, finding her nipple peaked.

She let out an exhale of a moan when I thumbed that precious discovery.

Then, in a strange fucking twist of events, the song cut out suddenly.

And a loud, high-energy country song swept in to take its place.

CHAPTER 4

WOULD YOU RATHER...

Jaxson

Everyone on the dance floor seemed used to the sudden change in tempo, save for me and Grace. They broke apart quickly, clearing the floor — or rather, getting into place for a line dance that they were all apparently accustomed to.

I all but threw Grace away from me, but she didn't react at all. She spun in a circle with her hands above her head like I'd meant to twirl her out, and then she pointed two finger guns at me and started moon walking backward.

I wanted to laugh, but I was too busy adjusting my fucking hard-on in my slacks and hoping the lights weren't bright enough for anyone to notice it. I checked where most of my teammates were at the bar, feeling a little relieved to find Vince still preoccupied with Maven.

Grace smirked knowingly, but then she fell right in line with a woman next to her and started watching her steps, attempting to pick up the line dance.

I took that as my cue to exit the dance floor.

I didn't make it four steps before I was being dragged backward.

"Oh, no you don't," Grace said, pulling me to line up next to her.

We were both nearly knocked over by the sudden turn and kick in the dance, and Grace laughed as I steadied her with my hands on her waist before we had no choice but to turn around again.

"Keep up!" she yelled over the music.

And I tried, I really did, but while Grace focused on the feet of everyone around her and eventually got the rhythm of the line dance, I just sort of maneuvered around everyone and tried not to be in the way.

I also watched Grace.

She was enthralling, all smiles and shiny eyes as she laughed and twirled and made friends with everyone around her. They were all giving her high-fives by the end of it, and then she turned toward me with a mischievous grin as a two-step began.

That was a dance I could somewhat keep up with.

Growing up in Alberta, I'd been to more than my fair share of country bars. Line dances never called to me, but any excuse to get close to a pretty girl had me chomping at the bit.

I took Grace by the hand and twirled her around the edges of the dance floor while another line dance took place in the middle, and then the cycle repeated itself.

We stopped dancing only long enough to take shots or refill our beers before Grace would be tugging me back out on the floor.

It had been almost an hour when I hit my breaking point, sliding through the crowd when Grace was tied up in another line dance. I checked to make sure the team wasn't leaving yet before slipping out the back door of the bar to a small courtyard.

It was mostly empty, just a few guys at a table in the corner and a couple making out on a bench under the Edison lights. I blew out a breath, leaning against the brick wall and sucking down half of my fresh beer in an attempt to cool myself off. I was a sweaty mess, my dress shirt sticking to my chest and arms like I'd just played an entire period without a line change.

I noted the guys were eyeing me kind of curiously then, muttering to themselves. I recognized that look on their face. It was the look I got from strangers when they wondered if they knew me, when they thought to themselves, *he looks so familiar*.

Only the true hockey fans figured it out.

I wasn't in the spotlight the way Vince was, didn't have a million groupies on the Internet — mostly because I barely posted there, anyway.

But these guys must have been fans, because one of them lifted his beer and said, "Hell of a season this year, Jax."

I tilted my beer toward him in a salute of thanks, and I really *was* thankful, because he and his friends left it at that. No one asked for a photo or an autograph, and I went right back to leaning against the brick wall and trying to cool down.

"I am a tipsy little nipsy!"

Grace wobbled out of the bar a little unsteady on her high heels, all but falling into me before she straightened and peered up at me.

"A what now?" I asked with a grin of my own.

"A tipsy little nipsy," she repeated — as if it'd make more sense the second time. Then, she shimmied her shoulders a little and leaned against the wall next to me, letting her head fall back against the brick on a sigh. "I love dancing. Dancing always makes me feel free."

"Funny. It makes me feel reckless."

She smiled without opening her eyes, like she already knew that, like it was her plan all along.

"Well, you needed to loosen up."

"Tell that to your brother when he knocks me back to last Tuesday."

"He didn't see a thing."

"How do you know?"

"You're still standing, aren't you?"

She peeked one eye open at me with that, a little smile on her lips, and then she turned where she was leaning against the wall until it was her shoulder on the brick instead of her back. She scrunched her nose up at me.

"Would you rather be a fish or a bird?"

I blinked.

And then I barked out a laugh. "Come again?"

"A fish or a bird, Brittzy. It's not a hard one."

I opened my mouth to respond, and then just laughed and shook my head instead. "Uh, a bird, I guess."

"Why?"

"I don't know. Flying seems cool."

Her mouth pulled to the side. "Fair. I'd be a fish, though. Imagine being able to breathe under water? And you know that feeling, when you're just lying on your back and floating?"

She spread her arms out and closed her eyes, her face softening in a peaceful bliss.

"Everything is so quiet. Nowhere to be. No *one* to be. You just... exist."

I thought I saw something sad tinge her expression then, but she dropped her arms against her sides with a slap before I could fully register it.

"Okay. How about this one. Imagine you have two miniature legs that are constantly kicking," she said, illustrating the scenario with her index and middle finger. She pointed them down in an upside-down peace sign and wiggled them back and forth like they were walking legs. "Would you want them attached to your chin, or your gooch?"

The laugh that barreled out of me was impossible to contain, and Grace smiled wider, moving the wiggling fingers under her chin before she popped them down in-between her legs in the most unattractive gesture I'd ever witnessed from a woman.

"Come on, you gotta pick one," she goaded.

I was laughing so hard I had a stitch in my side, watching her move those fingers back and forth between the options.

"This is the fucking weirdest question I've ever been asked in my life."

"Beats talking about the weather though, doesn't it?"

I wiped a hand over my mouth and shook my head before crossing my arms over my chest. "I don't know. My chin, I guess."

"Nice," she said. "You could join a circus. Or maybe have your own show in Vegas. Oh! Would you put shoes on the feet, or just let them be barefoot?"

"Shoes, of course. I'm not a monster."

Grace laughed, and the sound was so fucking sweet I felt it like a longing pain in my chest, the kind you get when you recall a memory of someone no longer in your life.

Maybe it was my body reminding me how off limits she was.

"I think you missed out on the gooch opportunity, frankly," she said, and then she reached down and thumbed off both of her high heels, holding them by the straps in one hand. "Imagine how fun it could be for your... *partner*."

"Is this you telling me you like to be kicked in the twat? Because weird but also intriguing."

She snapped her gaze to mine. "Why do you think it would ever be me?"

Grace held that serious expression long enough to make the smile melt off mine.

"Fuck, I didn't—" I cursed inwardly as my chest tightened with a zip of anxiety at what I'd said. "I was just—"

"Gotcha."

She pointed her finger at me, no doubt delighting in the way all the blood had drained from my face. I stood there with my mouth open like a guppy as her head fell back on a loud laugh before she pushed off the wall and did a little spin, her heels twirling in her hand over her head.

She stopped suddenly, her eyes wide like she just had an idea.

"Give me your phone," she said, holding her hand out.

I was still rebounding from her little joke, and I blamed the witchcraft she admitted to earlier for how I obeyed her command without hesitation.

Grace thumbed out her number and saved it in my phone before tossing it back to me.

"There. Now you have my number."

I'd no sooner caught the thing before Grace was twirling again, humming to herself as her bare feet danced on the dirty ground.

I slid my phone into my pocket just in time for her to trip and fall into me.

I caught her hips in my hands as she laughed, and then she smiled up at me, holding her heels in one hand while the other just *barely* curled in the fabric of my dress shirt over my abdomen.

All the jokes evaporated into thin air.

I was suddenly aware of everything — the music spilling out from the bar, the warm breeze blowing down from the oaks, the way the light played with the shadow on her face, how she was pressed against me, every inch of her, and how her eyes flicked between mine as she pressed up on her toes.

Those eyes fell to my throat when I swallowed, and her tongue slid the length of her lower lip before she dragged her gaze back to meet mine.

"Want me to read your palm?" she asked.

My jaw ached from how hard I clenched it, my restraint wearing thin as I removed a hand from her hip and held it between us.

She cradled my palm in her own, dragging her fingertips along the lines that creased my skin. She tilted her head side to side on a smile, tapping one that spanned the length of my knuckles.

"Says here that you're tired," she said. "Like you've been bearing the weight of expectation for so long that your knees are buckling."

I knew she was bullshitting, but the accuracy of that statement knocked what was left of my smile clear off my face.

Grace didn't look at me as she moved to the next line. "But this," she said with another tap. "This tells me you're on the path to rediscovery, that your priorities are about to shift, and you'll find true happiness."

Again, more bullshit.

But it intrigued me, nonetheless.

"Oh..." she mused, squinting at a small, faint line right in the center of my palm. She held my hand up as if to inspect it closer under the Edison lights. "This is interesting."

"What?"

"Well, you see this line here?" she asked, running her fingertip along it. "This really faint one that kind of splits into two different roads?"

I nodded.

Grace peeked up at me, the green in her eyes like a deep forest in the low light of the courtyard. "It says you're going to kiss me one day."

Those words hung between us, playful in nature and yet sticky like quicksand.

I swallowed, nose flaring when she guided my hand back to her hip, closing what was left of the space between us.

Don't be fucking stupid, Jaxson.

Teammate's. Little. Sister.

The warning might as well have been a flimsy spider web, for how easily I swatted it away.

"I thought you had a boyfriend," I ground out, my heart hammering in my chest. I told myself to let her go, to walk away, but my hands had a mind of their own, and they only gripped her to me tighter.

"I can't have friends if I have a boyfriend?" she asked, breathlessly — which fucked up her attempt to sound innocent.

"You kiss all your friends?"

"Haven't kissed you yet," she pointed out, but she pressed onto her toes, like she was daring me to change that.

And I must have been the dumbest fool in the world, because I gave in — just for a split second, long enough to run my hands gruffly over her hips and down to cup her ass.

It was a greedy, selfish motion — an urge I couldn't fight any longer. Even if just for a split second of insanity, I had to feel her. I *had* to.

She gasped, sucking in a breath and holding it as I groaned and squeezed her. For such a slight little thing, she had a great fucking ass. I wondered what it would be like to spank her, to bend her over, spread those cheeks, and feast on her sweet pussy like no boy her age knew how to.

Her eyes were heavy with want as she looked up at me, as if she could see every dirty thought playing out in my mind.

As if she had her own dirty thoughts playing on a highlight reel, too.

Fuck it.

I gripped her by the back of the neck and held her there as I lowered my mouth, ready to make her premonition come true. Grace's eyes grew wide with surprise and then drunk with desire, with need, and she gripped my dress shirt in her clutches, meeting me halfway.

But before our lips could meet, a rushing river of Ospreys barreled out of the bar, toppling over one another and bringing a chaotic blast of noise with them.

Grace was lightning quick when she tore away from me, and she spun in a little circle next to Carter as if she'd just blown out of the bar with them.

I was still shocked and leaning against the wall when Vince all but tackled me.

"There you are, Brittzy!" he said, ruffling my hair. He frowned then. "Where's my sister?"

Before I could answer, she jumped on his back with a battle cry, and he laughed and twirled her before taking off toward the bus. The rest of the team followed, all while I chastised myself for what I'd almost done and tried to regain my fucking composure.

I shook my head at what a moron I was as I finally pushed off the wall, following the last wave of my teammates as we exited the courtyard. Maven held back a bit, eyeing me curiously as I caught up.

"You alright, Brittzy? You look like someone else just blew out your birthday candles."

I forced a smile. "I'm great. Just drunk."

She arched a brow like she didn't believe me, and then we both turned when we heard a loud, shrill scream followed by peals of laughter.

Vince was sprinting circles around the bus with Grace on his back holding on for dear life, and the team cheered him on while I attempted to wrangle my common sense.

When they blew past me, Grace tilted her head back on a laugh.

Then, her eyes found mine.

Time slugged to a stop again, everything in slow motion, her hair blowing behind her and a slow, wicked smile spreading on her lips.

One night.

One balmy, rowdy night of chaos.

That was all it took for Grace Tanev to turn my entire world inside out.

CHAPTER 5

GETAWAY CAR

Now
Grace

Waking up the morning after a breakup felt a lot like waking up the morning after stupidly throwing back seven tequila shots in a row.

And I knew that from experience.

My head pounded as I winced and pushed myself up in bed, my stomach aching from being empty and yet roiling at the thought of food. I pressed my fingertips to my eyes next, feeling how they were still puffy and dry from all the crying.

I *hated* crying.

It was gross and uncomfortable, too many bodily fluids and involuntary breathing patterns for my liking. I rarely allowed myself to succumb to it. But last night, I hadn't had a choice.

Stupid boys.

I half-wondered if I had what it took to become a nun as I groaned and threw the covers off me, and then I padded barefoot and nearly blind to the bathroom, peeing and splashing water on my face.

I didn't know what time it was. I assumed early, since the sun was flirting with the horizon, but I didn't check my phone before making my way downstairs.

The house was quiet, Maven and Vince still sleeping, and I tiptoed through the living room, slowly and quietly sliding the back door open before shutting it behind me again.

My soul sighed when the first bit of salty air washed over my skin.

Every breath came easier as I made my way toward the water, the sun rising lazily behind me and slowly turning the water a brilliant turquoise. I sat my ass right in the sand, toes wiggling down into the cooler grains underneath the first layer, the briny smell of the ocean soothing my frazzled nerves and the breeze kissing my cheeks.

I instantly felt more grounded as I closed my eyes and inhaled deeply.

But that didn't change the fact that my life was a fucking mess.

I wanted to laugh at how pathetic I was, torn up over a guy who told me from the first time we met that he wasn't looking for anything serious. Except the laugh wouldn't come, not when my heart reminded me that his actions had completely combatted those words.

Trent had spent nearly every day with me, texting me nonstop when we weren't together. Any time we *were* together felt very much like we were in a relationship. He didn't just call me at two in the morning when he wanted to fuck. He took me to concerts. He talked to me all night until the sun came up. We cuddled on nights we could have spent having sex. We did cooking classes together, for God's sake.

The motherfucker even had the audacity to learn my favorite song on guitar and play it by the fire on a starry night when we were camping by the lake.

All those wonderful things made me want to fall for him, and perhaps that was what upset me most. In theory, the things we'd done, the time we'd spent together... it all should have led to me being madly in love with him. It should have me gutted here on this beach at the fact that I'd lost him.

But when he'd dropped me — cutting off all ties as if I'd never existed, as if I'd died and he'd wiped his hands clean — I'd almost felt like I was pretending to be hurt by it.

The truth was I'd actually expected it.

And *that* was what hurt most — not that I'd lost Trent the Camping Guy, but because I was tossed aside so easily. It was a move that had burrowed down deep into the recesses of my long-buried insecurities.

It reminded me that I'm forgettable, and never anyone's first choice.

The whininess of it made me dig the heels of my palms into my eyes, and I shook my head, letting out a frustrated groan before I blew out another long, steady breath.

I breathed in.

I breathed out.

Inhale.

Exhale.

And then, I dropped my hands from my eyes and looked around at the beauty before me.

I noted the cotton candy sky, pink and orange from the sun rising over the other coast of Florida. I noted the sand beneath my toes, the breeze wafting through my hair, the seagulls croaking out their good mornings as they swept the sky. I pressed a hand to my chest and felt where my lungs still worked, where my heart was still beating, my blood still warm.

And I smiled.

I was here.

I was alive.

I had a beautiful life ahead of me, just waiting for me to get started.

I didn't have time to mourn the loss of a man who clearly wasn't thinking twice about me, one who I wasn't even sure I missed, anyway.

And I didn't want to waste another second doing so.

A fierce, rolling ache in my chest protested, as if my body was telling me I needed to take a moment to feel sad.

But I fucking *hated* being sad. Life was too damn short to be sad.

Once, at a yoga training I took shortly after college, a kind woman named Marta, with silver hair and a belly button piercing, warned me that all those emotions I didn't take the time to feel had to go somewhere. She also said that they usually coiled themselves tight in areas like my hips.

So, I stood, moving into a gentle yoga flow as I shoved every emotion even remotely resembling melancholy into whatever crevice I could find.

We all had a choice. Every day we woke up, we could think of all the things we didn't have, and everything we'd lost, and every area we felt our lives were lacking. We could focus on where we fell short, where we could do more or *be* more.

Or, we could choose gratitude.

We could choose to focus on everything we *did* have, on all we were fortunate to experience, on everything around us that was beautiful and good.

We could choose new chapters and new beginnings.

We could choose to be happy.

And that's exactly what I did.

I'd no sooner flopped back down in the sand before my phone buzzed, and I frowned at the unknown number on my screen before reading the text.

Unknown: I've secured the getaway car.

I frowned, but then recognition had my stomach flipping.

Jaxson Brittain.

I just knew it was him, and I sat back enough to lift my feet and kick them in the air like a little girl being told she was going to Disney World.

I didn't take him too seriously when he offered a road trip last night, especially when he came back to the house after playing golf with the guys and saw how Vince fawned over me being upset.

My brother had cooked my favorite meal — beef and cheese pasties with ketchup — and then peppered me with questions at the dining table full of his teammates. He'd immediately followed me up to my room afterward to talk one on one and make sure I was okay.

It was honestly really sweet, and I loved my brother, but *fuck,* he was a cockblock.

There was no way Jaxson and I could have even walked into the kitchen alone last night, let alone hopped in a car together. And when he left at the end of the night, I filed that interaction in my room earlier in the cabinet labeled *jokes* and put it out of my mind.

Even if I was oddly disappointed, I wasn't surprised. I figured he'd come to his senses.

Seeing his text now had me hoping I was wrong.

Me: Took you long enough to text me.

Jaxson: Yeah, well, I couldn't exactly text you with your brother sitting right next to me.

Me: What's your excuse for the other two weeks?

Jaxson: I was a smart man who didn't want to die at a young age.

Jaxson: Besides — you had a boyfriend, remember?

I snorted at that.

Me: So, now you're a stupid man with no regard for life?

The little dots bounced for a while, telling me he was typing, and then they disappeared. I frowned when another text didn't come through, disappointment settling in deeper the longer I went without a response.

I chastised myself.

Fucking *really*, Grace? Have you not learned your lesson that boys are stupid and you're better off alone?

This was classic me — running headfirst into the next guy who showed me attention before the stench from the one who came before him was gone.

I was so desperate to be someone's priority, it made me a simpering fool.

My phone buzzed as soon as I'd set it face-down on my bare thigh, and at first, I told myself not to look at it, to make *him* wait.

But then I was fumbling the thing like a hot potato and unlocking it hastily.

Jaxson: Now, I'm your friend who hates to see you upset.

Friend.

I slumped a little, but then another text came through.

Jaxson: Get an Uber to this address.

A map location came through next.

Me: So bossy.

Jaxson: For obvious reasons, I can't pick you up there.

Me: Why not, if we're just friends?

Jaxson: Get your ass over here before I change my mind.

I stared at the text, biting my lip against a little laugh as I thought about all the reasons this was probably a terrible idea. And still, I scrambled to my feet and dashed inside to pack.

Because if there was one thing about me, it was that I never said no to a new adventure.

• • •

"So, let me get this straight," I said about an hour later, pointing at the sexiest car I'd ever seen in my entire life.

I didn't even know what it *was*, exactly — other than some kind of vintage Porsche. But I *did* know it was blueberry blue, shiny, and sleek as hell. It gave off every road trip vibe I could ever dream of, like riding windows-down through the desert with your hand waving out the window and Fleetwood Mac playing on the old radio.

But it was tucked away safely inside Jaxson's garage, not sitting in the driveway ready to go like it should have been.

"*This* is your car, but we're taking... that?"

I dragged my finger over to the 2023 G-wagon, wrinkling my nose as if it were a minivan.

Jaxson crossed his arms on a chuckle. He looked sleepy, like he'd just woken up or hadn't had a cup of coffee yet. He was also wearing glasses — which I hadn't known he needed, and *also* hadn't known would do very specific things to my nether regions.

Those amber crystal frames unlocked his sharp features even more somehow.

They also unlocked a new kink for me, apparently.

"I've never seen someone so displeased to be riding in a Benz," he said.

"Well, given the choice between the two?" I gestured between them again. "I mean, come *on*. This car was *made* for road trips."

"Actually, this car was *made* by hours and hours of restoring," he amended, petting the hood like it was a cat instead of a car. "And I'm not putting it on a highway, adding miles with no destination in mind. It wouldn't be the safest option, anyway. Plus, this one's a rental," he added, pointing to the Mercedes. "That way, we don't have to worry about driving back if we go too far. We can just fly home."

I pouted, eyes back on the cobalt beauty. "But it's so pretty."

Jaxson beamed a little at that. "She is, isn't she?"

"She? Oh, God. You're one of those. Next, you'll tell me *she* has a name."

He blinked. "You *don't* name your car?"

"I don't have one," I said on a laugh, shaking my head and dragging my suitcase over to the Benz. "So, no."

"How do you not have a car?"

"I don't need one. Not right now, anyway. Besides, I've got my eyes set on a camper van."

Jaxson opened his mouth to respond, but then ran over when he saw me trying unsuccessfully to heave my suitcase into the luxury SUV. He nudged me out of the way to do it himself, and then grunted as he tossed the behemoth into the back.

"Good God, woman. What do you have in there?"

"Basically everything I own," I admitted. "I'm in a nomadic state of mind, just going where the wind blows me."

I hoped I made it sound cool that I didn't have a home, like that was what I wanted, like it was a choice I made. *Look at me! A wild child living by each passing moment, never knowing what will happen next.* The truth rested more in the fact that I didn't know where the hell I wanted to be.

I'd graduated from college at Michigan in May, a task I completed only because my parents made me. I hadn't wanted to go for multiple reasons, starting with the fact that I wasn't exactly academically motivated, and ending with the bold-print bullet point that I didn't know what I wanted to do with the rest of my life at the ripe old age of eighteen.

I didn't understand why that was shocking to the world, but it was, and my parents had taken their eyes off Vince just long enough to tell me that if I wanted my trust fund, I had to go to college and get a degree.

So, I picked something random with the least amount required of me and ticked that off the list.

I was now the not-very-proud owner of a Bachelor of Arts degree in Philosophy.

As much as I was a little shit about it, I *was* very thankful for my parents, for that fund they'd put back for me. It wasn't enough where I didn't have to work, but it *was* enough to give me time to figure out where I wanted to go and what I wanted to do. Most people my age didn't have the same luxury.

How the hell we lived in a country that expected us to choose what we wanted to do for the rest of our lives before we were even legally old enough to have an alcoholic beverage was beyond me.

I'd never wanted to do the life society seemed so intent to push me into. I didn't care about college or getting some fancy, high-paying job that would allow me to live the same life my parents and Vince did. I didn't desire a corner office with a gold plaque on the wall with my name on it.

I wanted adventure.

I wanted limitless options, zero boundaries, and the freedom to make the most of every day I had on this Earth.

Of course, I still needed money to survive. So, going to college in order to secure at least a few years of stability? Worth it.

Jaxson eyed my bag with an arched brow before shaking his head and saying, "Alright, here's the plan."

He launched into our options for the road trip, which obviously started by heading north. I knew from experience it would take us hours just to get out of Florida. He then explained that we could turn around once we hit the Midwest, or keep going — as long as we were back here by August first for some training he had arranged with some of the other players on the team.

His eyes caught mine briefly then, like he wondered how long this road trip was going to be.

I didn't give him any hints.

It was fun to watch him squirm.

I also only half-listened to him, mostly because I was taking in the way he looked as he leaned against his car and prattled on.

He was dressed for a road trip, and yet somehow looked fashionable — the way only an NHL veteran with more money than God could. He wore a relaxed pair of cream-colored Nike shorts, crew cut socks and white sneakers, along with a black long-sleeve Tampa Bay Ospreys shirt that he'd bunched up at his forearms. Those forearms were thick and roped with muscle, and I found my eyes trailing the ink on the right one again. His left wrist sported a Rolex watch that fit him perfectly. It was a flex, and yet he somehow made it seem so casual.

And I had another kink unlocked, apparently, because the way that watch hugged his wrist had me salivating.

I had my answer from how I'd wondered if he had more tattoos to hide, too, because his left calf, shin, and knee sported an impressive sleeve of what looked like mechanical gears. It was like he was a robotic man, and the skin had been peeled back in various places to reveal the machinery operating beneath.

His hair was tousled, no styling whatsoever, and paired with his glasses and his outfit?

It made him look so fucking *cozy*.

I was particularly fond of those jogger-like shorts and the way they left very little to the imagination.

He couldn't hide that bulge even if he tried.

"Sound good?" he asked, and I blinked, slapping on a smile like I'd heard every word.

"It *sounds* like you're a Type-A planner," I said.

He frowned. "We can't just get in the car and drive without having some sort of plan."

"Why not?"

He opened his mouth, then shut it again.

"Look, we can use this as a guideline," I said, carefully taking the notepad from his hand. I found it a little irresistible that he'd taken the time to hand write it all down, and I smiled at the thought of him up all night with Google Maps making a plan. "But we need to be open to adventure. What if we want to drive a hundred miles off course to see the World's Biggest Soup Can? What if we see a sign for a state park we never even knew existed?"

"About the only signs we'll see in Florida will be for sex shops or Jesus."

I snorted at the accuracy.

"Fine," he consented. "My only requirements are that I have to be back in Florida by August, and I need to be in St. Louis for a charity golf tournament on the fourth of July."

That was just four days away.

"What is it with hockey players and golf?"

"It's about as close as we can get to hockey in the off-season. Plus, we can't help but be competitive. Asking us to go months without gloating over kicking each other's ass is like asking a giraffe not to be tall."

I rolled my eyes. "Fine, we'll make it to the golf tournament. Oh! I almost forgot," I said, jogging over to where the Uber had dropped me off. I grabbed the two reusable bags from the driveway, heaving them on to each shoulder. "I have the first round of snacks."

"*First* round?" Jaxson asked, using a finger to peek inside one of the overflowing bags. "You've got enough to feed the whole fucking league."

"The best parts about a road trip are the snacks and the music. You've got to be prepared."

"Do you have a playlist, too?"

"Obviously."

He shook his head, running a hand back through his hair on a grin. It faded quickly, though, his brows furrowing as he glanced at me, then at the SUV, and back.

"Listen... when I asked if you wanted to drive somewhere last night, I originally meant just like... around town or something. I didn't intend for..."

He paused, and my stomach sank.

"You don't want to go."

"No, no, I do," he said, but all the excitement in my chest was deflating like a pierced float at the Macy's Thanksgiving parade.

"It's fine," I said, grabbing my suitcase handle. "You were just being nice and trying to make me feel better. But I'm fine. I'll be fine."

"Grace, stop," he said, covering my hand to stop me from pulling my suitcase from the trunk.

Heat rushed from that point of contact all the way to my toes. It reminded me of the first time I'd taken his hand in mine and dragged him off that party bus in Austin, how the touch had sparked a flame under my skin and made me dizzy as hell.

Jaxson waited until I looked at him, until I had no choice but to see my image reflected in his blue eyes. "I want to go. I wouldn't have offered if I didn't."

I swallowed.

"I just..."

His words faded, and I couldn't help but smile a little at the fear on his face then. *That* was a look I'd seen on the face of dozens of boys before. "You're scared Vince will find out."

"More like I just don't think he needs to know."

"It's just two friends on a little road trip," I goaded.

He flattened his lips and leveled me with a glare.

"Relax. We already established that last night, anyway," I reminded him. "He doesn't need to know. No one does."

I hated the way my throat tightened a little with that last sentence.

I was so tired of being the girl who reduced herself to nothing to make everyone else happy.

But the thought had barely skimmed the surface of my brain before I shook it away, smiling and sticking out my hand for Jaxson's.

"Our little secret," I said.

"What did you tell him?"

"Vince is my brother, not my dad," I reminded him. "I left a note that said thanks for the food and the place to crash. He knows I don't stay in one place for long. Trust me — he won't think twice about it. He's got his own shit to worry about, anyway. New house, new fiancée, remember?"

Jaxson nodded, seemingly appeased.

"I just think we need to set some boundaries, too."

"Boundaries?" I asked, letting my hand fall.

He heaved out a long breath. "That night in Austin..."

The words hung between us, Jaxson eyeing me like I could fill in the gaps of what he *wasn't* saying.

"I meant what I said in the text, Grace. I want to be friends."

I swallowed. "What else would we be?"

His nostrils flared a bit, his eyes searching mine.

When he didn't reply, I shot my hand out again with a smile. "Nothing to worry about. You're a friend helping another friend get over a stupid boy. Just a couple of buds on the open road on a mission to have some fun." I held up my other hand, two fingers raised like a Boy Scout. "No hanky panky, I swear."

Jaxson eyed my hand warily for a long moment before he finally took it in his own, and when he did, another jolt of the night we'd spent together two weeks ago hit me like a freight train.

I felt that same hand sliding up my rib cage, felt a zap of heat between my legs when I remembered how he'd palmed my breast and groaned in my ear at the feel of it. I'd tested him that night, pushing him to the edge in every way I possibly could.

And just when I thought I'd broken him, when his hands were rough and needy, his mouth on track for mine...

My brother had ruined it.

Jaxson tore his hand away as if he was living the same memory, clearing his throat and pulling his sunglasses from his pocket. They must have been prescription, because he removed the ones he was already wearing before sliding the sunnies on, instead.

He rounded the SUV then, opening the passenger side door and gesturing for me to get inside.

As I slid in and buckled my seatbelt, I was already dreaming about all the ways I could test that friend boundary.

CHAPTER 6

PLAY WITH ME

Jaxson

Fuck, this was a bad idea.

I felt that notion in every inch of my body, which was buzzing in warning with Grace Tanev sitting cross-legged and barefoot in the passenger seat next to me.

She was singing along to some song I'd never heard before, the lyrics in a foreign language that I guessed was Korean. One of her hands was tapping on her knee and the other was feeding her sour gummy worms from the pack nestled between her legs. She had remnants of the beach on her feet and calves, white sand hugging her tan skin in a way that made me jealous. Thank fuck I'd gone with the rental. Snacks and sand, in my baby?

I shuddered even at the thought.

I could tell she hadn't slept for shit. Her eyes were tired, a little puffy, the edges of her smile still sad. She also looked like she'd rolled out of bed and grabbed an Uber without a second thought when I texted her this morning. She had on tiny, flimsy little sleep shorts and a spaghetti strap crop top with no bra underneath. Her hair was greasy and pulled into a ponytail, which had half-fallen out, the hair tie holding on for dear life at the back of her head.

She didn't wear a stitch of makeup, either.

I found that more irresistible than anything else.

I was so used to women getting dolled up for me. And don't get me wrong, I fucking *loved* that. There was something about a woman with her hair curled, her eyes lined, thick lashes and ruby red lips that just made me want to fuck. I liked having a woman like that on my arm. I liked the way *Grace* had looked all dolled up at the NHL Awards two weeks ago.

But this?

This was like having a backstage, all-access pass to the most mysterious woman I'd ever met. It was unfiltered. It was *real*.

And god*damn,* it was sexy as hell.

Those shorts revealed every slender inch of her legs, and with her sitting cross-legged the way she was now, I couldn't stop peeking over at the lean muscles of her inner thighs, and how that flimsy scrap of fabric just barely hid her pussy from view.

Yep.

This was a bad, *bad* idea.

Add in the fact that being in a car on the highway with no destination in mind gave me fucking hives, and you could say the first couple hours of our drive were not the most comfortable.

I wished I had fond memories of road trips from growing up, but for me, it usually meant one of two things.

One — there was an AHL player offering private lessons that my father was convinced I *had* to have, and he'd pawn every single thing my mother or I cared about to afford it if he had to.

Or two — he and Mom were fighting, and Mom had shoved me into the backseat as if I were a suitcase to take me with her wherever she was planning on blowing off steam for a few nights.

And that's all it ever was, a few nights max.

She always went back.

Which meant I had to go back, too.

"Let's play a game," Grace said, smacking her thighs.

I jolted a bit at the interruption of my thoughts, glancing over just in time to see her tucking the half-eaten bag of worms away. She then sucked the sugar from her fingertips in the most innocent, *I do this all the time* way.

But all my dirty ass mind saw was those pink lips wrapping around her digits and sucking them clean like it was happening in slow motion.

I tore my eyes away and back to the road, fists whitening a bit where I held the wheel. "Let's not."

"Oh, come on," she pleaded on a pout. Then, she narrowed her eyes on a knowing smile. "It would make me feel better. I was sitting here, getting all sad, thinking about Trent…"

She let out an exaggerated sigh, proving she could be an actress as tears glossed her eyes.

I shook my head. "You are a nuisance."

"That's what he said, too," she said, her voice soft and quiet.

The words felt like a kick to my chest, and when I looked over at her, she was staring out the window, hugging her knees to her chest.

Fuck.

"What game?" I asked.

And the little rascal whipped around with a huge smile, clapping her hands together.

I held the wheel with my left hand so I could reach over and tickle her with the right. "You think you're so fucking clever, don't you?"

Grace wiggled out of reach, sticking her tongue out as I put both hands back on the wheel.

"Hmm," she said, tapping her chin with her fingertip. "Oh! How about the picnic game?"

I cocked a brow at her.

"So basically, I'll start by saying that I'm going to a picnic. I'll tell you a few things I'm bringing, and you ask me if you can bring something, too. But you're trying to figure out the *category* of what you're allowed to bring. So, as you ask me if you can bring things, I'll say yes or no, and you have to put the pieces together to figure out the requirements."

I blinked. "And you find this *fun?* Sounds to me like torture equivalent to watching video in a room full of smelly hockey players."

She waved me off. "Stop being so grumpy. I'll give you an example. If I said I was going to the picnic and I was bringing strawberries, a tomato, and hot sauce, you'd say..."

"Gross."

She laughed, swatting my arm. "Come *on*," she whined, and then she leaned across the console, her top gapping in a way that made me work a little harder to keep my eyes on the road. Her next words were slower, softer, and laced with intent. "Play with me, Jaxson Brittain."

I cracked my neck on a slow and controlled exhale, refusing to look at her and see the wicked smile I knew she was wearing.

So much for those boundaries we'd set.

"I'd say... can I bring a red bell pepper?" I ground out.

"And I'd say yes, and you'd say, 'is it things that are red?' and I'd say YOU WIN and then it'd be your turn to throw the picnic."

She sat back down and shimmied her shoulders on a little victory dance, and I just shook my head.

This fucking girl.

In my normal day-to-day life, I was rewarded for being serious. I *had* to be serious — about hockey, about my team, about my career. I had to be serious when it came to negotiating my contracts, or finding the right trainers to work on my body, or about what food I ate.

My father had instilled that in me from the first time I held a fucking stick.

I didn't have time for games.

Yet here I was, on a road trip with no final destination, with a girl housing gummy worms and goading me into playing a game meant for children.

And the most unfamiliar feeling was sinking into my bones, lightening my chest, releasing the wrinkle that almost always rested between my brows. It was a foreign feeling, both soothing and anxiety-inducing, like I was enjoying the best meal of my life not knowing I had a fifty percent chance it would give me food poisoning and a night of hell later.

It was the kind of feeling that made you pause, that made you wonder if it *meant* something.

I didn't know whether to run from it or straight into its clutches.

An hour of the drive passed easily, Grace telling me what she was bringing to her stupid fucking picnic while I tried to guess what I could bring along. Eventually, I figured out that her category was *things that start with s and end with e*, and then it was my turn.

I was much less creative, bringing only fruits to my picnic.

When we were just outside of Lake City, I pulled into a gas station, ending the game at least for the moment as we both crawled out of the SUV and stretched.

"I'm getting snacks!" Grace said enthusiastically, and then she was skipping inside with me staring at the giant bags of food we still had in the backseat.

I didn't fight her on it, though. I just shook my head and watched her go before sliding my credit card and filling up the gas tank.

My phone rang when it was halfway full, and I frowned at the words DADDY P lighting up the screen. Will Perry was the best goalie in the league. He was also an unnervingly quiet bastard who kept to himself, which was why I was surprised to see that he was calling me.

I wasn't sure I'd ever heard his voice on the phone before.

"Hey, Daddy P. You calling to get some advice on your golf game? Because I gotta tell you, after yesterday, I think you might be beyond my help."

I heard him grumble on the other end before he said, "I don't have time for jokes. Are you free today?"

I frowned again at his serious tone, replacing the gas nozzle and taking my receipt. "Uh... not exactly."

"Goddamnit."

"What's up?"

Will let out a long exhale, and I could picture the way his brows would fold together on that sigh. I'd seen it a thousand times. "Nothing, I just... my nanny left me high and dry again, so now I don't have anyone to watch Ava and I was supposed to..."

His words cut off, another frustrated sigh mixed with a growl.

"It doesn't matter. Thanks, anyway."

"Sorry I can't help, you know I'd be there in a heartbeat to hang with my favorite girl."

Will paused before saying, "But?"

Shit.

"But... I, uh, decided to take a trip."

"A trip," he repeated, and then Grace was sprinting toward me with her arms full of chip bags, candy boxes, random ass drinks, and God knew what else.

"Yep, and I'm about to get back on the road so I better—"

I tried to cut the phone call before Grace got to me, but she was lightning fast, that little thing, and she nodded to the backseat as she scrambled closer. She had a crossbody bag on with a ring of keys and two outrageous keychains — one that looked like a leather whip, and one that was nothing more than a fuzzy puff ball.

"Hurry, open the door before I lose all this!"

I muttered a curse before swinging the door open, and she dumped the snacks with a satisfied smile before beaming up at me.

"I got the *weirdest* things. They had alligator jerky!" She stripped her crossbody bag off and tossed it into the car, those damn keys jangling like mad. She paused when she noticed I was on the phone. "Who's that?"

Daddy P's voice rumbled in my ear next. "My thoughts exactly."

"I'll call you later. Try Maven. You know she's always offering to help you out."

"Avoiding the question, I see," Will assessed. "Why do I feel like I need to warn you to be careful?"

I swallowed as Grace skipped around to the other side of the SUV, her flimsy shorts bouncing along with her perfect little ass as she did so.

"Probably because I'm playing with fire," I mumbled back.

Daddy P barked out a laugh. "Can't wait to hear about this at the tournament," he said. "Be easy on the girl, whoever she is. Later, Brittzy."

"Later," I said, and then I hustled inside the gas station long enough to piss and grab an energy drink.

When I got back to the car, Grace was head banging in the passenger seat to a Bad Company song, pausing only long enough to belt out the lyrics before she was drumming with the alligator jerky in both her hands and head banging again.

There was that feeling in my chest again.

Just as I slid inside, Grace held her phone out in selfie-mode, taking a video of the two of us.

"Today, I'm starting an adventure. A road trip with my new best friend — Jaxson." She smiled at me then. "Jaxson, tell me something good."

I cocked a brow at the camera, flattening my lips as I looked back at her.

"Calm down, no one will ever see this video but me," she said, reading my concern. "I take a video every day and tell future me what I was doing on this date. I always like to remind myself of all the good in my life, even on the seemingly ordinary days."

I laughed a little, staring at her like the bizarre creature she was. "And you don't post it?"

"Post it?" She wrinkled her nose. "Oh, on social media you mean? I don't have any."

That shocked the hell out of me, and my widening eyes must have told her so.

"Tell the camera something good so I stop wasting valuable space in my phone," she said, wiggling the camera in my face.

I shrugged, looking around like there was an answer floating in the air before I looked back at the camera, and at the girl sitting next to me, reflected on the screen. Her sunglasses were halfway down her nose, her smile wide as she took another bite of the fucking alligator jerky in her hand.

"It's off-season, and I'm on a road trip with a pretty cool girl."

Grace slid her sunglasses down even farther to smile at me. "Awww," she said, wrinkling her nose. Then, she popped her sunglasses back on and said, "Stop flirting with me, Brittzy."

She cut the video with me biting back a smile.

CHAPTER 7

ACTIONS SPEAK LOUDER THAN WORDS

Grace

"You're joking, right?"

I shook my head, popping another handful of white cheddar popcorn into my mouth as we pulled off the busy Atlanta midtown street into the valet line of our home for the night. "The fucking *Four Seasons*, Jax?"

Jaxson looked confused as he cut the wheel, pulling our Mercedes-Benz in behind a Maserati. "It's a nice place," he promised, as if that was my concern. "I stay here with the team a lot when we play the Stars."

"We're on a *road trip*," I reminded him, tossing a kernel of popcorn his way. "Not a bougie NHL overnight trip."

He grabbed the popcorn from between his legs and popped it into his mouth. "Are you seriously *mad* that I booked us a swanky hotel?"

"I'm disappointed."

He covered his heart with a fist as if I'd wounded him, but then smiled and pulled us in farther, a young kid in a valet uniform hustling our way. I rolled the top on the popcorn bag and put it away.

"That's funny, considering I'm pretty sure you stayed at the JW Marriott last time you visited Tampa."

"Again, *that wasn't a road trip*. Besides," I added as the valet opened my car door. "That was all my parents' doing, not mine."

I smiled and thanked the guy who helped me out of the SUV, as if it were a carriage and I a princess. I didn't miss the way his eyes darted over my sleep shorts, no doubt covered in dust from the various snacks I'd been munching on, before they found mine again.

His eyes widened when I smirked at the fact that I caught him staring.

I turned around, looking over my shoulder and running my hands over the back of my shorts. "Do I have anything on my ass?" I asked, feigning innocence as I batted my lashes at the poor kid.

I saw him flush crimson before looking almost green as a strong hand gripped me by the inside of my elbow and toted me away.

"You trying to give him a heart attack?" Jaxson growled into my ear.

I grinned up at him. "Maybe I'm trying to give him my number."

Jaxson's nose flared a bit at that, and he kept his hold on me as the valet crew struggled with my suitcase behind us.

"Aww, are you *jealous*," I teased him, and then I lifted his hand from my elbow until I was draping his arm around my shoulders. I leaned into him, putting my own arm around his waist. "Don't worry, Brittzy. I'm currently celibate, due to men being dreadfully disappointing, and the unfortunate fact that I am not sexually attracted to women. Besides," I added, my neck aching with the effort it took to look up at him — the tall motherfucker. "He's not really my type. I'm more of a *brother's grumpy teammate* kind of gal."

He closed his eyes and shook his head once, a long sigh leaving him, but I saw the way the corner of his lips curled *just* a little.

"Okay, you win tonight," I conceded, and I was content to stay there under his arm, but he released me when we approached the front desk.

I was suddenly very aware that I was in my dirty pajamas with no bra on in a Five-Star hotel lobby. I crossed my arms over my chest, and I swore I could hear my mom's voice whispering in my ear about my indecency, as if she was there with us.

s"But tomorrow night, *I* get to pick our accommodations," I added.

Jaxson looked like he was ready to argue, but he was next to check in, and I watched as every muscle in his face shifted as he approached the desk with a glittering smile.

Holy shit.

It was magic, how he completely transformed. I watched him tuck his true self behind some invisible wall as he lit up like a fucking Christmas tree, leaning one elbow on the desk as he fished his wallet from his pocket. He told the woman behind the desk that he was checking in for the night, and when he gave his name, recognition sparked in her eyes, as well as a few of her colleagues at the desks on either side of her.

Two of them began muttering to each other, smiling shyly as they watched Jaxson's every move. I swore I felt a hush come over the entire lobby, and when I glanced over my shoulder at the bar, there were various crowds of people with their eyes trained on Jaxson, too.

I was used to this with my brother. Vince Tanev was already a household name after just one season in the NHL. Add in the fact that Maven had followed him around all season and posted his every move on social media, and you could say he had a rabid fanbase. We couldn't even go to the damn grocery store anymore without him getting asked for both photos and autographs.

When I turned back to Jaxson, I realized he likely suffered the same fate. Not that he didn't enjoy it, from the way he was not-so-subtly flirting with the woman behind the desk. She played with her hair as she listened to him talk, and now *I* was the jealous one, a sinking feeling in my gut as I watched him turn his charm all the way on for her.

He's stayed here plenty of times with the team, he'd said.

How many women had he fucked inside these walls?

Jaxson tapped his credit card on the counter before sheathing it in his wallet again, taking the hotel keys and brochures from the woman and turning to face me. He didn't slip back into the Jaxson I knew, though — he kept that façade going strong as he gave our room number to the bellman with instructions to bring ice to our rooms, too.

"Ready?" he asked, handing me a trifold that had my room number written in Sharpie on the outside. Then, his eyes flicked behind me, and he muttered a curse before his smile grew strained.

"Hey, man, so sorry to bother you," a voice said, the *so* giving away that they were from somewhere in the Midwest. I turned to find four guys with their phones clutched in their hands. The boldest of them was the one talking. "We know you're just trying to get checked in, but we're huge fans. We both went to Ohio State, too."

"Go Bucks!" his friend chimed in.

"We were just wondering if we could get a picture?" the guy asked, cringing a little despite the hopeful look on his face.

I felt the way Jaxson schooled himself, how he forced a calm breath before smiling big. "Of course, man."

"Really? Oh, sick," he said, and then he looked around for someone to take the picture.

I held my hand out, and the guy thanked me before he and his buddies flanked Jaxson. There was another group watching us and slowly making their way over — this one looked to be three couples. I gave them a warning look that I hoped told them this was not fucking Disney World, and it seemed to work, because they paused their advance.

Once the photos were taken, Jaxson hurriedly pulled his hood overhead and slid his sunglasses into place even though we were inside. That notion also stopped a few other groups in their tracks before they could make their way over to us, and I wondered if he just didn't enjoy taking photos like he was some sort of zoo animal, or if he was more worried about pictures of *us* getting put into the world. Not that *I* wanted that to happen, either — God knew my brother would blow a gasket, and I didn't want that for either of us — but it still hurt a little.

I didn't have time to overthink it before Jaxson grabbed my hand and hauled me toward the elevators.

I stared at that point of contact, at where his hand completely enveloped my own, feeling another zap of a memory from the night we spent together in Austin. His skin was warm and calloused, and he kept his gaze locked on the elevators all while subtly looking around as if *I* was the one who needed protecting from the fans watching us pass by.

I chastised myself for the way my stomach took flight at that, at the thought of him wanting to keep me safe, to protect me like I was *his*. I had been single for all of ten seconds, and I was already dreaming of another relationship.

You are a stupid, lovesick girl, Grace.

Will you ever learn your lesson?

Add in the fact that he'd made it very clear before we even stepped into that rental car together that we were just friends, and I put an extra emphasis on *stupid*.

I needed to listen to those words, regardless of what his eyes said when they raked over me.

If I would have done that with Trent, I could have saved myself a whole lot of heartache.

What was it about me that I *didn't* take a man's word for the truth when he said shit like that? Why did I have this ridiculous fantasy about being the one to change their mind, about being special enough that the *I'm not looking for a relationship* guy would fall at my feet and declare his undying love for me?

I blamed all the 90's rom coms I watched growing up.

I mean, really — if Kat Stratford could make Patrick Verona fall in love with her despite him being a grumpy, unobtainable asshole who initially started talking to her only because some douchebag paid him to... how was I *not* going to think I had a shot with the guy who treated me like a girlfriend but swore I wasn't?

Actions speak louder than words, they say.

But just because they're the louder ones doesn't mean they're the truth.

The elevator dumped us off on the top floor with my mind whirring as it often did when I stopped long enough to let it. This was why I was always racing off to my next adventure.

If you never stopped moving, then you never had time to overthink.

"You're here," Jaxson said, nodding to room 5314. "I'm just next door if you need anything."

"Are you going to bed?" I asked, frowning when I looked at my phone. "It's not even seven."

He blew out a breath, running his hand through his hair and looking down at me like what he *should* do was go to bed.

But he also looked like he could be persuaded.

"Come on, let's shower and get dinner downstairs," I said. "Maybe have a few drinks?"

"I find it hard to believe you're anything close to hungry after how many Peanut M&Ms I watched you shovel into your mouth today."

"Interesting that you're paying so much attention to my mouth, Jaxson Brittain," I teased, stepping a little closer.

His next breath came slower, more controlled, like the exhale would burn if he released it too quickly. His eyes searched mine, jaw ticcing.

I waited for him to call me on it, to remind me of our little *boundaries* as he'd called them.

But he just stared.

And I took it as permission to step even closer.

"I'll be right here in an hour," I said, pointing to the spot beneath my feet. "If you want to join me for dinner, then meet me here. And if you don't," I added on a shrug, stepping back. I swore I saw his chest release when I did. "Then enjoy your slumber. I'm sure I can find someone else to hang out with."

His eyes flared at that, and again I found that stupid, misleading feeling swimming in my gut. He looked like the thought of anyone else hanging out with me but him was enough to drive him mad.

In all reality, I was likely just a pain in his ass — his teammate's little sister who he somehow felt obligated to care for.

I scanned my key card and slipped inside my room, where my bag was already waiting for me, along with a bottle of champagne on ice and a marble plate with petit fours.

Calling it just a *room* was laughable.

It was a luxury suite, complete with a king bed, city view, and giant bathtub that was already calling my name.

I chuckled to myself, leaning my head against the door I'd just shut behind me.

"Really roughing it on the road out here," I muttered, and then I stripped out of my shorts and top, leaving a trail of clothes on my way to the tub.

CHAPTER 8

FALSE REALITY

Grace

After a quick bath, I wrapped myself in the plush robe the hotel provided and sat at the vanity, applying moisturizer to my face. At the same time, I swiped a thumb across my phone screen and tapped my mom's contact from my favorites list, working the cream into my skin as the phone rang.

I'd sent a text to Vince just letting him know I was okay, which was about all he needed from me. He shot back a quick thumbs up emoji that told me he'd already moved on, assuming I was fine and handling myself. It was a fair assumption, since I'd been doing that since we were kids. I liked that he had faith in my strength as much as I disliked that I had to have it.

My brother would be there for me if I ever told him I needed him.

Sometimes, I just wish he could see that I needed him without being told.

"Hello, Gracie," Mom answered, a little breathless. "Everything alright?"

My chest deflated at the greeting.

To anyone else, it would have seemed like a mother answering her daughter's call with concern for her well-being.

But for me, I knew this was her way of quickly getting a pulse check on what kind of call this was. Because if I *was* okay, if I didn't need anything — she was busy.

"Everything's fine, Mom," I assured her. "Just checking in to let you know I'm in Atlanta."

"Oh! How fun! What are you doing there?" I could hear the distraction in her voice, the way you know someone isn't fully listening.

"Trying out for a circus."

"With your balance? Not the best idea."

I smirked a little, glad she was at least somewhat paying attention.

"You sure you're okay?"

I sighed. "Yeah."

"Good. Well, I hate to rush off the phone, but your father and I are heading out the door to go to dinner with the Marpets. They just bought a new Ferretti and want to take us out for a spin on the lake."

Only my parents would be casually going to dinner on their friends' new *yacht*.

"Oh! Will we see you at Vince's tournament in a few days?"

My stomach soured a bit as I swallowed. "Tournament?"

"He's doing a charity golf tournament in St. Louis. I thought maybe he would have told you about it. Anyway, we'll be there! We're happy to fly you in, if you'd like. And we can get you a room!"

This must have been the tournament Jaxson was playing in, too.

"I'll be there," I assured her. "But don't worry about the flights. I'm..." I decided less was more in the case of details at the present moment. "I already have it taken care of."

"Okay, my little adventurer. See you then. We're wearing our Ospreys t-shirts if you want to match!"

I didn't bother trying to not roll my eyes then, and with a kissy noise, Mom ended the call.

I sat there staring at myself in the mirror for a long moment.

She'd asked if I was okay, but I couldn't shake the feeling that she probably didn't actually care. I'd told her about the breakup when I was on my way to Vince's house, and she'd only half-listened to me then, too, it seemed.

She'd forgotten about it already, not even asking about Trent on the phone even though I'd dated him for months.

I snorted at the term *date*, because it felt like I'd been living in a false reality. To me, we were dating. But to him?

We were nothing.

I growled in annoyance at myself. I didn't even care. He was a smelly nomad with long hair who charmed me with his late-night thoughts on the universe. I didn't even feel that sad about losing *him*, specifically.

I was just sad that I was so easy to toss aside.

And, if I was being honest, I couldn't help but compare my mom's reaction to my heartbreak to the way she and Dad had fawned over Maven after meeting her for the first time. She and Vince weren't even together, and yet my parents were invested, probably planning a wedding well before there was an engagement even announced.

If *they* had broken up, my parents would have flown into Tampa and fussed over Vince, doing everything they could to fix the situation.

With me, it was almost as if they expected it.

Something sour bubbled in my stomach, something that felt a lot like it would pull me under the shadow of sadness if I let it. So, I snuffed it out before it had the chance.

Planting my hands on the vanity, I stood, shaking my head. "That's enough of that," I declared out loud, smiling at myself in the mirror. "Look around you, Grace. You're in a Five-Star hotel in one of the liveliest cities in the South. You're twenty-two years old, have money in your pocket, and don't have a single thing tying you down." I locked eyes with myself in the mirror, ignoring how much of my mother I saw in that reflection. "Tonight is not a night to mope around. It's a night to make new friends, to make new memories, to *live*."

I inhaled a deep breath and the resolve that came with those words, and then I hurriedly got dressed, picking one of my slightly nicer sundresses and my less-beat-up sandals from my suitcase. My hair was still damp as I ran my hands through it and tried to give it a little volume at the top. Then, I slid my hotel key card into my clutch and bolted for the door.

The hallway was empty, and I looked down at the time on my phone, noting that it had been an hour. I tried to ignore the zing of disappointment in my chest as I wobbled up onto my toes and back down to my heels, looking down the hall at where Jaxson's door was.

I waited four minutes before I straightened my back and made my way to the elevator.

It doesn't matter, I assured myself. And honestly, I shouldn't have been surprised. Jaxson Brittain was a grown ass man. I was shocked he'd dropped everything to take this trip with me. He likely only did it because he was the kind of guy to help everyone around him, the kind who'd give the shirt off his own back if it meant helping someone else out.

Or maybe he was just bored.

My chest was buckling under the pressure of the night when I stepped inside the elevator, and I soothed my rib cage with my fingertips, forcing a calm breath. I was already working out the words I'd say to Jaxson in the morning, how I could cut this trip short and set him free of whatever obligation he felt like he had to me.

But before the doors could shut, a hand shot out to stop them — along with my warring thoughts.

And Jaxson stepped into the frame.

Where I had very clearly just showered and thrown on the first thing I found in my suitcase, he looked like he'd had a professional tailor come up to his room to dress him for the night.

His hair was styled neatly, his short beard freshly trimmed, and he'd traded in the athletic shorts and Ospreys shirt for an olive-green Henley and cream dress slacks fastened to his waist with a belt. He'd shoved the sleeves of that Henley up to his elbows, his tattoos snaking out from under the fabric, and when he stepped inside the elevator, he twisted just enough to give me a view of his sculpted ass in those slacks.

And I understood *instantly* why he wore a belt, because his waist was narrow, but his ass was rock solid and big enough that I *knew* those pants had to be custom made to fit it — along with his tree-trunk thighs.

Fuck.

He was so hot it should have been a crime.

Jaxson arched a brow at me as he sidled up at my side, his hands casually sliding into his pockets. "You were just going to leave me behind, huh?"

My stomach fluttered with him looking at me like that, and now my mind was whirring with a completely different train of thought.

"You were late," I teased, lifting my chin.

"And if *you* were late, you would have been fine with me not waiting?"

"Of course not. Didn't you ever listen to Shania Twain? *I* can be late for a date," I said, pointing to my chest. "But you'd better be on time."

I sang those last words, shimmying my hips even though I knew I was a little out of tune.

"I'm Canadian. Of course, I know that song," he said. "But this isn't a date, so I guess I'm in the clear."

I wanted to keep the joke rolling, but those words hit me harder than I wanted them to — even with Jaxson smiling behind them.

I *knew* it wasn't a date, but the fact that he was so insistent on reminding me of that little fact had my eyes falling to my feet. I felt like a twelve-year-old again, a little girl crushing on her brother's friend with absolutely zero hope of him ever feeling the same.

I took only a split second to feel that rejection before I slapped on my happy face, just in time for the elevator doors to open and reveal the bustling second floor.

"Last one to the bar takes a shot!" I said loud enough to make heads swivel in our direction.

Then, I took off in a sprint, laughing at the curse word Jaxson muttered under his breath before he started jogging to catch up.

And I left all my sad girl emotions in my dust — right where they belonged.

CHAPTER 9

THE BAR IS REALLY IN HELL, ISN'T IT?

Jaxson

Grace reminded me of an Aston Martin DB5, the way she zoomed through the crowd in the hotel and pulled up at the first empty stool at the bar. She was enigmatic, stunningly beautiful without trying to be, the kind of girl who turned every head but never noticed.

She was classic.

Her long, platinum hair was a little darker tonight, still damp from her shower. She wasn't wearing makeup, nor was she wearing a bra under the spaghetti strap sundress that draped down to her ankles. Even in a crowded bar in Atlanta, she looked like she belonged on a beach, like she was a folklore goddess who'd just walked out of the sea.

I caught up with her just in time for the bartender to place a shot glass filled with some sort of amber alcohol down in front of me, his smirk telling me he both pitied me and was jealous I was there with Grace.

There was nothing to be jealous over, since she was anything but mine.

But I sure as hell wasn't going to tell him that.

"Drink up, buttercup," Grace sang, clapping her hands together when the same bartender started making her a martini.

"What is it?"

"Tequila."

I slammed it back without even a little grimace, and Grace's eyes widened before she blinked three times.

"Well, okay then," she said on a laugh. "I didn't realize I was partying with a monster. You didn't even flinch."

"Come on, babe," I said, taking the seat next to her. "I'm a professional hockey player. No one drinks like we do."

Her cheeks tinged pink, but she didn't reply, just picked up the menu in front of her and pointed to a dish. "I'm getting this. Strawberry Pavlova and lavender frozen Greek yogurt." She made a face like she was drooling just thinking about it, and then promptly did a little dance in her seat.

"That's dessert."

"And?"

"Don't you want dinner first?"

"Nope."

I opened my mouth to argue that she hadn't had a real meal all day and needed something with more nutrients than a fucking *pavlova,* whatever that was, but she held up a finger to signal the bartender and ordered it before I had the chance.

A heavy sigh left me, which made her smile like she'd won, and I told the bartender I'd have the grouper before he took our menus and left us be.

"We should toast," she said, holding up her martini glass. "To new adventures with new friends."

I grabbed my water glass and tapped it to hers before taking a drink, but she sucked her teeth.

"You can't cheers with water."

"Just did. Besides, *you're* the one who ordered me a shot instead of a drink."

"Fair," she conceded, sipping from her glass. She relaxed a bit when she did, her shoulders visibly releasing from where they'd been tied up by her ears. I saw then the strain at the edge of her eyes, like smiling was taking a little effort tonight.

It made me want to hunt down that motherfucker who made her sad and wring his goddamn neck.

Instead, I got her talking, asking her about college — which she had just graduated from in May. Although she didn't seem like it was her favorite subject, she indulged me, and I ordered an Irish whiskey and sipped it while she told me all her crazy stories.

The topic of conversation was a staunch reminder of how young Grace was, and how fucked up I was for wanting her.

I *knew* she was only twenty-two, but sometimes I forgot. She had this air about her that made her feel... ageless. She wasn't immature, but she wasn't *mature*, either. She wasn't childish, but she wasn't controlled in the way an adult who'd been hardened by experience was.

She was just this life force, this bundle of joy and adventure. She took the world head on, and I didn't know anyone else who did that.

When I thought about who *I* was at twenty-two, I wanted to kick myself for being a fucking pervert. When I was that age, I had no idea about life. I was just a kid who played hockey, hooked up with girls, and partied like it was my job.

Now, I was a thirty-year-old man getting a hard-on for a girl that same age.

She was eight years younger than me.

Hell, when *I* was twenty-two, she would have been just fourteen.

I was a sick bastard.

This was the kind of shit Taylor Swift would write a song about — and not the good kind of song, either.

I tried to convince myself it was just that I felt protective of her when our food arrived, watching as she dug into her little ice cream dish as if it were a steak, using her knife and fork to cut it into petite-size bites.

Maybe it was just because Vince was one of my best friends on the team, and I knew he'd want me to look out for her.

I actually laughed out loud at that, earning me a quirked brow from Grace as I forked off the first bite of my grouper.

I wanted to protect her, sure.

But I also wanted to hike that dress up and see if she was wearing any panties underneath that thin, floral fabric.

I shook the thought away, and both of us fell a little quiet as we ate. It was only when I saw her eyes losing focus as she drew circles in the leftover glaze on her plate with her fork that I broke the silence again.

"You okay over there?" I asked, dabbing the corners of my mouth with my napkin before I set it over my plate. The bartender appeared a second later to take it, but Grace glared at him like a feral dog when he tried to grab hers, too.

She smiled at me next. "Yeah, I'm great. Why?"

I narrowed my eyes. "Didn't you hear what I said the other night?"

"You mean your offer to kill my ex? Trust me, I haven't forgotten. Just trying to plan out the murder weapon."

The joke was her way of deflecting, and I ignored it. "You don't have to pretend like you're happy all the time."

Her hand froze where she was still drawing designs on her plate with her fork, and she slowly lowered it before letting out a sigh.

"What's on your mind?"

She ordered another drink before answering, sucking down half of her next martini before staring at where she held the stem of the glass between her fingertips. "I called my mom upstairs."

"Oh?" I asked, calmly taking a drink of whiskey while I internally freaked the fuck out. Because if she told her mom she was with me, Vince would find out by morning.

"Yeah," Grace said, still staring at her glass. "I told her I was in Atlanta. You know, just checking in so she'd know I was still alive," she added with a note of sarcasm I didn't miss. "Not that she'd care if I wasn't, or notice, for that matter."

I frowned, abandoning my drink and turning on the bar stool until I faced her.

She glanced at me and shook her head. "I know, I know. I shouldn't say shit like that. Go ahead and tell me I'm being dramatic."

"I didn't say a word."

"You were thinking it."

"All I'm thinking is that I'm sorry you feel that way, and I want to know why."

Grace froze at that, blinking once slowly before she turned to look at me. "You don't think it's stupid that I said that?"

"Not if it's how you feel."

Her brows knitted together, bright green eyes skirting between mine like she was looking for the lie. "Well... thank you," she said after a moment.

"For not negating your feelings?" I laughed a little. "The bar is really in hell, isn't it?"

"You have no idea," she said on a sigh, but she was smiling again, and this time it was genuine. She took another drink before adding, "Do you have any siblings?"

I shook my head, my stomach hollowing out a bit. Sometimes I wish I'd had a brother or sister, just so they could take some of the attention of my father instead of it being fixed on me all the time. I immediately felt guilty for that thought and shoved it away.

Grace smiled, but it fell quickly. "I love Vince. I do. He's the best big brother I could have ever asked for."

"But?"

"But," she conceded, like she hated that there *was* a but. "Living in his shadow is getting really fucking old."

I swallowed, and before I thought better of it, my hand slid from the bar down to cover her knee.

I didn't say a word, just squeezed her gently, letting her know I was listening. I also tried to ignore the way my hand wrapped around her so easily, the way chills washed over her arm at my touch.

"I know my parents love me," she added after a moment. "And they've always taken care of me. But... like, okay, for example. My mom knows I'm going through a breakup. She also, until this phone call, had *no idea* where I was in the world. And when I called her? She didn't ask where I was. I told her. And she also didn't ask how I was doing. I mean, she *did*," she amended quickly. "But not in the real way. Not in the concerned way a mother would when she knows her little girl is heartbroken. She asked in the obligatory way, just a quick pulse-check so she could tell me she was busy and needed to get off the phone."

I took another calm sip of whiskey to keep myself from commenting on that, because I was not the kind of man who would ever speak ill of one of my friend's mothers.

But also, *fuck her* for making Grace feel insignificant.

"And look, I get it, I'm an adult now," she added. I fought down the urge to argue that point. "And it's just a breakup, with some guy who really doesn't even matter, to be honest. But... if this were Vince? If Maven broke up with *him*?" She looked at me then, shaking her head.

"She would have asked," I finished for her.

"Oh, she would have already flown down to Tampa and set up camp in his house, cooking for him and doing his laundry and whatever else." She waved her hand in the air to illustrate. "Dad would be there, too. The same way they drop everything to go to his award shows or his big games."

I chewed my lip to keep from saying words I'd regret, watching as the sadness sank even deeper into her bones right in front of me.

"I just want to be someone's priority."

She whispered the words, so softly I almost questioned if I'd heard her right.

And those words broke my fucking heart as much as they made me grind my teeth.

"I'm sorry, Grace."

She nodded, and for a moment I thought she might cry. Her eyes glossed over, but she quickly inhaled and blinked several times with her gaze cast up toward the ceiling. Then, she pinned me with a breathtaking smile, lifting her drink to her lips. "What about you? Do your parents fawn over you the way mine do over Vince?"

Her question socked me in the gut — almost the way her masking her feelings with that smile did. I hated that she felt she had to put that mask in place, but I understood the need for it.

She leaned on happiness the way I leaned on apathy. She chose to smile where I chose to float through my life without any agency.

We all had our ways of coping.

"Not exactly," I answered.

Grace frowned, but before I could elaborate, I was tapped rather aggressively on the shoulder.

I spun in my seat just enough to look at the offender, a white, burly looking mammoth with an impressive beard and a smile that both terrified me and made me feel like we could be best friends.

"I knew it!" He turned back to a group gathered at the other end of the bar. "It is him!"

Their faces all lit up as they ambled closer, and I internally groaned, all while putting on my best fake smile. I could learn a lesson or two from Grace in that department.

"It is me," I confirmed.

"Man, you're a fucking *beast*," the guy said, clapping me hard on the shoulders as if we were family. "I used to watch you even when you played for the Assassins."

"Appreciate it, man," I said, clapping his shoulder in return. I was just about to tell him to kindly fuck off when he waved his friends closer.

"Can we take a pic?"

He asked, but by the way they were all crowding in, I knew it wasn't a question I could say no to.

"Sure," I said, already standing, but it was at the same time Grace said, "Tell you what."

Every head swiveled in her direction, as if they'd just noticed she was there. How they managed that was a magic

I wanted to learn how to harness, because I was nothing *but* aware of that woman any time she was near.

"If you can beat me at a game of quarters," she said, standing on the footrest of her stool long enough to swipe a shot glass from behind the bar. She slid it between me and the fan, arching a brow. "You can have a picture *and* an autograph. But, if you lose, then you have to pull up the Ospreys website and buy a Jaxson Brittain jersey right here at the bar."

Grace dug a quarter from her clutch next, flipping it between her fingers with a dare in her eyes that was fixed on the guy beside me. I had to bite back a smile as I turned to face him again, watching as confusion bent his brows, his gaze flicking from me to her and back again.

She was like a little bulldog when it came to me. I'd seen it earlier when she took a picture for a couple of fans then, too. She'd glared at anyone else who tried to come close, and now here she was again, doing what she could to protect my peace.

Fuck, that turned me on in a way not even slow grinding with her in a crowded Austin bar had.

When I just cocked a brow at the man — not jumping in to say it was fine and I'd take the pic regardless — he shrugged, looking back at his friends, and then at Grace.

"You're on."

She grinned like the Cheshire Cat. "Fabulous. Ladies first," she added, handing the quarter to him.

His friends chuckled a bit at that, the circle thickening around us. I heard someone call the guy Ben, so I assumed that was his name. And Ben lined up his shot, quarter balanced between his thumb and forefinger, before he slammed it on the bar in an attempt to make it bounce into the glass.

He missed.

His friends razzed him, and Grace slid the quarter toward her with a little smile. She framed it in her fingertips just like he had, and then closed one eye, her tongue sticking out as she bobbed her hand in the air.

One, two, three...

And the fourth time, she slapped the quarter down against the bar, and it popped up in a perfect arch before sailing into the shot glass with a satisfying *tink*.

The little crowd around us reacted in a mixture of cheers and groans, but Ben wasn't deterred. He fished the quarter out, pulling up a seat at the bar with determination etched in his brows.

"Best two out of three?" he asked.

Grace shrugged. "Sure."

Then, she winked at me, and the devilish smile she wore almost made me feel sorry for the guy.

Almost.

CHAPTER 10

LITTLE NOVA

Jaxson

Watching Grace mop the floor with grown man after grown man who challenged her at quarters was better than being front row at game seven in the Stanley Cup playoffs.

It was probably also more profitable, considering the amount of jerseys the Ospreys had sold tonight thanks to her.

Ben lost his *best two out of three* in less than sixty seconds, and then his friend was shoving him out of the way saying, "Let me try."

He lost just as quickly.

Soon, we had the attention of the entire second floor — including the bartenders, who watched from behind the bar with folded arms and smirks on their faces. Other than warning us not to scratch the bar top, they seemed content with the entertainment, too.

Grace slammed quarter after quarter into that shot glass, goading her opponents when they failed to challenge her. She even started asking the bartender for shots, claiming that she'd have to get her own ass drunk since no one could beat her.

It was fucking hilarious.

And somehow, *stupidly* hot.

It wasn't even the way the strap of her dress kept sliding down over her shoulder, or how her tits bounced a little in that thin material every time she threw the quarter down. It wasn't the winks she'd throw at the guys before handing their asses to them, or the way her lips caressed the shot glass every time she decided to get a little more drunk.

It was her laugh, wild and carefree. It was the little shimmy she did every time she bounced that quarter right into the glass. It was how no matter what was happening around us, no matter how loud and rowdy the crowd got... her eyes always found me.

Eventually, the crowd tired of losing, the energy draining because Grace fucking Tanev was unbeatable at this game. So, I called it, signaling for our check before I posed for a photograph with each group that had challenged her — regardless of the fact that they didn't ever win.

Grace almost pouted when I did, but I just smirked at her, shaking my head and scribbling out some autographs before saying goodnight to the guys.

They were happy as could be, laughing about the game and comparing photographs as they spread out through the bar.

And I turned back to find Grace looking up at me with drunk, lazy eyes.

"Hiiii," she sang.

I chuckled, signing our check to my room number before I reached for her hand. "Come on, little Nova."

She giggled as I hauled her off the chair, keeping her hand firmly in mine as I weaved us through the crowd and toward the elevator. She was swaying a bit, and a group of the guys who'd been challenging waved as she passed by. She waved in return, and then someone broke out a slow clap, and Grace yanked free of my grip long enough to jump on top of a plush chair and do a dramatic curtsy.

"Thank you, thank you, oh, you're all too kind," she said, blowing kisses around the room. The crowd ate right into it while I wiped a hand over my mouth, shaking my head.

But when she went to bow once more, she lost her footing, and I shot my hands out just in time to catch her before she tumbled to the floor.

"Wee!" she said when I swung her back upright. I held my hands on her arms to steady her, but as soon as I removed them, she swayed into my chest.

"Alright," I said on a laugh. "Looks like someone needs a ride upstairs."

Before she could agree, I scooped her into my arms, and she kicked her feet like a little kid the entire way to the elevator.

The crowd roared their approval as we passed, Grace waving at them over my shoulder until we slipped inside the elevator. The moment the doors closed, a heavy silence fell over us.

And I was suddenly all too aware of every place my skin touched hers.

Grace seemed completely unbothered, however. She laced her hands together behind my neck, staring up at me with lazy, happy eyes.

"Hi," she said again.

I laughed. "Hi."

Her eyes washed over me, pausing at various places
— my jaw, my throat, the tattoos on my forearm. Then, she
groaned, burying her head in my chest.

"If you're going to throw up, give me a warning," I
said just as we reached our floor. I stepped out and headed
for her room, still holding her tight.

"The only reason I'd throw up right now is from how
disgustingly hot you are."

I barked out a laugh at that. "Um... thank you?"

"No. *No*, thank you. It's a problem, Brittzy. A real
problem." She hiccupped. "I protected you down there. I'm
your princess in shining armor."

"That you are," I agreed, a smile curling on my lips.
When we made it to her room, I carefully set her back on
the ground in front of the door.

But she didn't let go.

Instead, she pulled me flush against her, fingers
wrapping into fists hard enough to untuck my shirt where
she gripped it. She closed her eyes as her head fell back
against the door, smiling for a long moment before she
peeked them open again and looked up at me.

Fuck.

Those eyes were like a neon sign the size of Texas
screaming all the dirty thoughts in that pretty little head of
hers. They danced with mischief, with an invitation — one
I couldn't accept, especially tonight.

"You called me Nova," she said, her words slurring a
bit.

"I did."

"Why?"

I swallowed, using my knuckles to sweep her hair out
of her face. A voice deep in the abyss of my mind screamed
that I needed to stop touching her, but I couldn't.

"Because you burn brighter than anyone else in the room."

Her lips tilted up, eyes wide like she couldn't believe I'd said that about her. She watched me like that for a pause before a little laugh rumbled in her throat, and she shook her head on a sleepy smile. "Stop flirting with me, Brittzy."

I laughed, taking that as an excuse to put much-needed space between us. I backed away only a few inches before she clamped my arm in both her hands, pulling me into her again.

"These fucking tattoos," she said, trailing one long line of black ink with her nail.

My whole body shivered without me being able to do a damn thing to stop it, and I didn't miss the way she smirked at the sight.

It seemed my reaction to her only made her bolder, because she fisted her hand in my Henley and dragged me in closer — until I had no choice but to frame her against the door.

Her hands snaked up under my shirt without an ounce of hesitation, scattering every thought in my brain other than the ones consumed by how it felt for this girl to touch me.

She pressed her palms flat against my abdomen, which stuttered at the contact, a breath hissing out of me.

"Mm..." she moaned, biting her lip before her smile spread wide again. Her eyes flicked up to mine, hands rubbing under my shirt like it was a nervous habit she had instead of a sure-fired way to turn me all the way on. "You're wearing contacts."

"I am," I managed, my voice rough.

"I didn't realize you did, not until I saw you in your glasses earlier." She paused, considering. "I like you in your glasses. Makes you look like a hot, nerdy bookworm."

"Well, I don't want to turn you on, but I *do* have a book with me. It's spread open," I teased, saying those words like I was whispering filth against her skin in my bed instead of talking about a fucking book. "Face down and waiting for me on my bedside table as we speak."

She faked a moan, biting her lip. "Stop it, it's too much."

We both laughed a little at the joke, which I desperately needed to take my mind off how her hands were still exploring the span of my abdomen. But then, her eyes were surveying mine again, the question she wanted to ask written in them long before her words followed.

"Do you ever think about that night in Austin?"

The question itself was enough to shorten my breath, but the fact that she slid her hands a little lower when she asked it, tucking her fingertips under the buckle of my belt...

Fuck.

I stayed silent, the muscles in my jaw working overtime as I used every ounce of willpower I had to stay rooted in place.

Teammate's little sister.

Eight years younger than you.

Don't. Be. An idiot.

I needed to say no. I needed to douse whatever flame she still had burning for me — all while fighting the roaring fire *I* still had burning for *her*.

But I couldn't.

I *also* couldn't confirm, because if I did, I knew she'd be pulling me into her, and she was in no mindset to consent to *anything* right now.

So, I just stood there, hoping she could feel everything I wasn't saying by the way I looked down at her, how my eyes searched hers, how I didn't shy away from her touch.

Of course, I think of that fucking night.
But we both know why I shouldn't.

After my prolonged silence, she deflated a bit, the playfulness leaving her eyes as she stared down at where her hands were on me. "I know, I know," she said on a sigh, releasing her grip. Her eyes found mine again. "You don't want me."

Damn it all to hell.

I swallowed, but didn't drop her gaze. I held it, praying once again that maybe she could see without me saying it that that was far from the truth.

Then again, maybe it was best that she thought that. Maybe that would keep us both out of trouble.

Grace looked sad for only a second before she blew out a long breath, stretching her arms overhead on a yawn. She smiled up at me next, tilting her head a bit.

"You know what?" she asked. "It's nice to have a friend, actually." She swallowed then, her eyes flicking to mine before they found the ground between her feet. "I don't have many of those."

Then, she pressed up onto her toes and kissed my cheek before unlocking her door and slipping inside.

And I stood in the empty corridor feeling like I'd doused her bright light in my own fucked up shadows.

CHAPTER 11

LET'S SEE WHAT YOU'VE GOT

Grace

Closing my eyes wasn't an option as I attempted yoga the next morning in the hotel gym.

Any time I did, the world spun, my stomach threatening to hit me with another wave of dry heaving. I'd already chugged water and popped some ibuprofen, but I had a feeling this hangover would hang around for at least half the day.

I couldn't sleep in — never could the day after drinking — so I'd dragged my ass down to the gym with the best of intentions. But even a slow yoga flow wasn't doing me any favors, so instead, I laid in a permanent corpse pose and stared up at the ceiling overthinking the night before.

Specifically — how I'd acted with Jaxson.

My memory was hazy, like I'd watched an old film rather than actively participated. I remembered all our conversations at the bar, and most of the chaos from playing quarters until Jaxson had quite literally carried me upstairs.

It was *there* that things got a little fuzzy.

I blinked, and a flash of Jaxson's crooked grin as he stared down at me knocked my next breath from my lungs. Another blink, and I could feel every smooth, hard curve of his abdomen, could remember how my fingertips had explored those muscles like uncharted territory. I blinked again, and there was no doubt in my mind that he'd shivered at my touch, that his jaw had been set like he wanted to touch me, too.

Do you ever think about that night in Austin?

That memory made me groan and cover my eyes with my hands, shaking my head in embarrassment. I was a drunk, silly girl asking a grown ass *professional hockey player* if he ever thought about a night that he was saddled with his teammate's little sister unwillingly. As if that night meant anything to him, as if he hadn't fucked at least a half-dozen women since then.

Of course, I didn't *know* that for sure... but it was a pretty safe bet.

Still... I wasn't *crazy,* was I? He definitely flirted with me, too. He definitely shivered under my touch last night. He definitely looked at my mouth like he wanted to do very dirty things to it.

Something like a fist around my stomach reminded me that the last time I'd trusted my instincts when it came to reading a man's actions, I'd ended up burned.

Listen to what he says, you idiot.

And what he *says* is that he's not interested.

There was a soft *snick* that interrupted my thoughts, and then the gym door opened, and I swiveled my head on the mat in time to see Jaxson swing through.

He stared at his phone in his hands as he entered, noise-canceling headphones covering his ears. And where I was pretty sure I looked like death warmed over, he looked like he'd had the best night's sleep of his life, like he'd just taken pre-workout and was ready to kick some ass.

I knew from growing up around my brother how brutal hockey season was on the body. By the end of it, especially if the team had any kind of playoff run, the guys were all leaned out and exhausted. It was impossible not to lose weight with how much and how aggressively they skated each day. So, in the off-season, they ate a shit ton of food and lifted heavy to try to build their muscle back up.

Staring at Jaxson, I had a hard time imagining *where* he could pack on any more muscle than he already had. He was fit as hell, and my eyes were naturally drawn over every inch of him, from his stacked traps to his monster thighs.

Jaxson swiped a towel and a bottle of water from the stand near the door before looking up from his phone, and when he spotted me, a little smirk curled on his lips.

I offered a two-finger wave from my mat, and he lifted his chin in response. Then, he headed straight for leg press while I pretended to do yoga.

I used to *love* yoga.

It used to calm me, center me, make me feel grounded. But nowadays, I just found myself... *bored* when I was on the mat. But I stuck to it, pretending like it was still my whole personality.

Because if there was one thing I hated about myself, it was how I never seemed to be able to stick to anything for long.

The joke with my family was that I had a shallow knowledge of everything, but a deep understanding of nothing. The truth was that not many things could hold my interest for long. Once I mastered a physical activity or hobby, I was immediately ready to move on.

About the only constant in my life was my desire to *move*.

Staying in one place for too long made me feel like I was suffocating.

Ever dedicated to my façade, I rolled onto my stomach and pressed up into a downward dog, but I watched Jaxson instead of my mat.

Holy. Hell.

I was pretty sure he had every fucking plate on that leg press when he finally sat down. He placed his feet shoulder-width apart on the platform and unlocked the machine, and then *easily* pushed ten reps before locking it again.

No wonder he had an ass of stone and quads to match.

In one breath, I brought my left leg up by my shoulder, dropping my foot next to my hands before windmilling up into warrior two. I tried to flow, giving it all my effort for about six minutes.

But all the while, my attention was glued to my *friend* and the way his body rippled with every rep.

Fuck it.

Letting my hands fall against my thighs with a slap, I abandoned my mat and marched right over to him, plucking a headphone off his left ear.

"I want to lift with you."

Jaxson arched a brow. "Well, good morning to you, too. How are you feeling?"

"Peachy," I lied.

His snort told me he knew it was a lie, but he didn't call me out on it. Instead, he wiped down the leg press that he was done with and mopped his face with a towel. "You want to lift, huh?"

"Yep."

"This is a lot different than yoga, you know."

"Don't box me in, Brittzy," I said, narrowing my eyes, but already I was smiling with the excitement I always felt when I was about to try something new.

He rolled his lips together against a grin, and then shrugged, gesturing toward the free weights. "Ever done RDLs?"

"Rapid Dick Licks?"

He nearly choked on the water he was taking a swig of as I skipped ahead of him over to the bench.

"Nah, I'm more of a take it slow kind of gal. You know, really swirl the tongue, use both hands, pretend like I have nowhere else in the world to be."

Jaxson let out a groan of an exhale, pinching the bridge of his nose. "You are a menace."

"To society, or to your mental health?"

"Both."

"Why, thank you," I said, and then I hung my hands on my hips. "Alright. Rapid Dick Licks. Let's do this."

I wasn't sure Jaxson accomplished much with me in the forty-five minutes he attempted to train me, but I was certain we both got one hell of an ab workout from how much we laughed. I was thankful there wasn't any sort of awkward tension hanging between us after I blatantly crossed our boundary line last night, and Jaxson — bless him — didn't call me out on it, either.

It made me cringe if I thought too hard about it, how he had to put his teammate's drunk little sister to bed while she tried to tear his clothes off.

Slowly, my headache began to fade, my stomach feeling more stable. I also started to get the hang of each exercise he showed me, and I liked the way it felt to push myself, to try something new and feel the way that burned my body in unfamiliar ways.

I was lifting approximately one percent of the weight *he* was, but still.

On my third and final set of bicep curls, Jaxson's phone buzzed on the bench where he'd left it. When he slid his thumb across the screen, tension furrowed his brows, and he let out a heavy sigh before texting something in return.

He all but threw his phone back onto the bench.

"Let me guess," I said, re-racking the weights and nodding toward his phone. "You got some girl pregnant."

It was a joke, and apparently a bad one, because Jaxson's smile was weak at best as he cracked his neck.

"Honestly, that might have been a better text."

Well, shit.

"Who was it?"

"My dad."

Through the haze of last night, I remembered me asking him about his parents, but we'd been interrupted before he could say much.

"Everything okay?" I asked.

He let out another long sigh. "Oh, fine. He was just reviewing film from our loss against Toronto that put us out of the playoff run and had some..." His jaw tensed. "*Thoughts* to share."

I blinked. "Wasn't that game months ago?"

"Indeed, it was."

He didn't elaborate. Instead, he jumped up to grab the bar that connected the two resistance machines in the middle of the gym. He repped out ten pull ups, exhaling little puffs of air at the top that told me he knew exactly how to breathe to best facilitate the movement that exercise required.

I hated that he changed the subject so quickly, but at the same time, I respected that distance he was silently asking me for. As someone who fucking *hated* getting into my sads, I understood that feeling of wanting a topic of conversation dropped.

So, I shoved down all my burning questions and skipped over to the bar just as his feet hit the ground.

"Me next!" I said, and I reached my hands up before jumping with all my might.

And I didn't even touch the bar.

My hands fell to my thighs and I pouted, looking up at the bar and then at Jaxson.

He smirked, shaking his head and nodding toward the bar. "Alright, little Nova. Let's see what you've got."

His hands found my waist then, and he lifted me like I weighed nothing — just like he had the night before. I couldn't fight back my smile as I found the height necessary to grab the bar, and once he was sure I had a good grip, Jaxson let go.

"Okay. Now what?"

He chuckled from behind me. "Engage your back, tighten your core, and lift yourself up."

I nodded with determination, sticking my tongue out a little as I attempted what he'd said.

And barely budged.

I laughed hysterically, letting my body fall limp as I held onto the bar. "Nailed it!"

Jaxson laughed, too, but then his hands were on me, and suddenly *laughing* was the furthest thing from my mind.

His hands were massive where they enveloped my rib cage, and he held most of my weight as he moved in close behind me.

"You want to think about lifting through here," he said, running his fingertips along my lats. I knew without looking to confirm that a wave of goosebumps had erupted at his touch. "And here," he added, ghosting those fingers over my deltoids and rhomboids.

And just when I thought I was safe from passing away at the feel of his warm hands on me, he wrapped them around my waist, one holding fast to my hip as the other splayed my stomach.

"Breathe," he encouraged — as if *that* was easy with him touching me. "And tighten your core. Use the energy here."

His touch lingered for a long pause before he pulled away, and I let out a shaky breath before feeling that determination sink back in.

With a grunt, I focused on all the areas he'd pointed out, using that sexual energy stirring in my gut to help propel me. I managed to lift myself halfway, and then I kicked my feet, tilting my chin up as if that would help it sail over the bar.

When I failed, I dropped limp again, hanging like a little kid from the monkey bars.

"I suck."

Jaxson chuckled. "No, you've just never attempted a pull-up before. These take a lot of strength. Here, let me help you so you can feel the proper form."

I waited for him to grab my waist again, but instead, he jumped, his hands finding the bar on either side of mine.

And that, of course, brought him flush against me — his chest to my back, our bodies in a tight-fitted seam.

Oh. My. Fucking. Fuck.

Heat rushed through me, from the point where his breath skated over my neck to where his massive biceps caged me in. He smelled like leather and fresh-cut cedar, the scent invading my senses and scrambling my brain just as much as his touch did.

"Oh, come on, Nova," he teased, lifting himself a little so his voice rumbled right behind the shell of my ear. "What was it you said to me that night in Austin? *Don't look so scared.*"

My eyelids fluttered shut, heart racing like I was doing cardio instead of weight training. Because that little jest, those four little words... they answered my question.

He *did* think about that night.

I swallowed, ready to drop from this bar and climb *him* like a tree, instead. But before I could, he wrapped his massive, watermelon-busting thighs around my waist, and pulled us *both* up.

"Oh, my God," I squealed. "You are a freak of nature!"

"Lift with your core," he said, but we both knew *I* wasn't doing any of the work as he powered us up for another rep. Instead, I just laughed, feeling like a little kid on a ride at the fair. I was weightless in his grip, but I felt every inch of his hard muscle where it pressed against me, and I was all too aware of a *particular* muscle nestled conveniently against my ass.

Being the brat that I was, I arched that ass *just* a little bit, enough to drag the length of him in a slow, imperceptible movement.

Or maybe it wasn't that imperceptible, because Jaxson let out a breath of a curse, and then he dropped to the ground, all contact broken.

I dropped, too, surveying my hands where they were red from holding onto the bar.

"Ouch," I said, shaking them out. "I can see why calluses are helpful."

I looked up at Jaxson with what I hoped was innocence, but the way he shook his head told me he saw right through the act.

"Menace," he said.

I grinned.

We wiped down the machines and weights in silence before gathering our belongings, and Jaxson held the door for me to exit the gym.

"Wait!" I said, scrambling for my phone while Jaxson rushed toward me like I was hurt. When he saw me peel my phone out from where I'd tucked it in the back of my shorts, his shoulders relaxed a little. I held it up between us with a little wiggle before unlocking it. "Video time."

I grabbed his arm and lugged him over to the full-body mirrors lining the wall, positioning him halfway behind me before I started the video.

"Today, Jaxson Brittain taught me how to do a pull-up." I used my fingers to zoom in on where Jaxson stood behind me with one brow in his hairline and both arms folded over his chest. "Jaxson, tell me something good."

"Well, it's damn sure not your form."

I elbowed him, the video going shaky with the movement as he chuffed out a laugh. Then, he rested his elbow on my shoulder and leaned on me like a crutch.

"We made a lot of money for the team shop last night."

I threw a fist in the air. "Fuck yeah, we did. Just call me the Quarters Queen."

I did a little curtsy with that, and Jaxson shook his head, throwing his towel over his shoulder and heading toward the door.

"Nah," he said, and I was glad the video was still rolling when he added, "You'll always be Nova to me."

CHAPTER 12

GOLD STARS

Jaxson

After a quick breakfast at the hotel, and another workout that involved using all my might to lift her suitcase into the car again, Grace and I were back on the road.

The first hour was quiet, neither of us talking as I navigated us out of Atlanta and back on the highway. My eyes were dry as hell after the late night, so once we finished at the gym, I changed out of my contacts, opting for my specs, instead.

Grace picked another playlist from her creations, this one titled *hot girl summer*. While the music wasn't exactly my taste, I didn't mind the pop music so long as I could watch her dance in the passenger seat as she sang along.

I was in my head for that first hour, anyway — for more reasons than one.

My father texting me with a mile-long list of all the ways I sucked wasn't anything I wasn't used to, but he usually gave me at least a *small* reprieve during the off-season. No such luck this year, I guessed. The fact that he casually tacked on a request for me to wire him money at the end without so much of a *please and thank you* added to my frustration, but again — I was used to it.

Those feelings had me gripping the steering wheel tight until I forced myself to calmly exhale and let it go. My father was who my father was, and I wasn't going to change anything about him now.

But when I let the topic of my father slip away, all my thoughts rushed back to last night.

I swallowed, glancing at where Grace was bopping along to the beat in the passenger seat next to me while she doodled in a notebook sprawled out on her lap. It was strange, but I *loved* that she wasn't on her phone, that she didn't even *have* social media. She was so present, locked into every moment happening in her life — even this one, which some might find boring, but she made the most of.

Watching her hands where one gripped the pen and the other held the notebook steady had me remembering all too well what they felt like pressed against my abdomen last night, and I thanked my lucky fucking stars that I had been strong enough not to give in.

How much longer I'd be able to resist, however, was yet to be seen.

I had to be giving the girl whiplash, because one second I had stone resolve, and the next I was jumping up behind her on a pull-up bar and wrapping my legs around her, my cock pressing against her sweet little ass.

It was as if I didn't have a choice. Common sense didn't exist. She altered my brain chemistry when she was near to the point that I couldn't control myself.

She was magnetic.

Even when I *did* manage to keep distance between us, I still felt a pull to her.

The interesting thing was that even being on this road trip was so out of character for me, it made my head spin. When I'd offered to go for a drive that first night at her brother's house, I'd meant just that — a drive. For like... an hour. *Maybe* two.

The last thing I'd expected was this, and yet I hadn't even hesitated when she'd suggested it.

It was like a part of me had been dormant my entire life, but it had stirred to life that night in Austin. And when she suggested a road trip conveniently when I didn't have shit to do, that part of me jumped at the chance, demanding to take the wheel.

I felt... reckless.

And yet, at peace.

I felt like I was running away and running home all at once.

The feelings were too messy and complicated to sort through, so I let them rest for now, deciding that — at least for the moment — I had permission to go with the flow.

In less than a month, I'd need to get back to Tampa. Preseason training and conditioning would take over my life just like it did every August.

But, at least for now, I didn't have a responsibility in the world.

Other than helping the girl next to me move on from her pain, which — truth be told — she seemed to be doing all on her own.

Suddenly, Grace leaned forward and cut the volume on the stereo. "Let's go for a hike."

I blinked at the suddenness of it, but I didn't know why I was surprised at this point. The girl was like the weather — reliable only in her unpredictability.

"We don't have any hiking gear," I pointed out.

"Fine," she said, sucking her teeth like she was annoyed with my rationale. "Let's go for an outdoor *walk*."

I shook my head on a smile. "You're a brat."

"A menace *and* a brat?" She shimmied her shoulders, already pulling up AllTrails on her phone to find a hike. "Out here earning gold stars left and right."

• • •

Grace somehow convinced me to pull off the highway near Chattanooga, even when I tried to argue that all the reviews on the hike said boots and poles were suggested.

So, here we were, slipping on the muddy rocks as we climbed, Grace skipping along with a bright smile while I grumbled like an old man.

"Please be careful," I said for what felt like the hundredth time as I watched Grace lose her step on a slippery part of the ascent. Her sneakers were covered in clay, with absolutely no purchase, which left her windmilling and just barely catching her balance more than I cared to witness.

"I'm *fine*, ya big fuddy duddy." She looked at me over her shoulder with a grin. "Maybe it's *you* who should be careful. First, you're flirting with me, and now, you're worried about my safety? People might get the wrong idea, Brittzy."

She giggled with the tease, sprinting up a particularly steep climb while I followed at a slower pace.

As much as I grumbled and complained, it *was* very beautiful — thick, lush trees surrounding us on either side of the trail, mossy rocks that looked like something out of a fairy tale, and the distant sound of rushing water. Even though it was July, it was comfortable in the shade. It felt like a spring day more than a summer one.

I didn't realize how much I missed seasons and cool weather, how much I longed for something that wasn't just a perpetual heat wave. Tampa was amazing in the short winter we had, but other than that, it was just... *hot*.

Still, I stayed there even in the off-season when I had the opportunity to travel — mostly because if I *did* travel, I knew I'd have no excuse not to go home.

And that was one place I did *not* want to go.

"I can't believe I'm the one leading," Grace called behind her. "With how much you skate, I thought it'd be your endurance outshining mine."

"Says the one huffing and puffing through that sentence," I shot back.

She laughed.

And then, she lost her footing again.

I cursed under my breath as I hiked faster to catch up to her, because I saw her arms flailing and sneakers sliding and knew this was one fall she wasn't going to be able to escape. I caught up just in time for her to fall backward into me, and had I not been there, she likely would have cracked her head wide open on one of those rocks I was just admiring.

"Besides, I *have* to walk behind so I can ensure there are no deaths during this hike," I said pointedly, helping her upright once more.

Grace just laughed, and then she looked over her shoulder at me, her eyes widening a bit at how close we were.

My hands were splayed on her hips, holding steady even now that she was fine on her own. She was wearing highlighter green biker shorts and a matching sports bra, leaving nothing but smooth skin for my thumbs to graze in-between the two fabrics.

Fuck, she was pretty.

Her pink lips curled into a soft smile the longer she looked at me, the longer *I* looked back. She had her long hair swept into a ponytail and covered with a baseball cap — the same one she'd worn that night at Vince's that said *asshole* on it. Her chest was sweat-slicked and heaving a bit from the effort of the hike, her eyes matching the pine around us and dancing with a playfulness that made me want to push her against the nearest tree and kiss her breathless.

I closed my eyes hard and tight, subtly gritting my teeth as I released my hold on her.

Teammate's little sister.

Eight years younger.

It was becoming a mantra at this point, one I repeated over and over hoping it would eventually sink into my thick skull. Sometimes, like in this moment, I had enough control not to be an idiot. But when I opened my eyes again, I kept them on the ground where our feet were until she started moving again.

Because my restraint when she looked at me like that was basically nonexistent.

Grace stood there for a long moment before she started hiking again, and I breathed a little easier once there was some space between us. I followed, and then she hit me in the gut with a question I didn't expect.

"What's the story with your parents?"

I paused mid-step, and Grace hiked another few feet before she turned and watched me with concern knitting her brows.

"Sorry," she blurted. "I... you don't have to answer that."

"No, it's fine," I promised her, and with a long inhale, I started moving again, signaling for her to do the same.

Maybe if we were talking, I could stop thinking about her ass in those shorts. "I'm just not used to much conversation outside of chirping my teammates."

Grace snorted at that.

I hated the way my chest grew tighter the longer I tried to find the words to answer her question almost as much as I hated the fact that it was such a hard one for me to answer at all. I also found it curious that I didn't change the subject, because any time any other woman had ever tried to get close to me, that was exactly what I did.

But with Grace... I *wanted* to tell her.

Maybe because, for some reason I couldn't explain, I knew she'd understand.

Before I could overanalyze it too much, I blew out a breath and started talking.

"My parents are... fierce," I landed on. "In everything that they do. They love hard, they fight harder, and they don't beat around the bush."

"That's kind of nice," Grace said, using her hands to help scramble over a tall rock.

"I never have to wonder what they're thinking, that's for sure."

"Are you close with them?"

I cracked my neck. "Not when I can help it."

Grace paused, waiting until I scrambled over the same rock. She looked up at me for a moment, her eyes searching mine, and then started hiking again.

"You were born and raised in Alberta, right?"

I nodded, trailing behind her. "Canmore, specifically."

"What was it like?"

"Beautiful," I answered immediately. "And there were adventures *everywhere*. Mountain biking, hiking, swimming, kayaking, climbing." I shook my head. "When we moved to Calgary, I missed it. Even though we were only a little over an hour away, it just wasn't the same as walking out your backdoor and having the world as your playground."

"Why did you move?"

"Hockey."

"Ah," she said with a grin. "Well, I'm sure you didn't hate that."

"You'd be surprised."

The words flew out faster than a blink, jarring both Grace *and* me.

She frowned. "What do you mean?"

I swallowed, and for a while, we were both quiet, me climbing behind her as the sound of rushing water got stronger with each step. We must have been close to the north creek, the one that had a suspension bridge hanging over it, according to the trails app.

"My dad played hockey," I said after a while.

"Professionally?"

I nodded. "Yeah, in the AHL. First for the Hawks, and then the Thunder. He was a fucking beauty too — a tough guy to play against and a real fan favorite," I added with a slight smile and shake of my head.

"So, he was great?"

"I was too young to really remember him playing, but I've seen the tape. If you think I'm a beast on D, you should have seen him."

"Who said I think you're a beast?" she teased, and I loved her for it, because it relieved the pressure on my chest when I laughed again.

"Anyway, he loved it. I mean, it was his whole *life*. He put a stick in my hands before I could even walk, because he was determined for me to follow in his footsteps." I swallowed, using a small tree to help me climb a rock. "But then he got hurt."

Grace waited for me to catch up, her eyes flicking between mine. "Badly, I'm assuming."

My throat was tight when I nodded. "Broke his back."

"*What*?" Grace gaped at me. "He... *how*?"

"Got plowed over by a winger hell bent on scoring, and he slid into the goal posts. He had pads on and everything, but it just... I don't know. It was the right angle, the right amount of speed that..."

My voice faded as the scene played in my head like a movie I'd seen a thousand times. I'd only watched that tape once, by accident, when I was trying to find the game my dad wanted me to study going into a tournament in high school. He and Mom had both done a good job shielding me from his injury up until that point.

But I watched it unknowingly that day. I saw the very moment my father slammed into the bar, watched as his body bent in an unnatural way around it before he lay lifeless on the ice.

I saw the last time he ever skated.

I sniffed, throat tight again. "Let's just say that accident changed him. Not just his way of life, but who he was inside, too. My mom... she swears he used to be funny and kind, that he was the life of any room he walked into." I cleared my throat. "But I only know him as harsh and abusive."

All the teasing had left Grace now, and we hiked along silently for a moment before she said, "He started projecting his dreams onto you."

"You're good at this game."

She shook her head, pausing when we hit the top of the ascent. We could see the creek now, which was more like a river, the water flowing beneath us.

"I don't fault him," I said as we started hiking down toward the bridge. "I can't imagine having everything taken from me like that. He's come a long way with surgeries and rehab and physical therapy, but... he can't walk, let alone skate. And if it wasn't for him pushing me the way he did, I probably wouldn't have made it this far."

"I'm sure it was hard," Grace said softly. "All that pressure."

The way she said it — it was as if she could relate.

And when I thought about what it would have been like growing up with Vince Tanev as an older brother, I imagined she probably really could relate in her own way.

"He started drinking on top of it all, and when he's drunk? He's a fucking monster," I said. "To me, to Mom, to anyone around him. And then he'll sober up and yell at you like *you* are the crazy one, like you're the problem. And the cycle repeats."

Grace stayed quiet, listening, and I didn't realize how much I needed to talk about this — not until more and more words tumbled from my lips like they'd been waiting to get free for decades.

"The funny thing is, the better I get, the further my career progresses... the angrier he becomes. He gets raging mad when I don't perform at the level he thinks I can, but then when I *do* perform..."

I swallowed, my body physically not allowing me to say anything more than that.

"And your mom?" Grace asked.

That made my jaw harden. "I don't even know who my mom is, past the shell of who she became taking care of my father. She has nothing but empathy for him, and she stands by him no matter what." I breathed a laugh. "As much as she can with the flimsy backbone she has, anyway."

My nostrils flared, but even as good as the words felt to say, my stomach soured. I loved her, and I didn't want to talk shit.

But she could have saved herself, could have saved us both — and she chose not to.

"True love," Grace said quietly, pausing at the foot of the suspension bridge.

"If that's love, then I don't want it."

She nodded, and then before I could prepare for it, she launched herself into my arms.

Her hug was ferocious for the tiny thing that she was. She crushed me to her like she could shield me from the world, and I stiffened only a second before I was hugging her back. My grip was soft at first, hesitant, but then I wrapped her up, closing my eyes when she rested her head against my chest and squeezed me with all her might.

My throat was tight for a completely different reason now.

I couldn't remember the last time I'd been hugged.

"Thank you for sharing all that with me," she whispered, her voice just barely reaching my ears above the sound of the creek rushing below us.

"Thank you for listening."

She squeezed me tight one last time before pulling back, her eyes a bit glossy when she looked up at me. But she smiled despite whatever she was feeling, the kind of smile that spanned her whole face and lit her up like a Christmas tree.

"Last one across the bridge has to jump in the creek!"

She took off like a lightning bolt, absolutely zero fear as she sprinted across the swinging bridge. She didn't care that it looked old and dilapidated, that it shook precariously the farther she got toward the middle of it. She just ran and laughed with her hands in the air, ponytail swinging behind her.

She was freedom personified.

I bit back a smile as I watched her run, hands hanging on my hips. I couldn't believe how much I'd just shared with her. It had me feeling a little crazy, like I didn't want to calculate all the risks before I made my next move.

So, I sprinted after her, following the sound of her laughter and silently praying the rickety boards of the bridge didn't give way. But I had a feeling it'd hold steady.

I was lighter than I'd been in years.

CHAPTER 13

FAVORITE SOUND IN THE WORLD

Grace

A cool breeze rushed across the top of the creek, sweeping up and over my slick skin. I sighed, instantly cooler, closing my eyes on a smile and tilting my face toward the sun streaming through the trees.

There was nothing like this.

It was easy to get swept away in how urgent everything seemed in life — get good grades, graduate college, go to work, pay your bills, find a husband, settle down, buy a house, make babies. It seemed we always had our eyes cast on the future, on following the grand master plan.

Meanwhile, life was happening all around us.

Jaxson and I had dropped our packs on the rocks at the edge of the water. I'd beat him across the bridge, and I was also the first one in the cool water of the creek. I waded in knee-deep, careful to avoid the current, and soaked it all in.

Distantly, I was aware of the sound of Jaxson wading into the water, too. I creaked one eye open, and then the next, before they both shot open wide.

He'd stripped off his shirt and abandoned it at the shoreline, along with his shorts.

He carefully edged himself into the cold water in nothing but a pair of black boxer briefs, his lips in an *o* as he made quick puffs of breath.

"Fuck, it's cold," he cursed, but he wore a smile, one more relaxed than I'd ever seen him have.

I, on the other hand, was shocked stupid, standing there with my mouth hanging open and no prayer of gathering my senses with him prowling closer in nothing but his underwear.

To be fair, I was in shorts and a sports bra. It wasn't like I was being modest.

Still, *I* didn't have muscles like *that*.

There was no better way to describe this man than *thick*. His chest was sculpted, pecs hard and round before they met the top ridges of his abs. And he didn't have an ounce of softness there — it was a rippling eight-pack, the sweat from our hike teasing me as it cascaded down the valley that ran over his belly button before disappearing at the band of his briefs.

I couldn't tear my eyes away from his arms, from the bicep muscles that were the size of a cantaloupe, or the black and blue ink that swirled from his right shoulder all the way down to his wrist. And as if the top half of his body wasn't distracting enough, those briefs left nothing to the imagination downstairs.

His thick thighs were corded with muscle, stretching the fabric, and between those thighs there was an unmistakable bulge.

Fuck, he was big.

I started sweating again the longer I stared, and when Jaxson cleared his throat, I jumped, ripping my eyes up to meet his gaze.

He chuckled, cocking a brow and folding his arms over his chest. "You checking me out, Nova?"

My cheeks warmed at the nickname, the heat nearly unbearable when a sly smirk spread on his perfect lips in the next breath.

"Don't act like you haven't been staring at my ass the whole hike up here."

"Me? I would never," he said, flattening a palm against his chest. "Now, your tits in that sports bra, on the other hand…"

I reached down for a handful of water, scooping it as best I could and launching it at him. His deep chuckle rumbled through his chest as he splashed me back, and then I was running, skipping over rocks as best I could to dodge his advance.

Which was pointless.

He caught up easily, his strides more confident and surer than my own, and he swung me up into the air with water spraying off me like I was a sprinkler. The river was freezing, but his body was hot against mine.

Until he took us both down into the water.

I emerged with my breath completely gone, lips trembling as Jaxson laughed and shook the water out of his hair. Once my breathing was somewhat even again, I chased after him, climbing onto his back in my attempt to take him down the same way he'd done to me.

But again, it was useless.

He was gargantuan in comparison to me, and he just laughed and dragged me with him toward the shore. Jaxson reached around for me and pulled me to the front of his body, where I tried to cling to him and continue my mission of dunking him. But before I could find purchase, he threw me over his shoulder like a fucking caveman.

Which left me with a glorious view of his ass.

His briefs were soaked now, hugging every inch of him, and I watched that indentation in the side of his ass flex with every step he took. I no longer fought him, and when we made it to the rocky shore, he carefully sat me down in front of him.

Water seared down his skin in rivulets from his hair to his chest, each drop rolling over his abs or along the line in-between them before they slid to the band of his briefs.

My mouth was dry again, seeing that bulge highlighted by the wet fabric sticking to it. I thought I saw it twitch, which made me clench my thighs together as I dragged my gaze up to meet Jaxson's.

He swallowed, his jaw tight, and then nodded toward our packs. "Let's eat."

We set up a picnic in the shady area by the bank, both of us keeping our distance now. I poured a smorgasbord of snacks out of my backpack while Jaxson retrieved two reusable water bottles from his, passing one to me.

We were quiet while we ate, the rushing water our soundtrack, and then Jaxson pulled a book from his bag and leaned against a tree. He was wearing his wire-framed glasses, and it was the hottest contradiction — this ripped, inked motherfucker leaning against a tree with a book in his hands and his brows furrowing over the top of those frames.

I would never pretend to be an expert on straight female sexuality, but there was just something about a man reading that made my brain short circuit every fucking time.

I studied the cover.

Healing the Masculine Soul by Gordon Dalbey.

Well, tits. He's even hotter now.

Carefully, I pulled my phone out and snuck a photo of him before tucking it away. If I was the social media kind of gal, I'd submit that shit to one of those accounts that posted hot guys reading. As it was, I saved it purely out of selfish greed.

"I saw that," he said without looking at me, licking his thumb before he turned a page.

I feigned innocence. "Saw what?"

"You being a creeper and adding a picture of me to your spank bank."

"I don't know what you're talking about," I said, hopping up from where I was seated on the one blanket we had with us on this trip.

The corner of Jaxson's lips curved up, his eyes skirting to me before he shook his head and went back to reading.

I strolled back down to the river, exploring a bit before I retrieved my slack line from my bag. Two large trees separated the clearing where we had our picnic, the perfect distance to set up. I attached one end of the line to each tree, pulling it taut enough to hold while leaving enough slack to play on.

Then, I stepped up, walking a few steps on the line with my bare feet, arms spread wide to help balance.

I took each step carefully, body leaning left and right to correct my stability when needed before I took the next one. I was relatively new at slacklining, which meant I didn't have any cool tricks unlocked yet.

That didn't stop me from trying, though.

Slowly, I started bouncing, making the line bend and warp until I had a little momentum. Then, I dropped down to my butt, sitting on the line like a trampoline for just a second before it pitched me into the air. I squealed with joy, stomach flipping from the drop before I landed on my feet. I threw my hands up in the air, turning to find Jaxson halfway up, book tossed aside like he'd been prepared to risk it all to save me from colliding with the hard clay.

I chuckled. "Ye of little faith!"

"What the hell are you doing, besides trying to give me premature gray hairs," he grumbled, climbing to his feet and walking over to the line.

"The salt and pepper look is hot. You should actually thank me."

He ignored the comment, and I hopped back onto the line, proud when I steadied myself and stayed on. That was a beginner trick, too, but it was getting easier.

"I picked this up in college," I explained. "I had some friends who would hang out on the mall, playing Frisbee or whatever. And one day this kid brought a line. I'm not very good at it," I added, stumbling off when I tried to turn around as if my body was keen to illustrate that point. I hopped back on just as quickly, though. "But it's fun, and challenging — which I love."

Jaxson folded his arms, watching me mess around for a bit. He nearly lost his shit when I did a front flip off the line, but I stuck the landing once again, winking at him when I saw his panicked attempt to catch me.

"What did you major in?" he asked when I climbed back on.

I snorted. "Does it matter?"

"I mean, for most people, yes."

"Philosophy."

"*Philosophy?*" he echoed on a laugh. "Good God, *why*?"

I shrugged. "I don't know, I just picked something that sounded halfway interesting."

"So, what do you want to do?"

"Right now? Land a flip on the line," I said before going for another attempt. My left foot caught the line, but the right slipped, and I tumbled off, rolling to the ground with a laugh.

Jaxson pinched the bridge of his nose as I dusted myself off and hopped up again.

"I meant, you graduated," he said. "So, what now? Do you want to... teach?" he guessed, but the way his voice raised, I knew he couldn't see me doing that any more than I could.

"I want to travel," I said. "I want to experience life through the eyes of a thousand different people. I want to watch the sun rise on the other side of the world. I want to eat foods I've never heard of and drink wine with the men who grow the grapes that make it." I bounced on the line, smiling, but then blew out a long exhale. "As for a job? Well, your guess is as good as mine."

"Meaning?"

"Meaning... I don't really care about a career. I'll do whatever job I can do in the place I'm at. Maybe I'll bartend. Maybe I'll be a waitress. Maybe I'll farm seaweed or be a kayak tour guide or serve lunch at a kid's camp." I shrugged. "Every new job will be a part of the adventure."

Jaxson smiled. "That's pretty cool."

His response startled me a bit. I was used to people hearing that little speech and promptly telling me I was irresponsible or lost, that I was a dreamer who would have to wake up one day.

"Is it?" I laughed. "I'm not sure my parents would agree, or most of America, for that matter. I'm living off the fund my parents promised me upon graduation. Past that? I have zero idea how I'll feed myself. All I know for sure is that I can't spend my life in an office." I shook my head. "I'd rather barely have two quarters to rub together than be loaded and stuck in a cubicle all day."

"Well, if you were *that* loaded, you'd probably have a corner office with a view."

"I don't want to look out at the world, though," I said, hopping off the line to stand right in front of him. "I want to swallow it whole, to take every experience it has to offer, learn every lesson it has to teach."

His eyes searched mine, the edges of them crinkling a bit as he did. "Anyone ever tell you you're not like other twenty-two-year-olds?"

"Well, I turn twenty-three next month, so maybe that's why. Your turn," I said, pointing to the line.

"*My* turn?"

"Come on, you big baby. Get up there." I smacked his ass with that, and he gawked at me before barreling out a laugh and planting his foot on the line. He stepped up easily, which made me slightly hate him.

"I really do think it's cool, you know," he said, his body shaking with the effort it took to keep his beastly frame balanced. He took a step, arms swinging out wide. "I admire that you're not just doing what the rest of your peers are."

"Well, don't admire it too much. It's more a sign of the fact that I'm not particularly great at anything, nor do I have a passion past seeing the world. It might be different, otherwise." I nodded toward him. "Unlike you and Vince, not many people in the world know exactly what they want to do at the ripe old age of five."

"Not many people have parents who don't give them a choice, either."

"You say that like you don't love it," I said, watching as he carefully turned around and didn't fall.

Bastard.

"Which I know is a lie, because I've seen you play."

He bobbed his head a bit, telling me without words that I wasn't wrong.

I could sense that he didn't want to dive in more on the subject, so I tried to edge the conversation away from his parents. Naturally, it led me to think of my own.

"I'm pretty sure my parents forget I exist until I show up at their house to do laundry."

Ugh.

I hated the words even as I said them. I wanted them to come out as a joke, to sound playful and funny. Instead, I sounded jealous and bitter and resentful — three emotions I didn't make space for in my life.

"Ew, sorry," I said on a laugh. "That sounded petty as hell. I know my parents love me and care about me. The fact that I'm living off their dime proves that. And I know they're interested in my life just as much as Vince's."

I didn't believe those words even as I said them, trying to convince Jaxson and myself that they were true.

"I just don't have as much going on at the moment. So, it's all good."

Jaxson paused, studying me before he hopped down from the line and walked over to where I stood.

"I fucking hate when you do that."

"Do what?"

"Act like you're not allowed to feel anything but happy, like being sad or angry or disappointed makes you a bad person."

Everything around us quieted.

The water stopped rushing, slowing to a hushed trickle. The wind ceased to blow, leaving the trees standing still.

All I heard was my heart beating overtime in my chest.

All I felt was a man seeing right through me.

His eyes held mine, not apologizing, not backing down.

My next breath stuttered out of me, and I was all too aware of how my chest rose and fell like I was running a marathon as opposed to standing still. There was a hot, enigmatic energy flowing off him — his eyes holding mine, his chest heaving just the same.

Then, those eyes fell to my lips.

Do it, the voice inside me urged.

It was a whisper at first, and then an incessant chant. He was looking at my mouth like he wanted to cover it with his own, and I silently begged him to without moving a fucking centimeter.

Suddenly, common sense pushed through, and I closed my eyes, laughing as I stepped away from him and turned all the way around for good measure.

Listen to the words he's told you, not your stupid heart, Grace.

God knows that thing can't be trusted.

Once I was composed, I turned around with a beaming smile, running past him and jumping up onto the line.

"Watch this!" I said.

"Stop ignoring—*shit, Grace!*"

His attempt to get me to face the truth he'd spoken went up in flames as I attempted a backflip off the line, only to overshoot and land on my butt, rolling backward and landing sprawled out like a starfish.

"Fuck, are you okay?" he asked, running to where I'd rolled.

My side was in a stitch from laughing, and I clutched my stomach before I opened my eyes again and found him braced over me, hands on his knees and eyes laden with stress.

"Oh, stop," I said. "I'm fine. I was a cheerleader, okay? I've had way worse landings than that."

He didn't seem convinced.

"Come here," I said, reaching my hand for his. "Lie with me."

That made the line between his brows soften, his eyes widening a bit.

"What — you too pretty to lie in the dirt?" I teased.

"No," he grumbled, carefully lowering himself beside me. "Are you so weird that you don't think lying in the dirt is anything out of the ordinary?"

"Shut up and close your eyes."

"Rude."

I didn't open mine again, just smiled as I felt him settle beside me with a sigh. Once he was quiet, nature spoke to us. The water rushed over the rocks and trickled down in streams. The breeze blew through the trees, whispering tales of history in our ears. Birds chirped somewhere in the distance, insects singing along with them.

"Hear that?" I asked softly. "This is my favorite sound in the world."

I inhaled a deep breath, reveling in the feel of the sunshine on my skin, the shade from the trees blocking it intermittently. When Jaxson didn't respond, I peeled my eyes open, shielding them with one hand as I turned to look at him.

And found him staring right back.

His eyes were so beautiful it hurt — bright blue, almost see-through the way the sun illuminated them now.

"Grace—" he started, but then a low, threatening roll of thunder made us both pause. Jaxson frowned, sitting up with his hands propped behind him as he narrowed his eyes at dark clouds hovering over the mountain in the distance.

"That doesn't look good," I said when I sat up to join him.

"We'd better get going." He stood, reaching down a hand for mine, and when I took it, he heaved me up so easily I nearly knocked into him. My hand flew out to steady me, catching his bare stomach.

We both froze.

Remove your hand, idiot.

But I couldn't.

My palm was glued there, feeling the heat of him trembling beneath my cool touch. I swallowed, staring at the contrast of our skin, at how his was inked and showing signs of his age, while mine was tan and smooth and young.

I thought my heart was going to race out of my chest the longer we stood there, both of us watching where I touched him and waiting for the other to make the next move.

Mine would have been to slide my hand lower, to roll my palm over the bulge growing in his briefs.

But Jaxson heaved a sigh, peeling my hand away like I was someone he needed to pity, like I was his friend's annoying little sister who had a crush on him.

My throat tightened with the truth behind that sentiment.

"Come on," he said, eyeballing the sky. "We need to get back to the car before this breaks loose."

Then, he started gathering our things with me still standing there like a fool.

CHAPTER 14

CONNECT THE DOTS

Jaxson

The group chat had been going off while Grace and I were on our hike.

We had driven toward Nashville once we'd loaded up again, stopping at an REI at her request. She'd made me promise to stay in the car, and so here I was, sitting in the parking lot still damp from our swim in the creek, as well as the rain we'd been caught in on our hike back.

I thumbed through my phone with my breaths coming a bit easier than before.

Truth be told, I needed a break from her. Not that I wanted one. But I'd come far too close to doing things I knew I shouldn't when we were down by that creek, and I had the amount of time she would be in that store to get my shit together.

I'd wanted to kiss her so fucking badly I still felt the desire churning in my gut like a spell I'd never be free of.

And when she'd touched me, when she'd looked up at me with those wide eyes and waited for me to make the next move...

Fuck. I'd been rock hard and ready to risk it all.

That storm rolling in was all that saved me.

I shook off the thought of what would have happened had I said *fuck it* and given in, pulling up the group chat that had dozens of unread messages, instead.

Fabio: Squad?

Fabio was Carter Fabbri's nickname. We let him think it was because of his flow, but the truth was it was a play off his last name and an inside joke about how his game with the ladies was absolute trash.

Poor kid. I was pretty sure he'd still be a virgin if we hadn't put that to rest thanks to an eager puck bunny his rookie season.

No, if anyone was going to get the title of Best Flow, that honor would go to Daddy P. Bastard had longer hair than the rest of us put together.

Tanny Boy: I'm down.

Daddy P: Can't. Currently interviewing another fucking nanny.

Fabio: Either you have shit luck with babysitters, or you're completely unaware of how terrifying you are when you're grumpy.

Tanny Boy: My money is on that option. I've witnessed more than two poor girls shit themselves when he yells at them.

Daddy P: I do not yell. And I wouldn't have to correct them if they weren't so fucking clueless.

Tanny Boy: Are they clueless, or are you just the most impossible person to please who's ever lived?

Fabio: I'll tack on that you're also an overprotective dad.

Daddy P: *middle finger emoji*

Fabio: What about you, Brittzy?

Fabio: Brittzyyyyy

Tanny Boy: He's probably practicing for the tournament. He needs all the swings he can get.

Fabio: Like that will help. I've seen basketball players with a better golf game than Brittz.

Tanny Boy: Yo, Brittz. Get off the shitter and come play COD.

Fabio: He'd have his phone if he was on the shitter.

Tanny Boy: Let's just keep texting until we annoy him so much he stops fucking whatever puck bunny he pulled in last night.

Daddy P: Did the part where I said I'm holding a goddamn interview go right over your thick skulls? Fuck off.

Fabio: Can't be going that well if you're able to text us.

I chuckled the more I read, and then skipped to the bottom and thumbed out a reply.

Me: Sorry — was driving. Decided to travel a bit before the tournament.

Fabio: Sure. It's okay if you were taking golf lessons, Brittzy. We won't shame you for it.

Tanny Boy: Nah, we'll just wipe the floor with you and Daddy P in a couple days — all in the name of charity.

Fabio: How'd the interview go, Daddy P? Got a new nanny secured?

Daddy P: For now.

Tanny Boy: We should start a prayer circle for the girl.

Carter sent a gif of a man making the sign of the cross, and I chuckled, even as my stomach sank with how I'd lied to them. Well — *technically,* I hadn't lied, but I'd carefully omitted the fact that my teammate's little sister was traveling *with* me.

I could still see how Vince had glared at me the first time I'd laid eyes on Grace, telling me without a word to not even think about it. Then, he'd told her to sit with me on the party bus that night in Austin.

"You're the only one I can trust."

My chest sparked with guilt, and then my heart sank when I opened a side text I had from Will.

Daddy P: We need to talk at the tournament.

Will Perry wasn't exactly one for sharing feelings, so if he needed to talk to me — it couldn't be a good thing.

I stared at that text for a long second before I nearly threw my phone, my heart leaping into my throat as someone beat on the passenger side window.

It was Grace.

With two arms full of camping and hiking gear.

• • •

"Only you would prefer sleeping in the dirt over a plush bed at a Five-Star hotel in Nashville," I said, eyeballing Grace as she put the finishing touches on the inside of our tent.

Tent — singular.

It was a good-size tent, at least, with room for two sleeping bags that Grace had elevated with inflatable pads beneath them. But that didn't change the fact that I'd be sleeping less than a foot away from her.

I swallowed down the risk that came with that, trying to focus instead on how happy Grace looked.

"Come on! *This* is what real road tripping is like," she said, sprawling out on top of her sleeping bag. She'd also secured two inflatable pillows, and she tested hers by lying on her left side and then her right, ending up on her back with a satisfied grin. "Perfect."

"You're a nut."

"It'll be the best sleep of your life. Trust me."

"On the ground with no sense of security in the Tennessee heat?" I flattened my lips. "Not sure I'm buying that pitch."

Grace groaned, flopping onto her stomach before she hopped up to her feet. She could stand fully in the tent, while I had to bend down — which was why I stayed at the opening of it, sweating even as the sun set.

"Those Five-Star penthouse suites have totally ruined your sense of adventure."

I stifled a laugh at the jest. She wasn't wrong. It'd been a long time since I'd slept in a tent — mostly because when you had access to the finest hotels, it wasn't usually an option you considered.

"Come on," she said. "We need to build a fire before we don't have any light left."

"Because it's so cold," I deadpanned as she swept out of the tent and past me.

"Because we need a fire to tell scary ghost stories and make s'mores," she said, as if that was the most obvious choice of activities for the night, and I was a dumb prick for not realizing it.

When I didn't budge, she grabbed me by the wrist and tugged with all her might — which wouldn't have moved me even an inch if I hadn't let her.

"Come *on*," she grunted, tugging me toward the wooded area that surrounded our campsite. "It'll be fun. I promise."

We separated then — me in search of larger logs of wood while Grace focused on gathering smaller brush we could use for kindling. She promptly elbowed me out of the way when I tried to take over starting the fire, pointing the lighter at me and warning that she was an independent woman who could do it herself.

And she did.

I helped with setting up our campsite and gathering that firewood, but I had zero doubts that she could have done it all on her own if I wasn't there. Still, I didn't like the thought of it — her being alone in this situation. A tent was about the least secure shelter in the fucking world, and I didn't care if there was a camper's code and everyone looked out for one another.

All it took was one selfish, sick bastard to put her life at risk.

I laughed at myself, shaking my head and that thought from it. I was not her fucking father. She was about to travel the *world* like this, and I was the last person who was going to be able to stop her.

But fuck if I couldn't halt the burning need to protect her while she did it.

"What are you laughing at?" Grace asked, watching where I was carefully rotating a marshmallow on one of the sticks she'd bought from REI. We'd eaten hot dogs for dinner — which I couldn't recall having since I was a kid.

I looked around us in lieu of answering, taking in the canopy of trees above us and the faint stars I could make out through the leaves. It wasn't quiet, but it was an interesting change from what I was used to. Instead of traffic and laughter and music as the soundtrack like it was in Tampa, it was the crackling of the fire, the occasional hoot from an owl, the wind rustling the leaves.

"Fine, keep your funny jokes to yourself," Grace said, and then she pierced a marshmallow of her own and plopped it right into the middle of the fire. It caught in a second, burning like mad as she pulled it out and watched it. She waited until the whole marshmallow was a black, crispy thing before blowing out the flame.

I blinked at it, then at her. "You're a monster."

"No, I'm a genius," she argued. "This is the only way to roast a mallow."

"Hard disagree. Look at mine," I said, nodding to where I was slowly rotating it just above the tips of the fire like it was a rotisserie chicken. "This thing is going to be perfectly browned."

Grace made a face that said that didn't impress her, and then she sandwiched her marshmallow and a piece of dark chocolate between two graham crackers and took the biggest bite known to man, making the marshmallow ooze out over her hands and stick to her lips.

She licked those lips in an attempt to get them clean, but all it did was draw my gaze to them, and I felt that spark of possession light between my ribs again.

I tore my eyes away and focused on the fire.

"I take it you never went camping as a kid?" Grace asked.

"What makes you think that?"

"Call it a hunch," she said on a laugh.

I shifted, not chancing looking at her again with that sticky white sweetness just begging to be licked off her.

"I did a few times in high school," I said. "Some friends and I would head out to Banff, spend the weekend there. Of course, we usually slept in our cars and drank beer more than we ate anything. But as a kid?" I sniffed. "No."

"Surprising, given where you lived."

"Camping isn't really easy for someone in a wheelchair," I said. "And the last thing Mom or I wanted was a situation that irritated Dad. I'm sure we went when I was younger, before the accident... I just don't really remember."

Grace nodded, and then yawned, the motion stretching her little mouth wide. She covered it with a sleepy smile. "Sorry."

"For yawning?"

She frowned, then chuckled. "For not being my usual peppy self, I guess."

"You don't have to be sorry for being tired."

That seemed to stun her — which was ludicrous.

"Here, finish that," I said, nodding to where she had stacked another burnt as shit marshmallow on a graham cracker with chocolate. "And let's get you to bed."

My marshmallow was finally perfectly cooked — lightly brown with an ooey-gooey center. I ate it without anything else, licking my fingers clean before I popped up from my seat.

When Grace finished, I walked with her to the bathrooms, brushing my teeth quickly before I stood watch outside the women's restroom like a fucking security guard. I felt my own eyelids growing heavy the longer I stood there, until Grace swung out of the bathroom in another pair of those damned sleep shorts.

Those things were going to be the absolute death of me — especially since it seemed like she had them in every fucking color.

They were so flimsy and thin, and paired with the little spaghetti strap shirt she wore — braless, of course — I could chart every curve and slope of her body. It was enough to drive me out of my goddamn mind, watching her walk toward me with those tan, lean legs and just a sliver of her midriff peeking out to tease me.

There were three freckles in a zig-zag line on the part of her stomach I could see, like the handle of the Big Dipper constellation.

God, how I wanted to lift that top a bit higher, to connect the dots with my tongue.

She walked up to where I was standing with the corners of her lips lifted.

"Who's the bulldog now?" she teased.

We were both quiet on the walk back to our site — Grace because she was tired, me because I was hammering my new mantra into my stupid head.

Teammate's little sister. Teammate's little sister.

Once we'd locked the car and all our belongings in it, I put out our fire and we climbed into the tent.

Grace acted like it was no big deal. She dove into her sleeping bag, letting out a groan of joy as she settled in and zipped herself up. "I'm going to sleep like a *baby* after that hike," she said.

That would make one of us.

I tried to smile, but I was too focused on making sure I didn't touch her as I laid down on my side of the tent. It was too damn hot to get into the sleeping bag, so I laid on top of it. And once I felt like we both were in place, I clicked off the flashlight on my phone, tossing it beside me. It was a good thing it had been on the charger most of the day in the car.

I stretched one arm up under my head, staring up at the ceiling of the tent. There were two vents letting in what little breeze there was, and I watched the trees playing with the moonlight above us as Grace worked to get comfortable.

I actually was pretty tired, but every noise around us had me on high alert. I didn't tell Grace, but I had a knife hidden under my sleeping bag.

Now, had I ever *used* a knife? Hell no. But I was prepared to learn real fast tonight if I had to.

It was a gift from my father, one that had stayed stashed in my bedside table ever since. He'd told me a man always had to protect himself and his family.

I'd snorted when he'd said it, and he'd backhanded me so quick I was tasting blood before I realized I'd been hit.

I hated that most of my memories of him were like that. It didn't matter how many good days I'd had with him, how many times he'd taught me how to play better and then celebrated my wins. He'd grown so resentful over the years that all that was covered by the rubble of the man he was now, the good buried under years of bad.

Still, there would always be a huge part of me that wanted his approval, that wanted to be like he was when he was my hero. Why, I would never fucking understand, but it was the truth. So, that knife — one of the only gifts I had from him — had been by my bed since the day he gave it to me.

Even when I traveled.

Tonight, it was a few inches under my head, sheathed and ready should I need it.

"What are you thinking about?"

I jolted a bit at the sound of her voice. "I thought you were tired."

"You aren't?"

"I'm getting there."

"So then what are you thinking about?"

I let out a sigh, wetting my lips. I'd talked about my family enough in one day that I never wanted to discuss it again. So, I lied. "Just thinking about our route for tomorrow."

In the darkness of the tent, all my other senses took over. I could hear the rustle of the sleeping bag as Grace shifted, could smell her hair as she moved closer — citrus and sea salt.

She smelled like the ocean, even in the forest.

More than anything, I felt the way my heart knocked against my rib cage when her body nestled against mine.

I waited for her to laugh when she realized turning had brought her flush against me, but she didn't. She stayed just like that — the front of her fitting to the side of me like a puzzle piece.

It didn't matter that her sleeping bag separated us. I felt her skin burning through it.

"Everything's okay," she promised on a whisper. "I know you think you have to be everything to everyone, but tonight — you can just rest."

All the air left me like a deflating balloon, my lungs emptying themselves completely. Those words comforted me as much as they made all my hair stand on edge.

I'd never been pinned down in one sentence like that, and this woman did it with ease — like she was telling me summer was hot and winter was cold.

I heard the rustle of the sleeping bag again, and then warm lips pressed to my jaw.

"Goodnight, Jaxson Brittain," she breathed against where her kiss had seared. Then, she rolled away, taking all her body heat with her.

Against all logic, a chill swept over me when she did — like it was twenty degrees instead of eighty.

"Goodnight, Nova," I echoed, throat tight.

She fell asleep almost instantly, her breathing growing deep and long.

To my surprise, I knocked out not long after.

And in the morning, I had to swallow my pride, admitting it out loud as we rolled up our sleeping bags and got ready to hit the road again.

Because she was right.

It was the best night's sleep of my life.

CHAPTER 15

OUR LITTLE SECRET

Grace

We were about two hours northwest of Nashville when my brother called me.

My phone was the one hooked up to the SUV, a map on the screen and my 70's playlist humming through the speakers. It was a mix of rock, pop, and disco, and "Hot Stuff" was interrupted by the call, BIG BRO sprawling across the screen in all caps.

Jaxson's nostrils flared as he looked at the screen, and then at me, and I held a finger to my lips as I answered.

"Don't tell me you want the game day dance for the stupid golf tournament tomorrow, because the answer is *no*," I answered, and the sound of my brother's deep chuckle filled the car.

Jaxson was as stiff as a fucking board in the driver seat.

"I was just calling to check in on you, but now that you mention it..."

"NO," I re-emphasized. "It's bad enough I got wrangled into doing this for every hockey game. All because I tried to be a good sister when you were in a bad mood in high school."

"Be honest — you love it."

I grumbled, but he wasn't wrong. I really did look forward to those calls before each game, knowing I was a part of his pre-game ritual — even if it was small. My brother was a professional hockey player. He had every reason to lose touch with me, but he never did.

"I love *you*," I corrected. "Which is the only reason I put up with it."

"Sure, sure. Where are you?" he asked.

Jaxson and I shared a look, and I swore he looked like he was about to shit himself.

"In the car with one of your teammates," I said, and Jaxson's eyes doubled in size, the car veering enough to hit the bumpy edge of the road before he re-centered it. "We were actually just thinking about pulling over for a quickie before you so rudely interrupted."

There was silence on the other end for a moment, and Jaxson's head was whipping back and forth between looking at the road and asking me *what the fuck* with his eyes.

I fought to hold in my laugh, and then Vince blew out a breath.

"Not funny."

"I thought it was."

Jaxson relaxed marginally when he realized Vince didn't believe me. He had no reason to. He'd scared all his friends off me his entire life, and he knew none of them would be stupid enough to test him.

I couldn't hide the smile that curled on my lips when I realized Jaxson knew the risk, but he was here, anyway.

I didn't know what that meant, but I liked to think about it.

Stupid.

This was the shit that got me into trouble. Jaxson had just offered to take me for a drive to make me feel better after a breakup that wasn't even really a breakup because technically, we weren't even dating.

And I'd roped the poor guy into a road trip.

Even when he agreed to it, he'd made sure to draw the line between us, to remind me what we were and what we weren't. He was telling me in every way possible that this was just him being a friend.

Still, if he didn't want to be here, he wouldn't be. He could have easily laughed me off and said no. I could still be loafing on my brother's couch and burritoing up in my sads.

Instead, I was in the car with Jaxson Brittain.

And maybe it was stupid, maybe I was reading into things...

But I *swore* he wanted to kiss me — just as badly as I wanted to kiss him.

Of course, right *now* he looked more like he wanted to strangle me. I guessed my little joke wasn't too funny to him, either.

"I'm in Kentucky," I said, not bothering to lie when I didn't need to. My family was used to my nomadic behavior, so me being in the middle of nowhere USA wouldn't be weird at all to them. "But don't worry, I'll be at your tournament tomorrow. Meeting Mom and Dad there."

"Good. You can watch me dominate in the name of charity."

"I see your modesty is even stronger in the off-season."

"Just confident, sis," he corrected. "Maven and I are packing now, flying into St. Louis tonight." There was a stretch of quiet before he asked, "You doing okay?"

"Oh, you know me. Sad for about twenty-four hours and then that shit is behind me."

"That's my sis. Don't give that loser any energy he doesn't deserve."

I smiled, but didn't miss how Jaxson subtly shook his head like he hated that answer. I thought about what he said to me at the creek yesterday.

"I hate when you do that — act like you're not allowed to feel anything but happy, like being sad or angry or disappointed makes you a bad person."

I swallowed.

Why *did* I feel like that?

When did being anything but happy start to make me feel like a burden?

"Well, I won't keep you. Just wanted to—"

"Hi, Gracie!"

It was Maven who interrupted him, and I smiled wide. "Hey, Mave."

"Can't wait to see you tomorrow! Livia is coming with us, too. So, while the boys hit balls with sticks, the *girls* can get drunk and pay a hot caddie to drive us around in a golf cart."

"Any caddie who values his life would know better than to come anywhere near my girl," Vince growled, and I rolled my eyes.

"Calm down, psycho. It'll be *me* the caddie rails at the end of the night."

I grinned proudly at the joke, which made Maven laugh and Vince ramble on about how he'd go to jail. I was laughing to myself when I glanced over at Jaxson.

But he looked just as murderous as my brother.

I narrowed my gaze at him, smiling even bigger at the thought that my little joke might have made him jealous.

I wanted him to be jealous. I wanted him to throw me over his shoulder caveman style again and tell me *he'd* be the only man touching me from here on out.

God, what was wrong with me?

"I'm going to go toss your brother in the pool before he overheats," Maven said over Vince still warning me to stay away from every man at the tournament. "Love you, see you tomorrow."

"See ya," I said on a laugh, and then ended the call, and "Hot Stuff" picked up right where it had left off.

An awkward tension settled over the car, and I was all too aware of how hard Jaxson gripped the wheel. Then, he reached forward and turned the music down.

"We need a game plan for tomorrow."

My chest squeezed at the insinuation, at the fact that while I'd been on the phone, he'd likely been freaking the fuck out realizing we were all going to be in the same place tomorrow. I didn't know why, but a small part of me thought maybe he'd just tell Vince that we'd been together. It wasn't like we'd done anything wrong. We were just two friends on a road trip.

Even as I thought it, I knew it was ridiculous.

Vince would never be okay with that, and we both knew it.

I didn't know which emotion I felt stronger — hurt that Jaxson wanted to keep me a secret, or elated that he was willing to risk what we both knew would be an unforgivable offense against my brother, all in the name of making me happy.

I couldn't remember anyone, ever, prioritizing me and my joy like that.

My chest squeezed again, but this time, it was less painful and more like hope — which I needed to squash down with a heavy boot.

"Don't worry," I told him, propping my feet up on the dash. "I've already got it covered."

"How so?" he asked, arching a brow.

"Easy. Drop me off at the airport, and I'll call my mom and dad, tell them I just landed. They'll pick me up, and then when the tournament is over, I'll have them take me back and you can pick me up again. Trust me — they don't check my flights anymore. They're used to me just taking off and going places. And this way, no one will see us together." I leaned an elbow on the console, then rested my chin in my hand as I smiled up at him. "Our little secret is safe, Brittzy. Promise."

He frowned at that, and I saw his fear wash away, something like guilt and regret taking its place. "Grace, I hope you don't think—"

"TAKE THIS EXIT!"

I cut Jaxson off with excitement buzzing through me, my eyes glued to the billboard until we blew past it.

"Wha—?"

"Now!" I said, grabbing for the wheel. I made sure the exit lane was clear, and then tugged enough to steer us toward it.

Jaxson slowed down, batting my hand away as he took over. "Okay, crazy, please don't get us killed." He shook his head, but he was watching me with both confusion and amusement as I bounced in my seat. "You have to pee or something?"

"Nope, I just found our next road trip pit stop."

He cocked a brow, pulling to a stop at the red light waiting at the bottom of the exit. And it was perfect, because all I had to do was hold my grin and point to the sign across the street.

IRIS FESTIVAL — 17.4 MILES

It had an arrow pointing to the right, and I waggled my brows when Jaxson looked back at me. I'd completely forgotten the Iris Festival was happening, and we'd just happened to drive through the right part of Kentucky that we ran into it. It was an EDM festival, a multi-day one with dozens of artists and thousands of attendees. I knew without looking that a general admission ticket would be all we could get this late, but that was all we needed to get in and dance.

Jaxson sighed like it was the last thing he wanted to do.

But he cut the wheel right, and I thought I saw him smile when I threw my hands up in an excited squeal of victory.

CHAPTER 16

BIG FUCKING TROUBLE

Grace

The Iris Festival sprawled the length of three football fields, with two grand stages and a playground of fair-like games and rides in-between. We heard the music before we even parked, and now that we were inside, it thumped through me like a heartbeat.

"This is heaven," I said, eyes wide as I took in the sparkly outfits, the creative flags flying from poles in every direction, the bubbles and the glitter and the lights. Everyone was smiling, laughing, dancing, and just... *vibing*.

"You think God likes to party, huh?" Jaxson asked, looking around with a mixture of awe and concern. He had on dark aviator glasses and had pulled his ballcap low to hide his face. I hadn't even thought about that — him getting mauled by fans — until we'd pulled into the parking lot. But when I'd given him an out, he declined, saying it would be fine.

He assured me he wasn't as recognizable as my brother was, that only real hockey fans tended to realize who he was.

Still, that had to be hard, to have to think about that any time you wanted to leave the house.

"Oh, she definitely does," I said. "She also approves of cute rave outfits and house music."

"God is a woman now?"

"Always has been. Keep up," I teased, and then I threaded my arm through his and dragged him toward the Ferris wheel.

Fortunately, no one realized who Jaxson was. My bet was they were likely high and wouldn't recognize their own brother if he were here, let alone a hockey player from Tampa. It may also have been that even if he *had* been recognized, everyone left him alone.

Whichever it was, I was thankful. It felt like I had Jaxson all to myself.

We didn't talk about how long we planned to stay, but hours passed in what felt like minutes. We rode the fair rides — bumper cars, the zipper, a huge slide we rode down on something that looked like a burlap sack. Our favorite was the Gravitron, a spaceship-looking contraption that spun us around so fast we stuck to the wall inside it. I tried to hold my hand out and ended up having it come back and slap me right in the face because I couldn't fight the centrifugal force. I'd never seen Jaxson laugh harder than he did then.

We ate turkey legs and funnel cake and drank blue lemonade out of a cup shaped like an alien.

We wandered the vendor booths, where I found a light-up pink cowgirl hat and a pair of yellow star sunglasses that I immediately had to purchase. I also wrangled Jaxson into an LED mask with lights that danced to the beat of the music.

Now, he *definitely* didn't need to worry about being recognized.

All the while, music blasted from each stage, the crowds around them bobbing in time with the music. Hands, flags, signs — all moving together like they were floating on the same wave.

"We should get going soon," Jaxson said when the sun started to set. It lit the festival up in a golden glow with a brilliant pink sky as the backdrop.

"What? We can't leave yet! Trust me — it's even better at night."

Jaxson chewed his lip, debating, the light-up mask flashing in his hand at his side.

"Come on," I said, stepping in front of his thinking face. "We're less than two hours from St. Louis. If we leave here at ten, we can drive an hour, get a hotel for the night, and head the rest of the way in tomorrow. When is your tee time?"

"Eleven."

"*See*," I said. "We've got plenty of time. Come on, Brittzy," I goaded, stepping a little closer. "Don't you want to dance with me?"

I was already tugging him toward the main stage, one brow lifted as I started winding my hips. We both knew damn well I couldn't pull him with me if he didn't want me to. He was twice my size and weight at least.

But he let me drag him, a smirk finding his lips as he looked up to the sky and shook his head.

Then, he took his hat off long enough to put his mask back on, and I knew I'd won.

I laughed, keeping his hand in mine as I turned so I could navigate us through the crowd.

I wanted to be close, to make my way as far as I could toward the stage. The trick was to just dance your way through, which was exactly what I did.

I held Jaxson's hand over head, twirling myself underneath it before I shimmied my shoulders and rolled my hips. With every step, I danced with the crowd, and this was what I loved about festivals — everyone danced right along. No one was upset, no one shoved us back like they had a right to their place by the stage. They all made room.

Everyone was welcome.

Still, the closer we got to the stage, the thicker the crowd was. Soon, there was barely enough room to wiggle through, and the dome of the stage stretched high over us like a bubble shielding us from the world.

The music was louder, heavier, every beat vibrating through me.

The lights were blinding, the fog swirling beneath them in a hypnotic dance.

Body heat surrounded us from every angle — hips moving, hands in the air, every person just surrendering to the music.

I found a small opening as close as I felt we could get, and then I turned to face Jaxson, making sure he was alright.

The last bit of sunlight was fading, the sky beyond the festival a dusty blue now. The crowd began to glow, costumes and signs flashing to the beat just like Jaxson's mask was. And it didn't matter that we were surrounded by thousands of people.

All I could see was him.

His hair was a mess when he whipped his hat off, the brown strands damp from sweat and a bit longer than they'd been that night in Austin. He removed the mask next, scrubbing a hand over his face on a smile, eyes cast up toward the lights streaming overhead. Those eyes were wide and curious. He was taking it all in, feeling this moment we had somehow found ourselves in.

I loved seeing him like that — relaxed, happy, *free.*

The throng of people around us pulsed like a living thing, slowly pushing in on every side. I was bumped from behind, and I braced my hands on Jaxson's arm to steady myself. He took a step to help right me, dropping the mask to the ground and putting his hat on backward as he did. But as soon as he moved, someone slid into the space behind him.

We were sandwiched together, every beat pushing us closer and closer, until there was barely an inch of space between us.

I studied the ink sprawling on his arm I held onto, the blue and black illuminated by flashes of yellow and white lights. My eyes traveled up from there, roaming his taut forearms, the swells of his biceps, all the way up to the neckline of his t-shirt.

I didn't realize my fingertips were tracing the same path my eyes were until I just gently touched his throat, and I felt him swallow, the motion tight.

My eyes shot to his, but I didn't remove my hand.

Instead, my other came to join it, just as another person squeezed behind me trying to make their way closer to the stage.

That annihilated what little space was left between us.

I shivered as his body heat encompassed mine, my hands against his chest as his just *barely* rested on my hips. It was like he was torn between only holding me enough to keep me steady or pulling me flush against him.

My fingertips drew circles on his chest.

Lazily.

Daringly.

And I didn't have a single ounce of alcohol in me, didn't *need* any drug. I was high off the feeling of him trembling beneath my touch as I dragged it lower.

Ecstasy was the way his hands grabbed my hips, grip tight enough to bruise as he warred between holding me where I was or pulling me closer. My buzz was driven by the low groan I heard even over the music when I kept one hand on his abdomen, but the other brushed over the seam of his shorts.

He was rock hard.

He was also fucking *massive*.

I couldn't help myself. It wasn't enough to just barely touch him, to just tease him when I knew my touch was affecting him like that. It was empowering, and that kind of power made me so greedy I couldn't hold back.

Slowly, I dragged my gaze up the entire length of his body, until I was staring up at him.

His eyes were dark blue like the night around us, his jaw set, body rigid beneath my touch like he was fighting with every ounce of willpower he had to stay still.

I kept my eyes locked on his, and then I slid my hand fully around him, palming his cock through his shorts.

His nostrils flared, his eyes darting between mine like he wasn't sure I realized what I was doing.

But I knew.

I knew when I gripped him firmer that it was me he was hard for. I knew when I slid my hand roughly over the long, thick length of him, that I wanted more than just a touch. I knew when I tilted my chin up, and his eyes fell to my mouth, and I licked my lips as my hand worked him through his pants that we were in big fucking trouble.

But *God*, I didn't want to stop. I *couldn't* stop.

Not when it felt this good.

Jaxson's hands had been frozen at my hips this entire time, but the longer I touched him, the more impossible it was for him to stay still. I felt his hands roughly roam my body as if they were being dragged against his will — along the slope of my waist, trailing the bones of my rib cage, brushing up over my arms and shoulders. They traveled up still until chills broke along my neck when he framed my face.

His hands were enormous — his thumbs spanning the entire length of my jaw as his fingertips curled around the back of my neck. He tilted my chin up so much it made my neck ache, his eyes ricocheting between mine with that same warning.

Stop this, he begged me without saying a word.

Instead, I squeezed him through his shorts, reveling in how his cock jumped against my palm.

His Adam's apple bobbed hard in his throat, nose flaring again as he slid his thumbs along my jaw. He smoothed one thumb along my lower lip next, spanning the length of it at a slow, heart-pounding pace.

My tongue darted out to chase that touch, and I tasted the salt of his skin for only a second before a growl ripped through him, and I swore all the music was gone because I heard that sound like it was the only thing that existed.

It was the sound of surrender.

His hands slid roughly back to frame my skull, fingers curling in my hair and pulling hard until I arched and gasped.

And Jaxson muted the sound with his mouth crashing down on mine.

We both inhaled, breathing each other in as his lips molded to mine — warm and bold and perfect. I wound my arms around his neck as his moved to envelop me at my core. He crushed me to him, my hands sliding up to twist in his hair enough that I knocked his hat off while his wrapped around me like he was trying to meld us together.

It was a kiss that shattered time.

I felt it stutter to a halt around us before snapping back with such intensity that it warped, taking us into a new dimension.

It was as punishing as it was reverent, brutal and yet tender, like Jaxson was pissed he was doing it just as much as he was certain he never wanted to stop.

One arm held me to him while the other slid down and palmed my ass, taking one cheek in a handful that he squeezed roughly. My leg hiked up automatically, dress riding up with it, and he slid his thigh between mine, biting my lower lip as I moaned into his mouth.

God, it was all-consuming. His hands rocked me against him, and I shook at the sensation, at the forbiddenness of it all.

This was my brother's teammate, his *friend*.

But right now, he was kissing me like he owned me — like there was no other choice for either of us but to give in.

His lips were so big, so warm, firm in their insistence, but soft in their execution. He kissed me long and slow, and then in a feverish frenzy, his tongue sending jolts of electricity straight between my legs with every swipe against my own.

And it wasn't *just* his mouth that was magic — it was his hands, his arms, his thigh pressing between my own. He didn't kiss me with only his lips. He touched me, squeezed me, ground against me like we were fucking with our clothes on.

It was the kiss to end all kisses, the kind that marked you like a tattoo, like a scar.

And it ended on a curse, Jaxson's hands sliding back up to cradle my face — except this time, he held me still, his hands trembling a bit as he pressed his forehead against mine.

I wet my lips, fingertips curling in the sleeves of his t-shirt. I held onto his biceps and pulled, trying to get him to touch me again, to meet my desperate rolls against his body with his own, to let me tilt my chin up enough for our lips to touch once more.

But he blew out a hot breath through his nose, shaking his head.

"We should go," he croaked out.

Three words. Three words that ripped through me like rusty scissor blades.

He winced as he released me, and my body shook at the loss of heat, at the loss of *him*.

Oh, God.

The realization of what we'd just done swept through me in a bolt of anxiety.

Jaxson swiped his hat and mask off the ground, tugging the ballcap on backward like he was angry with it. I half-expected him to just leave me there, horny and panting for him in the middle of a throbbing crowd, but he forced a deep breath before calmly, gently, taking me by the hand.

He made a path through the crowd toward the parking lot, tugging me along behind him in a daze.

I could feel so many emotions rolling off of him — regret, guilt, fear. But all of that was overpowered by what I felt burning through his touch the most.

Desire.

His body was still humming with the same energy mine was.

That wasn't just a kiss. That was unlike anything I'd ever experienced in my fucking *life*, and I knew without asking that it had been the same for him.

Right?

God, I needed to hear it. I needed him to look at me, to tell me it wasn't just me who felt that. I needed him to hold me. I needed him to kiss me, to *touch* me.

Whatever line existed between us, we hadn't just crossed it — we'd plowed over it, running so fast and so far it might as well have never existed to begin with.

Only one question existed as we climbed back into the SUV and headed toward St. Louis.

What now?

CHAPTER 17

BEND THE RULES

Jaxson

The nicest hotel I could find us in Mt. Vernon, Illinois, in the middle of the night was the DoubleTree. I threw my card down for two rooms next to each other, scrubbing a hand over my face as my heart still raced in my chest.

I was pretty sure it would never beat the same again after kissing Grace Tanev.

I swallowed, internally groaning because *fuck,* I was a stupid sonofabitch. It was one thing to toe the line with her, to flirt and know she was flirting back, to shamelessly check her out knowing she did the same to me. We were attracted to each other. We had been since the first time we met.

But until tonight, we hadn't acted on it.

Until tonight, we hadn't known what we were missing.

It had all been fun and games.

Until tonight.

Grace had been unusually quiet on the hour car ride to the hotel. She'd put on a mellow playlist, a mix of artists like Tame Impala and The Alchemist, but she hadn't sung along or danced in her seat like usual.

She'd sat there perfectly still, her hands folded in her lap.

That did nothing to ease my anxiety. I'd gripped the steering wheel like it was the desire I had pooling in my gut for her and I could somehow strangle it to death. My hands still ached from it, and I stretched them out before taking the key cards from the receptionist.

"And here are your cookies," she said with a smile, taking two from the warmer and handing one to each of us.

Grace lit up like a fucking Christmas tree.

"*Cookies!* I forgot you did that!" She unwrapped hers instantly, inhaling deep before she took a ginormous bite. She moaned as she chewed it, eyes fluttering shut. "*Hnggg, sho'guuud.*"

She opened her eyes and smiled up at me next, chocolate in her teeth.

And I laughed.

It was the biggest relief, how my chest unlocked itself and let that sound through. Grace looked like she'd just won the lottery with that fucking cookie and my laugh that came with it, like she'd been dying to break the tension as much as I had.

It was fine.

We were fine.

I almost believed it, too, as we made our way to our rooms — me lugging Grace's heavy suitcase as she carried my duffle bag on her shoulder.

It felt like maybe, *just* maybe, we could go right back to the way we'd been. We could forget what happened at the festival, chalk it up to being caught up in the moment.

But when I unlocked her room first, rolling her suitcase inside and propping it against the wall, that hope drained out of me. Because the door closed behind Grace with a quiet *snick*, and when I turned to face her, the silence fell over us like a shield.

We were alone.

In a hotel room.

With a bed just calling our fucking names.

My heart thundered in my chest again, and I cleared my throat, taking my hat off long enough to run my hand through my hair as I looked around at any and everything but the woman standing at the door.

"Alright, well. I'll let you get settled," I said. "Let's try to head out by seven thirty tomorrow. We can grab breakfast on the way."

I walked toward the door.

But Grace didn't budge.

She stayed blocking my path, shrugging my bag off her shoulder and gently setting it on the floor. "You should stay for a while."

"Grace..."

She hooked me by the elbow, not letting me argue as she dragged me back toward the bed.

Fuck.

Fuck, fuck, fuck.

She kicked out of her sneakers and peeled off her socks before falling back into the mattress, sprawling out like she was about to make a snow angel while I sat uneasily on the edge of it. She leaned up long enough to take off the pink cowgirl hat she'd bought at the festival, and then struggled out of her crossbody bag, tossing it on the bedside table.

The thing jangled every time she walked, a mess of keys attached to the clasp of it.

"Why do you have all those?" I asked, praying that if I got her talking, I could stop focusing on how her sundress just barely covered her when she laid out like that.

Grace looked at the keys with a smile, eyes lazy when they found mine. "Just collected them over the years, I guess."

There had to be at least seven keys on the ring, along with two keychains — one that was a fuzzy yellow puff ball and the other a baby blue leather tassel.

"Boyfriends?" I guessed, arching a brow. The question burned my lips even as I tried to make my voice light with it.

Grace's smile grew, and she bit her lip before turning onto her side to face me. "Since I'm on the go a lot, my parents wanted to make sure I had keys to all our homes." She held up her hand and counted off on her fingers. "Michigan house, Colorado house, Florida house... but then there's also my dorm room key that I forgot to turn in, a spare to Vince's, and one to Dad's wine cellar that I made a copy of without him knowing."

"Scandalous," I teased.

She made a little hum of agreement, but her smile was slipping in the next breath, heat glazing her eyes.

Fuck.

I have to get out of here.

I used what little willpower I had left to stand. "Alright, I—"

"Wait!" Grace rolled, her sundress riding up her thighs and showing the lower crease of her ass before she popped up out of bed. My perverted mind went straight back to the festival, to when I'd surrendered to the overwhelming need to touch her and felt that ass in one satisfying handful.

Jesus Christ.

I rolled my eyes up to the ceiling, fighting against a boner as she grabbed her phone and hopped back onto the bed. This time, she was on her knees, and she crawled over to where I stood, hitting record on her phone before holding it out so we both fit in the frame.

"July third. I succeeded in wrangling Jaxson Brittain not only into camping in a tent last night," she said, holding up a victorious finger. "But into wearing an LED mask — at a rave, mind you — and into dancing the day away. Oh," she added, reaching for her cowgirl hat and slapping it on her head. "And I got this hat, which looks *amazing* on me."

I chuckled, which drew her attention. She whipped the camera around to face me.

"Tell me something good, Jaxson."

Her eyes danced with a challenge, and I had to swallow down the flash of the festival that hit me like a freight train when she did. I could see the way her neck had arched for me, feel the heat of her thighs when I spread them with mine, hear the little gasp I elicited from her just before I lowered my mouth to hers...

There were plenty of good things about today.

And yet, every single one of them was bad.

"I'm sleeping in an actual bed tonight," I grumbled, which earned me a roll of Grace's eyes as she stuck her tongue out at the camera and cut the video. She set her phone down on the bedside table, and then crawled back over to me.

And I do mean she fucking *crawled*, on her hands and knees, long hair falling over her shoulders as she kept those emerald eyes locked on mine.

"That was the best thing you could think of?" she asked, and she kept crawling, knees pressing into the comforter each step of the way.

When she reached the edge, she stepped one foot down to the floor right in front of where I stood.

"Nothing... *good* about the festival?" she probed, and her other foot came down to meet the first.

She was standing less than half an inch from me, eyes glittering in the light as she looked up at me.

I had to shut this down.

Now.

But all I could do was stand there and stare back at her.

Grace waited for me to speak, her hands clasped behind her back as she swayed her shoulders side to side with an arched brow. When I didn't respond, she blew out a breath, falling back onto the bed and making the comforter fluff around her.

"Ugh," she groaned, covering her eyes with her forearm. She took a deep breath, and then...

The woman started listing planets.

"Jupiter, Mars, Saturn, Venus, Pluto — because yes, it *is* a planet — Uranus, Neptune—"

"What are you doing?" I asked on a smile.

Grace threw her arm from her face down to the mattress, leaning up on her elbows. "I'm trying not to be turned on."

She said the words unapologetically, and my mouth dried up like the desert when she did.

Her eyes stayed glued to mine, chest rapidly rising and falling, the strap of her dress sliding off one shoulder and catching on her arm.

"You have any tricks that are better than this?" she asked, but the tease was fading, her voice breathy now — needy. "Because I am still turned *all* the way on."

Possession rippled through me like the aftershock of an earthquake.

"I'm so wet for you right now, Jax," she breathed.

Each word struck me like a bolt of white-hot lightning, zapping what little self-control I was holding onto.

She writhed in the bed with her admission, one hand running through her hair as the other palmed her breast like she didn't even realize she was doing it — like it was the most natural reaction to the way she felt.

Fuck. Me.

Everything inside me wanted to catch those squirming legs of hers and spread them wide, to rake her dress up so I could investigate just how wet she was for myself. I wanted to hook my fingers under the band of her thong and rip it down her legs, wanted to hear the sounds she'd make the first time I slid my fingers inside her and tasted that sweet fucking pussy.

I shut my eyes tight, grinding my teeth.

Teammate's. Little. Sister.

Eight. Years. Younger.

God, the words were like a shallow whisper at this point. I could barely hear them, and yet I *had* to.

Nothing about this was okay.

But *everything* about her drew me in, like she was Medusa and I was locked in her gaze. Except the only thing turning to stone right now was my cock.

"Grace..." I warned, my voice gruff.

"I know, I know," she whined, huffing out a breath of air. "I read too much into that kiss, didn't I?"

She peeked at me, and I willed myself to keep my mouth clamped shut.

"God, I did," she said, letting her head fall as her eyes closed. "You don't want me. How could you? You're—"

"Don't do that."

The words shot out of me even though I didn't want them to. I should let her believe that, let her think it was a mistake.

But I just *couldn't*.

Her brows bent together as she leaned up on her elbows again, eyes on mine.

I took a step toward her, one that seemed to suck up all the oxygen in the room.

"You know damn well you don't believe that," I said. "You know damn well it isn't true."

She swallowed. "Then touch me."

"I can't," I croaked. "And we both know why."

The rejection on her face pummeled my heart like an iron fist.

Slowly, she laid back, eyes on the ceiling, those words hanging between us like the tentacles of a deadly jellyfish. My chest ached the longer I stared at her, and then my eyes flicked to the colorful keychains on her nightstand.

And a stupid, crazy idea bloomed before I could stop it.

I should leave.

I knew that to be truth even as my feet started carrying me in the opposite direction. I rounded the bed, walking over to her bedside table on the other side.

Go.

Now.

My brain tried again as I reached down and picked up her ring of keys.

And her key*chains*.

I smoothed a thumb over the fuzzy one first, excitement buzzing to life under my skin like the first purr of a Lexus LFA engine.

Drop the fucking keys and go to your room.

It was the last warning what was left of my common sense could manage.

I ignored it, fingering the tassel of the leather keychain next. The corner of my mouth ticked up, and I shut out what was left of my resolve before unclipping both of them and letting the keys drop back to the table.

Maybe I didn't have to break the rules.

Maybe I could just... *bend* them.

I rounded the bed again, my eyes glued to where Grace was still laid out on her back. She stared up at the ceiling like she was about to cry.

Until I stood above her, blocking her view, and I held up the downy yellow keychain.

"*I* can't touch you," I repeated, swallowing around the thickness of those words.

Then, slowly, I dropped the keychain until it met her shoulder, dragging it along the line of her collarbone.

A satisfying wave of goosebumps rippled across her skin.

"But I don't see why *you* can't touch yourself."

The words were a dare, a loophole.

A match strike.

Grace's eyes heated, and I dragged the keychain up the slope of her neck, along her jaw, dusting her lips with the fur.

"Do you want to touch yourself right now, Nova?"

With her shaky exhale, we caught fire.

And all the rules went up in flames.

CHAPTER 18

GOOD GIRL

Jaxson

There was no going back.

Not that I would have taken the last boat ride to safety even if it had presented itself. I was firmly standing in the aftermath of my decision to bend the rules, and the sight was enough of a drug to convince me it was worth any consequences that would follow.

Grace still hadn't answered my question. She laid there frozen, mouth parted and her doe eyes fixed on me like she wasn't sure she'd heard me right.

When I didn't move, a long, shaky breath shuddered out of her, and she managed a nod.

I wet my lips, removing the soft keychain from where it touched her. I took just enough time to turn my hat around backward and carefully take a seat on the edge of the mattress again.

Then, I traded out the soft keychain for the leather one.

I dragged the tassel across her chest, left and then right, following the movement with my eyes before I trailed them down and over the slight swell of her breast.

"I'm sorry, I couldn't hear you," I said, tickling her peaked nipple through her dress with the leather. Her chest heaved under the touch, and then I lifted, bringing the leather back down with a quick flick of my wrist.

It wasn't hard — just enough bite to make her gasp and arch, her fists twisting in the comforter.

"Do you want to touch yourself, Grace?" I asked again.

"Yes," she whimpered, and without any further instruction from me, she hastily shoved the straps of her dress off each shoulder, pushing the fabric down until her breasts spilled free.

My next breath lodged in my throat.

Fuck.

I couldn't do anything but stare at her — this brave, sexy, wild woman who was on her elbows again, smiling wickedly up at me with her tits pulled out of her dress. She kept my gaze as she ran her fingertips over one swell, tracing all around her nipple before plucking it between her fingers on a moan.

"Does that feel good?" I asked her, and the words made her moan again, my cock aching at the sound. I was so fucking hard it was uncomfortable, but I could handle myself later.

Right now, all my focus was on her.

"So good," she said, writhing under her touch.

Using the leather keychain, I swatted her hand until she removed it. Then, I opted for the soft one, gliding it along her sternum right between those perfect tits. She writhed under the sensation, and I teased the bottom swells of her breasts before tracing the tops, dancing around every inch of her except where she wanted it most.

"Jaxson," she begged, back bending as she tried to maneuver her body so the keychain would graze her nipple. I let her find the brief relief of contact only long enough for her to hiss in pleasure, and then I pulled it away.

"You said you're wet for me," I said, dangling the keychain from my index knuckle. "Show me."

I loved the sight of her spread out on that bed, the way her naked, perfect tits heaved with every breath. I'd imagined what she'd look like more times than I'd ever admit out loud, and just this glimpse put all my wildest dreams to shame.

She kept her eyes fixed on mine, not an ounce of hesitation as she placed her hands at her hips. I catalogued every inch of her, from where her long, blonde hair was fanned out over the white comforter to where her pink-painted toes curled.

Slowly, she walked her fingertips in place at her hips, pulling the fabric of her dress higher and higher, centimeter by centimeter, until her lavender lace thong came into view.

I groaned my approval at the sight of that purple fabric, at that beautiful apex of her thighs, and she preened under the sound like I'd just given her an A+ on an assignment.

I knew right then that she responded to praise, and my chest fired up with the need to make her work for it.

"So fucking pretty," I said, grazing her inner thigh with the softer of the two keychains. Whatever warning bells were left in my head faded into nothing, until all I heard was her labored breaths matching mine.

I dragged the velvety keychain up slowly, and her fists tightened where she held her dress, body writhing under the touch.

"Can you spread wider for me?"

She opened like a flower, knees falling to the side as her dress rode all the way up above her panty line. That motion alone showed me just how flexible she was, and my cock ached even more.

The ways I could twist this girl up...

I trailed the leather keychain from one of her hips to the other, taking my time, the tassel tickling the skin just above her thong. When I dragged it down between her thighs and right over her clit, she shuddered.

"Look at you," I said, trailing the tassel between her thighs. Her thong was so wet the keychain shimmered a bit when I pulled it up and dangled it from one finger. "Have you been like this all night?"

She nodded, her cheeks tingeing pink.

I trailed the keychain over her again, but this time, I lifted it with a quick *thwack* against her clit that made her gasp and bow off the bed.

"Show me how wet you are," I said, tickling the place I'd just swatted. "I want to see that pretty pink pussy."

Grace made the sweetest sound, squirming under my gaze before her hands were between her legs. And I thought she'd take her thong off, but she just hastily pulled it to the side, spreading her legs even wider and tilting her hips up toward the ceiling so she was fully on display.

She held the fabric out of the way with one hand, and the other slid over her clit, rubbing down and toying with her slick opening before she held her fingers up to show me.

"Fucking soaked," I said, and *damn* — I didn't know I needed this, to command her and have her so willingly give in.

All the tension that had been pent up since that night in Austin was going off around us like a bomb — and we were gladly in the rubble, desperate for another blast.

"You love this, don't you? You love me watching you, telling you what to do..." I shook my head, eyes on where her fingertips glistened. "Do you know how badly I want to suck those fingertips clean?"

She bit her lip, writhing in the mess she was making on the comforter.

"But I can't," I said. "So, you do it."

I braced a hand beside her on the bed, lowering until I was hovering just above her, no more than three inches between her mouth and mine.

"Suck those fingertips the way I know you want to suck my cock."

"Fuck," she moaned, and she dragged her fingers over her breast on the way up to her mouth, keeping her eyes glued on mine as she pressed them between her lips. It was only the tips of them that were wet, but she shoved them both as deep as she could manage, swirling her tongue and sucking them clean with a moan that made me see stars.

It was my idea to play this game, and here I was ready to bust in my fucking shorts without her laying a single finger on me.

"That's a good girl," I said, staying just above her. "Now, fuck yourself with those fingers. And don't be quiet — I want to hear my name on your lips when I finally let you come."

"*God*, Jaxson," she breathed, and then she reached out for me, wrapping her hands around the back of my neck. She tried to pull me down to kiss her, but I yanked out of her grasp, sitting upright again and removing all proximity.

"Ah, ah, ah," I said, holding the leather keychain over her. "Play by the rules if you want to win the game, Nova."

"Please," she begged, writhing.

"The relief you want is at your fingertips," I said, smirking at the literal weight of that statement. I bent just a little, lowering my voice. "Come on, baby. Let me watch you. Fuck yourself the way you wish I'd fuck you."

Challenge sparked in her eyes, and she tucked her hips even more, spreading her legs so wide she was practically in a middle split. Her hands dove down again, and she held her panties out of the way with one while the other rubbed her clit in circles.

And with those pretty green eyes looking up at me, she plunged two fingers inside.

The moan that ripped through her was pure ecstasy, and she bucked off the bed, toes curling as her eyes closed and her head fell back.

"How does it feel?" I asked her, and then I rewarded her with the soft keychain, rolling it in sweeps over both her nipples with enough friction to make them harden into points.

"So fucking good," she mewled, rocking her hips against her palm. I watched greedily as she pumped her fingers in and out, desperate to reach deeper.

"You look so fucking pretty right now," I praised, and I traded for the leather keychain, running the tassel over her swells. "These perky little tits bouncing," I said, and I swatted each one, leaving pink marks on her skin as she gasped and fucked herself harder. "The way you're making a mess of this hot little sundress," I added, twisting my fist in the fabric, but carefully enough that I didn't touch her while I did it. "How you keep spreading your legs wider for me."

She took the cue, stretching even more, and I bit my lip at the sight she revealed with it.

"*Goddamn*, you're so tight, baby," I said, watching her struggle just to fit those two fingers in the way she wanted to. "I want to watch that pussy stretch over my cock."

"*Yes*," she whimpered, and she stopped touching herself only long enough to rip off her thong before she spread herself again. I realized she needed both hands — one to fuck her pussy, and one to rub her clit.

I was a greedy fucking bastard as I watched her do just that.

Her legs shook, teeth pinning her bottom lip as her face turned red from the effort of reaching for her climax.

I bent over her again, even closer this time, my next words ghosting over her lips.

"I'm much bigger than those fingers of yours," I said, and her eyes popped open, flicking between mine as she continued working herself. "But you could take it, couldn't you? You could take me deep in this throat." I trailed the plush keychain over her open lips, and then I skated it all the way down to her clit, nudging her fingers out of the way. "Deep in this tight little cunt."

"*Fuck*," she screamed, and the way I was teasing her clit with that keychain wasn't enough. She pushed me out of the way and rubbed harder, fucking herself faster, deeper, her eyes rolling back.

"Look at me," I said, snapping my fingers above her face until her eyes shot open. I smiled, wetting my lips as I watched her. "That's it. Keep those pretty green eyes on me and *come*."

Her moans grew louder, her entire body trembling with the effort to reach the finish line.

She tried to capture my mouth, but I pulled away, smirking at the attempt, which only made her whimper and fuck herself with more gusto.

"Come on, baby. Just imagine it's me between these perfect thighs," I said, dragging the tassel of the keychain along her shaking leg. "Sinking in, deeper and deeper, stretching you."

Grace moaned and bucked and thrashed.

"I want you to come. I want you to squeeze my cock with that pussy and ride out every last wave."

That was it.

She went off like a firework, those filthy words the spark she needed to light. I moaned with her as she quaked beneath me, her eyelids wavering with the effort to keep them open and locked on me. But *fuck,* that's exactly what she did.

Grace Tanev let me watch her come, and she cried out my name when she did, her eyes never leaving mine.

It was better than any puck I'd stolen on the ice, than any goal I'd scored, than any game I'd ever won.

"Oh, my God," she cried, and then she fell limp, her chest heaving, sweat beading on her neck.

I kissed the leather keychain, and then dragged it over her lips.

"Good girl."

I pressed off the bed and away from her before she could respond, rounding the bed to set the keychains back on the table. Then, without looking at her, I bolted for the bathroom.

I was so ready for my own release, I could have come with just a stiff breeze.

I couldn't even make it to my own room, couldn't lock the fucking door. Hell, I barely shut it behind me before I ripped my shorts and briefs down to my ankles, palming my throbbing cock with a groan of relief.

But I didn't make it a step farther before the door slid open behind me, and Grace's eyes caught mine in the mirror.

CHAPTER 19

TELL ME WHAT TO DO

Grace

I didn't know what kinky spell Jaxson Brittain had me under, but I hoped it'd never end.

I was still in a daze from my orgasm, legs shaking under me as I followed him through the hotel room. Because that motherfucker had just rocked my world with his dirty mouth and made me come *without even touching me*.

And he was dead ass wrong if he thought I wasn't going to return the favor.

I didn't bother knocking on the bathroom door he'd shut himself behind, nor did I bother fixing my dress. It covered my ass now, but the straps were still off my shoulders, breasts exposed as I slid the door open.

And I found Jaxson staring back at me in the mirror, his shorts around his ankles and his cock in his hand.

"Get out," he rasped, voice tight like it pained him. Maybe it did. If he was even half as worked up as I'd been before finding my own release, then it had to hurt, how badly he needed to come right now.

"Not a chance in hell," I replied, and I stepped fully into the bathroom behind him. "I played your game. Now, you play mine."

"I don't like to be the one who receives the orders," he threatened.

"So then stop fucking around and tell me what to do."

His eyes flared in the mirror, and I arched a brow, running my fingertips over my shoulder and down to play with where my breasts spilled over the top of my dress. I grew even more confident when his gaze followed that touch, when he hissed a breath at the sight of me rolling my nipples between my fingers.

Jaxson turned to face me, and I didn't even attempt to not let my gaze fall when he did.

Fucking hell.

He was hung.

I couldn't help but study him, watching intently as he stroked that beautiful cock with one pump of his massive hand. He had to be at least eight inches long, at least two inches thick, and I both salivated and shivered at the sight of such a gorgeous specimen.

I swallowed, but I didn't back down.

My eyes found his again, and I tilted my head just a little to the left, waiting for instruction.

I swore Jaxson's chest swelled at the sight.

"Spit on it."

His first command lit me on fire, and rolled my tongue in my mouth a few times before stepping closer to him. My eyes didn't leave his as I spit, saliva dripping from my lips to where he held his cock.

He groaned when it hit, slicking himself with the lubrication.

"Knees."

Fuck, I loved this game.

Using the edge of the bathtub to support myself, I did as he asked, sitting on my heels with my hands in my lap.

Just that alone had him sucking in a harsh breath, his eyes raking over me as he pumped himself once, twice. He'd pushed his shirt up just enough that it was out of the way, and the view from the ground had me ready for another round — his tight abs, his monster quads flexing with every roll of his fist, the fact that he had been so desperate to come he hadn't even completely undressed.

And my particular kink rested in the fact that he still wore his fucking hat — backward. Watching him turn it around before he started commanding me in the other room had made me absolutely feral. That backward hat said he meant business, that he was about to get to work, that he was about to get dirty.

"I was ready to bust in my shorts out there," he said, squeezing the tip of his cock before rolling his fist over it again. "Just watching you writhe in that bed, listening to the sounds you made..."

"I wanted it to be you fucking me."

He let out a low curse at that, pumping himself a bit faster. "That right?"

I nodded but didn't move my hands.

I wouldn't — not until he told me to.

"You think you can handle me?" he asked, flexing into his hand.

"You already know I can."

The words earned me another satisfying groan, his eyes heating even more as they raked over me. Truth be told, I wasn't exactly sure I could back up that sassy attitude when push came to shove.

He'd stretch me, that I knew for sure. But I liked to *think* I could take it — liked the way he pumped himself faster when he thought about it, too.

"Sit against the tub."

I leaned back, pulling my knees to my chest as my ass hit the tile.

"Now reach under that dress and play with your wet pussy, baby. Spread your legs wide so I can see."

Fuuuuck, it was not okay how much my body responded to that. It should have felt degrading, and instead, it made me feel like a spoiled princess.

"Like this?" I asked, teasing him a little as I just barely spread my knees and touched myself under the dress.

He smirked. "We both know you can do better than that."

I loved that wicked gleam, the challenge in his voice. I propped one foot up on the toilet seat, the other hitting the wall on the opposite side, and I tucked my hips toward the sky, showing him as much of myself as I could from this angle.

"Goddamn, Grace," he cursed, and all bets were off. He fucked his hand mercilessly, and I thanked the universe again for the view I had — his balls pulled tight, his fist wrapped around his cock, the lower part of his abdomen I could see from where he'd moved his shirt out of the way. His muscles flexed as he pushed toward release, and I knew from how his breathing intensified that he was close.

I wanted him to unravel the way I had, wanted to bathe in the power I had over him in that moment.

So, I followed that boldness into the most delicious darkness I'd ever known.

"You like my tits so much," I said, one hand playing with my pussy as the other slid up to palm my breast. "Come on them."

"*Fuck.*"

He bit out the curse, chest heaving, fist pumping in long, hard strokes. I only smiled more, that power thrumming through me.

"Knees," he said again, this time the word barely rasping out of him.

I scrambled out of the stretch I'd been in, looking up when I was positioned at his feet.

"Open your mouth."

My clit ached at those words, desperate for me to touch it again. I felt absolutely unhinged.

I parted my lips, just a little at first, and then wider and wider, tilting my head back and locking my eyes on his.

He grunted something between a curse and my name — maybe both — and then he spilled, his release painting me like a canvas.

The first stream hit my chest, the next sliced across my neck, and when it reached my mouth, I licked his cum off my lips and rubbed that slick heat into my breast like it was an expensive serum.

It was disgusting — absolutely filthy.

And yet, it was so fucking *hot*.

"Holy shit," Jaxson said when he was spent, and he leaned back against the sink, holding on for just a moment before he sank down to the floor with me.

There he was, sprawled out, his cock wet and softening between his thighs.

There I was, still on my knees, playing with his release with a wicked smile on my face.

There we were — together, on the other side of temptation, completely fucking ruined.

Jaxson laughed, his head hitting the cabinet behind him as he shook his head. I giggled, too, hiding the blush on my cheeks now that the heightened emotions had passed, and I realized I was sitting on a bathroom floor with cum on my face.

Then, he looked at me, his brows furrowing, breathing steadying, eyes darting between mine.

"You're beautiful," he said.

I tried to bite down the smile that curled on my lips at his words, but it was no use.

"When I come?"

"When you exist."

I swallowed, and it was as if the tenderness of those words brought the reality of our situation crashing in like a tidal wave.

In less than twelve hours, we'd be at the same golf course with my big brother.

With *his* teammate.

And we'd just made each other come.

It didn't matter that he didn't *actually* touch me, or that I didn't touch him.

If there were any boundaries left, I sure as hell couldn't see them. The way Jaxson's brows were slowly furrowing, I knew he couldn't either.

And the heaviness of what we'd just done settled around us in that bathroom like a cloud of smoke.

CHAPTER 20

STICK TO THE GAME PLAN

Grace

There was no time to talk about anything the next morning.

Okay — so there was an *hour fucking drive*, actually. But we both stayed silent, Jaxson's eyes on the road and mine on the notebook I was pretending to write in. All I'd actually done was draw spiral after spiral on the page, because that little shape mirrored my state of being.

I was spiraling.

Do not freak out, Grace, I told myself for the thousandth time. *Do not read into this.*

But it was impossible not to.

Because whatever had just happened between us, it hadn't quenched my thirst for Jaxson Brittain. It had only proven that my thirst had been warranted, that he was even better than I could have imagined. The man hadn't even laid a fucking *finger* on me, and he'd given me the hottest night of my life.

I didn't want it to be a one-time thing.

I didn't want that to be all we ever had.

I wanted more. I wanted it *all*.

I burned for him — and not *just* from what had happened last night, either. I craved his laugh, the way it would burst out of him almost like he didn't want it to but couldn't help it when it came to me. I wanted to con him into more mischief. I wanted to soak up the way he looked when he gave in. I wanted to hear more about his childhood, about his family, about hockey and why he had a beautiful vintage car in his driveway, and which book he wanted to read next.

What had felt like a schoolgirl crush that night in Austin now felt like an insatiable *need*.

And that was a dangerous thought to have about my brother's teammate — especially when we were both in the car on our way to the same place as my brother.

I groaned internally, sinking down in my seat and scribbling another spiral.

Jaxson wouldn't even look at me.

I was over here dreaming up what could happen the next time we were together, and he was probably sitting in sticky, hot regret.

What if he drops me at the airport and that's the end of it?

What if it's over?

What if he goes home after the tournament... without me?

The possibility — and likelihood — of that made my stomach roil, and I shifted in my seat, shutting the notebook and tossing it down to the floorboard along with my pen.

I had to say something.

But before I could, my brother's name lit up the screen on the SUV.

This time, it was Jaxson's phone that was hooked up, and we both stared at where the screen said TANNY BOY like we were guilty criminals walking into our trial.

Jaxson cleared his throat, pushing the call to voicemail and promptly turning the volume up when the music started to play again.

I was so sick by the time we pulled up to the airport, I thought I was going to *actually* puke as I got out of the car on shaky legs. Jaxson rounded to the back before I could, retrieving my luggage and rolling it up to me.

There were a million emotions washing over his face, but I couldn't read a single one of them.

"Are you sure—" he started, but I quickly shook my head and waved him off.

"My parents are already on their way. Go. I'll see you there."

He nodded, turning like he was going to get back in the car.

But then he stopped, his back rigid, shoulders tight. He stood there for a long moment, each breath coming harder than the last. Slowly, he turned to face me again, his brows bent, eyes searching mine.

"Fuck it," he said.

Then he pulled me into his arms, swept my hair from my face, and kissed me.

My eyes shot open wide, because I was fairly certain I had blacked out and was dreaming. But one tender caress of that man's hand at the nape of my neck had me melting, my eyelids fluttering shut, and I threaded my arms around his shoulders.

We both exhaled a breath with that kiss, long and slow and pained. When I opened my mouth, Jaxson's grip on me tightened, and he held me to him as his tongue swept in to touch mine, tightening every nerve in my body all the way to my core.

He pressed his forehead to mine — which he could only do because he still held me off the ground — and his eyes were closed, the muscles working under his jaw.

He was kissing me goodbye.

"Grace, last night was—"

"Reckless," I finished for him, nodding my agreement even as the moment shredded me from the inside out. "A mistake."

Jaxson pulled back then, frowning before he carefully sat my feet back on the ground.

"Reckless, maybe," he agreed. "But not a mistake. And neither of those descriptions was what I was going to say."

Hope kicked in my chest like a wild mustang. "It wasn't?"

He sighed, tucking my hair behind my ear, his eyes following that motion. He seemed to be cataloguing every inch of my face.

"It was incredible," he whispered. "Filthy," he added with a grin, his eyes raking over me as my skin burned beneath the gaze. "But incredible."

There was that kick again, accompanied by a flurry of butterfly wings tickling my stomach.

And I realized then that hoping he felt the same for me was more terrifying than assuming he didn't.

"I don't know what happens next," he admitted, swallowing. "But... I know I don't want this to end. Not yet."

Oh, yes.

This was much, *much* scarier.

"Stop flirting with me, Brittzy."

The joke was barely a whisper as I said it, my nerves wound so tight they strangled it on the way out. But Jaxson laughed, and that sound made my next breath a little easier to take.

"I don't want it to end yet, either," I said, leaning into his palm. "I'm having too much fun."

He nodded, sighing another breath like he'd been just as torn up about the thought of this road trip ending as I had been.

"But today..."

"Trust me — I don't want my brother to find out any more than you do," I assured him.

He looked almost green at that, but he nodded again. "Let's just stick to the game plan, and we'll talk tonight. Yeah?"

"Yes," I said.

"Okay." He released me, but before he could go, I grabbed his hand and pulled him back to me.

"Kiss me one more time," I said. "Just so I know it's real."

A smile curled at the edges of his lips, and he slid his hands back into my hair, fingertips curling behind my skull, thumbs tilting my chin up. He kissed me even slower this time, his lips firm, his intent clear.

And I believed him.

Which was the equivalent of standing on the edge of a fourteen-thousand-foot mountain.

"Real enough for you?" he asked, his voice low against my lips.

"It'll do."

He chuckled. "Where's your phone?"

I pulled it out of the back pocket of my jean shorts, and he smiled, sliding his thumb over the screen. I didn't have a password on it, so it unlocked on that alone, and he pulled up the camera app. He pressed record next, pulling me under his arm as he did.

"Tell me something good, Grace."

I flushed so hard it looked like a sunburn, and I buried that blush in his chest, peeking up at him before I looked at the camera.

"Jaxson Brittain just kissed me at a crowded airport."

"And I'll do it again, too," he said.

And he did. He held the phone with one hand and held me to him with the other, searing me with another dizzying, spellbinding kiss.

My head was still spinning long after he left and my parents picked me up, chatting excitedly about the tournament and how they couldn't wait to see Vince. I didn't even care that they didn't ask me where I'd been or what I'd been doing. I didn't care that I had to endure another day that revolved around my big brother.

Because at the end of it, I'd be back in the arms of his teammate.

That was a reward well worth keeping a little secret.

CHAPTER 21

FIGURE IT OUT

Jaxson

Maven and Livia swept Grace away the moment she showed up to the tournament with her parents.

They linked their arms through hers and off they went, Maven pressing a quick kiss to Vince's cheek as they passed by us. They had their hearts set on margaritas at the club house, and to her credit, Grace didn't so much as cast me a lingering glance as they toted her off.

I, on the other hand, was so fucking aware of her presence the entire tournament that I was surprised I didn't have OBSESSED WITH GRACE TANEV written in neon on my forehead.

Even with it feeling a little like a reunion being back with my teammates, and even with my body humming to life at the chance to have a little friendly competition — my mind couldn't stop replaying what had happened the night before.

I was a dumb motherfucker.

It had sounded so logical at the time, when my cock-driven brain wasn't firing on all cylinders. I'd thought it would be fine to bend the rules, to play with Grace... as long as I didn't actually *touch* her.

I laughed out loud at that, earning me a look from Daddy P as he lined up for his first shot at the third hole. It was a fucking joke, that I'd *actually* used that mindset as justification. In turn, it had been maybe even hotter than if I *had* just given in and taken her the way I wanted to.

Keeping my hands to myself and watching her writhe in those sheets as she found her release didn't put out the fire burning between us. It stoked it, gave it oxygen, sprayed it with a gallon of gasoline.

I only wanted her more.

There was a battle in my head, two sides of me warring with each other while I attempted to remain calm and cool on the surface during the tournament. I laughed and joked with my teammates, took photographs for the press, played one of my best games of golf, and talked about everything and everyone else but me.

All while a highlight reel of the faces Grace made when she came played on repeat in my mind.

It had felt impossible to leave her hotel room for the night, to let her get some sleep and to give us *both* some much-needed distance. And I knew by how quiet the drive had been today that Grace was in her head just like I was.

We both knew it couldn't happen again.

And yet, it was all either of us could think about.

By the time we'd made it to the airport, I was sick to my stomach wondering what she was thinking. I was also desperate to ease the worry I saw etched into every single feature on her pretty face. So, I'd comforted her — and not with a lie, but with the truth.

I didn't want this to end.

But even as I'd said that to her, even as I'd been greedy enough to steal another kiss before her parents got there... I knew that, eventually, it *had* to.

She was twenty-two years old with an entire life ahead of her — one that looked vastly different from the one I was leading. She wanted to be on the move. I would be in Tampa at least until my contract ended, and then I hoped to get re-signed or find another team to settle down with. Where she wanted adventure, I wanted stability.

More than any of that, she was Vince's little sister.

Grace and I knew this road we were on led right to a dead end.

But we both wanted to keep driving.

For as long as we had the road, for as long as we had the summer... we had each other.

"Hey, Tanny Boy, can you show up and play today?" Carter asked on the ninth hole. "My back is about to break from the strain of carrying us."

Carter bent over like an old man, rubbing the middle of his back to illustrate, and Vince narrowed his eyes before kicking him right in the ass. Carter stumbled forward on a laugh, and the whole charade earned us some disapproving looks from the team that was wrapping up ahead of us and moving on to the next hole.

Putting four rowdy hockey players on the fairway alongside some of the classiest, most well-known golfers in the PGA Tour wasn't boding well.

"The only reason your back hurts is because you have to carry that off-season gut around," Vince said, poking Carter in the stomach.

Carter swatted his hand away and punched him in the arm. "Please. My abs put yours to shame."

He untucked his pink polo shirt from the khaki shorts he wore like he was ready to prove that point, but Will glared at him severely enough that Carter second-guessed, looking at our surroundings before he tucked his shirt back in again.

"Aw, come on, Daddy P," Vince teased, nodding at his caddy to hand him his club. He bent down to place his ball with his eyes on the fairway. "Let Carter show us his little abs if he wants to. God knows he's not showing them to any women."

"I never thought I'd say these words, but I'm glad I got sent down to the AHL this spring," Carter said, leaning on his club. "Better than putting up with you fuckers."

"Nize it, Fabio," I piped up. "You'll be back in Ospreys blue come fall."

"Yeah, and don't worry — we'll save up all our best chirps for the first day you're back on the ice with us," Vince said, and then he took his shot.

And it was terrible.

Carter laughed at his expense, and even Will cracked a smile before stepping up for his own shot.

The tournament was a scramble, which meant we'd each hit a tee shot before choosing which ball to play for the next shot. So far today, it had been mine or Carter's we'd been playing from. Vince was too busy goofing around to make a serious shot, and Will seemed distracted — quieter than he usually was, which was saying something.

"Maven is going to disown you after this," I told Vince when I stepped up to take my shot after Will. "She's already had one pussy golfer in her life. I doubt she needs another."

I barely got the shot off before I was thwacked in the back of the head.

"Oh shit, I forgot about that," Carter said, placing his ball. "Is that duffer here?"

"Fuck no," Vince said. "Probably because he doesn't have a death wish."

We all smirked at that. If there was anything I knew to be true, it was that Vince Tanev would go to jail if it meant he got to get in one good hit on the guy who had hurt his future wife.

Carter had the best shot again, and Vince grumbled about it as we headed down the fairway.

"You good, Daddy P?" I asked as we walked. "You're even grumpier than usual."

Will glared at me for a long second, long enough that I felt like a kid caught with their hand in the cookie jar. Something about the way he looked at me made me want to defend myself before he'd even accused me of anything.

Suddenly, I remembered the text he'd sent.

We need to talk at the tournament.

I swallowed, wondering what the hell that meant, but he cracked his neck and let out a long sigh, finally dropping his death glare.

"If putting up with you twerps doesn't send me to an early grave, trying to find a nanny for Ava will."

"What's wrong with the doe-eyed blonde?" Vince asked, nodding to the crowd gathered around the hole. We were still a ways away, but even so, I could see the girl Vince was referring to. She was maybe twenty-five, with platinum blonde hair and big...

Eyes.

It was almost comical watching Ava tug her around, and I hadn't missed the way the woman had cringed earlier when Ava had plopped down in the grass to play and insisted that her nanny for the day join her.

"Other than the fact that she couldn't cook macaroni and cheese from a fucking box?" Will grumbled. "She won't leave me alone."

"That's code for *she wants to suck his—*"

Will gave Carter a flat tire before he could finish that sentence.

"Honestly, Daddy P, I don't see the issue. It's not like she's unfortunate looking," Carter pointed out as we made it to the ball. "Let her ride. Maybe if you got laid, you'd be less grumpy."

"Please don't tell me the virgin is giving advice on getting laid now," I teased, and Carter chased me around like he was going to take me out at the knees while Will sighed and looked up at the sky like someone could save him from us.

Vince lined up to take the next shot, and we all clapped him on the back when it landed on the green. We'd have an easy putt to close it out.

"Hey, have you guys heard about Aleksander Suter?" Carter asked as we made our way toward the flag.

"Don't tell me — he got into another bar fight?" Vince guessed. "Oh! Or they found him with cocaine."

Will added, "The league fined him for a dirty hit again?"

"Too easy. My guess is they finally discovered he's the head of an organized crime unit," I chimed in. "Have you seen his team picture? Looks like a fucking mug shot."

Carter shook his head. "Apparently, Seattle has had enough of his shit. Rumor is they're looking to trade him."

That shocked us all silent. Jokes aside, Aleks Suter was one hell of a winger, with enough goals under his belt that even though the entire league gave him shit for his reputation, we still respected him.

"There's talk he may be coming to Tampa."

Carter's voice was drowned out by the rest of us erupting in a mixture of laughter and *no fucking ways*.

"Coach McCabe would *never*," Vince said. "You saw how quick he was to hand me my ass last season when I practiced at a rink with some kids? That was me being *nice*. That was *good* PR." He shook his head. "Zero chance he's letting a weapon with a bad attitude join our team."

"I don't know," Will said, like he knew something we didn't. "Coach may not like it, but he's not the one who calls all the shots, is he?"

"Dick," I said with a sigh when it clicked for me, too. Our General Manager was one for the dramatics. He was the only reason Maven King had unprecedented access to Vince and our entire team last season — all in the name of a publicity stunt to fill the stands.

And it had worked.

We had more fans in that arena last season than the past five seasons combined. Part of that was due to us just being better — but we'd be insane to think Maven hadn't played a huge role.

And that meant Richard Bancroft — or Dick, as we called him — was likely itching for another way to bring in fans this season.

"Christ," I cursed when I realized this could actually happen. "Just what we need — a fucking liability coming into the team when we're solid."

"It won't happen," Vince said with absolution I was certain he didn't actually feel.

Anything could happen in the NHL.

The conversation moved on to something lighter as we approached the green, knowing there were microphones and cameras everywhere. We got a birdie, and when there was a particularly loud chorus of female screams from the crowd, I didn't need more than one guess as to who it was.

Maven, Livia, and Grace were buzzed, plastic cups in their hands as they threw them into the air and did their little celly dances. The crowd around them was suffering from second-hand embarrassment — except for Vince's parents, who joined in the ruckus.

My phone vibrated in my pocket, and I knew without a second guess that it was a text from my father. He was watching the tournament — that I knew for sure. And it didn't matter that it was for charity. It didn't matter that it should have been more fun than competitive.

To my father, *everything* was a competition.

And I was expected to win.

Before we moved on to the next hole, Vince ran over to the tape, leaning Maven back in a kiss that had cameras flashing and the crowd roaring to life.

Carter put a hand on my shoulder, biting his knuckles. "Damn, you see Doc today?" He shook his head, looking like Squints ogling Wendy Peffercorn as he checked out Livia — Maven's best friend, and also, our team dentist. "That woman is *too* fine."

I chuckled, following his gaze just in time to see Livia pull down her sunglasses and arch a brow at him. But my attention was quickly pulled to the woman beside her.

I knew for a fucking *fact* that Grace hadn't got much sleep last night, and yet she still glowed like the sun. Her smile was bright as she looked up at her brother, no doubt razzing him about something because he took her under his arm and knuckled her head. I watched her laugh with a pinch in my chest, and even with her sunglasses on, I felt the exact moment her eyes trailed to me.

The corner of her mouth ticked up, just a bit, just enough for me to know she was looking at me. The way her cheeks flushed in the next breath confirmed my suspicion, and I felt that sensation in my chest grow even stronger.

My little Nova.

I couldn't wait to have her alone again.

I felt the eyes of someone else on me, too, and when I looked over my shoulder, Will Perry was glaring at me like I was the poor winger trying to score on him. He whistled through his teeth, calling Vince's attention, and signaled with his finger in the air that it was time to wrap it up.

His glare never left me, not until he turned and started slowly walking to the next tee.

• • •

We were actually doing pretty decent by the time we made it to the seventeenth hole. We weren't going to win it all, but we had a shot at second or third place, and that would still send a good chunk of change home to Tampa. We were playing for the Tampa Bay Babes Compassion Project, an organization Maven had started that benefited various areas of the community.

We were in the golf cart on our way to battle it out at the last two holes when Vince let out a breathy sigh. "I'm worried about my sister."

The words were like ice shoved straight into my boxers.

I stilled, not daring to be the first to comment, because I knew there'd be enough shake in my voice to give me away. I calmly took a drink from my water bottle, instead.

"I was meaning to ask about her," Carter called from where he and Daddy P were sitting on the back of the cart.

"When she showed up at your house crying last week... that didn't look good."

"She left the next day," Vince said. "Which, honestly, wasn't surprising. She doesn't stay in one place for long. But fuck, I'm just worried she's going to go back to that loser she was messing around with."

"She won't."

Fuck.

Every head spun in my direction when I said the words, and I shrugged, hoping none of them noticed how fast my heart was beating.

"I hung out with her that whole night in Austin, remember?" I said. "She knew then that he was a lost cause. My bet is she just needed one night to cry and then she was moving on."

Carter made a face like he was considering that option while Will stared lasers into the back of my head.

"That's pretty on par for her," Vince grumbled. "I love her so much. You guys know that. We've been close our whole lives. But the older we get, the less I feel like I know how to help her." He shook his head. "I swear to God, I'm going to have to start vetting the guys she dates. She's careless when it comes to that — always has been. This isn't the first time she's showed up at my door heartbroken."

My skin prickled, hands rolling into fists, but I clamped my mouth shut harder.

"Maybe she's a hopeless romantic," Carter offered.

Vince snorted, parking the cart when we made it to the hole. "More like just hopeless. She's always been a little lost. I think she just tries to find herself in any guy who gives her attention."

I gritted my teeth, hopping off the cart and rounding it to where Vince was slowly climbing out from behind the steering wheel. I'd had enough of him talking shit about her, especially since he was clearly fucking blind to how she'd lived in his shadow their whole goddamn lives.

She wasn't lost — she just wasn't like *him*.

Somewhere inside me, my common sense screamed for me to calm the fuck down. But I was already seeing red, and I opened my mouth to give him a piece of my mind when a hand slammed against my chest so hard it knocked the wind out of me.

Vince and Carter both turned with the sound of my breath leaving me in an *oof*, their eyebrows inching into their hairlines.

But Daddy P stood directly in front of me, his hand still on my chest, eyes murderous as he nodded his head toward the hole.

"You guys get started. I need to talk to Brittzy," he said.

Vince and Carter both made sounds like I'd been called to the principal's office, each of them flicking my ear or clapping my shoulder as they passed. When they were out of range, Will dropped his hand, but his scowl was just as present.

"Do you *want* to die, or are you really this fucking stupid?"

I swallowed, folding my arms over my chest. "I don't know what—"

"Don't," he warned. "You've been with Grace this whole time, haven't you?"

All the blood draining from my face must have been all the answer he needed, because he laughed through his nose, looking over to where Carter and Vince were at the tee before he brought that menacing gaze back to me.

"Look, I'm not your father. Do whatever the fuck you want to do. But, if you're going to be with one of our *teammate's sisters*, then you damn sure better be the one to tell him. If he finds out another way, we're all fucked — not just you."

I frowned. "Grace and I aren't..."

My words faded, because I didn't know what the fuck to say. Or maybe I just couldn't find it in me to lie to Will Perry. We'd been teammates for years.

"Vince is tied up in Maven right now," Will continued. "They just moved into a new house. It's off-season. They have a wedding to plan. So, yeah, he's preoccupied. And you're fucking lucky he is, because otherwise, he would have seen the video of you on social media that *I* saw — one where you were carrying his drunk little sister into an elevator at a hotel."

My stomach dropped.

"Yeah," he clipped at my expression. "Don't worry — I had PR handle it. They gave the guy some cash to take it down, and it hadn't gained much traction. Besides, after Vince was the center of the media circus all season, he hasn't been online at all this summer. But," he added, pointing a finger to my chest. "That doesn't change the fact that you were being a fucking dumbass."

I winced, pinching the bridge of my nose. "You're right."

"I know I am. I don't care if you just want to get your dick wet and leave it at that, or if you end up marrying the girl. All *I* care about is that you don't fuck up our season by being stupid." He waited until I looked at him again. "Vince will not be okay with this. You already know that. And I swear to God, if you fuck with our season when we finally have a chance at the Cup, he won't be the only one beating your ass."

Ouch.

Will leveled his gaze with mine. "Figure it out, Brittzy."

I nodded, cursing under my breath when he stormed past me and toward where our teammates stood.

Fuck.

I hadn't even thought about that possibility, that someone from that night at the bar in Atlanta would post a video of her. I knew they'd taken pictures with *me* — that had been the whole point of the quarters game. But I'd been so focused on getting her upstairs and to her room that I hadn't noticed any phones out when I was taking her to the elevator.

It was careless. It was *dangerous* — not just for me, but for Grace, too. I didn't want her name dragged through the mud, and it would be if something like that got out. I could see the headlines now.

Tampa Winger's Sister Seen Leaving Hotel with Teammate.

Does Vince Tanev Know Where His Teammate Was Last Night?

Tampa Ospreys Having a Family Affair.

I groaned, because something else I hadn't thought of until Will pointed it out was that this wasn't just about me and Grace.

If Vince found out, if he blew a gasket... that would impact the team's chemistry.

It could crash our season before it even started.

My head spun as I made my way over to the guys, and I numbly played through the last two holes in a daze.

We took second place.

But when the guys went over to the sidelines where family and friends waited to celebrate with us, I stood frozen in place.

I realized in that moment that while everyone else had someone to celebrate with, I had no one. And the one person who I *did* want to run to was out of bounds.

I watched as Grace hugged her brother, and then when her parents jumped in, her gaze slid to me.

She smiled, warm and unknowing, her eyes dancing with anticipation. I'd felt that same impatience less than a half hour ago.

Now, another less pleasant sensation was sinking into my bones.

She frowned a bit when I didn't come join them, and thankfully, my phone rang, giving me an excuse to tear my gaze from hers. When I saw my father's name on the screen, my heart lurched, but I turned my back on the crowd and started walking toward a pond, answering the call even when I knew what waited for me on the other end of it.

I barely said hello before Dad was drilling me, telling me where I went wrong at every hole, berating me with questions about the mistakes I made that he felt lost us the tournament. It didn't take long for him to transition from the tournament to how this related to my hockey game, too. He'd been sitting on this, I knew. He couldn't wait to tell me all his thoughts now that he had my attention.

And for the first time, I was thankful for his call.

Taking a lashing from my father was better than facing the sickening truth Will had just made so clear.

CHAPTER 22

GET YOUR KICKS

Grace

"Alright, bitch — spill the tea."

I blinked out of the daze I'd been in, looking up just in time to watch Livia plop down next to me on the green. She folded her long, brown legs under her and took a big swig from the open bottle of red wine in her hand before passing it to Maven, who sank down in a similar fashion right in front of me.

How she had an entire bottle of wine at a fancy golf club was beyond me, but then again, unsurprising. Livia Young struck me as the kind of woman who always got what she wanted.

"And don't give us that look, either," Maven added, waving her finger at me. "Like you have nothing to hide. We know better."

"Yeah, trust me. Being best friends with this psycho has given me the eye for things like this." Livia eyed Maven with that comment, who smiled and reached out to squeeze Livia's arm like she was flattered by the assessment.

I blinked again.

Maven and I had gotten close since she and my brother started dating, and that meant that, by proxy, I'd also hung out with Livia quite a few times. But after spending the entire day together, I couldn't imagine what else there was to talk about.

Until Maven handed me the bottle of wine and cleared any confusion I had.

"What's going on with you and Jax?"

Shit.

I must have had that word written all over my face, too, because Livia smirked like she'd just guessed how many gumballs were in the jar. She sat back on her palms. "I knew it. You don't stare at someone the way you were staring at him all day unless there's something juicy to tell."

"I have not been staring," I defended. In fact, I was very aware of how I had *not* been staring because it had practically killed me in the process. All day long, I watched Jaxson in my peripheral, wanting so desperately to look at him all while diligently keeping my eyes trained elsewhere. I had been stealth as fuck — or so I thought.

But the looks those women gave me told me I hadn't been as sneaky as I'd believed.

They were both strikingly beautiful. Maven wore white shorts and a blue bandana tied around her like a t-shirt. She had red hoop earrings hanging from her lobes that matched her lipstick. Livia, on the other hand, was much less patriotic. She wore a burnt orange romper and wedges, along with an array of gold that hung around her neck and dangled from her ears. Where Maven had light brown skin and curly hair that framed her face like a halo, Livia wore her black hair short and cropped at her chin, angled around her rich brown features in a way that let you know she was powerful without ever having to hear her speak a word.

I sighed, picking at the label on the bottle before I took a big drink. I grimaced when I did, immediately passing it to Livia.

I fucking hated red wine.

The tournament had been a rollercoaster of emotions. From laughing and drinking with the girls and hanging with my parents to sneaking glances at Jaxson, I'd had a multitude of highs. However, I'd also felt Jaxson's gaze grow more distant throughout the day, and felt sick at the thought of what I was hiding — what we were *both* hiding — from my brother.

Then again, I wasn't sure there was anything to hide anymore. Because Jaxson hadn't so much as said hello to me since the end of the tournament.

We all had dinner at the club together after the award ceremony, and then we'd gathered out here on the course for fireworks. It was America's birthday, but I didn't feel like celebrating.

Something had happened.

I knew it without confirmation. Everything Jaxson had said to me this morning, even if he'd meant it at the time, didn't matter now. He was shutting down. He was pulling back. He was *ignoring* me, for fuck's sake.

My mind raced all through dinner. Vince wasn't showing any signs of wanting to end Jaxson's life, so I imagined it wasn't that my brother had found out about us. It felt a lot more like Jaxson had been away from me for the day and realized what a colossal fuckup he'd made.

What a mistake *I* was.

Even as my throat constricted with the thought, I didn't know how to talk about it.

When I was growing up, my family was my best friends. Vince and I were inseparable. Our parents were always planning family activities or trips. I had other friends, sure — girls on my cheer squad, classmates in college — but I spent my weekends at home or on a new adventure.

I had a lot of acquaintances all over the world.

None of which I felt like I could call up with something like this.

Maybe that was why I looked at the two women staring at me expectantly on that course, heaved a big sigh, and gave in.

"You both have to promise not to say a *word*," I started, and Maven leaned in closer as Livia clapped her hands in glee. "I mean it — not to anyone, *especially* not my brother," I added with a pointed look at Maven.

She made a motion to zip her lips shut, and then they both waited.

And I told them everything.

From that night in Austin and the way Jaxson had accidentally agreed to a road trip to the Four Seasons, camping, and even the sordid details of last night — I spared nothing.

It felt good to tell someone, like keeping the secret had added an insurmountable pressure to my chest. I had always been an oversharer. I liked to talk, and I wasn't scared of anyone's judgment.

I was, however, terrified of what they'd tell me to do next.

For a long time after I finished talking, Maven sat completely motionless. Livia just kept taking small sips from the wine bottle and nodding. A few fireworks went off over the course, and we all watched them light up the sky before the silence fell over us again.

"Well?" I prodded. "Don't ask for the tea and then not drink it. What do I do?"

"I'm sorry," Livia said, trying to hand me the wine. She wrinkled her nose at me when I declined. "I'm just a little preoccupied trying to picture this whole keychain thing."

Maven snorted. "Perv."

"Come on! It was basically a baby whip," she pointed out. "You know that's my love language."

I frowned, then shook my head, not sure I wanted to know the details of Livia's bedroom preferences. I had picked up enough in passing conversations to know she didn't date anyone seriously — and that she had more toys in her house than a kid's seventh birthday party.

"Are you going to tell Vince?" Maven asked first.

I leveled her with a look that answered for me, and she sighed.

"I wish I could tell you it will be fine when you do, but..." She winced. "Even the first time I casually asked if you'd ever dated any of his friends, he had essentially said they wouldn't be alive anymore if they'd even tried."

I had to fight to roll my eyes.

"Well, I may not have to worry about it," I said, picking a few blades of grass at my feet. "Like I said, Jaxson has been ignoring me all day, and he's got regret written all over him."

"But he told you this morning that everything was fine, and you'd talk after," Livia reminded me.

"A lot can happen in a day."

We all fell silent again at that.

"Okay, let me ask you this..." Maven said, sitting up on her knees. "What do *you* want to happen?"

The question socked me in the gut.

What *did* I want to happen?

"Just start talking," Livia coached. "We're not making you swear an oath or anything. What do you feel?"

I blew out a breath. "Well, the most prevalent feeling is that I want him to blow out my back."

Maven and Livia dropped their jaws in sync, and then they both burst into a fit of laughter, clutching their stomachs and squeezing my arms as I fought back my own smile. When they were settled again, I continued.

"I don't know. I mean, I think this road trip started as a joke, but then it really happened, and now... we're having fun." I shrugged. "We haven't talked about where we'll go next, but I know I want to keep going. At least for a while."

"And the G-Wagon passenger seat isn't all you want to ride." Livia waggled her brows.

I covered my face on something between a groan and a laugh.

"Okay, wait, we can work with this," Maven said, hope lighting up her face along with another firework. The big show would start soon, the sky finally dark enough. "Brittzy will have to get back to Tampa in August for preseason training, anyway. So... what if you two just enjoy the next few weeks together?"

"Wait... I love this idea," Livia chimed in. "Get your kicks on Route 66 and then wipe your hands clean. That's my favorite kind of transaction."

"As long as you don't think you've caught feelings," Maven added. "Because that changes everything."

Before the lie could even slip through my teeth, my stomach roiled, chest tight. "Come on, we've been together *four days*."

"Five if you count Austin," Maven reminded me.

"Okay, five. That's less than a week. What feelings could I possibly have caught other than the very specific feeling of wanting him to take my clothes off?"

They both giggled at that, and the words themselves *sounded* convincing. Because it really was insane to think of catching feelings for someone in that short amount of time.

But if I was being completely honest with myself, I'd felt a spark that first night I met Jaxson Brittain. And the fire had only grown more intense with every second — like it was a wild one, eating up an entire forest and laughing at the helicopters dumping buckets of water on it.

Insatiable.

That's how I felt when it came to that man.

"My bet is this is just what you need," Livia said. "A few weeks of fun, and then you go your separate ways. And no one needs to know."

"Least of all your brother," Maven said, looking a bit green.

My mouth felt particularly dry as I searched the fairway for the rest of our crew. I found Will Perry talking to my mom and dad first, and then, standing next to a golf cart — my brother, Carter, and Jaxson.

It was stupid how delicious he looked in fucking golfing attire. Something about those gray, well-fitted pants made his ass even more tempting, and I didn't know a baby blue polo tucked into them would do things to me the way it did. The clothes battled with his messy hair, with the ink sprawled out over his skin. It was the most mesmerizing contradiction.

"And what if it's already over?" I asked, my voice quiet.

"Then you have to respect that," Maven said. "If he's thought about it today and decided it's not worth the risk... well..."

Livia sucked her teeth. "I would bet my year's salary on that not being the case. But, if it is, then continue the road trip on your own. That's what you want to do, anyway, right? Travel? See the world?" She waved me off. "Jaxson Brittain is just a pit stop. Enjoy him while you have him, but then leave him in your rearview mirror."

"What happened to all that sappy love shit you were hitting me with when I was trying to leave Vince in *my* rearview mirror?" Maven asked, crossing her arms and arching a brow at her best friend.

"Please," Livia said with a scoff. "You were so gone for that boy I was about to have to start forwarding your mail. And *I* was going to go insane if you didn't figure your shit out."

Maven tacked on something else, and then they were laughing and reminiscing while I stared at Jaxson from across the green, willing him to look at me.

He didn't.

The fireworks show started, and I knew I was in deeper trouble than I'd ever admit when a part of me longed for Jaxson to be able to hold me the way my brother came over to hold Maven. I wondered what it would be like to smile up at him as he pulled me under his arm, to kiss him as the bright light flashed across the sky.

My stomach was in knots by the time I climbed into my parents' rental car under the pretense that I was flying out tonight. Mom and Dad prattled on and on about Vince the entire way, though Mom at least had the decency to ask me where I was off to next when we pulled up to the airport.

"Wherever the wind blows me," I answered with a smile that felt more forced than ever.

Mom and Dad both got out with me, Dad grabbing my luggage while Mom wrapped me in a hug.

"I'm so proud of you," she said, squeezing me tight. "My little adventurer, taking the world by storm. I never have to worry about you."

My chest tightened. I wanted to believe her, but I couldn't imagine what she could possibly be proud of — that I'd scraped by with Cs in college and earned a degree? That I'd cashed in my trust as soon as they let me and was living off it rather than a salary? That I was technically homeless?

I couldn't bring myself to ask her — because I was scared I'd have to watch her falter and look at my father with panic in her eyes. She'd silently ask him to bail her out, and he would, because my father always knew what to say.

The other part of my sinking gut was spawned by that last sentence she'd said. *I never have to worry about you.*

What if I *wanted* someone to worry about me?

Mom climbed back into the car after making me promise to update her on my next stop, and then Dad pulled me in for his signature bear hug, a deep sigh leaving his chest.

"Be good," he said.

I pulled back with a smile, doing a little finger-gun dance. "Come on, Dad — do you even know me? I'm always great."

He tapped me on the chin. "That you are. My little ray of sunshine."

I beamed under the praise even though it felt like a lie, and with a quick kiss on his cheek, he loaded into the car, and they were gone.

I was alone.

I'd experienced this exact scenario more times than I could count — being dropped off at an airport with my next destination unknown. And yet, out of all those times, this was the first one where I felt lonely.

Or maybe, it was just the first time I admitted it to myself.

I stood there for a long pause before taking my phone out with shaky hands. Pulling up Jaxson's contact, I stared at our most recent texts, the jokes and the emojis, the texts we'd sent to find each other when we'd been separated at the festival.

Swallowing past the lump in my throat took more effort than I could manage.

Me: Coast is clear.

I waited for the dots to start bouncing, for a message to pop up and tell me he was on his way.

But nothing came.

It had been scorching hot all day long, sweat sticking to my skin even though I wore shorts and a spaghetti strap crop top. But now, a shiver rolled over me as I sat on the curb by my suitcase, hugging my knees to my chest.

He's not coming.

I felt that with absolution the longer I went without a reply, but I couldn't find it in me to make my next move. I had my luggage. I could easily get a rental car inside the terminal. I could get a hotel for the night. Hell, I could just get a ticket on the first plane out of here.

But I didn't want to do any of that.

Nearly half an hour passed, my heart sinking further as car after car drove right past where I was seated on the curb.

Just when I was ready to give up, to peel myself off that sidewalk and figure out what came next, a black G-Wagon pulled to a stop right in front of me.

My heart caught in my throat, and I jumped to my feet, lighting up at the sight of Jaxson crawling out of the driver's seat.

But he didn't say a word to ease my worry.

Instead, he heaved my suitcase into the back and then opened the passenger side door for me, shutting it softly once I was safely inside.

His jaw was set, his shoulders so tight it looked like they were attached to his ears as he rounded the car and slid into the driver's seat.

I didn't know if we were continuing the road trip, or if he was taking me somewhere to break my heart.

But the fact that he already had that power was all I could think about as the headlights blew by in a blur.

CHAPTER 23

TOO DAMN BAD

Jaxson

"You've got to be fucking kidding me."

I grumbled the words under my breath, but it must have been loud enough for both the women near me to hear. The one behind the desk swallowed uncomfortably, keeping her eyes on her computer screen.

And the one next to me stiffened like I'd hit her.

Everything had me on edge — last night, the talk with Will, the call from my dad. This state of agitation was one I was used to during the season. But during the season, I had ice to take this energy out on. I could skate. I could hit a puck, hit a fucking *grown man* if I felt like it. It was why I went out after every game, too — win or lose.

Because if I didn't *do something* with this energy, it would eat me alive.

I pinched my eyes shut, forcing a calm breath before I managed somewhat of a smile that I aimed at the receptionist. "We'll take it," I said, referring to the only room they had left.

The one with a single queen bed and no pullout couch.

I was too damn tired to keep driving any farther tonight, and we had found a small town that I was pretty sure only existed because a highway ran through it.

I was also anxious to talk to Grace, especially since she hadn't opened her mouth once to speak to me since I picked her up. She just sat with that goddamned fake smile plastered across her face, staring out the window, like she couldn't sense that something was off.

Which I knew was bullshit.

Then again, *I* hadn't said a word either — mostly because I didn't know where to start, or what to say, or what I fucking wanted.

Half of me felt pulled in the direction of obligation to, and respect for, my teammates.

The other, stronger half only felt pulled to her.

"Do you at least have a rollaway? A cot?" I asked. Having a room with only one bed certainly wasn't going to help me in my attempts to keep my hands to myself. And that was what I needed to do. I needed to back us up into friend territory.

Even as I thought it, I internally laughed at it actually happening.

Like I could be just her friend after I'd seen every slender curve of her body, after I'd watched her pin her lip between her teeth and ride out an orgasm with those jade eyes locked on mine.

The receptionist — whose name tag read *Emily* — grimaced. "Unfortunately, we have many families staying with us, and—"

I waved her off before she could finish. "It's fine. Thank you."

The words were clipped as I handed her my card, and when I snuck a glance at Grace out of my peripheral, she had her arms folded around her, a somber look in her eyes.

Fuck.

That was worse than her fake smile.

I didn't know what the hell I was doing. I could have called her after the tournament and told her I couldn't come get her. I could have picked her up and started driving toward Tampa. I could have encouraged her to leave me behind and get on a plane. I could have broken all this off and given her the choice.

Instead, I'd picked her up and made her suffer through an hour drive to the middle of fucking nowhere Missouri in complete silence.

I was a bastard.

I didn't know what to do, what to say. All I knew was that I didn't want to let her go, even when every fucking sign in the universe pointed to that being the right thing to do. I was a selfish prick, like a dragon sitting on its gold knowing I can't even spend it.

"Here you are," Emily said, handing me two plastic key cards. "You'll be on the bottom floor, right down this hallway to the left. Ice and vending are across the hallway, and our breakfast starts at six."

I tapped the keys on the counter with a muttered *thank you* before grabbing Grace's luggage and steering us down the hall.

I'd only taken a few steps before she dashed out in front of me, snatching a key from me as well as the handle of her suitcase. She dropped my duffle bag at my feet.

"I can handle my own shit," she said, lifting her chin. "And don't worry — I'll sleep on the floor. Wouldn't want you to have to suffer through accidentally touching me."

Grace landed her blow straight to my chest — especially when her eyes watered a bit with the words.

Of course, in true Grace fashion, those tears didn't get the chance to fully form before she whipped around and stormed down the hall, scanning the key and shoving through the door to our room so hard that it slammed against the wall.

I couldn't swallow past the knot in my throat, and I stood there in the hallway for a long moment before following after her.

When I did, I walked right into a Grace Tanev tornado.

A shirt hit me in the face, and I peeled it off me and dangled it from one finger as I shut the door behind me and set my bag on the floor. On closer inspection, I realized it was the little crop top she'd been wearing all day, and I looked up just in time to see her tug on an oversized Harry Styles t-shirt to replace it.

It was huge on her, and because it fell to her mid-thighs, I couldn't be sure if she had on anything underneath it.

There were more pressing things to attend to anyway — considering she had her bag half-opened and shoved to the side and was currently ripping pillows off the bed. She threw two down to the ground, leaving the other two on the mattress, and then she ripped the comforter off in one fell swoop that somewhat impressed me, given her size.

"Grace, you're not sleeping on the floor."

She ignored me, stomping past me and into the bathroom with her toothbrush and face wash in tow. She slammed the door shut, leaving me to look at the disaster of a room.

This is going splendidly.

I stepped out of my shoes, leaving them by the door before I crossed to the pallet she'd made on the short, hard carpet. I picked up each of the pillows and placed them back on the bed. I was resetting the comforter when she swung out of the bathroom, and she let out a frustrated grunt when she saw what I'd done.

"Stop," she said, nudging me aside so she could take the pillows off. Again.

"Grace."

"It's fine. I sleep in tents all the time, this is the same thing."

She plopped the pillows on the floor.

"What's wrong?"

"Nothing," she clipped, and she plopped down onto the floor, yanked the comforter from my hands, and wrapped it around her until she looked like a burrito.

"Don't do that."

She tried to glare at me, but her eyes betrayed her, watering again against her will. She shut them tight and burrowed deeper into the comforter without responding.

Slowly, I sank down next to her, careful to give her space, but close enough to let her know we weren't dropping this.

"Let's just get some sleep," she tried.

"Not until you talk to me."

"I don't want to talk."

"Well, that's just too damn bad."

Her mouth popped open as she looked over her shoulder at me.

"You don't get to do this," I said, pointing at her and then the space between us. "Not with me. You may have everyone else convinced that you're happy go lucky no matter what life throws at you, but I see through it. You're not okay right now. And that's fine. But you need to admit it, and you need to stop trying to hide your fucking emotions. Face them, and *talk to me*."

"Fine," she said, ripping the comforter off her and sitting up to face me. "You want to talk? Then let's talk. You want to be real? Let's be real. You," she said, pointing her finger into my chest. "*Kissed* me this morning."

Her little nostrils flared with that, and fuck if I didn't want to kiss her again.

"You held me," she continued. "You told me everything would be fine. And then, you ignored me. All day long. And I know it was part of our stupid *game plan*," she added, putting air quotes around the words. "But you didn't have to act like I didn't fucking exist. You say you can see right through me? Well, I see right through *you*." Her chin wobbled a little, but she held it even higher. "And you don't have to tell me. I already know what you're too scared to say."

She held my gaze for a long moment, letting the words sink in. Then, she turned away from me before emotion could warp her face again, wrapping herself up in the comforter.

My heart was pounding, breath wreaking havoc on my tightened lungs as I traced the curve of her back. This woman called to me the way nothing else in the world did. My entire body, my entire *being* responded to the sight of her balled up and hurting.

And whatever decision I thought I'd made, whatever *right thing* I thought I should do?

I fast pitched it all out the nearest window, and I crawled in behind her.

I tugged on the comforter with one hand, and she stiffened, clutching it tighter. But I slid in anyway, pulling again until she relented, until I could slip under the covers and lie on the floor with her.

She was so warm, so soft. I couldn't help the sigh that left me when I aligned myself with her — my chest to her

217

back, my hips behind hers, our legs curling around one another. My heart softened its pace as I burrowed my face into the back of her neck, inhaling the scent of her hair.

Sweet orange and salty air.

Grace was frozen until I pulled the comforter up around us like a fortress, covering even our heads. It was like blocking the world out, and she melted — just a little, but sufficient for me to know she'd lowered her walls enough for me to climb over.

"What is it you think you know?" I asked against her skin. "What is it you think I'm scared to say?"

The muscles of her jaw worked, and I heard her swallow several times before she could speak. She was trying not to cry, and some sick part of me wished she would just let it happen.

I hated that she was upset, but I hated that she was hiding that fact even more. She'd done it her whole life, masking what she really felt because she didn't think there was space for her.

"Grace," I prompted, nuzzling her neck. "What do you think you know?"

"That you don't want me."

She whispered the words so softly, and yet they broke me like a brutal hit against the glass. Then, she curled in on herself like a little kid.

I weaved my arm around her waist, pulling her into me again, lining us up in every possible place. I wanted her to feel my heart beating when I told her the truth.

"You think I don't want you?" I asked against the shell of her ear. Then, I laced my fingers over hers where she'd tucked it under her pillow, and I held onto her tighter as I rocked my hips.

She sipped in a shallow breath, arching her back and meeting my movement with tentative reach. I pressed my erection into the crease of her ass, tangling my fingers with hers and savoring the little moan she let loose.

"Does that feel like I don't want you?"

Grace rolled her ass against me, and I stifled a groan, letting out a heated exhale against her neck.

Both of us were barely breathing now, our bodies winding and rolling and intertwining in every possible way. She twisted in my arms to face me, and as soon as she did, we tangled ourselves up again — my fingers in her hair, hers curling around the back of my neck, my thigh sliding between her legs, her forehead dropping to mine.

"Then touch me," she pleaded, her words dancing over my lips.

I swallowed, gripping her to me even as I shook my head. "I'm too old for you."

"I'm not asking you to marry me," she combatted, and she ground herself against my thigh, trembling when she got the friction she was searching for. "I'm asking you to *touch me*."

Fuck.

"Your brother will kill me," I gritted through my teeth, but even as I said the words that should have made us both stop, my hand was traveling. I splayed my fingertips across her collarbone, her chest, trailing down until I felt the small curve of her breast.

I palmed her through her shirt, rolling my hard-on against her as she let out a simpering moan that I felt all the way to my toes.

My thumb roamed, running a line under the swell of her breast before I slid it over her hard nipple. I'd seen that fucking nipple pressing against the thin fabric of so many of her shirts, her dresses. The girl never wore a bra, and it damn near killed me.

But now, touching her, feeling her, hearing the sounds she was making...

I squeezed where I held her, one flawless handful, and we both let out low groans when I did.

I hadn't felt like this since I was a teenager, since I was hooking up with a girl for the first time. Everything inside me buzzed with awareness of each place our skin touched. Grace looked down at where I thumbed her nipple through her t-shirt, pinning her lip before she threw the covers off from where they covered our heads.

She climbed on top of me with a renewed sense of confidence, lowering her mouth until it hovered just above mine.

"Do you tell my brother everything?"

She said it with a teasing smile, throwing my own words right back in my face.

But she didn't close the distance, didn't kiss me — not yet.

She waited, straddling my lap with her hands braced on either side of my head. One roll of her heat against my shaft had me seeing stars, and I gripped her hips like I wanted to stop her, like I had a fucking prayer of stopping *anything* now.

I tried to breathe, tried to find reason, tried to remember all the ways this could go wrong.

But with my hands on that girl, nothing else made sense but her.

And over the sound of my racing heart, I heard the distant sound of my moral compass shattering.

"Come here," I growled.

One hand found the back of her neck, the other held fast to her hips, and I pulled her mouth down to mine.

Grace sparked to life under that kiss, under my touch, both of us hissing our next breaths like they burned as much as they healed. I was so hard my cock was threatening to break the zipper on my pants as I thrust it against her, reveling in the way she shook when I rubbed that sensitive apex of her thighs.

I fisted my hands in the fabric of her shirt like she was the bull I was about to ride, like I had any chance of taming the wild woman writhing in my lap. She met my bruising kisses with her own, and then she was kissing down my neck, biting the flesh just under my jaw.

"Fuck," I cursed, and then I rolled, pinning her on top of the comforter with her chest heaving, eyes glittering, lips curling into a daring smile.

She was so beautiful it hurt — her hair splayed over that pillow, her tan skin against the white comforter, her slight frame wiggling against my grasp like she needed more. I knew before I even fully succumbed to her that no other woman in the world would ever measure up.

"Before we do this," I warned, stopping only long enough to return the kiss she urgently pressed against my lips. "I need to know — are you still thinking about him?"

That made her still, confusion bending her brows. "Who?"

"Your ex."

The words felt like hot coals in my throat. I didn't want to think about anyone else touching her — not before me, not after. But I had to ask. I had to know before I gave in that she wasn't still hung up on someone else.

Grace nearly laughed when it dawned on her, and she shook her head, wrapping her arms around my neck and lifting enough to kiss me.

"I wasn't even thinking about him when we were... whatever we were," she said. "He was nothing. You, on the other hand..." She traced my jaw with her finger, shaking her head. "All I ever think about is you."

I closed my eyes, savoring the way it felt to hear her say that. If any of my logic was still here, I'd tell her she shouldn't. I'd remind her of all the reasons this was a terrible idea.

As it was, I didn't care if it was wrong. I didn't care about the possible consequences.

I'd face any of it, *all* of it, to have just one night with her.

She dragged her nails down my chest, ripping my shirt up from where it was tucked into my pants. "You, and your mouth." She pressed a kiss there to hammer that point home. "And this body," she added, a wave of chills breaking over my abdomen where she touched. One hand slid down lower, over my belt, and she wrapped it around me as much as she could. "And this cock that I want to taste."

"*Christ.*"

I sat back on my knees long enough to rip my polo overhead, and then I braced myself over her again, kissing her hard and biting that plump bottom lip. I rocked against her, and as soon as she had her arms around my neck again, I flipped us until she was back on top.

"Get rid of this," I said, tugging at the hem of her shirt.

That agitated energy in me transformed into something more focused, something primal as she obeyed.

This.

This was what I needed.

She peeled it overhead slowly, the fabric clinging to her in a way that made my hands ache to do the same. I watched the slow reveal of her hips, her stomach, the bottom swells of her breasts. When she pulled it up over her head, her long hair spilled down over her shoulders, and I let my eyes skate over her like she was fresh ice on an early winter morning.

I noted everything I'd missed before — the two, small beauty marks just above her left hip, the dip of an ab line that ran from above her belly button to just under her chest, the bell shape of her breasts, how her nipples were a shade darker than her skin. I registered it all with my eyes first, and then my hands, savoring the chills that raced across her body with every touch.

"These next," I said, tucking my fingers into the band of her boy shorts.

Grace stood, backing up a few steps so she could make a show of sliding those hot pink shorts down her tan, toned legs. My cock twitched at the sight of her completely bare, at how that apex of her thighs was dusted with just a slender trail of hair.

I took in the view greedily as my hands moved for my belt.

"You want to taste me?" I asked, and Grace's eyes fell to where I unfastened the leather.

She swallowed, nodding.

"Come on, don't get shy on me now, Nova," I teased as her eyes widened. "Where are those words you had before?"

I flicked the button open with my thumb, unzipped my pants, and lifted my hips enough to slide them down to my knees.

Grace's eyes were on the tent pitched in my briefs, and I savored her watching me as I slid those down next, my cock springing to attention the second the fabric wasn't restraining them.

"Fuck," she whispered.

That sound spurred me on as I stripped my pants and briefs the rest of the way off. Then, we were both naked — Grace standing above me like a statue of a Greek goddess, and me wrapping a hand around my cock with one slow pump that made me even more desperate for her.

"Now," I said, beckoning her with my fingers. I waited until she slid her hand into mine, and then I turned her, guiding her until she stood with her feet on either side of my head. "Sit that pretty pussy on my face and open your mouth wide."

I helped her lower to her knees, spanking her ass before I palmed it and spread her cheeks. I groaned my appreciation for the view — because I could see just how wet she was, how badly she wanted me, too.

"I'm going to eat this pussy while I fuck your throat," I promised, grabbing her ass and pulling her down more until she was straddling my mouth. I kissed the inside of each of her thighs before running my tongue in one long, flat sweep between her legs. "Let's see who comes first."

CHAPTER 24

THAT'S MY GIRL

Grace

I loved a good competition, but I knew before we began that this was a game I was destined to lose.

No way in hell was I going to be able to make this man come first, not when I was so sensitive to his touch that the first glide of his tongue had me quaking. I closed my eyes as all the awareness in my body zeroed in on that point of contact, on where he licked me from end to end before sucking my clit between his teeth.

"Oh, *God*." I rolled against that sensation, greedy for more, and Jaxson smiled against my pussy before he grabbed my ass in both hands and pulled me to him, my hips having no choice but to open more.

Then, I had an out-of-body experience, because the truth of it all came rushing in.

I was sitting on Jaxson Brittain's face.

The power of that swept over me as much as the next stroke of his tongue, and I trembled, palming my breasts and rolling my hips slowly to meet every inch of his tongue.

"Fuck, that feels so good," I cried, closing my eyes and tilting my head back. Jaxson sucked my clit, swirling his tongue around and around in the perfect way to build my climax. But just as the sparks started to catch, he pulled away, licking in softer, longer motions.

I whimpered.

"Oh, I'm *so* going to win," he said on another smile against my skin. Then, he hardened the tip of his tongue to a point and flicked it side to side over my clit, making me see stars.

I moaned, seeking his challenge through the fog his tongue was clouding my mind with. I crawled forward, bending over his body until I was face to face with the most beautiful cock in the world.

I balanced myself on one hand, reaching out to wrap the other around him as I wet my lips. The moment I touched him, he stilled.

And that power rushed through me again.

Slowly, I rolled my hand into a fist around him, sliding up long enough to coat myself in the drop of precum at his tip before I slid down the entire length of him.

I felt his groan vibrating through me, his next breath hot and needy on my pussy.

Jaxson flexed into my hand, teasing my clit with his tongue as he did. I pumped him once, twice, wondering how much of him I'd even be able to take.

I couldn't wait to find out.

Licking my lips, I lowered my mouth, twirling my tongue around his head before I sucked just the tip of him inside. He met my advance with a long sweep of his tongue between my legs, and we both moaned together.

He was so fucking *big*.

I stretched my mouth open wider and angled my head so I could take a little more, and then I pulled off, sliding my hand up to coat it in saliva. I squeezed my palm around him, fastened my lips to where my hand was, and pushed a little deeper.

"*Yes*, baby," he groaned, his hips curling like he needed more. "Just like that."

God, I loved that. I loved when he told me what to do, when he told me what he liked. I loved the thought of my touch driving him wild.

My tongue circled his head as my hand squeezed his shaft, and I worked them in time with each other, bobbing up and down until I hit a depth that made me gag.

"*Fuck*," Jaxson cursed, and then he slicked one thick finger and toyed with my entrance, teasing and gliding before he plunged it deep inside me.

My entire body clenched, goosebumps racing over my skin.

Jaxson exhaled like it was the best sight he'd ever had in the world, his finger inside me, and he curled it against a deep spot that made my legs shake violently around him. "I love when you gag on my cock. Do it again."

Those words alone were enough to make me come, my body humming to life under the praise. I slid my hand up and down his length, slow and calculated, and then I sucked him inside my mouth again and dove deep.

He was still fucking me with his finger, tongue circling my clit as a guttural groan ripped from his chest. Just when I thought I couldn't take any more, he flexed — just half an inch — and my throat stretched to let him in.

I held for a long second, and then gagged, pulling up to catch my breath. A string of saliva connected us, and I used it to fuck him with my hand as he smacked my ass.

"That is the hottest fucking sound I have ever heard," he rasped, rewarding me with a second finger curling inside me, and a torturous rhythm of his tongue against my clit. "I knew you could take it."

I bit my lip on a moan, both from his words and the perfect way he was stroking his fingers inside me. The combination of his tongue and his touch were too much for me to focus, and I couldn't help it — I sank down more, stretching my hips and rolling against him.

Then, before I knew what was happening, Jaxson flipped us, rolling until it was him balancing his weight on top of me.

"You want to come," he asked, spreading my legs wide and licking me from tip to seam. "Open wide and let me fuck that pretty mouth."

I writhed under his touch, under those words. I'd never gotten off from a guy going down on me before, but I was one swipe of his tongue away from bursting into flames. Add in the fact that him telling me in the most vulgar way that he wanted me to suck his cock actually made me even *wetter*, and this was going down as the most eye-opening sexual experience of my life.

Jaxson pressed up onto his palm, using his other hand to grip his cock and press it to my lips. He rubbed the tip of himself along the seam until I opened, and then he dipped in just enough for me to swirl my tongue around him.

"Wider."

Fuck. I opened more, and he slid in deeper, withdrawing only a moment before he pressed in again.

"Come on, baby. Open up for me."

I arched my head back, closing my eyes and doing everything in my power to school my breathing.

I can do this. I can take more.

Jaxson slid in again, slow and steady, and I felt that same sensation I had before even stronger. He stretched my throat, pushing in deep until I gagged.

"God*damn*," he praised, pulling all the way out and stroking himself while I caught my breath. As soon as I did, I pulled him back to me.

If Jaxson was surprised, he didn't show it. He let me take control, let me guide him into my mouth again, and I arched as much as I could to open my throat and let him in.

It was so fucking hot. He was literally on top of me *fucking my throat*.

The filthiness of that made me moan, the noise vibrating around his cock, and he flexed in deep with a groan ripping from his chest.

And I... was pretty sure I could come, just like this.

I reached between my legs, and just a brush of my fingertips against my clit told me I was accurate in my assessment. I bucked my hips against my hand as Jaxson cursed and slid in deeper, withdrawing, then pushing in again, over, and over, and over.

"That's my girl," he husked, palming my breast roughly. "Fuck your hand while I fuck your mouth."

He slid in so deep I gagged again, but the sound of it, the way he moaned like it was the hottest thing in the world made me circle my clit faster. I was so close. I was going to—

No.

Just before the flames could catch, Jaxson withdrew everything — his cock, his mouth, his hands. I was ready to whine and throw a fucking *fit*, but before I could, my ass was lifted off the ground.

Jaxson literally bent me in half.

My head, neck, and shoulders were still on the floor, but the lower half of me was suspended, ass resting against Jaxson's chest as he positioned himself between my legs. He looked down at me with a greedy sweep of his eyes over my body, and then he grabbed hold of my thighs and spread me more.

"Eyes on me, baby," he said, running his tongue flat and hot between my legs. I shook, my orgasm kicking back to life. "I want to watch you when you come on my tongue."

All words were gone after that.

He descended, and I realized then that everything before had just been a tease. Because he knew. He knew *exactly* how to lick me and suck me to make me unravel, knew just the right way to curl his fingers inside me and stoke my climax to the surface.

I writhed and bucked as he held me in place. It was both too much and not enough. I chased it as much as I ran from it. But my release caught me, fire licking at the edges of my vision before it took me under a roaring inferno.

I cried out his name, fisting my hands in the comforter as if that could tether me to the Earth. It was useless. I spun into outer space, my orgasm rocking through me in intense, body-breaking waves as Jaxson held me to his mouth and devoured me like eating my pussy was his favorite thing in the world.

I rode it out, every last drop, until I had no choice but to fall limp in his grasp. When I did, he smirked, pressing a gentle kiss to my clit that made me shake like a leaf.

Then, slowly, he lowered me to the ground, crawling his way up my body until he captured my mouth with his. I tasted myself on his tongue, and that, combined with his rock-hard erection pressing against my thigh, wound me up like a music box.

I was ready for more.

"Jaxson," I whispered against his lips, and then I bucked against him, telling him what I wanted without saying a word.

He kissed me hard, meeting my need with his own. Then, he pushed up long enough to reach for his pants. He grabbed his wallet out of the pocket and fished out a gold packet.

I tried to snatch it out of his hands, but he pulled back.

"Not even going to congratulate me on my win?" he asked, arching a brow.

I narrowed my gaze before grabbing the condom, ripping the foil with my teeth and tossing the wrapper aside.

Then, in a move bold enough it surprised me, I grabbed him — by the cock — and pulled him into me.

"It's not a win until I come with you inside me."

Jaxson slid his tongue along his lower lip as he watched me sheathe him, those deep blue eyes of his telling me that was a challenge he was happy to take.

Funny enough, even though it was me who'd issued that challenge, it was *me* now staring at his cock wondering how the hell it was going to fit.

Even *struggling*, I'd barely managed to fit a third of him inside my mouth. It was all my hands taking the rest of him. Then again, I had a small mouth. It would be fine.

Right?

I only half-believed in myself as Jaxson grabbed me by the hand and pulled me until I was straddling his lap, his back propped against the foot of the bed. The look in his eyes told me he had nothing but faith that I could take it.

That lit me up like nothing else could.

Bracing my hands on his shoulders, I pressed up onto my knees with my heart ready to race out of my chest. No number of deep breaths could soothe or prepare me. I was nervous. I was excited. I was more alive than I'd ever been with the anticipation of feeling him in the most personal, intimate way.

I rolled my hips, his shaft sliding into my wet heat. I was dripping from my release, and we both groaned at the feel of him gliding along that sensitive area. I didn't take him inside though, not yet. I just squeezed my thighs and rubbed him from tip to base, covering him, teasing him.

Jaxson's hands gripped my hips tight enough to bruise, like he was holding back from lifting me onto him and slamming it home.

So many times, we'd just barely touched — a gentle brush of a hand, an accidental graze of our bodies. But now, we were bared to each other, locked inside a room where we couldn't hear all the noise telling us to stop.

I moved a bit faster, rolling my entire body with the movement as I rode him without even a centimeter of penetration. When his head dropped back on a groan, he tightened his hold on me, biting his lip.

"You're killing me," he said roughly.

And I loved it. I wanted more of this — the power, the excitement, the anticipation. This was the last moment we'd ache for him to be inside me without actually knowing what it would feel like. This was the only first time we'd have.

I milked it for every last drop.

My hands slid into his hair, and I yanked, exposing his neck so I could kiss and bite along the slope of it. I tracked my way along his jaw, sucking the lobe of his ear between my teeth.

"Tell me what to do."

He shook with a vibration so strong he groaned, capturing my mouth with a bruising kiss. This was what he needed. The energy searing through him needed a release, and I knew he found it in commanding me — the same way I found my own power in knowing I could bring this grown man to his knees.

"Sit back," he said. "Let me see you."

I did as he asked, leaning back and bracing my palms on the floor behind me. I could just *barely* writhe against him like this, and he watched where his cock glided between my pussy lips like he was a starved man.

"Look at you," he said, reaching forward to touch me. He splayed his hand over my stomach, pushing it up slowly — between my breasts, over my collarbone, until he could wrap it fully around my neck. "Such a little cock tease."

My eyelids fluttered, stomach tightening. *Why* did that turn me on so much?

I dared him with my eyes to say more, to give me more, to stop tiptoeing around the words I was desperate to hear him say.

"You want to ride my cock, don't you?"

"Yes," I breathed, rubbing along his length until I sat right at the tip of him. I had to press up onto my knees to do so, and Jaxson tightened his hand around my neck to steady me.

"Sit on it."

My breath hitched, the desire to do what I was told taking over everything else. I fit him to my entrance, and then I sank down — only an inch, just enough for us to both curse and hiss and grip onto each other for dear life.

His hand slid higher on my throat until he could grip my chin and force me to look at him.

"That's it," he said. "But you can take more."

I whimpered, lifting a bit before I slid down even farther. The stretch sent a shock through me, but pleasure was right on its heels, sweeping in to wash away any pain.

"God*damn*, baby," Jaxson groaned. "So fucking tight."

Again, I lifted, dropping down and taking another centimeter. Again, and again, each time opening myself more for him.

"You listen so well," he coached, and his hand left my neck. He moved both his palms to my hips, splaying his fingers wide and helping to lift me and slide me back down.

Fuck.

I saw stars, felt myself stretching past the point I thought possible. It hurt a little more than it felt good, and I grabbed his forearms, halting us.

"You feel incredible," he said, and I knew by the way he didn't push me that he was well aware how fucking big he was. Instead, he let me sit there, let me gently lift and lower back down while his hands explored.

He trailed his fingertips lightly over my abdomen, drawing lines between the few freckles I had. Then, he palmed both my breasts, massaging them with just the *slightest* flex of his hips that sent another jolt through me.

I hissed, and he went even slower, paying special attention to my nipples and putting the power of our pace back in my hands.

"You're so goddamn pretty," he praised, his thumbs sparking electricity with every circle of my nipples. "You know that? You drive me fucking *mad*."

One hand continued playing with my breast while the other trailed up to my mouth. He slid his thumb over my bottom lip until I opened, sucking the digit inside.

That earned me a fierce groan, his nostrils flaring, and I knew he was fighting not to flex inside me again.

"You took me so well in this mouth, the way you gagged for me..." He swallowed, like he was weighing what he was about to say. But his eyes found mine, the decision made when he added, "Such a good little *slut*."

It should have shocked me.

It should have pissed me off and made me slap him hard across the face.

If anyone else in the world would have said it, that likely would have happened. But as it was, I had Jaxson Brittain inching his way inside me and looking at me like I was his whole fucking world.

And I wanted it.

I *wanted* to be his little slut.

I sucked his thumb harder as I pressed onto my knees, and then I sank down — fast and hard and as deep as I could.

I cried out when I hit my max, and Jaxson hissed, grabbing my hips to still me.

"*Jesus*, Grace," he cursed, looking at where we were fitted together. "I'm almost all the way inside you."

I used that as motivation, sliding up a bit to coat us before I went even lower.

"*Fuck*." He shook his head, and then his hand shot out, grabbing me by the back of the neck and pulling me to him. He crashed his mouth over mine, holding me tight, his hips rocking him out of me before he pressed inside slow and gentle. "No one takes this cock like you, baby. *No one*."

"I want it all."

He cursed again, withdrawing and pushing in as I rocked against him.

"Play with your clit," he commanded, releasing me enough so I could reach my hand down between us. He knew it was going to hurt, to take all of him, but he also knew I could.

I sucked in a breath, circling my clit as little bursts of sparks flew in my bloodstream. It felt so incredibly good, him filling me to the brim, his eyes soaking in the sight of me riding him. I could feel my second climax mounting as I spread my legs even wider, chasing the release.

"Good girl."

His hands found my hips again, and he slid me up, then back down — once, twice, three times — each one a little deeper than the last.

"You can take it," he told me again, and that praise tickled my skin for only a split second before he grabbed my shoulders and pulled me down, hammering himself all the way inside.

A sharp pain ripped through me, like a thousand knives had sliced right through my core.

"Shh, shh," Jaxson said against my lips, and he held me to him, not daring to move again now that I was fully seated. He just kissed me, over and over, across my jaw and along my neck and back up to my mouth. He swept my hair out of the way, his hands holding me to him, our breaths hot and labored in the space between.

And slowly, the pain subsided.

It washed away like a gentle wave, and when his cock twitched inside me, my stomach stirred with the promise of my release.

Carefully, I slid up again, not too far before I sat all the way back down.

"Oh, fuck," Jaxson growled, and he pulled back so he could watch when I did it again.

He shook his head, gaping at the view of me riding him, and then his hungry eyes found mine. He grabbed the back of my neck again and kissed me hard.

"You," he said, nipping my bottom lip. "Are fucking sensational."

I rocked against him, tangling my hands in his hair as I bounced slowly in his lap. And when he reached down between us and pressed his warm fingertips against my clit, I let out something between a moan and a prayer.

"I'm close," he gritted out, and then he took control — of everything. He bucked his hips, fucking me hard while I used my hands in his hair to steady myself. One arm wrapped around me to give him leverage, and the other rubbed my clit with the perfect amount of friction to give me what I needed.

"Jaxson, oh God, I... *fuck*!"

My second orgasm took me all the way out.

Numbness invaded me from head to toe, and then it was blasted away in a shocking wave of heat. My blood rushed to where he touched me, legs trembling with the effort to keep riding. I didn't have to do much. Jaxson bucked his hips to meet mine, fingers keeping their pace while he punished my mouth with another brutal kiss.

I was floating in space.

I was everything and nothing all at once.

I writhed in his lap, crying out his name, and when I did, he muttered a curse against my lips and shuttered.

I felt it, the moment he spilled inside the condom, the way he spasmed even as he managed to keep his pace and make sure I didn't lose my orgasm. The groan he let rip free gave me new life, and I took over, using his shoulders to help me bounce on his cock and drain him. I wanted every last drop.

I wanted to fucking wreck him — just the way he'd wrecked me.

The sounds he made when he came felt like the sweetest reward I'd ever earned. They were guttural, primal, completely untamed. And with every flex of his hips, he held onto me, pulling me down like he couldn't get deep enough to ever feel satiated.

A squeeze on my hip told me when he was finished, and I slowed, pressing up high enough to carefully remove the condom. I tied it off carefully and set it aside. When it was gone, I fisted my hand around him, savoring the moan he let out when I did.

"I have an IUD," I told him, pumping him slowly. "And I've been tested." I looked down at where he was hardening in my hand, and then locked my eyes on his. "I really want to feel you inside me, Jaxson. *Just* you."

His answer was a tightening of his jaw and his hands lifting my hips. I knew by that alone that he'd been tested, too — knew he wouldn't chance anything. But he confirmed it with words.

"You're safe with me."

Jaxson positioned me where he wanted, and then slid inside me — all the way, in one fluid motion that stole both our breaths.

God, it was so hot, to be connected like that, to feel him inside me without a barrier between us. And I was warmed up, lubricated, stretched enough to sit all the way down and wrap my arms around his neck, pressing my forehead to his.

It was my plan to just sit there with him inside me, to just... *feel*.

But soon, our breaths were slowing, and Jaxson was winding his fingers in my hair. Then, he was kissing me, unhurried in his perusal of my mouth. Before long, he was rock hard, flexing just deep enough to make me gasp.

"You have no idea what you're doing to me," he rasped.

The next round began before the first one was even done.

And as he moved me to the bed, pressing me into the sheets and sliding inside me again, all I could think was how wrong he was.

I knew exactly what I was doing to him, what he was doing to me.

What I didn't know was how we were ever supposed to walk away from each other now.

CHAPTER 25

JUST KEEP DRIVING

Jaxson

I woke to the feel of soft, warm fingertips gliding along my arm.

It was the first thing I registered, the way they both tickled and soothed where they ran from my shoulder all the way down to my wrist. The next thing I noted was the soft, slender heat touching every part of me — a leg hitched over my hip, a breast flattened against my chest, and a sweet little pussy nestled right against my thigh.

My cock twitched to life, but even as it did, I felt the rest of my body protesting.

I was pretty sure I couldn't fuck that girl again even if I wanted to.

I was usually quite proud of my stamina, considering I could skate non-stop and fast-paced for minutes at a time, take a small break, and then do it again — for *hours*. But Grace had pushed me to the limit last night in the best possible way.

Grace.

My eyelids fluttered open, and there she was.

Her hair was a fucking *mess* — dirty and matted from me burying my hands in it. Her eyes were tired but crinkled at the edges with a smile, her lips still swollen from my kisses and a slight bruise showing on her neck.

That made my heart stop, and I reached out to thumb the spot on a curse. "Grace..."

"I'm fine," she said before I could apologize.

I shook my head, swallowing, hating myself for doing that to her. But she covered my hand with hers and lifted my fingers to her lips, kissing each one until my eyes found hers.

"I'm *fine*," she promised. "I'm better than fine. I'm..." She lit up with a bashful smile, biting her lip. "I'm amazing."

That brought a relieved exhale to my chest, and I smoothed my thumb over her lip.

"Our *room*, on the other hand," she said, looking around us. "Is wrecked."

I frowned, leaning up on my elbow enough to survey for myself.

She wasn't wrong. Pillows and sheets were strewn everywhere, the comforter half covering our feet and half draped down to the floor. There were feathers scattered like we'd shredded a pillow. Maybe we had.

I glanced at the trail of soapy wetness that led from the shower to our bed. I hadn't been able to fuck her the way I wanted to when we were attempting to clean up, so I'd carried her right back out and thrown her into the sheets. We'd also broken the handle in the shower that was meant to be an accessibility aide, and it had scraped a line of paint off the bathroom wall when I'd hastily tossed it out of our way.

I blinked.

And then a laugh barreled out of me, and I wrapped a giggling Grace in my arms, kissing her hair.

"I told you you were a menace," I said, nipping at her earlobe.

"*Me*?" She poked me in the rib. "I'm not the one with muscles like the Hulk."

She squeezed one of my biceps, and then sat up again, balancing on her elbow as she brought her fingernail down to continue perusing my skin.

"I love your tattoos," she said, following the swirls of blue and black ink on my arm.

"Thank you. I'll send your compliments to my artist."

She smiled. "What do they mean?"

I couldn't explain it, but I felt a nervousness roll off of her with those words, like the rubble was settling around us and she'd just realized what we'd done. It wasn't regret, but rather... *fear*.

And I felt it zing up my spine, too.

We needed to talk about what this meant, but for once, I wasn't in a hurry to do so.

Maybe because I was scared of the answer.

"To be honest? Nothing," I said, watching as she traced the outline of a large eye on the inside of my bicep. "I found the artist online one day and just loved his work. I made an appointment, picked my arm to start, and told him to do whatever he wanted."

Her eyebrows shot into her hairline. "You let him put whatever he wanted on your skin... *permanently*."

"I did."

"That's insane."

I laughed, shrugging. "Maybe. It's art. I trusted him. Besides, I think..." I frowned, because before the words even left my mouth, I realized it was the first time

I was saying them out loud. It was maybe the first time recognition dawned on me at all. "I think so much of my life has been planned out, I wanted something that *I* had control over."

"And yet, you wanted freedom within that control."

We both fell silent at her assessment.

I felt even more naked than I was.

"Speaking of control," she said, biting her lip as her finger moved from my arm to my chest. "You called me a little slut last night."

"And you fucking loved it."

She buried her blush in my chest, and I smiled against her hair, pressing a kiss to it.

"*God*, I did. I really did. What does that say about me?" she asked, peeking up at me.

"Does it matter?" I brushed her hair from her face, tucking it behind one ear. "You don't need to be ashamed of what you like in the bedroom, Nova. If it turns you on, it turns you on. And for the record," I added, licking my lips as my eyes fell to her mouth. "It was fucking hot."

She smirked, leaning up on her elbow once more. Her eyes moved between mine. "Is it fair to say you had some pent-up energy last night?"

"What do you think?"

She touched my jaw, eyes following the movement. "It wasn't just from us, though, was it?"

I swallowed at that, letting out a long exhale. "My dad called me yesterday."

Grace snapped her gaze to mine, frowning with concern. "When?"

"As soon as the tournament ended."

"He wanted to congratulate you?" she guessed, but I could tell from her face that she knew that wasn't the answer even before she tried it.

"No," I answered simply.

Grace sighed, then nestled into me, wrapping her arm around me in the fiercest hug from such a small thing. "I'm sorry."

I closed my eyes, holding her, feeling something so strong it was almost overwhelming. I wanted to burrow into it as much as I wanted to shoot it down.

We laid like that for a long while — Grace smoothing her hands over my back while I pressed lazy, slow kisses on her forehead and in her hair. I was almost back to sleep when she tilted her head up, her lips against my neck.

"So... what do we do next?"

The question jolted me awake, but I managed a calm breath, smoothing my hand over her hair. "What do you want to do next?"

At that, she pressed up on her elbow, eyes searching mine.

"Can we just keep driving?"

I knew it was a bad idea. God, hadn't that been the theme of the whole fucking summer? Ever since that night she'd strutted to the back of the party bus in Austin and sat right next to me, pinning me with that spellbinding smile of hers.

We were driving fast and furious down a dead-end road.

And yet... I didn't want to stop. I didn't want to slow down. I didn't want a seatbelt or a fucking airbag.

I'd never felt this alive — not in all the thirty years I'd existed.

I knew, eventually, it would all end. I knew there'd come a day when I'd go back to Tampa, back to a new season with her brother as my teammate. And she'd go off on her next adventure with me as just a good story to tell.

But that was later. This was now.

I decided reality could wait.

Because we still had summer.

I kissed her nose, grabbed her by the hand, and put every other thought on mute in my mind as I pulled her up from the mess we'd made.

"Let's roll, Nova."

CHAPTER 26

GOOD AT KEEPING SECRETS

Jaxson

"**D**ear *God*, woman — what the hell is that?"

Grace bounced on the toes of her dirty white canvas sneakers, holding a plastic bag of something absolutely foul like it was a hundred-pound fish she'd reeled in on her own. She'd opened it while I was pumping gas, and the stench alone had turned my stomach.

"Pork rinds!"

I unlatched the nozzle and replaced it on the pump, closing the gas tank door next. "That sounds as disgusting as it smells."

"Come on — it's all part of the experience," she said, attempting to hand me one of the crisps.

"That's a hell no from me, Nova."

She shrugged, popping one in her mouth. She chewed it normally for a second before her movement slowed, and she grimaced, running to the trash can by the gas pump and spitting it out.

"Alright," she said, tossing the opened bag in next. "They can't all be winners. But look!" She dug into the bag slung around her arm and pulled out a small white pack of chocolates. "Valomilk cups!"

I blinked at her, rounding the SUV to open her door and help her climb in before I did the same. I fired up the engine, which was quiet and disappointing. I missed my Porsche.

"And what exactly are these?" I asked when Grace ripped open the packet and handed me a chocolate.

"Apparently, a famous Kansas candy. Marshmallow inside, I think."

She bumped her piece against mine and shoved the whole thing in her mouth, which made my eyebrow tic up.

"Hmm," I assessed, watching her chew. "Forgot just how much you can fit in that little mouth."

Grace's eyes shot open, and she laughed around a mouthful of chocolate and fluff, smacking my chest as a blush tinged her cheek.

"*Ash-hole.*"

I grinned, taking a bite of my own chocolate, which actually wasn't terrible. But it wasn't great, either.

I kicked us into drive, hitting the open road — and it was *quite* open as we drove straight through the middle of Kansas.

"I need to take you to Canada," I said. "We put your chocolate to shame. Everything we have is creamier, richer."

"Including the men," Grace piped up with a smile that told me she was proud of herself.

I took the wheel with my left hand and tickled her with the right until she was laughing and squealing and wiggling away from me.

When she was breathless, I stopped tickling her, and without me realizing what I was doing, I slid my hand between her thighs, hooking my fingers around the inside of her left one.

Fuck me.

Everything felt so good and right in that moment. I had one hand on the wheel, one wrapped around Grace's thigh, and she was smiling at me with pink cheeks as we drove without a damn clue where we were going next.

My heart pitched into my throat, but I swallowed it down.

"You've never had chocolate until you've had a Caramilk bar. Or a Wunderbar. Or, *fuck*," I dragged the word out, stomach grumbling. "A coffee crisp — with your coffee, naturally."

Grace leaned an elbow on the console, chin in her palm as she watched me. "So, take me to Canada."

I blinked. "Uh..."

"Come on," she insisted. "We're already halfway there, aren't we? Take me to your hometown."

I swallowed — not because I didn't want to take her, because I did. In fact, I wanted to so badly that my heart was ready to leap out of my chest and scream *yes* for me.

But going to Canmore meant being close to my parents — which I tried to avoid at all costs.

They'd moved back to our hometown once I was in the professional circuit.

"We don't have to tell anyone we're there," Grace said, like she was reading my thoughts. "We're pretty good at keeping secrets."

I thought about the video Will had seen, but decided Grace didn't need to know about that.

"In a town that small, we won't be," I said. "Everyone knows me."

Grace considered. "What if we just drove through it, then? These windows are tinted. You could show me around a little, and then we can run away farther north. Or west. Or whatever direction you want to. We can stay in a cabin in the mountains, order food in, and no one has to know."

"You really want to go, don't you?"

"I want to see where you're from. I want to feel the place that made you."

I looked at her then, at her wide green eyes and the way they assessed the world.

I'd never known anyone like her.

"Alright," I said, swallowing the knot in my throat. "To Canada we go."

"Really?!" Grace lit up like she thought she didn't have a chance to convince me — as if she didn't have me wrapped around her finger. "Yes!" She threw both fists into the air and did a little dance that had my hand sliding higher on her thigh. Then, she leaned into me, wrapping her arm around mine. "Okay, what other great snacks do you have?"

"Ever heard of All Dressed Chips?"

• • •

We drove until we hit a sign for Wilson State Park, and Grace insisted it was our home for the night.

It was a different kind of beautiful than the beaches of Florida, an almost barren piece of land surrounding the Wilson reservoir. The shoreline was rugged and colorful, with gorgeous cliffs and rock formations unlike anything I'd ever seen.

We got lucky, snagging up an empty campsite that someone had canceled their reservation for that afternoon. We were right on the water, the soft sounds of the waves lapping at the shore our background music as we set up camp.

There was still plenty of sunlight left before we needed to build a fire, so I grabbed Grace by the hand and we walked the shoreline. It was so peacefully quiet and serene, like all the campers were afraid to disturb Mother Nature. There weren't many of them, and I doubted anyone out here would know who I was. Still, I wore my hat and sunglasses just in case.

We hadn't made it more than a hundred feet from our campsite when my phone buzzed in my pocket, and I frowned at my father's name and photograph filling the screen. I pushed him to voicemail — a move I knew I'd pay for the next time I picked up. But for now, I didn't want to deal with it. With him.

Grace squeezed my hand as I slid my phone into my back pocket again. "He's persistent," she mused.

"This is nothing compared to the season."

"I don't understand," she said, shaking her head. "You're a professional defenseman, in the highest professional league, for a great team with a high likelihood of making the playoffs this season. You scored twenty-two points last season — *as a defenseman*. I mean, your plus-minus is twenty-five, for fuck's sake. That's like... *stupid*. Insane."

She shook her head, face reddening like it pissed her off that anyone would come for me. And that was *almost* as hot as the fact that this girl had just shot off my stats for the season like she was telling me the weather report.

"Little Nova," I said, stopping us and turning her to face me. I slid my hands to frame her face. "You googled me."

She flushed but tilted her chin higher. "And what about it? I was getting in the car with you. The least I could do was make sure you weren't a serial killer — or, worse, a shitty defenseman."

I tried to fight it, but I barked out a laugh before pulling her into my chest.

"You are so fucking cute," I said into her hair. Then, I spanked her ass and gripped it in a hearty handful. "But stop listing my stats, or I'm going to lose control and fuck you right here for the whole park to watch."

"Don't make promises you can't keep, seventy-seven."

My fucking number.

Christ.

"Woman," I threatened, picking her up and throwing her over my shoulder. But she laughed and promised to behave, and I dropped her again, threading my fingers through hers as we continued our walk.

"I just don't know what more he expects of you," she said, and my chest tightened with the conversation swinging back to my father.

"Perfection."

"Well, that's stupid. No one is perfect."

I nodded, a flash of my father's signature scowl striking like a branding iron.

"You *do* like it, right?" she asked. "Hockey, I mean. I feel like there's no way you fake playing as well as you do and looking like you're having fun while doing it."

"I love it."

The words rode out on a longing breath. It was true, but it hurt to admit.

"Sometimes I wish I didn't," I said. "Because he..." I paused, forcing a breath that I needed to loosen my chest. "He makes it so fucking hard sometimes. He makes me hate it, hate *myself*, even. I'll come out of a game on this... *God*, this unexplainable high." I shook my head. "And then he'll grab me by the throat and throw me to the ground."

"Jaxson..."

"It's fine," I said.

"No, it's not. I know this was his dream, and I understand that he helped you a lot with it. I'm sure he was a great coach, a great trainer. But he has no right to taint something that means so much to both of you. It's like he..."

She swallowed, biting back her words, and when I looked at her, I saw the regret on her face.

"Like he's jealous?"

"I didn't want to say it."

"Me either," I admitted. "But I've always wondered."

We walked in silence for a bit.

"It makes me sad," I confessed, chest tight again. "Because I love him. I care for him. I fucking *hate* that his career, hell, his way of *life,* got taken the way it did. I can't imagine having an injury like that. And I want his approval. I want him to be proud of me. But... *fuck*." I kicked a rock, cracking my neck. "I hate that when he calls me, my stomach drops. I hate that even when I play my best, I know he's on social media just looking for someone talking shit about me so he can rub it in my face and tell me how I fucked up."

Grace pulled me to a stop this time, and she placed her hands on my chest, right over where my heart felt like it was about to burst.

"Look, I'm not one to talk," she said. "But, for what it's worth, I think you're amazing. And I also think your father is hurting and doesn't know how to properly handle it. And I *also* think," she said, smiling a little, but it fell just as quickly. "That you are not the one who has to help him figure that out, nor do you have to be his punching bag."

I swallowed, covering her hands with my own.

"I know he's your dad, so I won't pretend like it would be easy to do. But... if you ever decided to draw a boundary, just know I would understand it. And you'd, at the very least, have me supporting you in that."

Fucking hell.

My chest hurt even more, and for a completely different reason.

"No fucking way are you just twenty-two," I said.

She laughed, and we started walking again. "Oh, trust me. I'm great at giving advice. Just don't ask me to take any for myself."

"You do really suck at talking about your feelings."

"Gee, thanks." She laughed, but then let out a long sigh. "I want to get better at that."

"Let's start now, then."

"Uh-oh." She looked at the lake, then up at the sky. "You know, I think we should head back, get the fire started. We—"

I grabbed her and pretended to drag her toward the water, which made her squeal and thrash until I set her back down. Then, I sat on a flat rock along the shoreline and pulled her into my lap. I turned my hat around backward and took my sunglasses off so I could see her better, so she could see me.

"You're not getting out of this."

She sighed, staring at where her hands were folded in her lap. "Fine. What do you want to know?"

"Just start talking. Tell me the first thing that comes to your mind."

Her eyes flicked to mine, and she swallowed, shaking her head.

"Okay," I said on a chuckle. "How about the second thing?"

Grace was quiet for a while, her eyes on the lake. Then, she did exactly what I'd asked her to do. She started talking.

And the words spilled out like she'd had them dammed up her whole life and I'd just busted the thing down.

"I'm so grateful," she started. "For *everything* in my life. I'm thankful for my parents, for how hard they worked to set me and my brother up with a life most people could only dream of. I'm thankful for the experiences I've already had, and I still have a whole life ahead of me. I'm thankful for Vince, for what *he's* done for our family, and for how he's always protected me."

I smiled, because I'd asked her to share something with me, and the first thing she'd thought of was to tell me everything good in her life. I didn't know a single other person who would have done the same. Not one.

But then, her eyes glossed, and she pressed a hand to her chest, letting out a shaky breath. "God, I hate this feeling."

"What feeling?"

She shook her head. "When my chest feels heavy and fluttery at the same time, when my throat closes in on itself and my nose stings."

"So... when you need to cry?"

She sucked in a breath, and her bottom lip trembled when she let it out. "No, no, *no*, I don't want to cry."

She fought it, and seeing that emotion choke her was like smoke in my lungs. I turned her in my lap, so she had no choice but to face me. "*Why*? Let it happen, Nova. Let it out."

She bit her lip and shook her head, holding her eyes open wide so they brimmed with the tears she refused to shed. "I'm scared that if I do, I'll never feel happy again. I'm so afraid this feeling will swallow me whole."

And with that, she broke.

The first tears slipped free, and she buried her face in her hands like she was ashamed.

That broke me.

I pulled her into my chest, covering her head with my hand and cradling her against me. I rocked her like a small child, soothing her with a hand on her back and my voice in her ear.

"You won't get lost in this feeling," I promised her. "As long as you allow it to exist, it will do just that — and then it will pass. Just like everything else in life."

She sobbed.

The girl full-on sobbed, clutching me to her and crying into my chest.

It killed me to feel that emotion escaping her, to know she was hurting. But I was also proud of her for letting it all be felt. It wasn't easy to do for anyone, least of all her.

I felt honored to be the one she could break with.

I held her for a long while, and then she sat up, her face red and streaked with tears. She batted them away. "I just... I feel like the only thing I'm good for is to make the other people in my life happy. When Vince was upset after a game, or before a game, or even in the off-season...

whenever he'd beat himself up, I was always there to remind him how great he was, to push him on, to tell him he could do anything he put his mind to."

I thought about how Vince called her before every game so she could do some little dance she'd done one time in high school to cheer him up. He'd won that night, and so it had become a superstition, part of his routine.

He needed her, and she was there — every fucking time.

"And my parents," she said, sniffing. "When they were worried about Vince, or about work, or about some stupid party they were hosting or — *whatever*." She waved her hand in the air. "I loved to be the one to cheer them up. I loved to make a joke, to bring them comfort, to turn their anxiety into laughter. With my friends, it's always felt... surface level. Like, if someone has a bad breakup, I'm the one they call for a good night out on the town. Or if we're at a party and it's dull, I'm the one they look to. I'm the one they expect to jump up and dance on the bar or challenge someone to a drinking game. And don't get me wrong," she said quickly. "I *love* to be that person. It feels natural to me. I *enjoy* being the life of the party. I just..."

She took a breath, fidgeting with her hands.

"Somewhere along the way, that's what I became to everyone I loved. I was the one they went to when they wanted to feel better." Her face crumpled. "But because I was always okay, because I was always happy... no one ever checked in on *me*."

I swallowed the knot in my throat, pulling her to me again.

"I sound like such a brat."

"No," I said, pulling back so I could look her in the eyes. "You're not a brat because you want someone to ask you how you are, Grace. And because I can feel it in how stiff you are right now, I'll also tell you that it doesn't make you selfish, either." I took a breath, framing her face. "You are allowed to be sad. You're allowed to not be okay. And you're damn sure allowed to wish for someone to notice when you're not."

She nodded, eyes watering again. "I think sometimes I'm just a joke to them. Cute little Grace, always getting into something. I'm always on the go, always dating someone new and then heartbroken a week later. But the truth is..." She sucked in a breath like she just realized the truth she was speaking of, and it killed her. "The truth is I'm always on the go because I don't feel like I have a safe place to land."

I closed my eyes, suppressing a curse as my heart cracked at her admission.

Then, I tilted her chin, and I made sure she was looking at me when I said, "You always have a safe place to land with me."

Her eyes flicked between mine, and then she crushed me in a hug, her arms winding around my neck as she buried her face in mine. I held her tight, letting her feel it, feel *me*.

After a while, she pulled back, and the tears seemed to be drying out. She let out a long sigh. "That actually felt good."

"Told you so."

She chuckled. "I love traveling, by the way," she said. "I don't want you to think I don't."

"You can love traveling and still want a place to call home."

Her lips curled, and she didn't have to say another word for me to hear her. She felt seen. She felt understood.

KANDI STEINER

I knew, because I felt the same way.

"Give me your phone," I said.

She handed it to me, wiping her nose with the back of her hand as I turned on the camera and faced it toward us.

"Today, Grace Tanev cried," I said, looking at her as she let a laugh bubble up. She swatted my chest, but then leaned into me, looking up at the camera. "And it was the most beautiful thing," I added.

I kissed her temple, and she tilted her chin up at me.

"Tell me something good," she prompted — just like always.

A million things crossed my mind, but every single one of them felt too heavy. So, I sighed, pulling her under my arm as I pretended to think.

"Oh, I don't know... that blowjob last night was pretty fucking great."

She elbowed me, earning her a puff of a laugh as I cut the video. She tucked her phone away again and then wrapped her arms around my neck.

"Thank you," I said, squeezing her leg. "For sharing all that with me."

"Thanks for listening."

"And see? It didn't pull you under, you're not a depressed dark cloud roaming the Earth."

She laughed.

"Everyone gets sad sometimes," I said, knuckling her chin.

"It's nice when you don't have to do it alone."

I nodded.

And then my stomach twisted into the most awful knot.

I knew, right then, on that craggy shoreline in fucking Kansas, that I didn't want her to ever have to do anything alone again. That *I* didn't want to be alone.

That I wanted her — not just for the fucking summer, and not in secret.

I also realized I couldn't have what I wanted.

It was like I was the moon wishing to be the sun.

It wasn't just us that we had to think about. It was her brother, my teammate — my *team*. It was the fact that I was eight years older and in a literal contract that kept me in one city for the foreseeable future, and she was young and hungry and ready to see the world.

I could see the same thoughts tracking through Grace's mind as we stared at each other.

We didn't fit. We didn't work.

Except right here, right now, in this eclipse of time.

"Take me to the tent, Jax," she said, curling her fingers in the hair at the nape of my neck.

So I did.

I laid her down and stripped her bare, sinking inside her on a longing sigh we both released in sync.

We knew what we were, and what we were not, and what we could never be.

We understood the risk we took with our hearts, and yet we did it anyway.

One day, we'd have to walk away from each other. One day, we'd have to say goodbye.

But that day wasn't today.

And we were going to make the most of every second we did have.

That was a promise we both could keep.

CHAPTER 27

JUST A LITTLE HIKING

Grace

I was living in a dream.

A bright pink sunrise, warm afternoon wind through your hair, scent of fresh-cut grass and mountains in the distance dream.

I'd known from the first moment I met him that I wanted Jaxson Brittain. I wanted to kiss him, to feel his hands on me, to see if he was as good in bed as he was on the ice.

But *that* had all been a pipe dream, a fantasy, one I knew would never play out. He was my brother's teammate. That was all I needed to know to understand nothing would ever happen between us.

And then it did.

It was one thing for us to give in to the way we craved one another. That fire had been burning hot since the moment I pressed my ass against him in a crowded Austin bar.

But it wasn't just a one-time, fuck-and-get-it-out-of-our-system deal.

I didn't know how we ended up here. I didn't know how many stars had to align for him to have been at my brother's house when I showed up crying, suitcase in hand. Or for him to follow me upstairs, to make a joke about taking a drive that turned into an actual road trip. I didn't know what had shifted in him to make him break, to make him give in and kiss me and touch me knowing the possible consequences.

All I knew was that it all felt like a dream, and if it was, I never wanted to wake up.

After the night at Wilson State Park, we slowed down.

We woke up later, spending more time wrapped in our sleeping bags or sheets — depending. Which meant we didn't hit the road until later, and for obvious reasons, we didn't care to drive very much farther before we were pulling off for the night.

It seemed like there was this invisible clock ticking in the car with us, and the longer we were in that car, the more we heard it. When it got too loud, reminding us of the impending end of summer, we'd climb out, run away, and lose ourselves in each other like we had all the time in the world.

We drove through Kansas and into Colorado, swinging through the Rocky Mountains because neither of us had ever been before. Well, *technically* Jaxson had grown up in them, but not the ones in Colorado. The range was different this far south, and I'd marveled at the tree-covered slopes just as much as I marveled at the way *he* looked at them.

It was one thing to travel alone, to not have to report to anyone or ask anyone's opinion when deciding what to do. There was a freedom in that, in being with your thoughts as you explored, in meeting new people and opening yourself to new experiences.

But driving on the road with Jaxson... it was something *more*.

I lived for what the day would hold, which usually, we didn't know. We'd see a sign and follow it. We'd pull off for gas and ask a local the best way to waste an hour. We tried new food and hiked new trails. We laughed and played, sneaking kisses when no one was looking, and every night, whether we slept in a tent or a Five-Star hotel, he was right there beside me.

Inside me.

Every chance he got.

A week blew by like that — with everything heavy left in Kansas, and only the light and playful following us on this leg of our trip. The only tension came when I had to field calls from my brother, which would sober both of us in an instant. But we never let that sink in for long before we were off on the next adventure.

Jaxson indulged me in my silly questions and even sillier road trip games, and where he'd been a bit grumpy and hesitant in the beginning, he said yes to everything now.

I loved that — that he left his reservations somewhere in the middle of the US. Right now, he wasn't thinking about all the reasons to say no. He wasn't thinking about the season waiting for him back in Tampa.

He was just here, *living*, with me.

We were getting ready for bed at a hotel just outside the Rocky Mountain National Park when my phone buzzed on the bathroom counter. I was brushing my teeth, but I smiled when I saw Maven's name on the screen.

I slid my thumb across it, revealing a group text she'd started with me and Livia.

Maven: So, Livia and I are having martinis. Naturally, we thought about you and your predicament at the tournament, and we need updates.

Livia: That's code for DID YOU AND JAXSON GET IT ON YET?

I bit down on my toothbrush, laughing to myself as I looked through my GIF app. When I found one of the Route 66 sign, I sent it, closing my phone and setting it back on the counter.

It promptly blew up with messages.

Livia: THATTA FUCKING GIRL.

Maven: Okay, first of all — happy for you. Second of all, this feels like a betrayal to Vince, so I feel like you should not tell me anything further.

Livia: Come on, Mave. Chicks before dicks. Do you tell Vince how you wipe, too?

Maven: You're disgusting.

Maven: I just gave her a tittie twist for that, Grace. Just so you know.

Livia: Joke's on her though, because I liked it.

Maven: *eye roll emoji* It's true. She asked me to do it harder.

Livia: ANYWAY — forget what Maven said about not telling us more. I need details. How is it?

Me: A lady never gets railed within an inch of her life and tells.

Livia: YOU TEASE.

Maven: I apologize for my best friend's lack of boundaries. You'll get used to it eventually.

Livia: If you drive by one of those highway sex stores, stop and get a peg. Something tells me Jaxson Brittain would love a good pegging.

I spit out a laugh loud enough to make Jaxson ask if I was okay.

Me: I'll leave the kinky shit to you, Doc. For now, just know I'm doing great, and there's nothing for either of you to worry about.

Only half a lie. I *was* doing great.

How I would feel when this all had to end, on the other hand...

I batted that thought away like a baseball pitched right down the middle, reading the flurry of texts and emojis that came in with a goofy smile on my face. Maven and Livia felt like the kind of girls I could be best friends with, the kind who would keep even a secret as big as this one.

The next day, when we crossed over the Colorado border into Wyoming, we saw a sign for a car show in Cheyenne, and Jaxson parked us with a giddiness I'd never seen flowing out of him.

He wore his hat and sunglasses, even though I didn't see a single person so much as giving him a second look like they might know him. The opposite had been true in Colorado. He'd been recognized when we were getting gas, and for that reason, we'd had every meal either in our car or hotel room while we were traveling through.

But at the car show, he seemed not to care — at least for the moment. He dragged me by the hand through an aisle between two rows of cars, pointing at each one and rattling off things about them that might as well have been him speaking in a foreign language.

I had zero idea what a cabriolet or brougham was, but I knew Jaxson lit up when he told me about them, and that was enough for me.

I mostly marveled at the beautiful paint jobs and gorgeous leather interiors. And when some of the owners let us sit in the cars, revving up the engines, I swore Jaxson got a hard-on when he saw me gripping the steering wheel and pretending to drive.

Back on the road, we originally planned to drive straight up through the state. But we didn't get far before signs for Yellowstone National Park were begging us to take a detour.

I pulled up my phone and began researching, tapping my bare feet on the dash to the mellow beat of "Rose Colored Lenses" by Miley Cyrus. Halfway through the song, Jaxson reached over and slid his large palm along the inside of my thigh, hooking his hand there and holding tight. I glanced up to find him smirking at me.

"What?"

"I like this song," he said.

I paused, listening to the lyrics, and then my cheeks warmed.

"Don't worry — I won't tell any of your teammates you like a Miley song," I said.

"If you don't, I will. We need this banger on the warm-up playlist."

I laughed, then leaned over the console and angled my phone screen toward him. "Okay, so. Here's the sitch for tomorrow. Most of the camping sites are booked, *but*," I added, wiggling in my seat with excitement. "There are some backcountry options available. And I already applied for a permit."

"And what exactly does a backcountry camping site entail?"

I bit my lip. "Just a little hiking."

"How much is a little?"

"Like... fifteen miles or so?"

Jaxson coughed. "Fifteen *miles*? We haven't trained for that, Nova."

"Oh, please," I said, pinching the skin over his abdomen — because there *was* no fat there. "Says the man who probably *skates* fifteen miles a day. You're fit as hell, and I hike all the time. We'll be fine. We can take it slow."

He shook his head, cocking a brow at me, but when he saw the excitement in my eyes, his resolve wavered.

"It'll be an adventure," I promised. "Think of everything we'll see. The stars! Can you imagine the stars?!"

"I imagine they'd be just as bright from the parking lot of a hotel."

I clapped my hands together and held them under my chin, batting my lashes up at him. "Please, please, *please*."

He sighed, glancing at me and then back at the road as a smirk painted his lips. "We better find a store. We'll need more than the few supplies you picked up in Tennessee."

I threw my hands up at him giving in, doing a little dance before I leaned across the console and kissed him.

It was just a peck to his cheek at first, but then I kissed along his jaw, his neck, and back up to claim his mouth with a moan vibrating between us. I slid my hand into his hair, tugging on the strands, heat flooding to where his hand still held my thigh.

A dream. It was an absolute *dream*. How could I just touch this man, *kiss* him, any time I wanted to? How were we existing in this world where no one and nothing else mattered?

My stomach tightened a bit when I remembered it would end.

Eventually, it had to.

But I swallowed that truth down. That was future Grace's problem.

"Woman," Jaxson said, kissing me back but breaking contact to look at the road. "I'm driving."

"What's wrong? Can't drive when you're... distracted?" I teased, and I slid my hand down between his legs, rubbing the length of him through his athletic shorts.

He sucked in a hot breath, pinning my wrist before I could stroke him again.

"You want us to wreck?"

"I want you to wreck *me*."

At the next exit, we were off the road and he was granting my wish.

• • •

I found myself wondering again about the stars aligning the next day when we pulled up to the Bechler Ranger Station at Yellowstone, because not only were we able to score a camping site in the backcountry, but we got the one right across from a hidden gem of a hot spring — Mr. Bubbles.

I was never the best at planning when I traveled, and sometimes that bit me in the ass. Reservations filled up weeks, and sometimes months, in advance for things like this.

We got lucky.

And I felt like that was the theme of the summer.

After talking to one of the rangers at the station, I grew more and more excited. What I thought would just be a hike and overnight camping adventure was now a trek to a hot spring that was one of Yellowstone's best-kept secrets. It was where the river met the springs, which meant it wouldn't boil us alive like some of the other thermal spots in the park, and it wasn't illegal to hop in, since *technically,* it was the river — and swimming in the river was allowed.

We just had to *get* to it, which required a fourteen-mile hike.

After quick research and a shopping trip the day before, Jaxson and I were both loaded up with giant packs.

We had our tent, sleeping bags, cooking supplies, and food — including the various snacks I insisted on being essential, like Peanut M&Ms and sunflower seeds — plenty of water, rain gear, knives and multi-tools, a GPS, a satellite locator beacon, trekking poles, headlamps, water-treatment tools, toiletries — including toilet paper — bear spray, a fire starter, and more.

We also made sure to pack extra clothes and — after advice from one of the employees at the store — a pair of rugged sandals to help us cross the rivers, along with sunscreen, insect repellent, and other necessities.

It was only one night, but it was one night in the backcountry. Where I likely would have just winged it, Jaxson was more sensible. He decided he'd rather we be over-prepared than under.

Once we were loaded up and had our permits and camping site in hand, Jaxson grabbed a map and led the way.

"You look so hot with that bear spray on your hip," I said, waggling my brows.

"Is this your kink? A backcountry hiking man?"

"You know my kink," I said, and just saying the word had my cheeks heating.

Jaxson smirked, pulling me under his arm as best he could with my pack in the way. He lowered his lips to the back of my ear.

"You want me to tell you how pretty you were on your knees last night? Or how much I loved the way you moaned when I called you my little whore? Because I'm happy to relive the moment."

Electricity zipped through me, the memory bright and blinding. I'd never felt as free to explore what I liked in the bedroom, never *knew* what I wanted at all. But Jaxson had known. He'd known without me having to ask.

I bit my lip before playfully shoving him away. "We have a big hike today. Save your energy."

"Oh, believe me — I will."

His smile was promising, and my body hummed with anticipation as we snaked our way through the woods.

Yellowstone was just... *breathtaking*. There was no better way to describe it. From the thick woods to the vast meadows, every turn on the hike led to another view that ripped a gasp from me. I couldn't take it all in even when I tried. My camera was also completely useless. It couldn't capture the way it felt to hike along the rushing rivers, or how magnificent the mountains sprawling along the horizon line were when you were standing in the middle of a wide-open space.

I pulled out my phone and recorded my daily diary, laughing when I asked Jaxson to tell me something good, and he said that if a bear came, he had a good amount of faith he could outrun me.

When we made it past the first couple of miles, I played music on a speaker hanging from my pack to help

269

ward said bears off. As certain as I was that he'd die trying to save me even with that little joke he'd made, I wasn't keen for us to have to test that theory.

After a few hours, when we had to cross over a bridge suspended over the river, we stopped for a snack and a little rest.

"Okay," I said, crossing my legs under me as I handed a stick of beef jerky to Jaxson. "Would you rather…"

"Oh, God, here we go."

I grinned. "Would you rather be mauled by a bear, or sprayed by a skunk?"

"I'm not sure if that question is morbid or hilarious."

"Both, now answer it."

He chuckled, biting off half the jerky stick in one go. "Bear."

"*Bear*?" I shook my head. "Explain."

"Well, you said mauled — not killed. I'd come out of it with a great story and some bad ass scars. Whereas the skunk option would just leave me pissed off and smelly."

"Fair point," I said, chewing on his reasoning. "What is it with hockey players and scars, by the way? I swear, you guys get *excited* when you lose a tooth."

"It's a rite of passage."

"How many have you lost?"

"Only two," he said. "One from a high stick and one from a fight."

"A *fight*?!" I gaped at that. I had seen my brother get in countless fights during the games, but never one so intense anyone lost a tooth.

"It was my first year in the NHL," Jaxson explained, eating the last of his jerky. "And another asshole rookie thought it was funny to slide into our goalie." His jaw tensed. "No one fucks with my goalie."

"Wow," I said, noting his scowl. "That's hot. Okay, now ask me one."

I was sure he'd argue that it was a stupid game and he wasn't going to play, but he must have been used to my antics, because he sat back on one palm, thinking.

"Would you rather have a third eye or a third nipple?"

"Oh, this is hard!" I tapped my jerky stick against my chin, chewing off a bite as I considered. "Nipple."

"Nice. I was hoping you'd pick that one."

"Perv. Okay, here's one. It's heavy," I warned, waiting until I was sure Jaxson was ready. "Would you rather tell your parents you need to set boundaries, or get a call from my brother telling you he found out about us."

"Parents. Easy."

I laughed, even as the weight of that answer hit me square in the chest.

He'd rather face something that has torn him up for years than our secret be revealed, which told me everything I needed to know about where we were headed.

Not that I didn't already know, but a small part of me...

I shook my head, brushing the thought away.

"Your turn," he said, stuffing the wrapper from his jerky into his pack. "Would you rather have to buy a house and never be able to travel out of that state you're in, or sit down with your parents and Vince and tell them how you've felt living in your brother's shadow."

"Like I'd *ever* subject myself to talking about my feelings," I answered just as fast.

"But you'd stay put, knowing you couldn't travel the way you want to?"

I sighed. "Obviously, I hate both options. But, if I had to choose... I guess I'd just need to find a really cool house in a really cool place. California, maybe. That's like seven states in one."

Jaxson stood, reaching a hand down to help me up. Once we had our packs strapped on, we continued on the trail.

"Here's one," I said. "Would you rather kiss me right now, or spank my ass?"

"Both," he growled, and then he did just that, slapping my ass and holding it in a handful as he pulled me into him. He swiped my hat off my head for better access, and then he kissed me long and deep.

We'd only passed one other group on the trail so far, and I was thankful we were alone then, that there was no rush as his tongue swept over mine and my body melted into his.

I wished the *would you rather game* was real, then. I wished someone would ask me if I'd rather go back to my life before Jaxson Brittain, or stay right here in this moment with him forever. I wished the answer became reality, that there was magic in this world.

I knew without a doubt I'd choose option two.

We talked and laughed the rest of the hike, stopping a lot along the way to take photos or just sit and admire how beautiful everything was. We celebrated when we survived fording the river — not once, not twice, but *three* times — and we marveled at the waterfalls we found along the path, complete with a rainbow I could only dream of.

My body was beginning to protest when we hit the last few miles of the hike, hips and knees and feet aching and begging to stop. But Jaxson distracted me, sharing stories of his time in the league and asking me about college. And before long, we'd made it to our campsite.

Setting up a tent after an all-day hike was definitely *not* going on my list of favorite things to do, but it was all worth it when we changed into our swimsuits with a couple hours of sunlight left, and just a short, half-mile hike to the hot springs that had brought us all this way.

We followed the trail, Jaxson carrying a container of wine and two reusable mugs with him. I had cheese and meat locked in a bear-proof container. Together, we had the dinner of champions.

I was mid-laugh over a rookie party story Jaxson was telling me when we hit the top of the trail, and there below us was the most breathtaking sight I'd ever seen.

The sun was low, the light golden where it touched the colorful, nature-made hot tub. That same light reflected off the rivers that rushed into the hole from either side, the hot mixing with the cold in a natural phenomenon that felt so precious I was almost afraid to touch it.

We could feel the heat from the various springs around us, and then the breeze would flow down from the icy river. In the distance, trees ran thick and lush along either side, and at the river's end, the mountains rolled along the horizon.

"Wow," I breathed, shaking my head at it all before I turned to look up at Jaxson. His eyes were just as wide, his lips parted, chest heaving like he was experiencing the same flood of emotions I was.

"This is unreal," he whispered.

I didn't know why tears pricked my eyes, but I didn't stop to think about it. We'd come all this way, and I damn sure wasn't going to get up in my feels and ruin the moment.

I grabbed his hand in mine, and together, we ambled down the rocky edge of the spring until we found a place to shed our packs and the clothes we'd put on over our suits. Then, we tested the water with just a toe, making sure it wasn't too hot.

I waded in first, dragging Jaxson behind me, and the more my body sank into the steamy water, the more alive I felt.

"Oh my *God*," I said, speaking quietly as if I didn't want to disrupt the maker of the bubbles steaming up from the center of the pool. "It feels amazing."

"*Fuck*," Jaxson added on a groan when he was submerged. He released my hand so he could float on his back. "I think my muscles are crying in relief. I'm sore as hell already."

"Oh, that's too bad."

Jaxson frowned, sitting up in the water again. He waded until he found a place he could touch, and I swam over to him, my eyes just above the water.

When I reached him, I threaded my arms around his neck and latched my legs around his hips, kissing a trail along his jaw. "I was just thinking how we have this place all to ourselves, how there probably isn't anyone else for miles..." I rubbed myself against him, reveling in how quickly he responded to my touch. His cock was already growing hard, his fingertips digging into the flesh at my hips. "How hot it would be to... *play* here."

Jaxson groaned when I nibbled on his ear, but before he could pull me in for a kiss, I released him, swimming away on my back.

"But I guess if you're *sore* — eeek!"

I hadn't made it even two feet away before he grabbed me by the ankle and pulled me across the top of the water and back into his arms. He wrapped me up again, one hand snaked around my waist as the other slid into my wet hair and pulled me in for a bruising kiss.

"I'm never too sore to fuck my girl."

CHAPTER 28

DIRTY FUCKING GIRL

Jaxson

Chills swept over Grace's body at my words, and I sealed the promise by propping her ass on a low rock and spreading her legs wide. She was still half under water, but now I could see where her nipples peaked against the baby blue triangle top of her swimsuit, could see how her chest heaved when I wrapped my hand around her throat and tilted her chin up.

"Someone could walk up at any moment," I pointed out, squeezing just enough to make her lips part and a soft breath hitch out of her. My free hand slid under the water, and I dipped my fingertips beneath the fabric of her swimsuit. "I need you to come fast for me."

Her body shook when I pressed my fingertips against her swollen clit, but I didn't apply pressure yet. Instead, I teased her, gliding over that sensitive spot with the lubrication from the water.

"Can you do that?" I asked, tightening my grip on her neck and lowering my mouth to hers. I didn't kiss her. I hovered, our lips brushing, the heat of her exhales ghosting over my skin.

She ground her pelvis against my hand under the water, and I pressed against the movement, giving her just enough friction to wind her up.

"Mmm, look at you," I mused, smiling against her lips. She tried to kiss me, but I pulled away, keeping less than a centimeter between our mouths as she bucked her hips again. "Fucking my hand in the middle of a national park. What if someone's watching you right now, Nova? What if someone is behind those trees, seeing how desperate you are?"

She moaned, struggling against my grip on her throat enough to kiss me. I nipped at her bottom lip when she did and slid my fingers down between her pussy lips. Pressing one deep inside her, I swallowed the cry she let rip free when I did.

"I need to hear you say it," I said, curling that finger inside her. "Tell me you can come fast, baby. Tell me what you need."

Her hands slid into my hair, and she tightened her grip, kissing me hard.

"Your mouth."

I smiled against her next kiss, removing my finger from inside her as she let out a soft whimper.

Fuck, I was insatiable when it came to Grace.

Every morning, afternoon, and night wouldn't be enough. When she looked at me like this, her eyes hooded and lips pouty with need... it obliterated my self-control. All I could think about was making her feel good, hearing the sweet sounds she made when I touched her, feeling her body clench and release, watching the blush that always crept up her neck to her cheeks when I said something filthy that I knew she fucking loved.

My hands found her hips, and I picked her up easily, carrying us through the water to another spot in the pool where I could balance her ass on a rock. This one was out of the water completely, and I propped her up on it with a wicked grin.

"Dirty fucking girl," I said, biting my lip as I curled my fingertips over the slim band of her swimsuit bottoms. "You're going to be splayed out for everyone to see if you want my mouth on you."

She nodded, pinning her lip between her teeth as she watched me pull that fabric over her hips and down her thighs. She had such a gorgeous body, one I could spend hours paying homage to. But we didn't have hours here.

I kissed along her shin and ankle as I stripped her the rest of the way, and then I slung the wet piece of cloth so it stayed on the rock behind her.

"God*damn*, Grace," I said, pressing my hands against the inside of her knees. I slowly opened her, cock hardening to stone at the sight of her slick, pink pussy glistening, at how she was propped up on that rock like a fucking offering. "I'll never get tired of this sight," I said, sliding my hands up her inner thighs. "Of seeing my girl wet and swollen and fucking aching to be filled."

"*Yes*," she breathed, squirming under my touch.

"Come here," I said, hooking my hands at her hips and tugging until her ass hung off the rock. I slung her legs over my shoulders next, kissing and licking along the inside of her thigh until I hit the spot she wanted me most.

I teased her with just one lash of my tongue that had her moaning and looking up at the sky.

"You look so fucking pretty right now," I said, sucking her clit and letting it go with a pop. "Take those tits out, baby. I want to watch you playing with them while I taste you."

"*God*, Jaxson."

I growled at the sound of my name ripping from her throat, at how she desperately pulled her breasts up out of her swimsuit. She listened so goddamn well, and it turned me on every single time she did.

One hand held her steady against the rock, and the other plucked at her nipple, her legs shaking when I timed a long lick of my tongue right where she needed it.

As much as I wanted to drag this moment out, to stretch it through eternity and savor what Grace looked like spread out under the golden sun in the middle of nowhere with her tits pushed over the top of her swimsuit and her thighs balanced on my shoulders, I really didn't know how long we had before someone else showed up.

So, I dropped my mouth to where she wanted it most, and I ate her sweet pussy like it was the first dessert I'd had in years.

Grace writhed and moaned as I feasted, holding her thighs to me so she couldn't wiggle free. I licked and sucked and reveled in the feel of her tangling her fingers in my hair and holding my mouth to her. She was ravenous, and I savored every little sound she made as she chased her climax.

When I knew she was close, I released one thigh and used my free hand to snake under her, toying with her slick entrance. I pressed one finger inside, slowly, stretching her as I sucked her clit.

Part of me was a sick bastard, because I almost *wished* for someone to see us. I wanted them to walk up and find my girl like this — toes curling, thighs quaking, lips wet, and eyes heavy. I wanted them to see how fucking gorgeous she looked when she was about to come — and to know *I* was the one with the power to make her do it.

The other part of me knew I'd have to kill any sonofabitch who *did* happen to walk up and see us, because this view, this body, this *woman*?

She was *mine*.

My heart thundered at the thought, and I ate her with even more fervor, as if I could brand her with my name like a tattoo if I touched all the right spots. Something whispered in the back of my mind, something reminding me how *not mine* she really was...

That only made me work harder.

Suddenly, Grace reached for me, maneuvering me away enough for her to slide off the rock. Her ass splashed against the water as she found her footing, and she reached for my board shorts next, hastily untying them.

"I want you inside me."

I shut my eyes on how fucking incredible it was to hear her say that, at how it had every muscle in my body tight with anticipation. I reached under the water to help her shed my shorts, and then I slung them up next to the lower half of her suit on the rock.

"Turn around," I said, spinning her. Her hands flew out to catch herself against the gray stone when I did, and then I hiked one of her legs up, too.

Which left her sweet ass out of the water, slick and round and *mine*.

I groaned, running one hand down her spine and over her cheek. I slapped it hard enough to make her yelp, and then I squeezed it, shaking it a little so I could watch her ass jiggle.

"*Fuck*, baby," I said, fisting my cock and sliding it between her lips. I toyed with her entrance, slicking my crown up and down and in-between before I inched myself inside her. "Play with your clit and come for me like a good girl."

With a moan, Grace used one hand to hold herself up, and reached the other down between her legs, knowing my grip on her hips would hold her steady. She circled slowly, and I was careful not to push in too fast. If I gave into the animalistic urge inside me, I'd slide all the way fucking home right now. I'd fill her with a brutal thrust and feel her pussy hugging my cock the way I was desperate for.

But she was so fucking slight. We'd fucked multiple times a day for a week now, but every time, we had to work her open.

I took my time, sliding in a half inch before I'd pull out and then sink a little deeper. Thrust after thrust, she took me in, moaning and shaking as I stretched her.

"Just like that," she said, her voice a ragged whisper. "Slow. Deep. *Fuck*, Jax."

"I wish you could see this view," I told her. "You always look so pretty when I fuck you, but like this?" I shook my head, reaching down to spread her ass cheeks. "I can watch every inch you take, can see the way your pussy hugs my cock when I pull out."

"*God*." Grace circled her clit faster, pushing back against me until she took me whole.

I hissed a curse, hooking my fingers at her hips and keeping our pace slow and steady.

She didn't have to tell me. I knew she was coming the second her orgasm caught. She stilled, fingers working her clit while she let me take control of the rest. I picked up my pace *just* a bit, enough to hit that spot inside her in a rhythm that would drive her to the edge.

I felt her clench around me, and then, spasms.

Grace cried out my name, and I reached up to wrap a hand around her mouth and muffle the noise as I fucked every last wave of her orgasm out of her. I saw stars at how she pulsed around me, stoking my own release to the surface. Her legs trembled, and she met my thrusts with her ass like she needed more, like the orgasm was never ending.

I took her harder, faster, and that quickening in pace had all the blood in my body rushing to my cock.

"*Fuck*, Grace. You feel so good. So *fucking* good."

I was close, but I needed more.

"Hold on, baby," I told her, and then I gripped her hips forcefully, and I gave in to my need.

My drives grew harder, more urgent, and I slid balls-deep inside her. Grace bit out something between a moan and a scream at the fullness, and I groaned, feeling my release rushing through me.

"You can take it, baby," I coached her, smoothing my thumb over her hip where I held her. "Take that dick like the good fucking girl you are."

She moaned, and I couldn't be sure if she was still coming, or if the thought of making *me* come had her screaming like that. Either way, the sound pushed me on, and when Grace started slapping her ass against me in her effort to meet me thrust for thrust, I lost it.

"Fuck!"

I spilled inside her, pumping in and out at a brutal pace as black invaded my vision. Her tits and ass bounced wildly as we both lost control, as she took every drive, and I gripped her hips hard enough to leave that mark I was so desperate to leave.

Moving to grip her cheeks in my hands, I spread her wide again, and my orgasm stretched at the sight of my cum leaking out of her and down her thigh. I plunged my cock back inside her, slower now, and each time I withdrew, more cum spilled out of her — only for me to push it back in.

"*Jesus Christ*," I mused, biting my lip as we both slowed, our breaths heavy in the quiet air around us. "Come here, I want you to see this."

Swiftly, I pulled out of her only long enough to spin her around and prop her ass on the rock again. Then, I spread her wide and pushed back inside her, using my cum as the lubricant.

Grace leaned up on her elbows, tits spilling over her swim top as she watched me slide in and out.

"Holy hell, that's hot," she whispered, and then her fingers trailed down, and she covered my cock with her hand, feeling where we were slick from our releases.

I groaned, everything hypersensitive, and then I slid back in, first through where her hand was fisted around me, and then all the way inside her.

Her eyes ran up to meet mine, and for a moment — everything stopped.

Time slogged to a standstill, the sun lowering and reaching us only through the trees now. I stayed deep, rooted inside her, feeling the way she squeezed around me, hearing her heartbeat so loud I felt it as my own.

"Jaxson..."

Grace leaned up to wrap her arms around my shoulders, pulling me to her for a long, deep kiss. I cradled the back of her neck, holding her to me and kissing her with the same neediness that she gave me. And when she rolled just enough for me to slide out of her, I pressed in again, both of us shivering at the feel of it.

Fuck, one round was never enough with this girl.

All of a sudden, Grace cursed, shoving me hard backward until I splashed into the water.

It was a shock to my system — one second I was inside her ready to fuck her again, and the next I was under water.

The push such a surprise that I'd lost my footing and fallen into the deeper part of the spring.

I resurfaced on a laugh, ready to make her pay for that, but her eyes were wide, her top back in place, and both our swimsuits gone from where they had been on the rock behind her before.

She shoved my trunks into my hands under the water, nodding behind me.

And I turned to find an older couple at the top of the trail where we'd had our first look of the spring.

"Shit," I said, but it was through a laugh — one Grace matched as her cheeks flamed red.

I knew the water was clear, but I hoped to God that older couple had terrible eyesight as they ambled down toward us while we both hastily tugged our clothes back on.

"Oh, it's just beautiful!" the older woman called when they were twenty feet or so away. "Glen, would you look at this?"

"I see it, sweetheart," her partner grumbled. He was moving a bit slower than she was, puffing each breath, but I didn't miss how he watched her with a smile as she lit up at the sight.

It made my chest pinch.

"How's the water?!" the woman called to us next.

I cocked a brow at Grace, fighting back a laugh.

"It's perfect!" she said over her shoulder, her eyes still on me. "*Blissfully* hot."

I dunked under the water so I could let out the laugh I'd been suppressing.

When I resurfaced, it was just in time to watch Grace climb out of the water like nothing had happened, grabbing our bag on the shore. "Would you two care to join us for some wine?"

I shook my head, chuckling to myself. I'd just had her bent over a rock and crying out my name, and now, she was making friends with the elderly couple who almost caught us.

That's my girl.

CHAPTER 29

NO CHOICE

Jaxson

It turned out the elderly couple who almost caught us was staying at the campsite next to us.

Nora and Glen were married and retired. They'd been traveling for years, seeing all they could in this world together. And even though there was quite a bit of space between our sites, Grace embraced them like they were our neighbors,

We spent a long time at the springs, Grace asking the couple for their life story as they slipped into the hot water to join us. We drank the bottle of wine while the sun set, and once the cheese was gone and we were all starving, Nora and Glen invited us to their campsite for dinner — and then surprised the hell out of us when they offered us a joint as dessert.

Grace partook while I opted to stay sober, but I'd be a lying bastard if I said I didn't take advantage of her heightened sensitivity when we were alone in our tent later that night. Just trailing my fingertips over her skin had her writhing in need. And when she finally couldn't take anymore and climbed on top of me, she rode in slow, smooth movements that tested my ability to last long enough for her to find her release first.

We woke with the sun the next morning, packing up our supplies and stopping long enough to wish Nora and Glen a happy life before we started trekking back to the ranger station. We were exhausted after the back-to-back hikes, so we slept in a nearby hotel that night before hitting the road the next morning.

And then, we were headed north to Canada.

There was so much to see, so much we wanted to stop and explore as we crossed through Idaho and Montana. We seemed torn between taking in all the sights we could, and getting to our end-destination before we ran out of time.

In the end, we landed on a week of exploring the area, losing our days trying our hand at fly-fishing, hiking, and exploring while every single night was spent discovering more about one another. The book I'd brought with me still had a bookmark in the same place I'd left it that day we'd hiked in Chattanooga. I couldn't remember the last time I'd gone this long without reading.

But I had better things to do with my hands now than turn the pages of a book.

When we weren't fucking each other into oblivion, we were talking — Grace's head on my chest, my fingers rubbing lazy circles on her skin. She made me laugh. I made her feel safe enough not to fake a smile. And it didn't matter how late we stayed up or how much we talked on the road, I never got tired of hearing about her life — her past, what she was thinking now, where she thought she might be in the future.

I'd only known the girl for a month, and yet it felt like I'd been living under water before I found her. It was like she'd pulled me to the surface, like I'd taken my first breath and looked around and saw the world with fresh eyes.

And now, I couldn't imagine living without her.

Which fucking gutted me — because I didn't have another choice.

One night, when she was sound asleep and letting out the most adorable, annoying little snores in the world next to me, I let myself entertain the thought of asking her to be with me. *Really* be with me.

And then I instantly realized how fucking stupid an idea it was.

Vince would never let it happen. The moment he found out, he'd fight me. He'd threatened all of us on the team within an inch of our lives to stay away from his sister. And it wouldn't be just me and Grace who would suffer. Vince was our strongest winger. He was our point-leader. If Will wasn't our captain, it would be Vince. He pulled us all together, made us stronger, made us want to work harder for each other.

But this... this would tear us apart.

My stomach tightened at the memory of Will cornering me at the tournament, at what he'd reminded me of.

This was bigger than just me.

And even if I did decide to say fuck Vince and fuck the team, too — what did I honestly expect? Grace was twenty-fucking-two years old. She still had so much growing to do, so much to see and experience.

I would hate giving her up when the summer came to an end.

But I'd hate holding her back even more.

I shoved all those thoughts to the back of my mind whenever I could, committing myself to soaking up the present moment. Because right now — she was mine.

It was the wildest sensation when we finally decided to cross the border, handing over our passports at the Canadian checkpoint with Grace bouncing excitedly in the passenger seat. I felt both like I was coming home and like I was jumping headfirst into a pit of needles.

I smiled and pointed out landmarks to Grace as we drove, all while my stomach twisted into an awful knot. We stopped at Tim Horton's for a double double and timbits, and I stretched my hands against the numbness threatening to invade them.

It was amazing.

And yet, it was terrifying, too.

Because I was back in my country — but I was also closer to my father.

We stopped for the night at a little manor in Glenwood, a small village not far from the border with a gorgeous view of the mountains we'd be driving toward the next day. The host was a huge hockey fan, and about lost his shit when he saw us walk up to check in. He went above and beyond to make sure we were comfortable, even going so far as to make us dinner — bison burgers and poutine.

Grace was fucking thrilled.

I was just happy the guy didn't ask to take pictures or beg me to sign anything. He treated me like a VIP, but without the need to brag about being in my vicinity. It was refreshing, and it also brought me peace knowing Grace and I were safe there.

After dinner, I listened to Grace humming a song I didn't recognize as she did her nighttime routine in the bathroom. I was stretched out on the bed, one arm behind my head as I stared up at the ceiling.

We were just three hours from my parents.

The proximity made anxiety swim in my gut. I felt like a fucking asshole for not wanting to see them, but in the same breath, my self-preservation reminded me on repeat why seeing them would be a bad idea.

It was hard enough to put up with my father's constant attack on my performance over the phone. In person? He was relentless. And it was always harder to listen to him when I could also see what hockey had taken from him, what a shit hand he'd been dealt.

It made me feel sorry for him instead of feel like I had any right to ask him to leave me the fuck alone.

"Holy shit!"

Grace gasped, and I shot up from where I was reclining. "You okay?"

She bounded into the dark room, her eyes wide and bright like a kid on Christmas morning. She leapt into the bed, balancing on her knees and pointing at her forehead.

"I have a wrinkle!"

I blinked, and then blew out a breath, shaking my head. "Fucking Christ, woman. I thought you were hurt."

"Look!" she said, ignoring my concern. She leaned closer to me, into the light from the lamp on our nightstand, tapping that spot on her forehead again. "See it?"

"No," I answered honestly.

She scowled, which made her skin fold on itself. "See it now?"

"That doesn't count."

She sighed, slapping her hands against her thigh. "You're being grumpy. I *totally* have a wrinkle."

"Why do you want me to confirm this? Weren't you just moisturizing your face to *combat* wrinkles?"

"No, I was moisturizing my face because it's dry as hell up here," she said, and then she climbed into my lap, threading her arms around my neck. *God*, I loved when she did that, when she touched me like it was natural, when she wrapped herself around me like we were the perfect fit.

"I like wrinkles."

She said the words as she reached up to remove my glasses, and then her fingers traced my skin — around my eyes, my mouth, over my forehead.

"They're proof you've laughed, you've cared, you've hurt." She swallowed, her fingers lingering over the line I knew existed between my brows whether I was frowning or not. "Proof that you've lived."

I covered her hand with my own, pulling her knuckles to my lips for a kiss. Her face was so bright and open and honest, this girl who continued to surprise me no matter how much time we spent together. Here she was tracing the deep lines in my skin like they were beautiful, all while saying she was happy to earn a wrinkle of her own.

She lived this life like no one I had ever met before.

And right there in that dingy fucking hotel room, I felt three words slam into my chest like a semi-truck.

I loved her.

Fuck.

I loved her the way I loved breathing, the way I loved the feel of fresh ice under my skates and fresh snow on the mountains. I loved her as if there was no choice.

And maybe there never was.

Maybe it didn't matter that it was cruel and impossible, that loving her was sentencing myself to a life of pain.

I'd been drawn to her since the first moment I knew she existed, like my soul wouldn't allow me any other option.

I loved her — even though I could never fully have her.

The urge to tell her danced on my tongue, forcing my mouth open. But I clamped it shut again and swallowed the words down, burying them deep.

"There's no one in this world like you, Grace Tanev," I said instead.

She smiled, leaning into my palm when I reached up to touch her face.

"We'll be in your hometown tomorrow," she said.

"We will."

"You okay?"

I heaved a sigh. "Yes and no."

"We don't have to stay long."

I swallowed, looking at where my thumb smoothed the line of her jaw. "Actually, I was going to talk to you about that."

Grace stiffened even before I said anything more, and the words felt like lead as I tried to push them out.

"Remember when we started the trip, and I told you I had a training booked with some of the team?" I asked.

I waited, wondering if I'd need to explain further, but hockey had been a part of Grace's entire life, too. Vince was one of the guys who went in on booking the ice, so she probably already knew about how it all worked.

This would be the first time back on the ice since the season ended for most of us, and it wasn't just Osprey players, but guys from other leagues, too. We'd meet to just get some ice time in, run drills, and play a few scrimmages — anything we felt we needed to do to get prepped for camp.

Staying in game shape was a commitment to my team — one I couldn't break. And it didn't matter that I wanted the summer and this trip to last forever. Reality was knocking hard on the door.

The season was coming, and I had to get ready for it.

Grace deflated a bit as she put the pieces together.

"The first?" she asked.

I nodded, searching her eyes as she did the math.

"One week," she breathed.

"Six days, to be exact. I'll need to catch a flight on the thirty-first."

Her nostrils flared, and for a split-second, I thought... I thought I saw *something*. But she nodded immediately, smiling and leaning down to press a swift kiss to my lips.

"Well, that's actually perfect! I'm meeting some college buddies in Costa Rica for a birthday yoga retreat. So that will give me just enough time to stop by Mom and Dad's, do some laundry, maybe see some friends, and then head out."

My chest hollowed out. "Oh."

I searched for any sign of her hiding her emotions again, for any sign of tears she was holding back. I was pretty good at spotting it in her now — the fake smile, the sadness that would tinge the edges of her eyes.

But this time, I found nothing.

My next swallow felt like I was working a wine cork down my throat. Of course, she had plans. She knew this wasn't going to last forever just like I did. It shouldn't have hurt that she already had her next destination planned. In fact, I should have been *happy*. She had somewhere to go. She had people waiting on her. She had the rest of her life to live.

But I was a selfish fucking prick, and it killed me to think about her moving on without me — even when I knew, deep down, it was what I wanted for her.

"It's going to be *amazing*. Oh! Let me show you our bungalow!" She rolled off me, grabbing her phone and pulling up the listing. She leaned against me as she thumbed through the photos, rattling on about how they'd have yoga on the beach, sound baths, daily meditations, and a bunch of other shit that I tuned out.

Not that I didn't care — because I did. And that was the fucking problem.

I cared so deeply for her that I knew now I would be a fucking wreck when we said goodbye in a week.

I'd told myself not to fall for her. I'd told myself not to even *think* about touching her, because I knew — I fucking *knew* this would happen.

And yet, it was like it was inevitable, like we had no choice but to crash into each other and exist in the wreckage when the time came for us to part.

Swallowing, I wrapped my arms around her, my chin on her shoulder as I listened to her detail the trip. I felt the excitement rolling off her, and in the same breath, felt my heart give way to a single, deep crack.

But I closed my eyes against it, inhaling her scent and committing it to memory.

One more week.

I had her for one. More. Week.

CHAPTER 30

YOURS AND YOURS ALONE

Grace

We pulled into Canmore just before noon the next day, and I felt like a freaking puppy.

I hung my head out the window, eyes wide as I attempted to take it all in. The air was crisp and light even in July, the sun shining but with a cool breeze right on its heels.

As if the breathtaking views of the mountains all around us weren't incredible enough, the town itself was adorable. There was a little main street lined with shops and restaurants, a boardwalk along a gorgeous flowing river, and people *everywhere* soaking up the beautiful weather. There were bike-riders and families on skates, hikers with packs and locals taking their dogs for a walk, young couples blowing up paddle boards and friends joking around as they geared up for a climb.

It was unlike anything I'd ever experienced — which was my favorite feeling in the world.

Add in the fact that Jaxson was right beside me, smiling as he watched me, his hand on my thigh... and it was the most perfect moment.

Deep in my chest, a stone hand was wrapped around my heart in a tight fist. It was a constant sensation — my heart struggling to beat against it, my lungs tight as they forced every breath. But I ignored it all, pretending like the end of this week wasn't something that would kill me, like right now was all that mattered.

I was good at that. It was one of my best qualities.

I could always turn my attention to the bright side.

I could always pretend like nothing could hurt me.

Jaxson had found a modern little cabin to stay at, an A-frame with tall windows and a gorgeous claw-foot tub that I couldn't wait to soak in. It was right on the river next to the boardwalk that led to the main street of shops, and apparently it was owned by an old friend of his. We popped in long enough to unload the car, and for us both to put on sunglasses and hats, and then I was dragging him by the hand out the door to explore.

We didn't have any plans for the day, but as we walked in and out of shops and ate lunch at a place with the best pierogies I'd ever had in my *life*, I made a list of everything I wanted to do.

I wanted to paddle board the reservoir. I wanted to drive up to see Lake Louise and Moraine Lake. I wanted to hike Grassi Lakes and eat fondue at the Grizzly House in Banff and take a boat tour of Lake Minnewanka. I wanted a picture of us by the Banff sign, wanted to make out in the gondola on the ride up to Sulphur Mountain. And I was definitely not leaving here without indulging in *every* weird Canadian snack I could get my grubby little hands on — starting with ketchup chips.

I wanted to do and see and experience *everything* that made Jaxson Brittain.

He listened patiently as I rattled it all off while we ate lunch, jotting line by line down in a special notebook I'd purchased from one of the stores. It had an illustration of the Three Sisters mountain peaks on the front and said *Dare to Live Big*.

But even as Jaxson chimed in with his suggestions, I could feel the tension radiating off him as he picked at his poutine.

I tried to keep the conversation light, but I was dying to get inside his head.

"Wait," I said when the waitress brought us our second beers — an IPA for Jaxson, a watermelon sour for me. "Did you just speak *French*?"

The waitress had said something to one of her co-workers behind the bar, and when Jaxson heard it, he responded to her in the same language. She'd seemed somewhat surprised, and then I filled in the blanks that he told her he was from the area.

He cocked a brow. "I did."

"What the actual fuck?"

"Surprised?"

"Very," I said, waving my hand for him to fill in the blanks.

He just shrugged. "We all learn French in school here."

"That's so cool," I said, leaning an elbow on my open notebook. "Say something in French."

"*Tu es une si bonne fille*, Grace."

Fuck me. Even the way he said my name sounded French.

"What did you say?"

Jaxson leaned forward over the table, his eyes dancing between mine. "I said — you're such a good girl, Grace."

My neck burned, and I immediately sat up and picked up my pen. "Yep. *Definitely* adding Fuck Jaxson Brittain While He Whispers Dirty French Things to the list."

I scribbled it out with a smile, but when I looked up at Jaxson again, he was watching me like his stomach was sick.

"You okay?" I asked, closing the notebook and setting the list aside.

His gaze swept over my face, over and over, like he was committing me to memory. "I'm great, Nova."

His voice was soft and sad, and I reached across the table to cover his hand with mine.

"You're pulling a Grace."

He chuckled at that.

"Is it your dad?" I guessed.

He swallowed, squeezing where my hand held his, and nodded.

"Do you want to go see him?"

"Hell no," he answered quickly, and then let out a long, pained sigh. "And that makes me feel like such a piece of shit."

"You're not a piece of shit because you don't want to see the man who constantly uses and abuses you."

Jaxson frowned, cracking his neck. "He's not all bad, you know. I have a lot of good memories with him — how he taught me to skate, taught me to play, taught me all the things to look for when I'm studying video." He swallowed. "It's just..."

"Tainted," I finished for him. "Because most of the time, he's yelling at you or asking for money."

His brows bent together, and he nodded again. Then, he blew out a breath and sat back, releasing me and flattening his palms on the table. "What do you say we finish these beers and go back to the cabin?"

"So you can whisper dirty French words in my ear?"

"I can't think of a better way to spend a night."

I smiled, watching as he thumbed out some of the Canadian cash we'd picked up from the bank. He left it on the table and grabbed my hand in his, leading us back out into the street.

When we made it to the river, I pulled him to the side, sliding my hands up to hook on his shoulders. I waited for him to look down at me, and then I framed his face as best I could for being so much shorter than he was.

"You don't owe him anything," I said, holding his gaze and hoping he believed me. "You can love him and still need distance. You can respect him and still withdraw the power he's had over you. Your dad has helped you — no doubt about it. But this gift?" I said, placing my hand over his heart. "It's yours and yours alone. Don't let him steal that from you."

He sighed, covering my palm, his large fingers lacing over mine.

"How do you know exactly what I need to hear?"

I shrugged, pressing up on my toes to kiss him.

"The same way you can tell when I'm faking a smile, I guess," I said. "I just know... *you*."

CHAPTER 31

ONE LAST TIME

Grace

Time was my number one enemy.

I felt like I was free falling, hurdling toward a certain death while I grappled to hold on to anything I could grasp. A tree branch, a rope, a jagged rock — but nothing would catch, and nothing could stop me.

One by one, we checked every item off my list.

Day by day, we explored and laughed and lived like we were the only two people in the world.

And night by night, I fell in love with Jaxson Brittain.

I didn't even try to fight it. I think a part of me knew it would happen from the moment I jumped into his passenger seat. It was impossible *not* to fall for him — for his smile, his hands, his drive, his passion, the way he held me, the way he kissed me, the way he *listened* to me, like he wanted to know everything that made me who I was.

I didn't just slip into loving him, either. I sky-dived. I flipped off a cliff and swam in the warm waters of loving him like the gift that it was.

I knew we were saying goodbye. I knew it was all coming to an end.

Just like every other relationship I'd ever had, I knew before it even *started* that it would be over soon.

But for the first time, I found it all worth it.

This summer with him had been worth the pain that would come.

It was almost laughable, how it had all started with him wanting to make me feel better after a stupid boy had broken up with me. *That* was not a relationship. That was *nothing*.

The very man who wanted to heal me had only given me something even harder to lose.

It was easy to pretend we had forever that week in Canmore, when every minute of every day was filled. There wasn't any spare time to think. There wasn't ever a silent moment to let reality sink in.

Until the night of the thirtieth, when Jaxson and I were packing our bags.

And this time — it wasn't to get back in the car and set off to the next place together.

My throat was impossibly tight as I rolled a pair of jean shorts, trying and failing to find enough space in my bag for them.

We'd decided to sell our hiking and camping gear at the local outpost so they could in turn sell it used at a good price to someone in the area who might need it. But still, I'd bought so many little things along the way, there just wasn't enough space.

Which was also very unlike me.

In all my travels, I never bought souvenirs. I was always taking my memories and photos with me and nothing else. But with this...

I'd found myself desperate to find and hold fast to any tangible object I could, to take any and all proof with me that this wasn't just a fever dream.

That it was real — that *we* were real.

I had a coaster from the bar in Atlanta, a Chattanooga magnet, my sunglasses and hat from the festival, a golf ball from the tournament, a Wilson State Park t-shirt. There was the coffee mug from Rocky Mountain National Park, a keychain from the car show, a tiny bottle of water I snuck from Mr. Bubbles. And in the last week, I'd purchased something from every stop in Canmore and Banff, desperate to fill this bag with reminders of Jaxson and the place he grew up, of every memory we made here together.

Now, combined with everything I'd already had in my bag before, it was overflowing.

"Did you check in for your flight?"

Jaxson's voice startled me a bit from where I was lost in thought, and I held my hiking boots in one hand, staring at my bag and trying to figure out where I could shove them. My speaker played softly in the corner of the room, "Almost Lover" by A Fine Frenzy setting the solemn mood.

"Yeah," I answered, but the word was like a croak from my dry throat.

"And you have your passport?"

My nose stung, and I shoved my shoes forcefully into my bag. "Got it."

"We'll need to leave pretty early in the morning," he said from where he was zipping up his own bag. "Calgary Airport is about an hour and a half from here, and I have no idea what security will look like. It's peak season here."

I sniffed, cursing myself as tears flooded my eyes.

Stop it, Grace. Pull it together.

I felt the moment Jaxson saw me, felt how the energy in the room shifted when he froze. Then, slowly, he moved across the room, wrapping his arms around me from behind and pulling my back to his chest.

He kissed my hair before resting his chin on my head. "Not all fitting, huh?"

I slumped against him. "No."

The word garbled out of me, and Jaxson held me tighter with a little chuckle.

"Hey, it's alright. We'll stop and grab another suitcase in the morning. My treat."

I wiped my nose with the back of my hand, shrugging out of his grasp. Then, in a final attempt to shove all my emotions down, I started ripping things out of my suitcase.

"I don't even know why I need all this... all this *stuff*," I said, tossing one item after the next over my shoulder. "It's stupid. It's wasteful. Why did I buy all this? Why did I—"

Before I could launch the neon cowboy hat from the festival, Jaxson grabbed my wrist. He took the hat from my grip, dropped it back into my bag, and turned me until I was facing him. Then, he wrapped me up in a bear hug, his arms enveloping me, one hand at the small of my back, and the other holding my head to his chest.

"Shhh," he said, running his fingers through the strands. "It's okay."

My face crumpled, and I squeezed him as tight as I could.

"I'm going to miss you."

The second I whispered the words, tears pooled in my eyes too fast for me to stop them.

We both stiffened.

I was the first to acknowledge it, the first to call what we both were feeling to the surface.

And with that realization, I broke — shoulders shaking, tears rushing, all that pain that had been suffocating me breaking free at once. I couldn't hold it down any longer, couldn't fight it, and it took me under like a tidal wave.

I felt the way Jaxson's next breath hitched, heard how hard he had to swallow before he responded. When he did, his voice was gruff and tight with emotion.

"I'm going to miss you, too, little Nova." He let out a ragged breath. "So fucking much it kills me to even think about it."

I squeezed my eyes tight, burying my face in his chest, and he wrapped me up even more. It was like we were trying to meld ourselves together, like maybe if we could become one person, we could have everything we wanted.

Take me with you.

The words were on the tip of my tongue, but I swallowed them down, fighting back another sob. I hated this pain more than anything in the world. I was so terrified of never being rid of it, of committing myself to a life of unhappiness.

But this was what we'd known all along.

I had to believe there were better days ahead. I had to believe that one day, I'd look back on this time in my life, on this summer with Jaxson, and I'd feel nothing but joy. One day, when my heart was healed — and it *would* heal — I would tell our story to another lover, or maybe to my kids or grandkids, or maybe just to a fellow stranger roaming the Earth.

I'd tell them and I'd smile, thankful for what we had, grateful for the time in my life where I belonged to Jaxson Brittain and he belonged to me.

But right now, in *this* moment, I was sad.

I was *ripping* at the seams.

It was foolish to think he would ever want to be tied down. As much fun as we'd had, that was just what we were — *fun*. We were a summer of being reckless, an unplanned road trip with no destination, and yet a most definite dead end.

He was my brother's teammate.

He was thirty years old.

He was a professional hockey player with women quite literally throwing themselves at him and begging for his attention.

It made me sick to think of any of them getting it, of anyone else getting to touch him the way I had, to feel him inside them. Did he want to settle down? Did he want a family? Why *would* he, when he could live a life of taking any woman he wanted to bed?

Regardless — I wasn't the girl for him in either option.

I didn't want to settle down. I wanted to fly, to explore, to see the world. I didn't want kids now. I maybe didn't want them *ever*.

What did I expect — him to ask me to be in a long-distance relationship? To stay faithful to his teammate's twenty-two-year-old sister while she ran all around the globe? To ignore every woman far more attractive than me who presented themselves? Did I really think we could tell my brother, he'd be just fine with it, and then we'd have a relationship where we barely saw each other?

None of it made sense.

I couldn't ask for what I wanted because I didn't even fucking *know*.

Inhaling a long, deep breath, I swiped the tears from my face and grabbed Jaxson's hand, leading him to the bed we still hadn't made from when we'd trashed it that morning.

One last time.

I needed to feel everything that he was *one last time*.

And then, I'd do the impossible.

I'd let him go.

My hands trembled as I reached for the hem of my dress, pulling it up and over my head in one fluid movement. I made quick work of my bralette and panties next, and then I stood there — stripped to my soul in front of a man I knew I'd never forget.

Something in Jaxson's gaze told me he wanted me to talk to him, that he wanted to heal my pain. But I think he knew as much as I did that he couldn't — just the way I couldn't heal his.

We only had one option, and that was to break together.

Slowly, he shed his clothing, too — piece by piece until the floor at our feet was covered. He swept me into his arms then, pulling me into his lap as he sat against the headboard.

There was no time for foreplay, no playfulness or dirty talk. I reached down and placed him where I needed to feel him most, and then with my hands braced on his shoulders, I worked myself onto him, slowly lowering inch by painful, blissful, heartbreaking inch.

Jaxson held my hip with one hand, the other sliding into my hair, fingers curling behind my neck. I dropped my forehead to his, our warm, shallow breaths mingling in the space between us as I rode him.

I moved slow, rolling my body into his, savoring the way it felt to stretch and open and be consumed by him. I didn't miss how he trembled, too. I didn't miss how he pinched his eyes closed and swallowed hard before kissing me, his tongue sweeping in to dance with mine.

Neither of us reached for our climax. It was like we both wanted to stay just like that for as long as we could, connected in every possible way, inhaling the other like our last breath.

I rode him until my legs were so sore I couldn't move, until he rolled me into the sheets and started his own slow pace between my legs. His ocean blue eyes searched mine, piercing my soul deeper with every thrust until I thought maybe we'd succeeded in our mission.

Because he felt like a part of me, like a permanent piece of who I'd be when we left this cabin.

I welcomed the new addition, riding out the first orgasm and then digging my nails into his back to beg for another.

My bag stayed half-packed for the rest of the night, our cabin an absolute mess that we'd have to deal with in the morning. But we pushed it off as long as we could, losing sleep and losing ourselves in the possibility of what we could have been in another space and time.

I catalogued every brush of his hands against my skin, every flex of him inside me, every kiss he ghosted over my lips. Every one was a whisper of *farewell*, of *I'll miss you and this and us*.

And I whispered it back, clinging to him as I kissed his shoulder, his neck, his beautiful, sacred mouth — all while my heart splintered in my chest.

Goodbye, goodbye, goodbye.

The morning came too quickly, and when we had no choice but to finish packing and roll our suitcases out of that cabin, I knew only three things for certain.

I loved him.

He changed me for the better.

And I'd never get over him — not as long as I lived.

CHAPTER 32

NOT NOW. NOT EVER.

Jaxson

I remember the first time I had a major injury in hockey.

I was seventeen — which, all things considered, was pretty late. I knew plenty of kids who had teeth knocked out and bones broken well before that age. Hockey was a brutal sport, one that had the ability to humble you in a split second. But I'd been lucky. I'd fallen, sure. I'd had some cuts and bruises and sprains, but nothing serious.

When I was seventeen, playing in the WHL, my time ran up.

It happened so fast. I had just stolen the puck and shucked it down the ice to where our center waited for the pass. Then, I was hit hard from behind, and I went flying into the boards shoulder-first.

My collarbone snapped.

The shock of it hit me more than the pain at first, my body sending all the adrenaline rushing through me to help quell my suffering. It wasn't until later when it wore off that I really felt the torture — not just of the break, but of the realization that I'd have to undergo surgery, that I'd be off the ice for months, and that my season was over.

It was the first time I realized something you loved could hurt you.

The memory of that feeling, of that specific type of affliction sat with me the entire drive from Canmore to Calgary on the morning of the thirty-first. My eyes burned from the late night, so much so that I hadn't even attempted putting in contacts. I held onto Grace's thigh just as tightly as the steering wheel, both of us silent, her face blotchy and red from crying the night before, and my heart firmly seated in my throat.

There was no rush of adrenaline to help me, no doctor who could patch me up and send me home with a rehab plan.

There was only agony — ripe and all-consuming.

We'd booked flights as close together as we could — hers for Grand Rapids, mine for Tampa. But mine still left an hour before hers did from a gate on the opposite side of the terminal, and I was cursing how fast the minutes passed, how quickly the moment was sneaking up where I'd have to walk away from her.

After I made a quick purchase of an extra suitcase for Grace to fit all her souvenirs in, we turned in the rental car and checked our luggage, holding hands as we made our way to security.

Like I'd predicted, it was busy.

Someone recognized me in the line, which led to a flurry of people wanting autographs and photographs. I internally groaned, biting back the urge to tell them all to fuck off while Grace pretended not to know me.

We were pros at it now. When someone recognized me, she got lost just in case some asshole decided to take a photo of us and post it.

I was so fucking pissed at the world, at the circumstances we were locked in.

I didn't want to hide her.

I didn't want to *lose* her.

She shot me a text that she would meet me in the lounge. I'd booked us first-class flights, and I knew at least in the lounge, we could exist in peace. So, I forced smile after stupid smile for photos until security helped me escape the throng.

By the time I made it and took a seat next to Grace, I was a bundle of anxious energy.

My foot bounced, hands wringing together where they hung between my knees, every breath harder than the last. I couldn't get enough oxygen, couldn't will my heart to steady.

Closing my eyes, I forced an inhale as slowly as I could and let it out just the same. Then, I reclined, putting my arm around Grace.

"I think we should do one last video, don't you think?"

"*That*," she said, digging into her carry-on. "Is an excellent idea."

She was trying so fucking hard to keep it together. Her smile was bright, her emerald eyes shining as she looked over her shoulder. Then, she leaned into me, resting her head against my chest and holding her phone up so we were in the video frame.

"Today," she started, letting out a long sigh before plastering her smile back in place. "I get to fly first class. I get to see my parents. And I get to say goodbye to one adventure and hello to the next."

A heavy boot crushed down on my rib cage hearing her say those words. It was what I wanted for her — to move on — and yet it fucking shredded me.

"Tell me something good, Jaxson," she said next, looking up at me before she found my eyes on the phone screen.

I swallowed, hooking my arm around her and pulling her into me even more. I opened my mouth to speak, but then paused, feeling how the emotion was strangling me.

God, I couldn't remember a time in my life that I'd felt like this. Not when I was climbing into the car with my father after a game knowing he'd be screaming at me the whole way home, not when my college hockey team lost the one time we made it to the Frozen Four, not even when I played in my first NHL game and felt sick nearly the entire time.

There was nothing as raw as this.

I cleared my throat, shaking it off as best I could, and then I tipped Grace's chin until she looked at me, until I was looking at her instead of the camera.

My eyes searched hers, scanning every inch of her face before I found her gaze once more. I took a mental photo and tucked it into the pocket of my heart to hold forever.

"I have had the best summer of my life with you, Grace Tanev," I said, and every fucking word ripped at my throat on the way out.

Her bottom lip wobbled, but she smiled despite it, and then she leaned up to press a kiss to my lips with the camera still rolling.

We spent the next hour holding one another — Grace asking me *would you rather* questions that had us both laughing even as our hearts threatened to break out of our chests. I smoothed my thumb over her knuckles where I held her hand, soaked in every smile she threw my way, and tried my best to face the situation the way she was.

I reached for the positive, for all we had to be grateful for instead of all we were losing. But where that came naturally to Grace, it was like pulling teeth for me.

Flashes of the last month played like a movie reel in my mind. I saw every smile, heard every laugh, felt every tremble of her body beneath mine. And far before either of us were ready, time ran out.

I had a ten-minute walk to my gate, and my flight was about to start boarding.

I pushed it off as long as I could, and then when we had no other choice, we both stood, facing each other like nervous school kids. Grace's cheeks were pink, her hair falling in front of her face as I hooked a hand on the back of my neck.

Then, I let out a shaky exhale, and I reached for her.

My hands wound around her waist, pulling her close as her arms stretched up around my neck. I dropped my forehead to hers, both of us closing our eyes and inhaling together.

And my body rioted.

My chest squeezed so painfully tight I let out a gasp of an exhale. My heart surged, thrashing in my rib cage as my stomach dropped. I felt the uneven pulsing of blood in my ears, felt how the agony ripped through me and demanded to be felt.

"Fuck, Grace," I whispered, the words breaking us both. "I don't want to do this."

I squeezed my eyes shut with the admission, and with that, the tears I'd been fighting back broke free.

They seared a burning path down each of my cheeks, my chest stuttering with the sob I refused to let out. My father had beaten into me that men don't cry — but *fuck*, I couldn't stop it. I couldn't hide the fact that I was shattering.

Grace wrapped me up tighter, and when I opened my eyes to look at her, she was shaking her head, shedding her own tears as she wiped mine from my face.

"Hey," she said, sniffing on a smile. "This isn't goodbye. I'll see you soon, yeah?"

I nodded, biting my lower lip and trying to feel that that was enough. Another tear slid down to my jaw where it met her thumb. She wiped it away as I cursed.

I was fucking crying.

I was fucking *crying* for this girl.

Had I *ever* cried, other than when I was a child?

The thought made me pause and feel just how significant that was. Then again, that seemed to be how everything was with Grace. I couldn't remember ever having a hug before her, or laughing so hard my stomach hurt, or longing for something so badly I was willing to risk *everything* to have it — even if I couldn't keep it.

"Go, go," she said on a laugh, pressing her hands to my chest and pushing me away a few inches. "I'll see you soon. I'll be in Tampa for a game before we know it. And it was fun, right?" Her face twisted a bit with that, but she smoothed it out so quickly — an expert at her craft. "We had fun."

"Yeah," I said, sniffing. "Yeah, we had fun."

Now *I* wanted to laugh — but not because it was funny. Because it was sick. It was a fucking *joke* to call what we'd shared fun, to give it such a simple, shallow label.

We stared at each other a moment more, and then she pushed me again, smiling as her eyebrows raised. "Go," she said on a laugh. "Before you miss your flight."

I grabbed my bag off the floor, slinging it over my shoulder and turning for the exit. I took four steps, but every one felt like I was walking in quicksand, like time was moving in slow motion. And I felt it again — my body rioting, refusing to work properly, refusing to let this be the end.

Suddenly, I halted.

I didn't have a choice. My legs stopped moving, and I stood there with my back to Grace, heaving each breath that burned all the way down.

I shook my head, nose flaring as I dropped my bag to the floor and turned. I crossed the space between us in long strides, Grace's chin wobbling as I did. She looked half surprised and half devastated when I ran back to her, and I swept her up in my arms, crushing my mouth to hers.

"You have to go," she said against my lips, even as she clung to me, even as she kissed me hard like she never wanted to stop.

"I love you."

The words ripped from my chest, loud and broken.

And they cracked her wide open.

She sobbed, fingers curling in my hair as I kissed her again and again.

"I know that's selfish to say," I said between them. "I know everything feels impossible and I have no fucking idea what comes next for us, Grace, but I do know that this isn't over. I cannot — *will not* — leave you behind without you knowing that."

She sobbed harder, and I ran my hands through her hair, framing her face until I could look her right in the eye.

"I love you," I said again. "I didn't know what it was to live before you came into my life. I didn't know there could be joy like this, or adventure, or pain so fucking deep in my chest."

I beat my fist against my rib cage, wincing as I confessed everything I'd shoved down.

"I didn't know that I could be with you — every second of every day — and *still* want more."

Grace nodded, like she understood, like she felt it, too.

"I don't know what I can ask of you right now, and I don't know what I can give you in return." I let out a slow breath, my heart evening out now that I'd told her the truth. "All I know is that I need you to understand that I'm not walking away from you, from this, from *us*." I shook my head. "Not now. Not ever."

Her brows bent together, face warping as she nodded over and over and pulled me down for another long kiss.

I breathed her in. I ran my hands through her hair and behind her neck and down until I could crush her to me. I wanted to leave my mark with that kiss. I wanted to seal everything I'd just said with a promise so strong she could never question it.

"I love you, too," she whispered.

I inhaled her even more, beaming, every cell in my being rejoicing at what it felt like to hear her say it.

"We were never supposed to happen, and yet I love you still. I can't tell you how many times over the last month I've wondered if the stars aligned for us. And I agree," she added, sniffing. "I don't know what happens next. But I know I'll never let you go, Jaxson. You'll always be a part of me."

That elation I'd felt was still there, but a fist was crushing it like a soda can now.

Because her words sounded an awful lot like a goodbye.

An announcement interrupted us from the lounge speakers — a call for all passengers to board my flight.

"You have to go," Grace said.

"*Fuck*." I claimed her mouth again, and then she pressed against my chest, and I had no choice but to rip myself away from her.

I didn't dare look back as I jogged to my bag, swiped it off the floor and raced for the exit. I ran and ran through the airport, feeling the pressure crushing my lungs all the way to my gate.

I made it just before they closed the doors.

I texted Grace as soon as I was in my seat, breath still coming hard and shallow. Then, I put on my headphones, pulled my hoodie up over my head, and replayed her words until they were branded into my memory.

She loved me, too.

I still didn't know what would come next for us — if anything. But I'd told her the truth. I'd left nothing unsaid. I'd laid it all out on the line, and I knew now that she felt the same.

The plane took off, carrying me home.

But I left my heart with her.

CHAPTER 33

BE HERE

Jaxson

I was a pathetic piece of shit for the first few weeks back in Tampa.

I wished I could channel Grace's energy, that I could pop right back into the life I'd been happily living before I knew what it was like to lose myself in her. But it was impossible.

I went back to my house, to my vintage cars, to my books and my team and my routine — but it all felt off now.

The guys were desperate to go out as soon as I got home, all of them giving me shit for not being around for the off-season. Fortunately, they didn't press past me telling them I had family stuff to take care of. I wasn't sure how much more I could lie right to their faces.

I couldn't act the same around them. Any time I was with Vince, I was caught between wanting to punch him in the throat and let him punch *me* for disrespecting him. He had trusted me, and I knew I was sitting on a betrayal so deep I wasn't sure it was forgivable. It made it impossible to act normal around him, to laugh and joke like we used to when I was keeping such a secret.

Carter dragged me out to Boomers a couple times, the local bar that was more like a club where all the puck bunnies knew to find us. He then promptly gave me shit for sitting in the corner and drinking alone. I laughed at his jokes about my dick being broken all while swallowing down the truth, which was that there wasn't another woman in this fucking city — in the *world* — who could make me want them now.

Desecrated. That's what I was.

I could feel the weight of Will's gaze on me, too. He knew I wasn't the same, but he didn't press. Every now and then, he'd clap me on the shoulder and ask, "You good?"

A nod was all he got in return.

Driving my cars down Bayshore Boulevard didn't give me the same rush as before. I couldn't read more than a page in any book. I didn't feel the usual excitement humming under my skin that I usually did with a new season ahead. I just felt... numb.

It was like I was playing pretend in someone else's life, like I was trying to walk in shoes too big for my feet. I was off kilter in every possible fucking way.

I hadn't been eating enough or working out enough on the road trip, so when I returned, I had to force feed myself to put on weight — which was especially hard considering my appetite was nonexistent.

My trainers had me lifting heavy every fucking day, and we were back to skating again, playing practice games and running drills as the preseason was just around the corner.

I was thankful at least for that — for hockey. The one place I felt mildly like myself again was on the ice.

Will was usually the first one to the arena when we had skate time, but I was beating him to it these days, and staying until my trainers all but dragged me away. The more my muscles burned, the more I had to think about where the puck was and where *I* needed to be...

The less I thought about her.

I didn't know why, but now that we were thousands of miles apart, things between us just didn't feel the same. Grace and I had texted a lot in the first few days, but then she went to Costa Rica, and her service was so unreliable, I didn't hear from her for a week.

I couldn't even talk to her on her birthday.

When she got back, she FaceTimed me, and I felt a little piece of my heart click back into place at the sight of her. She was sporting a fresh tan and a bright smile as she told me all about it — how she'd done yoga every day, how she'd tried her hand at surfing, how much she loved the sound baths and the days at the beach and the nights meditating.

She was doing okay. And *fuck*, I was so glad she was.

But I was also gutted — because *I* was at the opposite end of the spectrum.

Still, time has a funny way of pushing us forward whether we drag our feet and kick and scream against it or not. Soon, August slipped into September. Camp and preseason took over my life, and I jumped willingly into that pool, desperate to drown myself in anything that wasn't the longing in my chest for Grace.

We still texted, almost every day. She sent me pictures and videos, and I hid my screen from Vince when I sent my replies. There were a couple nights when we were both alone and our video chats turned into her fucking her fingers while I stroked my cock and remembered the way it felt to be inside her.

But the longer we were apart, the more I felt the distance Grace was putting between us.

Soon, texting every day turned to every other day, and then just a few times a week. She was in and out of service, so our calls faded, too. We went from having everything to say to each other to only talking surface-level to eventually just sending a joke or meme in a text.

I knew it wasn't because she didn't care for me, or that she didn't want things to be different. It was the opposite.

Grace was an expert at running from pain.

And right now — I was the source.

Our lives moved on.

Just like we both knew they would.

Except I still had this hole burning into my chest, reminding me of what once had been there, whispering for me not to let it go just yet.

On September twenty-seventh, our first preseason game at home, I had barely taken my pads off before my phone was ringing. Just like it did every time, my heart leapt into my throat, wishing for it to be Grace.

When I saw my father's name and photo on the screen, I sighed, running a hand through my wet hair before I ducked into an empty training room and took the call.

"Well, I don't know what to say, son, except you're damn lucky Tanev had a monster night."

The familiarity of his voice grated like nails on a chalkboard.

"Hello, Dad," I said, leaning against the wall. I let my head fall back against it.

"What was that shit in the second? You were too busy puck-watching, and Hankin attacked like you were a fucking watch guard sleeping on the job."

I pulled the phone from my ear, letting my father scream into the void of the empty room while I forced a calming breath. He raged and rambled and recited garbage I knew he was just pulling off the Internet from other trolls who loved to talk shit — all while I tuned him out.

This was nothing new.

But the more he went on and on, the harder my breaths came. I felt something stirring inside me, like I'd woken a sleeping giant and he was climbing up out of the depths.

I realized I'd had enough of this being my normal.

And before I could decide if this was really the fight I wanted to pick, the giant was breaking free.

"*Enough*, Dad!"

I brought the phone back to my ear, cutting him off mid-sentence in a baritone I knew surprised him — that was the only explanation for why he actually shut the fuck up.

"God, do you hear yourself? Aren't you fucking tired of this?"

A moment of silence stretched between us, and I pinched the bridge of my nose on an exhale.

"Every fucking game, *every* game, since I was a *kid*," I said, shaking my head. "Now that you can't yell at me in the car ride home, you call me. And you know I'm going to answer. You *know* it. Did you ever stop to think why? Did you ever ask yourself, 'why does my son always answer when he knows I'll either be shitting on his game or asking him to send a check?'"

My chest was heaving.

Dad didn't say a word.

"It's because I love you," I filled in for him when he didn't dare to answer. "I love you, Dad. And I respect you. I'm so, *so* fucking thankful that you brought hockey into my life, and that you taught me everything you did. But I'm done with this."

I shook my head, waiting for him to speak.

I was pretty sure he was having a heart attack, considering I'd never talked back to him before.

"I'm sorry about your accident, Dad. I'm sorry it took the sport you love from you. But that doesn't give you the right to do the same to me."

My chest sparked at that, and suddenly, I was picturing Grace in the room with me. I could see her nodding, encouraging me. I could feel her holding my hand and telling me to keep going.

"I am happy to help you and Mom. I always have been. I want you to be comfortable. But I also want you to call me without my stomach dropping when you do. I want you to ask about my life. I want you to be a *part* of it."

"Is that a fucking joke?"

I reared back as if he'd slapped me — especially when he started laughing.

"You want us to be a part of your life, eh?" he asked. His voice was terrifyingly calm. "So much so that you spent a week in Canmore and didn't so much as tell us, let alone stop by?"

Shit.

I swallowed, my throat tight. I'd wondered why I hadn't heard from him before tonight. Usually, he was chewing my ass as soon as camp started.

I had my answer now.

"You're right," I said. "I should have come home. And I would have, under different circumstances. But as it stands..." I shook my head, searching for my strength. "I don't want to fucking see you. Okay? I don't care to receive my lashings in person. Or at all, for that matter."

He puffed a laugh. "My son, a keener. You want me to pat you on the head and tell you what a good boy you are?"

"I just want you to be my dad!"

I screamed the words, chest heaving in the silence they left me in.

Dad sniffed on the other line, and I swore I heard the distinct sound of him slinging back a shot from his mickey. "Well, I am. Any good father lets his son know when he needs to do better."

I closed my eyes.

This was never going to work out in my favor.

"Listen, I love you," I said again, voice softer this time. "But I don't want this energy in my life anymore. So, if you want to be a part of it, I'm going to need you to get on board. No more calls after the game. If I want advice, I'll ask you for it. I'm happy to provide for you and Mom, but I want phone calls that don't involve hockey. I want you to ask how I am, and tell me how you are. I want family holidays that don't make me sick to my stomach just thinking about them. I want you two to come see a fucking game, for Christ's sake. And then," I said, holding up a finger. "Not say a fucking word about it after other than *good job, great game.* Do you think you can do that?"

The sounds on the other end were muffled. I thought I heard the TV. I also thought I heard Mom sniffling, which broke my fucking heart. But if she could hear the conversation, then she was also close enough to speak.

Neither of them did.

I swallowed, nodding. "Well, then I guess we have nothing left to discuss."

I ended the call just as the training door swung open, and Will slid through it with one brow arched into his hairline.

"You good?" he asked — just like always.

"Not now, Perry."

My hands were shaking as he stilled a breath, clapping me on the shoulder before he hopped up to sit on one of the training tables. He folded his hands together. "Not your best game."

"Trust me — already heard it from my dad, don't need to hear it from you, too."

"Well, since I'm your goalie and your captain, you're going to have to."

I sighed.

"I know you're fucked up, alright? You have been since August. And I know that because I remember exactly what it feels like to try to show up for your team when you're fucking numb inside."

His words sucked the air out of the room.

We all knew what happened to him. We all knew his wife had passed away and left him to raise their daughter.

But he never talked about it — not when it happened, not in any time since.

So to hear him even reference that time in his life felt like seeing a pig fly across the sky.

"Now, I may not know exactly what's going on, but if I had to guess, my money wouldn't be on your shit-for-brains father who you just cut out of your life — which I agree with, by the way," he added. "No, I'd place my bet on the fact that you're heartbroken over a girl you never should have touched to begin with."

My jaw tensed, and I stared at the ground, unable to look him in the eye.

"It's none of my fucking business who you get involved with," he said. "*Except* for when it bleeds into here." He pointed his finger down at the floor. "I warned you in St. Louis, and from the way you've been moping around, I know you didn't listen. That's fine. You're a big boy. You can make your own decisions."

He hopped down from the table, walking over to where I stood.

"But the way you played out there tonight is not the Brittzy I know, and it's not the one we need on this team — especially not while we try to navigate having new blood on the roster."

I nodded.

He was right. Between the rookies who were still learning and adjusting to their first pro year, and that rumored trade of Aleks Suter to Tampa being true, we were in new and unfamiliar territory. We had the strength of last season with a dash of uncertainty. The rookies needed guidance. Suter needed to be tamed like a fucking wild animal.

We could either fine tune our new machine, or we could watch it break into shambles — and the latter was bound to happen if we weren't all focused.

"I don't have to tell you that Vince will have your fucking ass if and when he finds out," Will said. "But if that's what needs to happen, then get it over with so we can move on. And if that's not the option that's on the table? Then we both know what the other one is."

Let her go.

Those were the words he didn't have to say.

And at this point, the first option he mentioned wasn't even one to entertain. Grace was out living her life. She had already left me at that airport — right where she should have.

It was *me* holding on to the impossible.

"Life is unfair. It's a kick in the ass more days than not. But whatever you think you've lost, I can tell you one thing you still have, one thing you will *always* have." Will poked a finger hard into my chest. "You have this game. You have the ice. You have this fucking *team.*"

I nodded, over and over, letting his words sink in.

"We need you," he finished, removing his hand. "So, either *be here*, or get out of the way so someone who wants to be can take your place."

He left me on that note, and the quiet of the training room suffocated me the moment I was alone.

My head was spinning — from the shit game I'd played, from the boundary I'd set with my parents that I never thought I'd have the balls to, and now, from every word my goalie had left me with.

Everything inside me wanted to reach for my phone, to text or call Grace and tell her about it all. I knew she'd be proud of me for standing up to my father. I knew she was the only reason I had the strength to do it.

But Daddy P was right.

I was holding on to a dream, a fantasy, a life that Grace already knew we couldn't live. And it was fucking killing me. It was murdering my game, my teammates' trust in me, my *spirit*.

She was already letting go and moving on.

And it didn't matter how badly it fucking hurt.

It was time for me to do the same.

CHAPTER 34

THOROUGHLY RUINED

Grace

I'd always heard people say you change a lot in your twenties, and to be honest, I thought it was a crock of shit.

I had been the same person ever since I could remember. I embodied everything that a Leo was. I lived for the fun of it all. If someone asked me to write my bio for *The Bachelorette*, I knew exactly what I would say.

Grace Tanev: sunny, adventure-seeking, big-hearted and always down for a good time.

I wasn't going to change. I didn't *want* to change. Because at the end of the day, no matter what happened to me, I had the uncanny ability to look at the bright side. I could always dig my way out of any hole. I was resilient. I was *untouchable*.

But as a freshly twenty-three-year-old, sipping coffee on the porch of a one-bedroom cabin in New Hampshire all by myself... I finally understood what they meant.

Two months.

It had been two *months* since I'd felt my heart ripped out of my chest when Jaxson left me in that airport.

I didn't know what hurt more that day — the silent drive to an end we both knew was coming, watching him break down in that lounge, hearing him confess that he loved me, or staring at his back when he finally had no choice but to walk away.

It was death by a hand I'd dealt myself.

But just because I knew it was coming didn't make the kill any more merciful.

Now, I felt like a hamster on a wheel, chasing the high I used to feel from traveling to a new destination but never able to reach that high. I had now officially spent more time *away* from Jaxson than I had *with* him, and yet he still consumed my every thought.

I couldn't rent a car or hitch a ride without wishing it was him in the driver's seat. I couldn't sleep a single night in a tent or a cabin or a hotel room without longing to curl up with him under the covers. I couldn't paddle board or dance or sit by a fire or hike a mountain or do *anything* without imagining what Jaxson would do if he were there with me.

I was thoroughly ruined.

Every experience in my life felt dull without him, like an old film photo or a VHS tape from the 90s. Life was happening. I was moving forward. But nothing was as sharp, as colorful, or as clear as it had been with him by my side.

Now, I was watching the yellow, orange, and red leaves slowly fall, one by one, as I ticked another day off the calendar and sat fully in my sadness. That was a new development for me, too — a way I had *changed*.

I wasn't running from the pain.

It had been nearly two weeks since the last time Jaxson and I spoke.

I missed his voice like I missed the innocence of childhood. I longed to call him, to text him, to run to him. Two weeks without any contact had me thirsting for him like I'd been walking a week in the desert without a sip of water.

It was for the best. I *knew* that, deep in my gut. It was why I fought every urge I had to send him a photo of where I was, why I didn't text or call him even though I was desperate to hear his voice.

The old me would have been fine by now. Two months? That might as well have been a lifetime. I would have left him in my rearview mirror. I would have already been dying over someone else, crushing so hard I felt butterflies every time I saw them. I would have traded in that pain so fast it would make a head spin, reaching instead for the next person who had the ability to make me feel good.

But as the wise old *they* had predicted — something in me had changed.

It wasn't that I still didn't opt for the bright side, because I did. When I longed for Jaxson, I reminded myself how amazing it was to have the time we did have together. I listed off every experience I was thankful for with him.

But something he'd shown me was that it was okay to sit in our sadness every now and then, to feel the pain that life shells out to us.

That pain is what makes us human.

That pain is what makes us appreciate the overwhelming joy when we're blessed with it.

The old me *never* cried. I would have sooner sawed my arm off with a rusty pair of scissors. But the new me cried almost every day — and *liked* it. God, it was wild, how something I used to fight so hard was something I welcomed like an old friend coming home now. But I did. I embraced that tight zing in my chest. I smiled when the first tears rolled down my cheeks.

Because for the first time in my life, I had someone to miss.

Every night, when I closed my eyes, I replayed the way he'd sprinted back to me in that airport. I watched his brows bend in anguish, heard his voice when he broke and confessed that he loved me, felt his hands clinging to me so hard it was like he would fade into nothing without feeling my skin against his.

It was my favorite memory — even when it ripped the scab off any attempt my heart had made to heal itself.

He loved me. And I loved him.

If only it were like a movie where that was enough.

I swore to myself that I would leave him alone. I swore I would let him move on and heal, and that I would pay myself the same respect.

But on my second day in New Hampshire, I woke to a text from my mom that broke my resolve like a dam made of toothpicks.

Mom: Hey, little globetrotter. We're heading to Tampa for the first home game. Meet you there?

CHAPTER 35

AND YET...

Jaxson

"TIME TO HIT BOOMERS, BABY!"

Carter slid across the locker room floor Tom Cruise style, wiggling his hips in a way that made me laugh and cringe at the same time. Vince wound up a towel into a tight spiral before snapping it on Carter's ass.

"Why, so you can sweat any time a bunny tries to dance with you and then go home alone like always?" Vince ducked out of the way when Carter tried to hook him with a punch to the arm after that remark.

"You know what, Tanny Boy? Not even you can get me down. Because we just won our first game of the season, and I," he said, pointing a thumb to his chest. "Was a star of the game."

There was a scoff from the other end of the bench, and we all turned to find Aleks Suter shaking his head as he took off his jersey and pads.

He looked like he belonged in prison more than a professional hockey league locker room. His hair was buzz cut short to his head, his lip in a permanent snarl, and he had the body build of someone who fought for a living. He was scrappy and terrifying as hell.

He was also really pissing me off.

The man was new to this team. I didn't give a rat's ass if he was bigger and badder than Carter — he hadn't been on this team as long. And he needed to show some fucking respect before I made him show it.

"Got something to say, Su Man?" I asked, trying to keep my voice level.

Suter hit me with his signature death glare, and then shrugged, stepping right up to Carter's chest. "Enjoy your star, kid. Because if what you brought tonight was the best you have, you'll be sent down within the month."

I jumped up off the bench, ready to make Aleks shut his mouth since he apparently needed help in that department. But Vince landed a palm hard to my chest to stop me.

I didn't miss how Carter's face fell a little. And truth be told, Aleks had a point. Carter had a decent game, but we opened with our easiest opponents. He was good on the ice, but if he wanted to stay in the NHL, he needed to be *great*. He needed to be unbelievable. He needed to up his game.

Still, it wasn't the fucking new kid's place to tell him that — not when he hadn't even been here three months.

"Guess that means you're not joining us, huh, Suter?" Carter asked, bouncing back just like he always did. Nothing kept him down for long.

Aleks grunted, and Carter chuckled, pointing to Will next. "What about you, Daddy P?"

"No."

His answer was barely more than a grumble, and judging by the way he was hastily packing his shit, I had a feeling he was still struggling in the nanny department. It made me feel sorry for him. He was just a year older than me. I couldn't imagine having a kid right now — let alone one who I had to raise on my own.

"Vince?" Carter asked, spinning to point at our winger next.

"You know I would be there, but the family flew in for the game. I'm going to spend some time with them back at the house."

Carter let his hands fall to his thighs on a groan, stomping like a little kid. "Are you serious? Do you guys not realize the responsibility we have to the puck bunnies of Tampa? We're going to break hearts tonight — and not in the usual way." He shook his head, clapping me on the shoulder next. "Looks like it's just me and you, Brittzy."

But I was frozen, my brain hung up on the word *family* like it was a jagged nail sticking out of the wall.

I cracked my neck. "So the whole family is here, huh, Tanev?" I asked, hoping I sounded only mildly interested.

"Yep," he said, stripping out of the last of his gear. "Poor Maven is going to have to field wedding questions from my mom all weekend. At least Grace is here to be a buffer. She's always been good at that."

My heart stopped, excitement and anxiety flooding my bloodstream in equal measure.

Just hearing her name made every nerve ending buzz to life.

Carter asked Vince something about the mentioned wedding, but I was too busy carefully removing my cell phone from where I'd shoved it in my bag well before the game. When I saw a missed text from Grace on the home screen, my heart skipped another beat.

Nova: Got room for a hitchhiker in the passenger seat of that hot little Porsche you drove to the game tonight?

The text was followed by a photo of her in front of the Tampa sign at Sparkman Wharf — and she was dressed for the game, sporting her brother's jersey in a size that swallowed her.

A million thoughts warred to be the first one through the fog in my head. There were the warnings and the reasons not to respond, the reminder that we'd both started moving on, that this would only reopen a deep cut trying to heal itself.

But I couldn't hear any of that over the loudest voice of all, which was screaming for me to find the fastest way to get her in my arms.

Me: Where are you?

Nova: Waiting for Vince in the family lounge with Mom and Dad.

Me: Vince said you're heading back to his place.

Nova: We are, but I've been laying the groundwork for having a headache all night. Mom keeps telling me to go to our hotel and get some rest, so as soon as we see Vince, I'll be free.

My heart pounded like a sledgehammer in my chest.

Me: You're bad.

Nova: I am. You might have to spank me and teach me a lesson.

I cursed, cock twitching to life in my briefs. I looked around to make sure no one noticed when I adjusted myself before I fired a text back.

Me: You're going to regret saying that when you can't sit tomorrow.

Nova: Promises, promises.

I couldn't help the smile that curled on my lips. My entire body was flooded with energy like it was after every game, but it was tripled now, every nerve on edge as I thumbed out my address, gate code, and door code to her.

She was here.

Grace was *here*.

All the work I'd done to try to let her go in the last couple of months swirled down the drain in an instant. I didn't care about what was right and wrong. I didn't care about our age difference or who her fucking brother was.

The only thing I cared about was getting to her as fast as I could.

I tucked my phone away and schooled my expression, sliding up next to Carter as he made his way toward the showers.

"Hey, man," I said, keeping my voice low so only he could hear. "I'm going to pass on Boomers tonight."

"What?!" I thought the grown ass man was about to whine. "Come *on*, man. We just won our first game of the season! What the hell is wrong with everyone tonight?" Then, something caught in his expression when he saw mine. "Wait... what's with that face?"

"What face?"

"That one," he said, pointing right at my nose. "You look like you just found out your dick was made of gold." He snapped his fingers on a knowing grin. "Oh, shit. You're seeing someone, aren't you?"

I looked around to make sure no one had overheard him before I pushed him farther toward the showers. He laughed when I did, rubbing his hands like a greedy sonofabitch.

"*Please* tell me it's that actress we partied with in New York last season," he said when I shoved him into a corner. "I know she's married to that director, but the way she was hanging all over you that night in SoHo tells me he's more of a speed bump than a roadblock."

"I just don't feel like going out tonight."

"Sure," he said, winking conspiratorially and elbowing me in the ribs.

I shoved him off. "Can you be fucking cool?"

"If you tell me who she is."

I ground my teeth. Carter was like a brother to me, but *fuck,* I needed him to stop talking so I could take my shower and get home to my girl.

"I can't," I said.

His eyes widened. "Oh, shit. It *is* her, isn't it? You homewrecking dog." He shook his head on a click of his tongue. "I feel like I should give you some advice here, like tell you to be good or something. Cheating is wrong, man." He wagged his finger at me with a mock stern expression, his eyebrows furrowing. But then he tapped his chin on a thought. "Then again, if it's not technically *you* who's doing the cheating..."

"It's not her," I gritted. "Look, I'll tell you one day, alright? But right now, I need you to just nize it."

He threw his hands up. "Alright, man. Calm down. I'll let you off the hook for tonight. But you owe me," he added with a finger to my chest. He watched me with a narrow gaze. "Why do you look so nervous about it?"

I swallowed, the reality that I was going to see her after two months apart eating at my chest. She had texted me. She wanted to see me, too. But in what capacity? Did she want to hang out as friends, shoot the shit, catch up and go our separate ways again?

Her text told me there was at least one part of that friend boundary she wanted to cross.

Did she want to be... *fuck buddies*?

My stomach tightened again at the realization that I wasn't going to be able to differentiate. There was no way in hell I could just be a Tampa hookup for her. I was already too far gone.

"Let's just say I'm playing with fire," I admitted. "One that's already burned me to the ground once before."

Carter whistled through his teeth, then clamped a hand on my shoulder. "Well, here's hoping you survive. But if you don't — can I have your cars?"

• • •

I got to my house before she did, and I threw my car into park in the garage before kicking out of it like it was on fire. I didn't even bother with my bags — just stood in the middle of my driveway with my eyes on the gate.

I knew the Tanevs well enough to know getting away wouldn't be as easy as she thought. My bet was that her brother and Maven probably begged her to come back to their house. I could hear how Maven would offer a guest room and a whole bottle of Advil if it meant she could have Grace with her.

When ten minutes had passed, I thumbed out a text asking what her ETA was, but there was no response.

Finally, headlights slid over the landscaping in front of the gate. The car pulled to a stop, and I jogged down the drive as Grace climbed out of a taxi.

A fucking taxi?

I hadn't seen anyone use a taxi in years, but that surprise was with me for only a moment before every thought turned to the fact that Grace was in my driveway.

Her long hair was even lighter where it fell straight over her shoulders, her legs a dark tan like she'd been soaking up the sun every day since I'd last seen her. She was still in Vince's jersey, and it was bulky and far too big for her. It fell down to her knees, leaving me to assume she had on shorts underneath. I spotted the keychains on her crossbody bag, and a memory of the first time I touched her knocked my next breath from my chest.

That jog turned into a sprint.

The taxi was already pulling away as Grace hastily typed in the gate code, and the metal slid open just enough for me to squeeze through before I had her swept up in my arms.

Her scent enveloped me, arms wrapping around my neck, legs around my waist as I hauled her up and held her tightly to my chest. She smelled like citrus and sunshine just like always, but she also smelled like the Colorado Rockies, like Yellowstone and Banff, like loud music and the open road.

It was everything I loved and missed back within reach as I held her tight. It was the first sip of air that didn't burn on the way down. It was a quick release on all the pressure mounting in my chest. It was familiar and comfortable and the source of the joy I hadn't felt since the last time she was in my arms.

Home.

That's what she was for me.

And I knew, right then, before either of us said a word, that I couldn't walk away from her a second time.

I didn't care what it took or who we hurt in the process. For once, I wanted to be selfish. I wanted *her* to be selfish with me.

All I knew in that moment was that I belonged to Grace — and no one, and nothing, would keep me from making her mine.

"*Fuck*, Nova," I said, inhaling her deep. "I've missed you so much."

She pulled back, her eyes glossed even as she forced a smile past the emotion. "I've been fucking miserable without you."

She said it on a laugh, and I laughed with her, but not at what she'd said. I laughed at the stupidity of it all, of the absolute ridiculousness that we both thought what we had was something so trivial as a flash in the pan summer romance. But I also heaved the biggest sigh of relief to hear her say that she'd been feeling the same way, to know she hadn't already forgotten me the way I thought she had.

I needed her like I needed ice under my skates, and trying to move on from her had proven nothing except the truth I'd always known — which was that I couldn't.

Not then. Not now. Not ever.

"You?" I said, sweeping her hair from her face. "I've been a pathetic fucking mess."

She laughed again, the sound so sweet it made my chest hurt. Her eyes searched mine, and she shook her head, trailing her fingertips along the stubble on my jaw.

"I tried to stay away from you," she whispered. "I tried to just move on and live my life without you. But I—"

"Can't," I finished for her, and then I couldn't take it any longer. I tilted her chin and claimed her mouth with my own, kissing her with all the words that had been left unsaid between us. "I know," I said against her lips. "I can't either."

She almost cried at that, wrapping herself around me more and kissing me like I'd disappear if she didn't hold the connection.

"I've cried more in the last two months than in my entire life. Everything I do, I wish you were doing with me. Everywhere I go, I feel empty without you being there, too."

I swore my body was breaking down with how fast my heart raced, how hard each breath came. Her words soothed me and revved me up at the same time, and my body couldn't keep up with the emotions flooding through me.

"I know, I know," I assured her, smoothing a hand through her hair and kissing her again. "Nothing feels right without you. Not this house, not my cars or my books, not even hockey. I feel like I've been carrying a hundred-pound weight and walking on the ocean floor. Everything is muted and slow." I shook my head. "I... I am a fucking simp for you, Grace."

She barked out a laugh. "I don't know whether to laugh or cry. I didn't know if you'd feel the same, but now that I know you do... God, Jax." She bit her lip. "What the fuck are we going to do?"

"Right now?" I was already walking us up the drive toward the house. "Many, *many* filthy things."

"And after?"

My heart stuttered. "I don't know," I confessed. "But... we'll figure it out. Together."

She nodded, sliding her hands into my hair. "Together. *Oh God,* is this real? Please tell me this is real."

"It's real, baby," I promised, kissing her as I unlocked the front door and we tumbled inside. I blindly felt for my security keypad to disarm the system, and then I was pressing Grace into the nearest wall. "I have no fucking idea how we're going to do this without causing a shit storm," I admitted. "But I don't care. I love you, you little weirdo."

She tilted her head back on the most beautiful laugh at that.

"I do," I said, kissing her throat. "And I'm so sorry, Grace. I'm so sorry I left you, that I couldn't see that any consequences are worth it if I get to have you in the end."

She shook her head. "It wasn't just you. It was me, too. I didn't see a way past it. Our lives don't match up. We don't make sense."

"And yet..."

She pressed her forehead against mine. "And yet."

My eyes closed on a long, relieved exhale. All the nervous energy drained out of me at once, and I basked in the longing and the pure fucking ecstasy it left behind.

"Grace."

"Yes?"

"Why were you in a fucking taxi?" I shook my head. "You should have told me, I would have sent a car."

"Well, about that... I planned on taking an Uber, but I *might* have lost my phone."

My eyes widened. "Are you serious?"

She bit her lip and groaned. "I'm the worst, I do this shit all the time. I had it in the bathroom with me when I was texting you after the game, and I think I left it on the toilet paper roll dispenser."

I blinked, and then chuffed a laugh, pinching her side.

"I know, I know!" She let her head fall to my shoulder. "By the time I realized I didn't have it anymore, Vince, Maven, and my parents had already left for the beach house. I tried to get back into the stadium, but of course, they weren't letting anyone in. So, I did things the old school way. I used a stranger's phone and called a taxi."

"Shit. Do you want to go get it real quick? I can get us in."

She leveled me with a look, winding her fingers up into my hair and tugging just enough to make my body wake all the way up. "There's only one thing I want to do right now, and it doesn't involve my stupid phone. It can wait. It was in the family and friends lounge bathroom, I don't think there's anything to worry about. We can get it tomorrow."

"You sure?" I asked, but my hands were already roaming, palms splaying the curves and lines of her body that I could chart like constellations at this point.

"Take me to your room, Jax," she breathed against my lips.

"Mmm," I hummed, kissing her deep before I started walking us through the foyer. "I think a tour is in order first. Let's start with the kitchen." I sucked her ear between my teeth before adding. "I'm a little *hungry* after that game."

CHAPTER 36

A VERY BOOKWORM FANTASY

Grace

Everything was right again.

My body hummed with the relief of that truth as Jaxson carried me through his home. We wouldn't make it far before he was pressing me into a wall and kissing me breathless, and then we were on the move again.

My fingers twisted in his hair. His pressed into my hips and my waist. It was as if I'd been living in an alternate universe, one where my heart didn't beat properly and my world revolved too slowly around the sun, and now everything had snapped back into place.

"God, I've missed the way you taste," he breathed against my lips, and I tried to take in his beautiful house, but couldn't admire much before my ass was propped on the cool granite of his kitchen island. "The way you smell, the way you *feel*."

The moment his hands didn't have to carry me up any longer, they slid up into my hair, framing my face and holding me to him.

"Every night, I thought about how I'd never get to do this again, how I'd never be able to kiss you and hear the sweet moans you let loose when I do."

I took the cue, moaning just like he'd said as he bit my lower lip and sucked.

"It drove me mad," he confessed, his voice gravelly like he was savoring that sound he'd elicited from me. "I was absolutely fucking *crazy* without you."

He paused then, pulling back enough to let his eyes roam over me. They searched my face before sliding down over my chest, and his jaw tightened a bit.

"I know he's your brother," Jaxson said, tugging on the Ospreys logo sprawled over the front of the jersey I wore. "But *fuck,* this pisses me off."

"What does?"

"Seeing you in any jersey that isn't mine."

The possession in that statement rippled through me, and I squirmed at how it shot electricity right between my thighs.

"Hmm..." I said, curling my fingers in the hem of the jersey until I had a good grip. "Maybe we should get rid of it, then."

"Please," Jaxson agreed, all too eager to help me.

But when I peeled off the jersey, he stopped, blinking as he took in the one he didn't know I was wearing underneath — the one *no one* knew I was wearing all night.

I didn't give a fuck if it looked like I was wearing a burlap sack the entire game, if I looked frumpy as hell. Wearing two jerseys was worth it to see this look on Jaxson's face.

His lips parted, fingertips trailing over the blue fabric, and every spot it clung to my skin. He traced a line from the collar to my shoulder, and then his fingers danced down to skate over the number stitched on the sleeve.

Seventy-seven.

"You had mine on this entire time?" he croaked, and *fuck*, it was so hot seeing how that unraveled him.

I nodded, threading my fingers through the hair at the nape of his neck. "You're the one I wear closest to my heart."

Jaxson let out a long, slow breath like he was trying to garner control. Then, his hands snaked up under the jersey, hooking around the top of my jean shorts. He felt blindly along the waistband until he found the button and zipper, making quick work of them before his mouth crashed down on mine.

"Up," he said, landing another bruising kiss, and he smacked the side of my thigh to hammer home what he meant.

I pressed my palms into the island, lifting enough for Jaxson to drag the denim fabric off my thighs and down to my ankles. He flipped my sneakers off next, sliding the jeans the rest of the way off and flinging them behind him before he removed my thong in the same swift motion.

I reached for the hem of the jersey, but he clamped his hands over my wrist.

"Not a fucking chance, Nova," he said, pressing into me until I had no choice but to prop my palms behind me again. "That jersey stays on until I get my fill of you in it."

He spread my legs wide before I could respond, hands pressing against my inner thighs and sliding up until he had my hips in his grasp. He yanked me forward, tongue sweeping in to claim my mouth as my ass hung off the ledge of the counter.

Jaxson cupped me roughly, both of us exhaling a shaky breath when his warm palm covered my aching pussy. I rocked against him, desperate for friction, and then whimpered a moan into his mouth when I got what I was seeking.

"God*damn*," he whispered, his thick fingers sliding between my lips. "You're fucking drenched."

He nestled his middle finger in more, toying with my entrance and smiling against my lips as I bucked my hips in an attempt to have that finger pressing inside me.

"Mmm, so impatient," he mused, licking along my jaw as I let my head fall back. "I should make you beg for it."

"Please," I ground out without him having to ask twice.

"I love that sound. I love how fucking needy you are for me." He pressed inside me, just the tip of his finger, just enough to make me squirm and writhe for more. "You want me inside you, baby?"

His words sent chills racing down to my toes, which curled in anticipation. He wasn't the only one who thought about this every night for the last two months, who thought it would never happen again.

I was savoring every touch, but I was also eager to be filled.

Still... my insecurities were quieted, but they weren't altogether silent.

"Have you... has there been anyone else since we..."

Jaxson's hands stilled, his muscles taut in a way that made my heart leap into my throat.

Oh, God.

He pulled back, nestling between my legs and framing my face with his hands. His eyes searched mine as he let out a heavy breath.

"Nova, don't you understand?" He shook his head. "You fucking ruined me for anyone else. There will *never* be anyone else. Not after you."

He kissed me hard with those words, sealing them like a promise, and then his hands were exploring again, revving me up with every touch. He started crawling back down my body, his eyes set between my thighs.

"I haven't been with anyone else, either," I whispered.

That made him snap his gaze to mine, his jaw tight. "That's because you belong to *me*."

"Yes," I breathed, shivering as he ran his finger along my slick heat. The feminist inside me didn't even pretend to rage.

I wanted to belong to him.

I loved that he belonged to *me*.

"Talk to me, baby. Tell me what you want," he said, teasing me with just a centimeter of penetration again. "You want my mouth on this swollen clit?" he asked, hiking one of my legs up onto his shoulder. The other grappled for purchase on the counter as he descended, shoving his jersey up enough for him to kiss down my navel.

"God, *yes*," I breathed, pinning my lower lip as I watched him suck and bite along my inner thigh. He was such a beast of a man, and he had to bend to accommodate, to kiss me where I was sprawled out on that counter.

I loved that thought, that sight — of Jaxson Brittain bending for me.

Every touch of his mouth and tongue sent shivers up my spine, reminding me he knew *just* how to use them. And when he slid that thick finger all the way inside me, curling it deep as his tongue swept from where he penetrated me up to circle my clit, it was pure ecstasy.

I shook violently at that first touch, that first taste, at what I thought I'd never have again crashing back into my life like a train. I was in his house. He was touching me, kissing me, fucking me with his finger and mouth with a promise to give me more.

It was every fantasy come true, every nightmare that had killed me over the last two months coming back to soothe me and make me whole again.

Because this wasn't a dream, and it wasn't something I would ever have to lose again.

I didn't let myself think too much about *how* the fuck we were going to figure this all out, not when Jaxson settled in-between my thighs and worked me like I was a machine only he knew how to program.

My legs shook where I held them apart — one slung over his shoulder and the other spreading wide along the counter. I wanted to watch him, to soak in the way it felt to slide my hands into that messy head of hair as he licked and sucked in the perfect rhythm to coax my orgasm to the surface.

When he added a second finger to the first, I cried out, giving in and letting myself lie fully back on the counter. My back bowed off it when he sucked my clit and curled those fingers inside me, wiggling them and calling a hot flame to lick along my spine.

"Jaxson," I breathed, popping back up with my eyes hooded. I clawed at his arms.

He knew without me asking what I wanted.

As soon as his mouth released me, his fingers withdrawing and leaving me empty, I shuddered. He pulled me into his arms, my legs like Jell-O as I wrapped around him and held on for dear life. Jaxson walked us through his house with his mouth punishing mine, and I tasted myself on his tongue, felt his heady urgency like a drug through my system.

"Where are we going now?" I asked breathlessly.

We swung into a dim room, Jaxson taking only enough time to push his foot on a pedal that illuminated it with the soft glow from a lamp. My back hit a shelf before I could ask again, before he could answer, and I gasped as we sent several books and something that sounded a lot like glass spiraling to the hardwood floor.

"When I was in my most masochist of states," he said, pinning me against the wood with his hips so he could strip his jersey over my head. He kissed me as soon as the fabric was discarded, his hands snaking around to unfasten my bra next. "I'd imagine bringing you here to my house, to this room, and fucking you against these shelves."

"This is a very bookworm fantasy," I teased, though the words came out breathier than I wanted when he palmed me again, rolling the hot heel of his hand against my clit. It called my orgasm right back to the surface, and I ground my hips against him, gasping a little as my climax teased me.

It was within grasp, my blood ready to rush to that spot where he touched me, but it seemed to hold back, like it didn't want to let go until I had him inside me.

"Are you complaining?" he teased.

"Definitely not. Now put me down and get naked."

He smiled against my urgent kisses, dropping my feet to the floor only long enough to strip. I leaned against the shelf and watched eagerly, one hand plucking at my nipple as the other slid down between my thighs.

Jaxson watched me playing with myself as he toed out of his Oxfords, and he kept those deep blue eyes on me as he shrugged out of his suit jacket next. Button by button, his dress shirt opened, and if I'd thought it was hot to watch him strip out of his usual joggers and t-shirts, it was *nothing* compared to watching him slowly shed a suit.

If I wasn't so focused on him slowly revealing his godlike body that I'd been missing so much, I might have taken the time to appreciate the beautiful library we were in.

As it was, I couldn't give a damn where we were.

I was entirely focused on where his hands wrapped around his belt, how excitement fluttered in my stomach when he flicked the top button of his slacks through the slit and then slowly unzipped them next. He pulled them down along with his briefs, kicking out of them when they hit his ankles.

I bit my lip on a moan when his cock sprang free, my core firing up at the memory of what it felt like to have him inside me. It had been months, and yet I could still remember the distinct combination of pleasure and pain that came with him stretching me.

"You need a napkin?" he asked with a smirk as he descended on me again. "You're drooling a little bit..."

He thumbed the corner of my mouth with the tease, but I couldn't find it in me to joke back as I mounted him, climbing into his arms until he had no choice but to take my weight again.

"Please," I begged, holding on tight as he pressed me into the shelf again. A few more books knocked to the ground, but I didn't care. I hooked one arm around his neck, and my other hand flew up and over my head, gripping the first shelf I found.

I bucked against him, reveling in the way we both trembled at the feel of his thick shaft sliding in-between my legs. I rolled my hips, riding his length without taking him inside me until we were both shaking and cursing and seeing stars.

I could feel the restraint Jaxson was using as he pinned my squirming hips and lined himself up at my entrance. He rocked in only an inch before stopping, his nostrils flaring as goosebumps paraded over every inch of my skin.

"God, *yes*," I breathed, rocking against him. "More."

I used my grip on the shelf and his shoulder to help lift me before sinking down another inch.

"Christ," he cursed, dropping his forehead to mine. "I don't want to hurt you."

"You're not hurting me," I promised him. "You're *healing* me."

He sucked in a stiff breath before kissing me hard, and a flex of his hips had him burying himself another two inches inside me.

I gasped, but the pain zipped through me only a second before pleasure washed in to take over. Gripping his shoulders, I rolled until I took more, until he was meeting me thrust for thrust and stretching me open to fit him all the way inside.

"You have consumed my every waking thought. You have wrecked every dream I've had," he cursed against my lips, kissing along my jaw and my neck next. "I am *obsessed.*"

I couldn't handle the emotion that swirled inside me, the combination of having him after thinking I would never again and the way he whispered those words against my skin.

"I've been thinking of this every night," I confessed, riding him as we sent more books to the floor. "I'd fuck my fingers or my toy and think of this, of *you.*"

"*Damn*, baby," he breathed, sucking my earlobe between his teeth. "You're so filthy, aren't you? Fucking yourself to the thought of me." He held my hips hard enough to make me gasp, and then he slammed into me, stealing my next breath. "I want to hear it. I want you to come and scream my name loud enough to make up for all those times I missed."

I was so close, I knew he wouldn't have to wait long to get his wish.

He fucked me harder, hips slamming into me as the shelf rattled against the wall each time. More books and décor slid off, the crashing sounds around us like a symphony as Jaxson claimed my mouth. And when I slid one hand down between us, it took only a few circles of my clit for my climax to catch.

"Oh, God. Oh, *fuck*, Jax," I breathed, circling faster as he fucked me in a pace that matched my need.

And I combusted.

I thought I'd had orgasms before. I thought I knew what it was like to have the best release of my life ripping through me. But every time before was *nothing* compared to this, to how the wave consumed me from the inside out and drowned out my cries.

I knew I was screaming his name. I knew I was digging my nails into his back hard enough to draw blood. But it was like watching from above, like an out-of-body experience as my body shook and my pussy pulsed around him.

"*Fuck*," he cursed in my ear, and I felt him spill inside me, rocking in so deep I blacked out for a moment. My orgasm was still wrecking me as he found his, and each flex of his hips slammed me into the shelf. I knew the wood would leave bruises on my back. I knew no orgasm in my life would ever feel as powerful as this one.

And I knew even if we were about to set fire to the world we lived in now, I would gladly live in the ashes if it meant I got to be with him.

We surrendered everything.

We laid our old lives to rest, knowing there would be hardship and pain ahead of us. We jumped headfirst into the risk, hand in hand, willing to forsake it all in the name of each other.

There was no walking away this time.

There was no end to this summer.

Jaxson Brittain branded me against that bookshelf, and I inked myself into his skin. One round ended only for the next to begin, and neither of us could get enough, not even when we were too sore and exhausted to go again.

We were desperate, like it wouldn't be enough until we were one person instead of two.

I didn't know what would happen after tonight, but one thing was certain.

We were forever.

We were always.

And there was nothing, and *no one*, who could ever keep us apart.

CHAPTER 37

PRETTY LIES

Grace

I yawned and stretched like a cat the next morning — or maybe it was after noon? I couldn't be sure. All I knew was my muscles were aching as I arched my back and pointed my toes, stretching my arms up overhead and soaking in every deliciously sore area.

Every muscle that protested my movement sent a flash of a memory of the night before striking behind my lids. I bit my lip on a smile as it all replayed — the kitchen, the library, the shower, the bed.

Now, the sun was peeking through the blinds, the shadows playing with the light on my skin as I let out a heavy, sated sigh.

"Waking up to this sight every morning is going to be a real fucking problem."

I peeked one eye open and then the next, and my heart squeezed tight at the view — Jaxson in nothing but a pair of navy-blue boxer briefs holding two mugs of something hot and heavenly smelling.

I want this life.

The thought made my stomach do a flip, a thousand butterfly wings tickling the edges of it. I knew there was still so much in this world that I wanted to see, so many places I wanted to explore. But waking up to Jaxson half-naked and bringing me something warm to drink after fucking my brains out all night brought one truth into focus.

He really was my safe place to land.

And I didn't feel that urge to fly as much anymore, not now that I had a home.

I winced a little as I leaned up in bed, propping myself against the headboard. Just like the hotel outside of St. Louis, we had destroyed his room last night. Hell, we'd destroyed his entire *house*.

I, for one, couldn't wait to go investigate the library or wherever he'd had me that we'd trashed his shelves.

As it was now, I was thoroughly enjoying the view of his abs and chest, of his massive arms and the ink that sprawled along his skin. I thanked him when he handed me one of the mugs and climbed into bed to sit across from me, folding his legs under him.

I took the first sip and moaned. It was some sort of black tea with cream and sugar, sweet and warm and cozy.

"And why is it such a problem?"

"Because today is an off day, and I have nowhere to be, but on the days when I'm supposed to get up early and get to the rink for practice, I'm going to be fucked." He shook his head, his eyes trailing over my body. I didn't bother putting any clothes on yet, and the sheet pooled in my lap, leaving the top half of me exposed. "No way will I be able to walk out the door without touching you."

"Hmm... maybe I'll have to be the responsible one, then." To illustrate that point, I kicked one leg out from under the covers and pressed a foot to his chest to stop him when he leaned in to kiss me.

Jaxson hit me with a sleepy grin that made my chest ache, and then he snatched my ankle and brought it to his lips, kissing along the sensitive skin.

"Is this another challenge to see who will break first? Because I—"

Jaxson stopped mid-sentence at the sound of a strange voice coming from down the hall. It was feminine and yet robotic. I couldn't be sure, but I thought it said something like *front gate*.

He frowned, climbing out of bed and setting his cup of tea on the nightstand.

"What is it?" I asked.

"Someone passing through the front gate," he said. "I forgot to close it last night."

"Delivery, maybe?"

He swallowed, but he was already pulling on a pair of shorts and a t-shirt to investigate. "Maybe. Stay here."

That made my heart leap into my throat, but before he could take even one step toward the door, we both got the answer to our question of who it could be in the form of four loud, insistent knocks on the door.

And my brother's voice.

"Open this fucking door, Brittzy."

Jaxson's eyes shot to mine, and my stomach shriveled to the size of a raisin.

Fuck.

Another lashing of knocks rumbled the house, and Vince yelled even louder. "Open the goddamn door *now*, or I'll kick it down!"

My heart thundered in my ears as Jaxson swallowed, both of us realizing that we didn't have time to talk about our game plan. We were about to face our biggest obstacle right here, right now.

"He doesn't know I'm here," I whispered. "I can hide."

But Jaxson was already shaking his head. He disappeared inside his closet as more knocks sounded, and I swore Vince was actually attempting to kick the door down. Jaxson emerged again and tossed me a t-shirt and a pair of his sweatpants.

"Put these on," he said, and then he walked out the door and down the hall.

"Shit," I cursed, pulling the fabric overhead. "Shit, shit, *shit*."

I barely had the oversized sweatpants pulled up over my hips when I heard what sounded like a body hitting the wall and shaking the whole house. Then, irate footsteps were pounding down the hall.

I pulled the sheet up over me as if I were still nude, or as if it could shield me from what was about to come. But it was no use.

My brother swung through the door, and when his eyes locked on me, his neck and face turned a bright, beet red.

He looked at me, at the absolutely wrecked room, at the mugs of tea we'd abandoned on the table, and then back at me again.

"I'm going to fucking *murder* him."

"Vince, wait!" He had already turned before I could scramble out of bed, and he didn't stop when I asked. I heard him storming down the hall, and I slid into the doorway just in time to watch him shove Jaxson hard in the chest.

"You are a fucking dead man. *Dead*."

Jaxson held his hands up as Vince pointed a threatening finger right in his face. "Vince, take a breath."

"Take a *breath*?" my brother repeated incredulously.

He laughed then, backing up with his tongue pressed against his cheek. He stared at Jaxson like he was Brutus, like he was still holding the knife he'd used to stab my brother in the back.

"We can talk about this," Jaxson said.

"Oh, can we? Sure. Which part would you like to start with?" Vince asked, thrusting his hands out. "Do you want to start with how I trusted you to be a fucking gentleman around my sister and instead, you took her on a fucking road trip behind my back? Would you like to go into detail about how you *both*," he gritted, turning to look at me only briefly before his murderous gaze was back on Jaxson. "Lied to me, to everyone? Would you like to tell me how funny it was to be at the tournament sliding under all our radar?" He shook his head. "Or should we skip to the good part, where I found out along with the entire fucking nation when videos were leaked from Grace's phone this morning?"

Ice slithered through my veins, my next breath so hard to take that black tingled at the edges of my vision.

"What?" I asked, voice barely a breath.

"Yeah," Vince answered with his eyes still hard on Jaxson — who looked like he was going to be sick. "Someone found your phone and posted everything. It's all over the fucking news right now." He gritted his teeth, stepping back into Jaxson's space. "You should see the headlines. They're fucking fantastic. My personal favorite was *Jaxson Brittain Shacking Up with Teammate's Little Sister*."

I pinched my eyes shut, heart threatening to beat out of my chest as I tried to process what he was saying.

Someone had found my phone.

Someone had found my phone and broken into it.

It wouldn't have been hard to do. I didn't even have a password on it. I just thought with where I'd left it, it would have been safe. No one was going back in. The only person who could have even found it would have been a teammate's family member, maybe a wife or girlfriend, or a janitor.

I realized then how fucking stupid I'd been. Who's to say there wasn't a girlfriend or a wife of a player who would have jumped at the chance? Who's to say a janitor wouldn't have sold to the highest bidder to make some cash?

I'd been so desperate for Jaxson that I didn't care about anything other than getting to him, and once I did, I couldn't stand the thought of either of us leaving.

I thought it could wait. And now, we were both paying the price of my ignorance.

The word *leak* replayed in my mind on a loop, and then I covered my mouth with my hands as I catalogued everything they would have found.

The pictures I took of Jaxson when he didn't even realize it.

The videos of us — some innocent, some far from it.

All of that was supposed to only be for me. I didn't even have social media. That phone was more like my journal than anything else.

Now, the rest of the world had access to my most private thoughts and experiences — whether I wanted them to or not.

When neither of us spoke, Vince shook his head, over and over, eyes washing the length of Jaxson as if he was seeing him for the first time. Suddenly, he turned and stormed toward me.

"Get your shit. We're leaving. *Now*."

I almost shot into action at his words. My instinct was to do exactly as he said, but my heart refused to let me move.

"Grace," Vince warned, steaming. "Get. Your fucking. Shit."

"Vince, I need you to take it down a notch," Jaxson tried just as I said, "I'm not leaving."

"The hell you aren't!" Vince ignored Jaxson and pointed at me, his jaw tight. "We have a PR *nightmare* to handle. Mom and Dad are already at the house with Maven making a plan with the team."

That made my stomach crawl. What would Mom say? Oh, *God*... what would *Dad* say?

"I'll come, too," Jaxson tried, pushing off the wall.

"You," Vince growled, spinning and pressing his finger into Jaxson's chest. "Will stay the fuck away from her, and from me, and from my entire family."

"Vince, *stop*. You're overreacting," I said to my brother. "It'll all blow over, we'll—"

"Sorry, sis, but I'm pretty sure a video of my fucking *teammate* telling you how good you were at sucking his cock isn't going to *blow over*."

Shame and horror washed over me as I remembered the exact video he was referring to — the one we'd taken at Wilson State Park. That moment had meant so much to me. It was the first time I'd cried in... I couldn't even remember how long. It was me baring my soul to Jaxson and him listening, holding space for every feeling I had.

He'd said that last part as a joke to make me smile, to lighten the mood. It wasn't crude. It was... beautiful.

But now, everyone would judge it, judge *us*.

Suddenly, my brother was shoved hard from behind, and Jaxson cornered him, absolutely seething.

"Watch your mouth when you're talking to my girl."

"Your *girl?*" Vince laughed, shoving him back. "That's my fucking *sister,* you punk!"

He wound up to hit him, and I screamed, running until I could step between them. Jaxson hauled me up out of the way and put himself as a barrier between me and my brother, which made Vince even more pissed.

He was shaking, face redder than I'd ever seen it as he looked at where I was hiding behind Jaxson. I knew, even in the heat of the moment, that he wasn't just angry. He was hurt. He was upset we'd lied to him. He was likely devastated about what the news was saying about me, because he cared about me.

But right now, all he could reach for was rage. And I didn't know how to get through to him.

His eyes flicked between us, and then he forced one long, calm breath, smoothing his hands over his shirt.

"Grace, I need you to get your belongings and go to the car," he said, his voice more level.

"No," I tried, but Jaxson turned to face me, his hands on my arms. I knew before he even spoke what he was going to say, and I shook my head violently. "*No,*" I said again.

"Just for now," Jaxson promised me. "Go be with your family and let me talk to the team's PR agency. We will get this figured out."

"I don't want to leave you." Tears flooded my eyes, and Jaxson framed my face, lowering his gaze to mine.

"We will work this out together. I promise. I'm not going anywhere. Okay?" He waited until I nodded, and I knew he could see everything I could about my brother in that moment. There was no reasoning with him. "But right now, your family needs you to go be with them, and I am not welcome."

Vince snorted behind him, but Jaxson kept my attention on him.

"We'll figure it out," he promised again.

I wanted to kiss him, to feel the comfort and security of his lips on mine. My entire body was trembling now, the facts of what my brother revealed sinking into my skin like claws.

Someone had leaked our videos, our photos, our texts.

It was such a personal invasion of privacy, I could barely breathe.

With one last squeeze, Jaxson released me, and I numbly gathered my clothes off the kitchen floor. I ambled toward the front door with my head spinning and my heart pounding.

Through my haze, I heard my brother hit Jaxson with one final blow.

"I trusted you."

I froze at the sound of it, knowing those words would break Jaxson. But I couldn't turn around, couldn't comfort him — not right now.

Vince's hand found my shoulder and guided me out the door.

He must have shut the gate after he came through it, because there was already a small gathering of paparazzi, and their cameras all began to flash when we emerged.

Vince shielded me, and with the landscaping around Jaxson's property, none of them got a clear shot before I was ducking into the passenger side of my brother's Maserati. The windows were tinted far past the legal shade of darkness, but I still hid my face as we pulled out of

Jaxson's driveway and Vince sped us across town toward the beach.

I didn't even have my phone to text Jaxson and tell him I loved him, that we would get through this, that everything was okay.

The weight of the morning socked me right in the gut, panic zipping through my chest and making me curl in on myself.

And I realized maybe it was a good thing I couldn't text him.

Because those last two statements were just pretty lies.

Nothing was okay.

I wasn't sure it ever would be again.

CHAPTER 38

WITH MY LIFE

Jaxson

I walked into the morning skate the next day with my chin held high.

I knew Vince would have loved to have seen me with my tail between my legs, with my head hanging. But I refused.

I wasn't sorry.

I wasn't sorry for the way I felt about Grace, for the way she felt about me, or for anything we'd done. The invasion of our privacy was against our will, and the only thing I was mildly apologetic for was that we couldn't be the ones to tell Vince and everyone else about us. I hated that they found out this way, but again, that wasn't on me.

The locker room buzz died in an instant when I walked through the door. I had on headphones, but nothing playing in them. I just didn't want to field questions — especially not after spending all fucking day and night with the public relations team doing just that.

After Grace and Vince left, I had screamed. I'd thrown shit and stormed around like a beast until my rage could simmer. Then, I'd called coach, asking him where he needed me to be and what I needed to do to get this shit handled.

It wasn't as easy as I would have liked. I wished we could threaten the news outlets with lawsuits, but they hadn't leaked anything that was in the realm of revenge porn. It was all relatively wholesome content — other than the fact that they kept replaying the video where Grace had asked me to tell her something good, and I'd responded with my stupid remark about her going down on me.

Every time I thought about it, I had to pinch my eyes shut and force a breath. I was murderous thinking how many people had seen something meant for only us.

Still, I had to focus on what I could control — which wasn't much. I had the team working on a statement, one I wanted to give as soon as I talked to Grace and got her permission.

As much as it hurt to know I'd let my team down, it hurt worse to think of the pain I knew she was in.

And I couldn't even reach her — because she didn't have her fucking phone.

I didn't say a word or look at anyone in that locker room as I got dressed for our morning skate. We were facing off against New York tonight, and I had to find a way to get focused. Because if there was one way to make it up to my teammates, it was to show up and help us win a fucking game.

Tomorrow, we'd be flying to Atlanta for our first away matchup. My chest was tight with the resolve to get this all figured out before then.

I refused to leave Grace without her knowing that this changed nothing for me.

I still wanted her. I would give up *all of it* for her.

I just hoped she felt the same.

It killed me not knowing what was going through her head right now. I also hated that I couldn't be there to hold her hand as we faced her parents — together. If I were her father, I'd want to kill me.

This wasn't the way any of it was supposed to happen.

I jumped when a hand squeezed my shoulder, and I slid my headphones off one ear, turning to find Will and Carter behind me. Carter had a solemn smile, and Will wore his signature hard ass expression, but even that was tinged with sadness.

"You good?" Daddy P asked.

"No," I answered honestly. "But I'm ready to play."

He nodded, satisfied with the answer. Carter, on the other hand, looked like he wanted to hug me. I turned and slid my headphones back into place just in case he actually planned to.

Vince showed up late, looking like he'd slept just as poorly as I had. He froze at the sight of me, like he was surprised I showed up. All of our teammates watched us with bated breath, but Vince just scowled and stormed to his locker as I finished up and made my way out to the ice.

I wanted to talk to him. I wanted to squash all this shit. I hated the way he looked at me, like I'd double-crossed him, like I'd gone from one of his best friends to his number one enemy overnight. He was like a brother to me — and I didn't know if I'd ever get the chance to make it right.

But for now, we had a game to focus on.

The morning skate before a match was always chill. It was a way to get loose and ready, and we were usually rambunctious during it. We'd chirp each other and play stupid games on the ice to shake off all the nerves.

But today, the rink was deadly quiet.

All we could hear were blades skidding across the ice and pucks hitting the net or the bar. Our DJ even seemed to play the music softer, like he was afraid blasting rap music too loudly would instigate a fight.

For the first part of practice, Vince stayed away from me, and I did the same. But somewhere around the thirty-minute mark, he shoulder-checked me into the boards.

I hadn't expected the hit, and I slammed into the glass, staying there a long moment to force a calming breath. That little move alone told me how much all of this was affecting him, because if coach would have seen that shit, his ass would have been toast.

I went right back to skating and ignoring him.

Until the fucker did it again.

"That's enough, Tanny Boy," Will warned from the goal, but Vince didn't so much as acknowledge him.

And five minutes later, as he was skating in the opposite direction I was, he slung his stick out lightning-fast and tripped me.

I hit the ice hard, breath knocked out of me the instant my chest made contact, and I didn't miss the *ohh* that came from my teammates when I did. I hadn't been skating at full speed. If I had, I knew Vince wouldn't have tripped me — no matter how pissed he was. He wouldn't want to put me at risk of getting truly injured, of putting our team out of a defenseman.

No, he'd known I'd be alright, but he wanted to make a point.

And now, my jaw was set with the determination to do the same.

I tried to calm myself down, tried to find that breath — but it was no use. I popped up off the ice and skated fast and furious across the rink to where he was watching me.

"You wanna do this now?" I asked. "Let's fucking go."

I ripped the Velcro from around my wrists and then slung my gloves off just as I reached him, and Vince dropped his stick, his eyes hard on mine as he got rid of his own gloves. I didn't stop or slow down, didn't wait for him to be ready. I plowed straight into him and landed the first punch right to his jaw.

It was madness after that.

Our teammates screamed for us to stop, several of them trying to break us up as fists flew. Every time they'd tear one of us off the other, we'd break free and go again.

I was distantly aware of the punches he landed, of how my lip split and I tasted blood — but it wasn't enough to make either of us stop. We fought like it was game seven of the Stanley Cup playoffs, and the other had gotten a cheap shot on one of our teammates.

Daddy P had the most successful attempt at putting an end to it, standing between us with his hands hard on our chests. But Vince swiped his arm out of the way and shoved him hard, clearing the space long enough to connect his fist to my ear.

I hissed as the pain struck, my head ringing, and then I attacked, taking Vince to the ice in a tackle that would have earned me some attention from the NFL and pinning him there as I sat up and raised my fist.

A whistle blew, loud and long and right in my ear, making me wince and giving Vince just enough time to kick free. Then, all of our teammates stepped in, peeling us apart and holding us back from one another.

And in the middle of it all was Coach McCabe.

It didn't matter that he wasn't much older than I was. Coach commanded respect — he always had. He was severe and intentional in everything he did, and he had a way of making me feel like a child when he wasn't happy.

Right now, he was fucking murderous, his chest heaving as he looked at me, then Vince, and back again.

"You've got to be fucking kidding me," he said, his jaw tight. Then, he grabbed us both by the neck like we were little boys, and he steered us toward the bench.

He kept his grip firm even when we were off the ice and walking through the tunnel, and he didn't stop when we hit the locker room. Instead, he walked us into the back hall and threw us into a dark conference room where we typically met to watch video.

Coach flicked on the lights, pointed at the space between us, and said, "Figure it out."

Then, he left, slamming the door so hard behind him that I swore the entire arena shook.

Vince and I were both breathing heavy in the otherwise silent room, each of us wiping our faces and staring at the blood on our hands when we did. I flopped down in one of the chairs, and Vince leaned against the wall, folding his arms over his chest.

He wouldn't look at me, and neither of us spoke.

I ran over it in my head a thousand times last night — what I would say to Vince when I got the chance to speak. But now, it all felt trivial and like it wasn't enough. It was one thing to tell him I had feelings for his sister, but to have to try to explain it all after the phone leak was another beast altogether.

He was furious, and that was the easiest emotion to reach for. But I knew more than that, he was hurt. And he needed to be the one to speak first, to let it all out.

So, I waited, bending down to unlace my skates and pull them off. Vince did the same, ignoring me as our breaths evened out.

When the silence was heavy around us, Vince sniffed, wiping his nose with the back of his wrist and grumbling when he saw blood again. He blew out a long breath, then looked at me for the first time.

"I have nothing to say to you," he growled. "And to be quite honest, if I had it my way, you'd be off this team and out of this fucking league. But we can't always get what we want, can we? So, let's just agree to stay clear of each other and focus on winning."

He pushed off the wall like that was his final word and we were done, but I stood just as quickly, blocking his exit.

"That's not going to fly."

Vince tilted his head to the side like he was surprised at my audacity. "I don't think that's your call to make."

"It's not. It's Coach's, and our teammates out there who will feel this rift between us whether you decide to face it or not. Now, stop beating around the bush and say what you want to say."

"I don't have—"

"Liar."

"YOU BETRAYED ME."

His chest heaved with the burst, and I nodded, holding my tongue until he got it out.

"My whole life, I have been protective of Grace. Because she's needed it. She's too fucking good for this world, and my bet is that you know that, too. So, when I see my teammates or my friends drooling when she walks past them, I put an end to it quick. She's not a fucking puck bunny, and she's too fucking young for any of you pricks. I have always done what I could do to keep her from having her heart smashed, and I thought sitting her with you that night in Austin was the best bet to do that. Because I thought we were friends. I thought you respected me and would, in turn, respect her." He shook his head. "Turns out I was feeding her to the wolf."

"I never intended to cross a line — not that night and not after," I explained. "I knew you trusted me, and I took that to heart."

Vince scoffed. "Clearly."

"I did," I insisted. "But something happened that night that I couldn't explain even if I had a fucking book to write it all out. You're right. Grace *is* too good for this world. She's also the kind of woman who has the power to walk into your life and shake you out of a haze — which is exactly what she did to me."

Vince gritted his teeth, moving for the door again, but I slid in front of him.

"I understand that she's your sister," I said. "But she's so much more than that, Vince. She is a beautiful human being who is autonomous of that label — but you and your family have never seen her that way."

"Fuck you," he said, slamming his hands against my chest. "Don't talk about my family like you know us."

"How would you feel if the roles were reversed, huh?" I asked, stepping right up to his face. "What if it was Grace who was the successful athlete, who your parents doted on and revolved their entire world around? What if you had no choice? What if you never asked yourself what *you* wanted to do because you didn't feel like there was space for you? What if you were always just *Grace's brother*? How would you feel?"

He narrowed his gaze, scoffing, but before he could refute it, I jumped in again.

"Don't act like it isn't true. Grace has always felt an unbearable pressure on her shoulders to be the happy one — no matter what. She's never shared what her dreams are with you or your parents because there was never any room for her to *have* a dream.

"When you were upset or not playing your best, she did anything she could to make you feel better. When your parents were stressed about where you would go to college or what team would draft you, she was there to put a smile on their face. Every game, she was there for you. She *still* is," I reminded him, hoping that would conjure up how she always answered every call before a match to do the dance for him that had become part of his pre-game rituals.

I thought I saw his brows smooth a bit, like I might have been getting through — so I kept on.

"Have you or your family ever asked her what *she* wants to do for a holiday, or how *she* wants to spend even one fucking night? It's the Vince Tanev show, and to Grace's credit, she's been fine with that. In fact, I'd say she's been your biggest fan since she was born. But you don't get to sit here and tell me she's your sister, like that gives you some fucking right over who she dates and what she does with her life. Frankly, you're a fucking idiot if you can't see that she is more than capable of handling herself. And she is allowed to make her own choices."

Vince's expression definitely sobered then, the line between his brows softening the more I spoke, as if he really never saw it until now.

"Grace has opened me up in a way no one else ever has," I continued. "From the first fucking night we spent on that stupid bus. She made me laugh. She made me feel something other than numb. And when I saw her come to your house crying over that dumbass punk, yeah — I jumped at the chance to make her feel better. I asked her what she needed, and she said she wanted to drive. So, that's what we did.

"And I know I should have told you then. I understand the risk I took and the way I broke your trust by going behind your back. But honestly, I had no fucking idea what I was doing. All I knew was that I felt a pull to her that I had never felt before in my life. Judging by the way you asked Maven to marry you after knowing her for less than nine months, my bet is you can understand that kind of crazy."

Vince swallowed at that, his eyes falling to the floor.

"I *see* her, Vince," I said, my voice softer now. "Not just the happy-go-lucky side of her, either. That girl has been looking for a safe place to break her entire life, and I gave her one. I could talk to you all day about it. I could make a fucking PowerPoint, but it wouldn't change the fact that you will *never* understand what we have. No one will.

"What happened on that road," I added, pointing toward the door. "It was something meant only for us. You think I don't fucking hate that her phone got leaked? You think it doesn't make my stomach turn that her privacy was violated, that the world is making assumptions about her based on jokes that were meant to stay between us? It fucking kills me. Alright? But we will handle it. Together. Me and her. Because I don't care whether you forgive me or not. I don't care if you hate me for the rest of your life. I am never, *never* letting that girl go."

Vince lifted his gaze, looking at me for what felt like the first time since he'd stormed into my house. I felt like he was both sizing me up and seeing me in a new light. He narrowed his eyes a bit, like he was looking for some sort of sign that I might be lying. Then, he blew out a breath and ran a hand through his hair, slumping into the nearest seat.

He was silent for a long time, and then he shook his head and said, "I hear you."

My next breath deflated out of me, and I realized then that I was shaking. I made my way to the seat next to him and flopped down, too.

"I didn't know she felt like that," he said quietly. "Which tracks, since clearly I've been so caught up in my own life, I haven't thought to ask about hers. I've always been so protective of her..." He shook his head, pain etching his brows. "And really, I didn't know her at all. It's like she's always been the ten-year-old little sister to me. I didn't realize..."

"That she's grown up now?"

He sighed, nodding.

"You know, if you would have just fucking *told* me you were interested in her—"

"You would have told me to fuck off," I finished for him.

He opened his mouth to argue, but shut it again just as quickly. "Well, you still should have told me."

"You're right. And I planned to. *We* planned to. But just like the rest of her life, you don't get to dictate when or how things happen. It's her decision, and mine. You think we didn't see how this would all blow up? You think we didn't realize all the reasons we couldn't and shouldn't be together?" I laughed at that. "Trust me — *no one* has run over that list more than me. She's younger than I am. She's my teammate's sister. She wants a life of adventure when I'm bound to the team and what it wants for me. We don't make sense, and we *tried* to walk away from each other. We let ourselves have the summer and were willing to sacrifice what we felt because we knew what we were up against."

I let out a soft laugh, eyes losing focus on my hands.

"But it was like fighting against a rip current, man. We couldn't do it. We made ourselves both *miserable* in our attempt. And last night, we decided we'd face whatever consequences we had to, but we were going to be together." I swallowed. "It fucking sucks that you found out the way you did, and I'm sorry for that. But I'm not sorry for loving your sister. I will never apologize for that."

Vince frowned. "You love her?"

"So much so I was willing to face your wrath and every judgmental prick who had something to say about it. So much so that I was ready to walk away from everything if I had to — including hockey. So much so that I couldn't walk away from her even knowing she could do better, *be* better without me."

He sighed, sinking into his chair, and I knew without him saying it that he understood.

He felt the same way about Maven.

"I can't undo what's already done," I said. "But I can promise you that I will do everything I can to clean up this mess. More than that, I can promise you that no one in this world will love her harder than I will, and I will protect her with my fucking life." I balled my hand into a fist and hit my chest. "With my *life*, brother. I know that, in your eyes, no one will ever be good enough for her, and I'm not arguing that fact. All I'm asking is that you let me try to be.

I'm asking that, for once, you listen to her and what *she* wants — and trust that she's old enough to make her own damn decisions."

Vince smirked, cocking a brow at me. "Did you rehearse that?"

"Maybe a few hundred times when I couldn't sleep last night."

He chuckled, sitting up and planting his hands on his knees. "I hate that you lied to me," he said. "But... I understand why you did. And I know what it's like to have to keep a secret like that when all you want is for the world to know. I... I'm sorry," he said, shocking himself and me both. "For being such a beast that you couldn't come to me and tell me the truth. I couldn't help it. She's my little sister and I just..."

"I know," I said, clamping a hand on his shoulder. He stiffened at first, but then relaxed, nodding.

"You're one of my best friends, Jax," he said, lifting his gaze to meet mine. "I know we don't talk about the heavy stuff much, but we don't have to for me to know you've been through it. I know you work harder than anyone, other than maybe Daddy P — and that doesn't count because that man is a machine."

We both chuckled at that.

"And I also know that if anyone will take care of my sister the way I have tried to, it's you."

Emotion hit my throat like a fist with those words, and I swallowed, nodding. "Thank you."

The corners of his mouth tilted up, and then he stood, wiping a bit of dried blood from his knuckle. "So, do we hug now or what?"

I stood, too, opening my arms for him to bring it in.

But before he could, I nut tapped him, and then took off running down the hall.

Vince hobbled after me, half-groaning and half-threatening my life as I swung into the locker room where our teammates were just coming in off the ice. I weaved through them with Vince chasing me, but this time we were both laughing, and when he finally caught me, he grabbed my underwear and pulled hard, giving me the worst wedgie of my life.

Carter jumped in on the fun, grabbing the back of Vince's jersey and pulling it up over his head. That made Vince run straight into a locker door that was open and curse before he was chasing Carter — all while I attempted to dig my underwear out of my ass.

Daddy P rolled his eyes, but I saw the smirk he hid.

My chest was instantly lighter, my heart beating steadier. I knew there was still a shit show to navigate with the media, but with Vince's blessing, I felt like everything else we had to face was like a basket full of kittens.

Today, I would focus on showing up for my team, on kicking New York's ass and starting our season off with two home game wins in a row.

And tonight, I'd start my next adventure with Grace.

With *just* Grace.

I couldn't wait to see where the road would take us this time.

CHAPTER 39

THE IDEA OF A HOME

Grace

My parents wouldn't let me go to the game.

For once, I didn't feel like kicking and screaming and demanding to make my own decisions like the adult I was. Because as much as I wanted to be there for Jaxson *and* for Vince, I knew I wasn't ready to face the swarm of cameras — professional or otherwise.

The entire country had their mind made up about me at the current moment, which was fine. I didn't care. But I also didn't want to hear their assessment of me screamed loud enough for the whole arena to hear. It was bad enough reading the headlines.

So, I sat on Vince's couch with my parents and Maven, watching numbly and counting down the minutes to when it would all be over. I didn't know *what* had happened, but my brother and Jaxson were both sporting fresh cuts and bruises on their faces and knuckles, and Jaxson had reached me earlier by calling Maven's phone.

He'd assured me things were okay, and asked if he could see me tonight.

As if that was a fucking question.

Now, I was wishing I could fast-forward time to when I was in his arms.

Maven sat curled up next to me on the couch, and she squeezed my wrist when the first period ended. "Want to take a walk on the beach?"

I looked over to my parents, as if they might tell me no, but Mom smiled and nodded. Dad still looked a bit green from the events of the past few days, which was understandable provided the things being said about his little girl, but even he managed a slight tilt of his lips.

"You're not in prison," he said. "Just be careful and call us if there are any lowlifes with cameras out there."

My eyes filled with tears — which had been a common theme for the last thirty-something hours. I was pretty sure my parents had seen me cry more in that time than in my entire life.

But this time, I cried because I was thankful, because in a situation where my parents could have been nightmares — they'd surprised me. Mom had held me and soothed me and assured me more times than I could count that nothing was my fault, and that I hadn't done anything wrong. And Dad, though I knew the things being said about his little girl were driving him mad, was just as supportive. He had held me as I sobbed and told me he was there, that I wasn't alone.

Neither of them had said a single bad word about Jaxson.

Then again — Vince had done enough of that for all of us.

I flung my arms around them both, hugging them tight as Mom let out a surprised, "Oh!" and Dad stiffened before hugging me in return.

"I love you," I whispered.

They softened, leaning into me. "We love you, too, sweetheart," Mom said.

When I pulled back, I held her hand in mine. "I want to talk to you guys and Vince," I said. "When all the dust has settled."

"Any time, whenever you're ready to speak, we'll be here to listen," Mom promised.

I squeezed her hand, and then Maven and I ambled out into the humid Florida air.

I sighed when my toes hit the sand, finding comfort in that and the soft waves rolling in the distance. Maven threaded her arm through mine and led the way.

"I'm proud of you."

I laughed. "For being stupid enough to leave my phone in the bathroom?"

"For handling this whole situation with grace. See what I did there?"

She winked and I nudged her, both of us toppling a bit in the sand before we found a straight line again.

"I mean it," she said. "What happened to you... it's completely fucked. I know very well how nasty people on the Internet can be, and I know this can't be easy for you. But you've held your head high. You've faced your parents and your brother, and I know that had to be hard to do."

"Especially when Vince essentially turned into a dragon."

Maven chuckled. "I think it's kind of hot when he's ragey," she confessed. "But not toward you."

"I wonder what happened between them today."

"Judging by their faces, they fought it out," Maven guessed. "But, if Vince's texts earlier, and the fact that Jaxson felt bold enough to call you through my phone is any indicator... my guess is that *after* they fought, they talked."

My chest filled with hope. "Why do I still feel like I'm going to be sick?"

"Well," Maven said. "You had your privacy violated, which never feels nice. And even though things are smoothing out, you're still in very choppy water. The media isn't going to quit." She sighed with that. "And I imagine you and Jaxson have a lot to talk about."

I swallowed. "Yeah."

"What are you most nervous about?"

"I would have said my brother before all this," I said. "But now... I don't know. I guess just everything we've been hiding behind up until now, all the ways we don't make sense."

"Why, because he's older?"

I nodded. "That's part of it."

"And because you want to travel the world and he's stuck in Tampa?"

I chuckled. "That's been part of it, too. Except..."

"Except now, you don't feel that call to roam as strongly as you did, do you?"

I stopped, pulling her down into the sand with me. "You're far too good at this."

"Livia has rubbed off on me. I swear, that woman is a Jedi."

"It's not that I don't want to travel anymore, because I do. There's so much I want to see and do..."

"But you also love being with Jaxson. Here. You like the idea of a home."

My eyes welled again. "Yes."

"It's okay to want both. Who's to say you can't travel while he's busy with the hockey season? Meet him at away games when you can, come home to Tampa when you want to. And during the off-season, you two can travel together."

My chest expanded with that dash of hope again. "You really think it could be so simple?"

"Judging by the way that man literally risked it *all* for you?" Maven shook her head on a smile. "He's down bad, sis. And you are, too. The rest?" She waved a hand in the air. "Just logistics."

I leaned a head on her shoulder, stomach floating on the wings of a hummingbird as I thought about it all.

If my brother really was okay with it, and so were my parents — I didn't care what the rest of the world thought. Truthfully, even if they *weren't* okay with it, it wouldn't have mattered.

I wanted a life with Jaxson Brittain — rain or shine, hail or blistering snowstorm.

In just a few hours, I'd tell him that.

And we'd face whatever came next together.

• • •

After the game — which the Ospreys won by two — my parents, Maven, and I waited up for Vince and Jaxson. The second we heard cars in the driveway, I was sprinting out the door, and I didn't stop until I was launching myself into Jaxson's arms.

He'd just stepped up out of his vintage Porsche, but he caught me with a spin, holding me to him and breathing in deep like I was his own personal brand of oxygen. I threaded my fingers into his hair and kissed him, all the tension in my chest instantly releasing once I did.

"Are you okay?" he asked, sweeping my hair out of my face like *I* was the one with the bruises.

I thumbed the one coloring his left eye. "I think *I* should be asking that question."

Jaxson grinned, and as he sat me down, my brother made a loud gagging noise.

"Yeah, listen," Vince said, slinging his bag over one shoulder and draping his other arm around Maven. "I'm going to need to never see that shit again."

"As if I haven't had to watch you hang all over her," I pointed out.

Maven held up a finger. "She's not wrong."

"That's different," Vince combatted. "We're not as gross about it."

"I call bullshit," Jaxson interjected. "Pretty sure you mauling her in your lap on the party bus is the whole reason your sister couldn't even stand to sit next to you, which led you to sending her back to sit with me."

Vince blinked. "I really did this to myself, didn't I?" He shook his head then. "Still, it's not the same. We don't make out in public," he tried, looking to Maven for backup.

She grimaced, shrugging as if to say, "Well, if I'm being honest..."

My brother continued arguing his point as Maven laughed and dragged him inside.

When they were gone, Jaxson slid his hand down to intertwine with mine, and we both slowly made our way to my parents.

My father stood tall, chest puffed, and Mom smiled sympathetically at us both.

"Mr. Tanev," Jaxson said. "Mrs. Tanev. I just want to say—"

"I'll tell you what I told her," my mom interjected. "You have nothing to be sorry for. Your relationship is your business and yours alone. I'm just sorry for what happened to you. It's a horrid thing, and I hope whoever did it gets their karma."

I leaned into Jaxson's arm, hiding my giggle and blush. My mom was usually so proper. I loved when she let the mama bear side out.

"I hope so, too," Jaxson said, shaking her hand.

He reached for my father's next, who eyed that hand like a bug before finally taking it in a firm shake. He let out a throaty exhale like he was suppressing the urge to shoot flames. "We'll talk more later, but for now, I just need you to know that's my little girl, and if you hurt her..."

"Dad," I groaned.

"I will do everything in my power not to," Jaxson promised.

Dad seemed satisfied with that, at least for now, and he hooked an arm around Mom to lead her inside, leaving me and Jaxson alone.

At last.

He let out a long breath, tucking me into his side for a hug as he bent to kiss my hair. His scent made me nostalgic — the leather and fresh-cut cedar. It brought me back to our road trip, my heart squeezing at the memories.

"It's been torture to be away from you through this," Jaxson said. "I am so fucking sorry for what's happening."

"It's not your fault," I said, peeking up at him. "I'm the dummy who left my phone in a bathroom."

"We all do that," Jaxson argued. "This is on the piece of shit who decided they had a right to what was inside that phone."

The team was doing everything they could to find out who the "source" was who'd leaked everything from my phone. Part of me hoped they'd find out who it was so that person would get fired or exposed. The other part of me thought that they must have been very sad and very desperate for money to do something like this, and I pitied them for that enough to not wish them any harm.

"Either way — what's done is done," I said. "We can't control any of that."

"I want to make a statement," Jaxson announced, threading his hand in mine again and steering us toward the beach. "I'm so fucking angry at them for making you out to be some..."

"Whore?" I finished for him, and his jaw tightened, so I leaned into him on a smile. "I'm *your* little whore, remember?"

He growled, attacking my neck with kisses as his fingers dug into my side. I squealed with laughter until our feet hit the sand, and we both kicked off our shoes before continuing toward the water.

"I want to set the record straight," he continued. "I want to tell the whole fucking world that we're together, and that those photos and videos and texts were private — between two consenting adults. I'm also still trying to figure out if we can press charges against—"

"Why does it matter?"

He frowned.

"I'm serious," I said. "Listen, I hate it as much as you do, but making a statement, defending ourselves... it only calls more attention. And trust me — those people who are posting those awful things about us? They've already made up their minds. Nothing we do or say is going to change how they think about the situation. If anything, it'll just give them more ammo to drag us with."

"Fuck," Jaxson cursed, running a hand through his hair. He slumped down in one of Maven's loungers by the water, and I took my seat in his lap. "You're right."

"Mmm, say it again," I teased, kissing his neck. "Slower this time. Drop your voice a level."

He tickled my sides until I was squirming, and then wrapped his arms around me, bringing my forehead down to his.

"I want to protect you," he said. "I want to keep you safe."

"From the media?" I laughed. "Babe, there's a reason I don't have social media. I don't give two shits what strangers think about me. I've been weird my whole life. I'm the subject of a million drunk night out stories for people who don't even know my name." I shrugged. "Who cares what they think?"

He slid a thumb across my jaw, shaking his head. "You're something else."

"What *I* want to know is what happened between you and my brother."

"Oh, we brawled on the ice this morning," he said, and I laughed as I smoothed a finger over the cut on his lip. "Coach all but threw us into a conference room and made us stay until we figured it out."

"And did you?"

"Yeah," he said. "Yeah, I really think we did. But you know, I think you should talk to him, too. And your parents."

"I plan to," I promised. "I think there's a lot I have been needing to say for a long time."

"That reminds me," he said, smoothing a hand over my thigh where I sat in his lap. "I didn't get to tell you, but I set boundaries with my dad."

My eyes shot wide. "You did?"

He nodded. "I did. I told him if he wanted to be in my life, he needed to *be* in it. No more coaching, no more shit-talking, and no more unwarranted advice. I told him I'd still support him and Mom, but that I wanted a real relationship between us."

"And?"

He deflated a bit. "And I'm pretty sure I don't have parents in my life now."

My heart cracked, and I wrapped him up in a hug. "I'm so sorry, Jaxson."

"Me, too," he said. "I could hear Mom crying on the other end, which tells me she heard the whole thing. But, you know... she's an adult, too. She could have grabbed the phone and talked to me. She could have put her foot down with Dad. Unfortunately, I don't think that will ever happen, but I'm done making it my problem. I'm done being the punching bag."

I squeezed where I held him. "I'm proud of you, but I hate that it went down like that."

Jaxson pulled back until he could search my eyes with his own. "It's okay. Because you're my family now."

My chest expanded, eyes prickling with tears. I groaned and swatted them away before they could fall. "I am so fucking tired of crying! Stop being cute."

He chuckled, his hand sliding farther up my thigh. "I can be dirty, if you prefer."

Heat rushed to my core at those words. "I will absolutely be taking you up on that later. But for now..." I played with the hair at the nape of his neck. "I want to talk about us."

"What about us?"

"What happens now? What... *are* we?"

I hated the insecurity that slipped through with that, but I needed to know. I needed to hear him say it. After years of looking too far into situationships, and giving more feelings than I was getting in return, I didn't trust my judgment — even when my heart begged me to. I needed words to affirm me, to soothe the anxiety rioting in my rib cage.

"Are you asking me to be your boyfriend?"

I scrunched my nose at him. "Maybe not, if you're going to be such a brat about it."

"Oh, now *I'm* the brat?" Jaxson smirked, tapping my ass for me to lift it so he could reach into his pocket. Then, he had me hold out my hand, and he dropped a small, cool chain into it.

I frowned, holding it up to try to inspect it under the moon and soft light coming from Vince's house. Jaxson pulled out his phone and shined the flashlight on it, and I sucked in a breath at the charm at the end of a chain.

A tiny silver star.

"I remember thinking you were insane when you read my palm in Austin," he said, smirking to himself. "And I was fairly certain you were bullshitting."

"*Completely* bullshitting," I confirmed.

"But you nailed me down. Even then. You could see the weight I was holding, could see how stuck I felt before I even realized I felt it. Against all logic, I wanted to kiss you that night. I wanted to claim you even then. And when you swung back into my life two weeks later, it was as if I didn't have a choice." He swallowed, his eyes finding mine. "I don't think I did. I don't think I've ever had a choice when it comes to you."

My heart swelled so big it felt like my rib cage was a prison.

"I told you in Atlanta that you burn brighter than anyone else in the room, little Nova," he said, taking the chain from my hands. He began fastening it around my neck. "And if you're a star, then you're *my* star — my sun. From this moment on, I only want to exist in your orbit."

I thumbed the charm where it sat on my chest, twisting to face him.

"As long as you'll have me," he added.

"I have a question first."

"By all means. Ask anything."

I twisted until I could straddle his lap, winding my arms around his neck. "Would you rather... spend next off-season on another road trip, or should we try something new. Say... a cruise? Maybe the Bahamas? Oh! Or the Med!"

He licked his bottom lip on a smile, framing my face with his hands and pulling me closer. "Oh, *definitely* the Med. But let's charter something private. There are too many dirty things I can think of for us to do on a boat for us to have an audience."

He covered my laugh with a kiss, holding me tight to him as I did the same. Every sweep of his tongue lit my heart on fire, and I clung to him like I'd never be close enough.

Before I could take that kiss where I really wanted to — which was to unlock my fantasy of being railed on a beach — Jaxson pulled back, holding his phone out again. He turned on the flash and pointed the camera right at me, making me laugh and shield my eyes against the light.

"What are your notes about today, Grace Tanev?"

I smiled on a breath, letting my hands slap against my thighs. "Today, I got a boyfriend."

"Future husband," he corrected, which made heat crawl down my neck as I smiled. I knew there was a lot I wanted to do before I had a wedding, a lot I needed to figure out before I could even *decide* if I wanted babies. But at the same time... I could picture it all with Jax. I could see us eloping to a national park, could see us jumping into a lake and trashing our tux and gown while a photographer caught it all on tape. I could see us raising a family, a little boy or girl who looked just like him.

Stealing the phone from his hand, I leaned against his chest, snuggling in as he draped his arms around me, and I held the camera out to capture us both.

"Tell me something good, Jaxson," I whispered.

He swallowed, looking down at me instead of at the camera, and he pressed a slow, sweet kiss to my temple.

"I have you."

CHAPTER 40

HOW'S THE WEATHER?

Jaxson
One Month Later

I was pretty sure Daddy P was going to kill our new guy.

We were on a hot streak, one that Aleks Suter almost ruined when he decided to get in a fight for no fucking reason. He'd been sent to the penalty box, and then we'd been scored on — bringing us to a tie with Toronto.

Fortunately for Aleks, Vince had answered that goal with one of his own less than three minutes later, and we'd pulled off the win. But as soon as we made it to the locker room, Will grabbed Aleks by the jersey and steered him down the hall to chat.

I did not envy him — especially since Daddy P seemed particularly grumpy lately. My guess was that it had a lot to do with the fact that he couldn't find a reliable nanny to save his life, and he was trying to captain a team that had an unpredictable enforcer who liked to shake shit up.

When I made it to my locker, I high fived my teammates as they passed, peeling off my jersey and pads in-between. The energy wasn't quite the same as when we won at home. There was no DJ to play our win song as we skated the rink, but there was something particularly satisfying about beating a team on their home ice.

I frowned when the last of the team had filed in, because Carter hadn't been among them — and I hated it.

He'd been sent down to the AHL again.

I knew from experience how badly that shit hurt. When I'd started in the league, I'd flopped back and forth between the two until I upped my game. I had faith Carter would do the same eventually — he'd find his permanent spot here in Tampa.

But until then, I knew how it stung, how it made you question if you were good enough.

It also sucked for us, because Carter's energy was one no one else could match. I missed the little fucker.

Reaching into my bag, I pulled out my phone, smiling when I saw a few missed texts from Grace.

Future Wife: How's the weather in Toronto? Because I'd be willing to bet it's not as great as here.

Her next text was of her in a tiny swimsuit sprawled out on a lounge chair by a pool. She had found a random house-sitting job in Thailand where she took care of the plants, packages, and a fat cat named Gegee, which meant she got to explore a new place like she loved to do.

I missed her like fucking crazy, but seeing the content smile on her face made me happy she went.

I snapped a pic and sent it back.

Me: It's cold as balls. But I'll be using that pic you sent to warm myself up when I'm back at the hotel.

Future Wife: Perv.

Me: You're just mad you'll miss out on the fun.

Future Wife: Or, you could FaceTime me and we could both have some fun...

Me: Nah.

I chuckled at the tease, putting my phone down so I could continue taking off my gear. When it buzzed again, I opened it to another photo.

This time, with her top off.

It was just ten in the morning there, the sunlight playing with the palm tree leaves above her and casting lines of shadows across her gorgeous body.

And now, I had a boner.

Me: Fucking hell, baby. You've got me rock hard in another team's locker room.

Future Wife: In one week, I'll have you rock hard in me.

Me: Now I'm definitely calling you when I get to the hotel.

Future Wife: Hmm... maybe I'll answer. If I feel up to it.

She sent a winky emoji with that, and I smirked, shaking my head. Then, Vince popped up right beside me, and I hastily shoved my phone away before he could see the screen.

"I think Daddy P is going to need a stiff drink tonight," he said, eyeing where Will and Aleks had just walked back through the door. Aleks looked smug, and Daddy P looked like he'd aged ten years.

"I can't remember the last time he went out with us."

"Well, I think we need to try tonight."

I nodded, packing my shit away as Vince went over to talk to Will.

The last month had been a whirlwind. Between the team being on a hot streak with a promising spot in the playoffs ahead of us, my personal life was in the best shape it'd ever been in. Grace and I had found a way to be a couple while also not sacrificing anything that made us individuals.

Grace had spent a couple weeks in Tampa with me, neither of us wanting to be apart longer than when I had to go to the arena for practice or a game. But eventually, she was ready to roam, that adventurous part of her heart striking to life like a match.

So now, she had various trips planned — from Thailand to New Mexico. I was happy she was going. I was even more happy that the road always led her back to me in the end.

As for me, I had hockey — and for the first time in my life, it was well and truly *mine*. My father hadn't tried to contact me since the day I told him how I felt. Some days, that hurt like hell. But most days, it felt like I'd cut myself free, like I'd shed the chains binding me to an abuser.

What soothed more than anything was that my mom had shown up in Tampa two weeks ago.

It was the night before Grace was leaving for Thailand, and when I'd gotten the call from my front gate and found my mom on the other side of it, I'd nearly shit myself.

I couldn't remember the last time she'd left the house, let alone the country.

I'd made us tea, Grace launching into action and setting up the guest room while Mom and I talked. She'd left my father — and she'd told me it had been me who had given her the strength to do it.

Still, as happy as I was for both of our freedoms, it killed me to think of Dad being alone. But this was his choice, and all we could do was love him and ask him to show up for us. If he didn't, that was on him.

Mom stayed with me until a few nights ago when we moved her into her own little condo near the beach — one I was happy to pay for. It would take time for us to heal our relationship, and I knew it wouldn't be easy. But she was in Tampa, and we were trying. That was the only first step I needed.

Grace had faced her family shortly after the media frenzy died down, too. I sat by her side and held her hand as she told them how she'd felt her entire life. I knew it wasn't easy for her, nor was it easy for her family to hear. Facing trauma of any kind makes everyone involved uncomfortable. But they listened, and so did she, and in the end, they were hugging and crying and making promises to change.

Vince was the one who jumped on board first. I'd never seen him take such a high interest in anyone other than Maven. But now that Grace was living in Tampa at least part time, he took every advantage he could to hang out with her and get to know her better.

It made Grace happy — which, in turn, made me happy, too.

Now, I was counting down the days to when I would have her back in my arms. This was apparently a common theme for me now, but as much as I longed for her, I loved that she was still the woman I met that night in Austin. We were together without her having to lose herself. I would have been in pain if it were any other way.

She was a bird with a need to move, to travel, to explore. I would never clip her wings, nor would I let her cage herself.

I wanted her to fly.

And in the end, she always came back to me.

She always came back home.

CHAPTER 41

SEASONS

Grace
Two Days Before Christmas

Sitting in the wives and girlfriends' suite watching Jaxson and the rest of the Ospreys play hard against Washington, D.C., felt a lot like Christmas had come early.

It wasn't often this happened. Most of the time, friends and family had an area dedicated for us, a place where we all sat together in a higher-level section of the stands. But every now and then, there would be a suite open, or the GM would buy a suite at an away game for us as a little gift.

Like I said — it was like Christmas coming early.

I was reveling in the feeling of being at a game, period — at getting to watch my boyfriend in his element. It was one thing to strip that hunk of a man down in the privacy of our home, to have an up close and personal view of every muscle, every lean line and hard edge and sprawl of ink. I cherished those moments.

But *fuck*, it was nothing compared to watching him dominate on the ice.

He was so hot. From the moment he stepped out to warm up and stretch, to the very last second of play, he was determined. I salivated each time he skated out to play a new game, especially when he wore his Ospreys hat backward with a little tuft of hair popping through the front and around the sides. My core would fire up when he did his groin stretches — of course, I wasn't alone in that. I had to share my fantasy of Jaxson with thousands of other hockey fans, female *and* male.

I didn't mind, though.

Because at the end of the night, it was *me* he took to bed.

Warmups were just a tease. It was when he skated into action for the first play that the real sex appeal started to ooze. He was just such a *beast*, blocking goals well before they got to Will Perry, and applying pressure to any opponent who skated into the defensive zone. My favorite was when everything would line up just right for him to score a goal. That wasn't even his job, but when he had the chance, he took it.

Watching him slice that stick through the air, hearing the sweet sound of the buzzer when the puck finds the net, getting the up top view of him celebrating? It was magic.

I especially loved when he pointed up at the box. I didn't have to see his face to know he was winking, and that he was looking right at me.

The game was an anxiety-inducing shit show, the 2-2 tie lasting long enough to send us into overtime. We won — thank God — and I immediately bolted from the suite and made my way down to the waiting area.

I'd been on a ski trip with some friends in Tahoe and hadn't seen Jaxson in ten days.

I couldn't get to him fast enough.

It was always the worst part of the night, twiddling my thumbs and waiting for him to do his after-game bike session or shower or both. At least he wasn't the last one out. He was usually far from it, in fact. But still, the wait killed me.

Finally, about an hour after the last buzzer sounded, Jaxson swung through the door with a wide grin. He dropped his bag just in time for me to leap into his arms, and then we were making out while a symphony of groans, giggles, and catcalls played in the background.

Jaxson's hand splayed the side of my face when he pulled back, his forehead against mine and a longing sigh leaving his chest.

"Fuck, I missed you."

"Missed you, too, Brittzy."

He smirked, setting me back on the ground. He grabbed his bag in one hand and my hand in the other, steering us toward the parking lot.

"Great game tonight."

"I did it just for you."

I smiled, leaning into his side.

"I got a rental car," he said when we hit the parking lot.

I cocked a brow. "Oh?"

"Our next game is on the twenty-seventh in Tampa," he reminded me, as if I didn't have the schedule memorized. "That gives us... three nights, if you count this one, before I need to get back for practice."

"So, basically — Christmas Eve and Christmas."

"Precisely. I know your parents are going to Tampa, but..."

"I think my family can survive a Christmas without me," I said. "They have Vince and Maven, and Maven's parents will be there, too."

Jaxson slung his bag into the trunk of a G-Wagon, which made me smile, all the memories of summer rushing back just at the sight of it.

"Your stuff at the hotel?" he asked.

I nodded.

"Mine, too," he said. "What do you say we swing by there just long enough to change that."

I folded my arms over my chest, leaning my weight on one hip. "What exactly do you have in mind, Jaxson Brittain?"

He crooked a grin, fisting his hands in the jersey I wore — the one with his name on the back — and pulling me into him.

"Wanna go for a drive?"

"Where?"

"Anywhere."

"Careful, that got you into trouble last time," I warned.

"It was the best kind of trouble."

He kissed me with that, and I wound my hands around his neck as I breathed all of him in. My heart never beat the same as it did before I met him. It was smoother now, steadfast — the way only a heart that belongs to another can. I felt safe in his arms. I felt at home no matter where we were.

"Well, since we missed the sunset... I guess we ride at dawn?" I asked.

"How about *you* ride at midnight," he teased, sucking my earlobe between his teeth. Chills swept my body as I bit my lip.

"You know, for all the road tripping we did, we never tested getting freaky in the car."

"Not true. We pulled off the road more than a few times, if I recall."

"Hmm... I guess my memory has just faded, it's been so long..."

Jaxson growled, swooping me up into his arms and carrying me to the passenger side of the SUV. Except he didn't open the front door. He opened the back.

"Allow me to remind you," he rasped against my lips.

"Good thing these windows are tinted."

"Think you can be quiet?"

"No chance."

"Then I really hope this sucker is soundproof, too."

I giggled as he laid me down, locking us inside and pinning me between him and those plush leather seats. As we fogged up the windows and made a new memory, I counted out all that I was grateful for — just like I had that morning I was heartbroken on the beach in Florida. That was before I knew I'd be driving with Jaxson less than two hours later, before I knew I was about to embark on a summer that would change my life forever.

It was winter now, the air frigid outside the car we were steaming up, and one truth was as clear as the night sky had been in Yellowstone.

Jaxson and I had a love that transcended the seasons.

And there was nothing I was more grateful for than that.

EPILOGUE

YES, SIR

Will

"**Y**ou've got to be fucking kidding me."

I growled the words, ripping my mask and helmet off as I skated past our wide-eyed assistant athletic trainer. She was new to the team, joining us for her first season, and I didn't mean to make her pale as a ghost with my reaction to the message she'd delivered — but I couldn't help it.

Grumpy was my natural state of being lately.

And I was *extra* grumpy at the moment from being interrupted in the middle of our practice by a trainer telling me my daughter was here.

Ava was my fucking world. Other than hockey, she was all that mattered to me. I looked forward to every minute I got to spend with her.

The issue was that she should have been at home right now with the newest nanny I'd hired — not standing in the penalty box next to the home bench.

I tried and failed to school my breathing the closer I got to Ava, and Coach McCabe gave me a nod as I passed him to let me know it was fine — but to make it short.

Ava was perched up on the seat inside the box, pressing up onto her toes to get a better look at the rink through the glass. She was watching the rest of the team as they ran drills, her mop of dark brown curls falling out of the ponytail I'd tried to wrangle them into earlier that morning.

Like me, my daughter didn't smile much. It was an unfortunate side effect to having me as a father and the only steady parental figure in her life.

But right now, her eyes were big and filled with excitement. The kid loved hockey just as much as I did, and any time I let her come to the stadium, she lit up like I'd taken her to Disney World.

Except this time, I hadn't let her come. She was supposed to be at home — playing house or running in the yard or swimming in our pool.

Instead, she was watching pucks fly.

And it wasn't her nanny standing beside her and making sure she didn't fall.

It was Chloe Knott — her kindergarten teacher.

She stood out like a sore thumb, not just because the stands were empty, but because that woman wouldn't be able to blend in *anywhere* no matter how hard she tried.

Her bright copper wave of hair was lobbed just above her shoulders and parted down the middle, her brown eyes framed with thick, dark lashes that dusted her rosy cheeks every time she blinked. Other than that blush, her skin was like porcelain, pale and smooth like she bathed in sunscreen every morning before leaving the house.

She wore a long black skirt with white polka dots and a white t-shirt with a rainbow on it. Under the rainbow, it said *no rain, no rainbow.* Jade green arches dangled from her ears to complete the look, and they shimmered in the stadium lighting the closer I got.

I remembered the way I'd felt the first time I'd met her. It was a mixture of annoyance and relief.

Annoyance, because no one had a right to be that damn bubbly.

And relief, because she'd lit up at the sight of Ava as if she were her only student.

Chloe had bent down to her level on that welcome night, looking my daughter right in the eye and talking to her like an adult. She'd managed to get Ava to smirk, which was a feat, and I'd felt the weight on my chest dissipate.

It was one thing to have Ava in a half-day of early learning last year, but to have her officially in school had put my emotions through the wringer. I didn't want her to grow up. I wanted her to hold onto her innocence forever, to always stay this young.

Knowing she was in good hands with Miss Knott made me feel at least marginally better about it all.

"I'm so sorry, Mr. Perry," she said when I was close enough to hear her. She smiled apologetically, looking at Ava and then at me. "I didn't know what else to do."

I could put the pieces together before I even got an explanation.

After the run of bad luck I'd had with nannies over the summer, I'd made sure to let Miss Knott know when I hired a new one. I'd also written consent for Miss Knott to be able to drive Ava to me should anything happen. She had already been added to my approved list from when she'd tutored Ava in the first semester of the year, but I didn't revoke that access even now that we were in the second.

The last thing I wanted was for my daughter to be stuck at school waiting on me when I was out of reach — and we didn't have any other family nearby to help.

When I joined them in the box, I immediately shut the door behind me just in case a puck came flying our way. And even though it didn't do much to block out the noise of practice, I was instantly aware of how the three of us fit in the tight space.

I was particularly aware of how close I stood to Chloe.

The modest skirt and t-shirt she wore did absolutely nothing to hide her curves, and I was as irritated as I was surprised by the fact that I noticed those curves at all.

I thought that side of me was dead. I hadn't so much as cast a woman a second look since my wife passed.

But the awareness buzzing beneath my skin proved my theory wrong.

Because I was *very* attuned to my daughter's teacher at the moment.

"What happened?" I grumbled more forcefully than I meant to.

"Hi, Daddy," Ava said, not bothering to take her eyes off the rink.

I softened, just a bit, leaning in to sweep her hair off her face and kiss her cheek. "Hey, Pumpkin."

Chloe lowered her voice a little, all while keeping a close eye on Ava to make sure she didn't fall off the bench she was standing on.

"I tried calling," she explained, her eyes sympathetic. "No one came to pick Ava up. We tried the number you left us for Ava's new nanny, and when that failed, we tried your cell, and then the emergency contact you have on file.

When we didn't get an answer, I took it upon myself. I tried your home address first, but no one was there. So..."

"You came here," I finished, pinching the bridge of my nose on a sigh. The emergency contact I'd put down was my uncle — the closest thing I'd ever had to a father. But he was a lineman, and he was on the road more than he was home anymore.

"I'm sorry," she said again, and when I looked at her, she was biting her lower lip as if *she'd* done something wrong.

I blew out a breath. "Not your fault I seem to have a knack for finding the worst nannies in the world."

"It's okay, Daddy. We are doing our best."

Again, Ava didn't take her eyes off the rink when she said those words. When I messed up, which was often, those were the exact words I used. Now, she was echoing them back to me, and Chloe smiled, glancing at my daughter before her eyes found me again.

I couldn't even find it in me to be pissed off — mostly because, at this point, I was just *tired*. I'd tried everything, from personal recommendations from my teammates' wives to working with a recruiter.

So far, every nanny I'd hired had either been unprofessional, under qualified, or unavailable for the hours I needed them. I'd dealt with everything from older women who couldn't keep up with Ava's energy to younger women who pretended to be a nanny only to attempt to shoot their shot with me when Ava was asleep.

Why was this so goddamn difficult?

If Jenny were here, she'd know what to do.

Then again, if Jenny were alive, we wouldn't need a nanny in the first place.

My chest tightened the way it always did when I thought about my late wife, the mixture of complicated emotions all too familiar.

"It's *me* who should be sorry, and I am," I finally said to Chloe, ruffling my kid's hair before I looked at her teacher again. "Thank you for bringing her here."

"Of course."

Chloe's eyes flicked between mine, those impossibly wide brown irises watching me with uncertainty.

"I can watch her," she offered suddenly, her voice louder than it had been. The offer seemed to surprise her as much as it did me, because she nervously grabbed her elbow with the opposite hand. "I mean, it seems like you're a little tied up. Unless you want to call her nanny?"

"Oh, I want to call her *ex* nanny many things," I grumbled.

Chloe smiled. "I'm happy to take her to my place, or to yours — whichever you'd prefer."

I tilted my head to the side. "Really? I'm sure you have plans."

She snorted at that — like actually *snorted*. "Trust me — I have nothing better to do."

I grabbed the back of my neck, looking at the time on my watch before I glanced behind us at where practice was in full swing. I knew if I needed to leave, Coach McCabe would understand. It was rare for me to ask for *anything*, and I was a leader on the team.

But I didn't *want* to leave.

We had a big home game tomorrow night against a team fighting us for a spot in the playoffs, and I needed the ice time.

"If you're sure you don't mind... just this one time," I clarified quickly. "And I'll pay you."

406

"Oh, that won't be necessary."

"I'll pay you," I reiterated.

Chloe offered a soft smile, her fingers twiddling with her skirt. "Yes, sir."

My nostrils flared at that, for a reason that was entirely inappropriate, and I mentally slapped myself before turning my attention toward Ava.

"You're going to go spend the afternoon with Miss Knott, okay?" I said, lifting her into my arms so I could look her in the eye. "And I'll pick you up after work."

"Can't I stay here?"

She didn't whine those words. In fact, she said them as if she didn't actually care what I responded with. Her lips were turned down, her eyes seemingly bored.

She had my feigned indifference down pat.

I hated that I'd rubbed off on her.

"Not today, Pumpkin," I said, kissing her temple. I sat her down then, squeezing her hand. "But if you behave, we can talk about you coming to the game tomorrow."

She considered that, and then nodded, but still didn't show any emotion when she said, "Okay."

Chloe arched a brow at Ava, then at me, and shook her head on a soft smile. "I'll bring her home around six?" she suggested.

"That would be perfect."

I wondered if she heard the relieved exhale leaving my chest. Knowing Ava was with her meant I could focus on practice.

Of course, I still had rage for my former employee simmering under my skin — but I'd deal with that later.

"Maybe you could have dinner with us," Ava said, and she did so on a shrug that indicated she didn't care either way. "Chef Patel always makes too much food for just me and Daddy."

I tried to give my daughter a warning glare that would tell her not to put me on the fucking spot like that, because as much as I was thankful for her teacher stepping in to help, I wasn't eager to have *anyone* joining us for dinner.

Chloe peeked up at me, and for a moment, I thought she looked pleased by that idea. But the second she saw my face, her smile dropped.

She cleared her throat. "Oh, that's okay, sweetie. You and—"

"You're more than welcome," I cut in. I hoped the words didn't sound as forced as they felt, that she didn't notice how much my teeth gritted together when I said them.

At that, Chloe tilted her head a bit, as if she could read right through the lie.

Then, she smiled. "Okay, then. Dinner it is."

I blinked.

I hadn't expected her to take that offer seriously.

I certainly hadn't expected her to accept it.

And something about her satisfied smile as she took Ava's hand and led her through the tunnel told me she knew it, too.

What happens when the grumpy goalie collides
with his daughter's sunshiney kindergarten teacher
on his quest to find the perfect nanny?
Find out in Daddy P's book: *Learn Your Lesson*
(https://amzn.to/3PtBIOY).

Can't get enough of Jaxson and Grace?
Get back on the road in this steamy bonus scene!
(https://kandisteiner.com/bonus-content/)

Don't miss out on Vince and Maven's story in
Meet Your Match (https://amzn.to/44HShes).
Enemies to lovers, forced proximity, and he falls first!

MORE FROM KANDI STEINER

The Kings of the Ice Series
Meet Your Match
One Month with Vince Tanev: Tampa's Hotshot Rookie – twenty-four-seven access on and off the ice. The headline says it all, and my bosses are over the moon when the opportunity of a lifetime lands in my lap. Of course, they aren't aware that they're forcing me into proximity with the one man who grates on my last nerve.

Watch Your Mouth
My brother's teammates know not to touch me — but that doesn't stop me from daring Jaxson Brittain to be the first to break the rule.

The Red Zone Rivals Series
Fair Catch
As if being the only girl on the college football team wasn't hard enough, Coach had to go and assign my brother's best friend — and my number one enemy — as my roommate.

Blind Side
The hottest college football safety in the nation just asked me to be his fake girlfriend.
And I just asked him to take my virginity.

Quarterback Sneak
Quarterback Holden Moore can have any girl he wants.
Except me: the coach's daughter.

Hail Mary (an Amazon #1 Bestseller!)
Leo F*cking Hernandez.
North Boston University's star running back, notorious bachelor, and number one on my people I would murder if I could get away with it list.
And now?
My new roommate.

The Becker Brothers Series
On the Rocks (book 1)
Neat (book 2)
Manhattan (book 3)
Old Fashioned (book 4)
Four brothers finding love in a small Tennessee town that revolves around a whiskey distillery with a dark past — including the mysterious death of their father.

The Best Kept Secrets Series
(AN AMAZON TOP 10 BESTSELLER)
What He Doesn't Know (book 1)
What He Always Knew (book 2)
What He Never Knew (book 3)
Charlie's marriage is dying. She's perfectly content to go down in the flames, until her first love shows back up and reminds her the other way love can burn.

Close Quarters
A summer yachting the Mediterranean sounded like heaven to Jasmine after finishing her undergrad degree. But her boyfriend's billionaire boss always gets what he wants. And this time, he wants her.

Make Me Hate You

Jasmine has been avoiding her best friend's brother for years, but when they're both in the same house for a wedding, she can't resist him — no matter how she tries.

The Wrong Game

(AN AMAZON TOP 5 BESTSELLER)

Gemma's plan is simple: invite a new guy to each home game using her season tickets for the Chicago Bears. It's the perfect way to avoid getting emotionally attached and also get some action. But after Zach gets his chance to be her practice round, he decides one game just isn't enough. A sexy, fun sports romance.

The Right Player

She's avoiding love at all costs. He wants nothing more than to lock her down. Sexy, hilarious and swoon-worthy, The Right Player is the perfect read for sports romance lovers.

On the Way to You

It was only supposed to be a road trip, but when Cooper discovers the journal of the boy driving the getaway car, everything changes. An emotional, angsty road trip romance.

A Love Letter to Whiskey

(AN AMAZON TOP 10 BESTSELLER)

An angsty, emotional romance between two lovers fighting the curse of bad timing.

Read Love, Whiskey – Jamie's side of the story and an extended epilogue – in the new Fifth Anniversary Edition!

Weightless
Young Natalie finds self-love and romance with her personal trainer, along with a slew of secrets that tie them together in ways she never thought possible.

Revelry
Recently divorced, Wren searches for clarity in a summer cabin outside of Seattle, where she makes an unforgettable connection with the broody, small town recluse next door.

Say Yes
Harley is studying art abroad in Florence, Italy. Trying to break free of her perfectionism, she steps outside one night determined to Say Yes to anything that comes her way. Of course, she didn't expect to run into Liam Benson...

Washed Up
Gregory Weston, the boy I once knew as my son's best friend, now a man I don't know at all. No, not just a man. A doctor. And he wants me...

The Christmas Blanket
Stuck in a cabin with my ex-husband waiting out a blizzard? Not exactly what I had pictured when I planned a surprise visit home for the holidays...

Black Number Four
A college, Greek-life romance of a hot young poker star and the boy sent to take her down.

The Palm South University Series
Rush (book 1)
Anchor (book 2)

#1 NYT Bestselling Author Rachel Van Dyken says, "If Gossip Girl and Riverdale had a love child, it would be PSU." This angsty college series will be your next guilty addiction.

Tag Chaser

She made a bet that she could stop chasing military men, which seemed easy — until her knight in shining armor and latest client at work showed up in Army ACUs.

Song Chaser

Tanner and Kellee are perfect for each other. They frequent the same bars, love the same music, and have the same desire to rip each other's clothes off. Only problem? Tanner is still in love with his best friend.

ACKNOWLEDGEMENTS

This series wouldn't be possible without Rhiannon Gwynne and her husband, Josh Brittain. Thank you for indulging me with multiple interviews about what it's like to be a professional hockey player as well as the WIFE of a professional hockey player. Your guidance and patience has made all the difference. I hope me naming Jaxson after you showed my appreciation.

To my husband, Jack – thank you for your endless support and love. My life is better with you in it.

To my momma, Lavon, and my bestie, Sasha – thank you both for always being my biggest cheerleaders.

To Tina Stokes, my Executive Assistant and dear friend – you are an absolute angel and I cannot put into words how thankful I am for all the hours you've spent on graphics, PR boxes and more for this series. Thank you for loving these books as if they were your own.

A huge thank you to all the amazing women in this industry who have been my writing buddies through various parts of this book. Laura Pavlov, Elsie Silver, Lena Hendrix, Maren Moore, Jessica Prince, Fiona Cole, Karla Sorensen, Brittainy Cherry – I'm honored to be on this journey with you.

Thank you to the crew at Osys Studios for bringing these books to life in audio.

To my team of beta readers: this book was THICC and I can't thank you enough for loving these characters as much as I did and for helping me polish this book to a sparkly shine. A huge and heartfelt thanks to Frances O'Brien, Patricia Lebowitz QUEEN MINTNESS!, Allison

Cheshire, Kellee Fabre, Sarah Green, Marie-Pierre D'Auteuil, Janett Corona, Jayce Cruz, Gabriela Vivas, Carly Wilson, Nicole Westmoreland, Anna, Lily Turner, Diana Daniel, and Jewel Caruso. I am so happy to have you all on my team.

To the team who helps bring my vision to life: Elaine York with Allusion Publishing, Nicole McCurdy with Emerald Edits, Nina Grinstead, Kim Cermak, and the whole team at Valentine PR, Katie Cadwallader and Staci Hart with Quirky Bird Cover Design – THANK YOU. From editing and formatting to photography and promotion, it truly takes a village. I'm so thankful for each and every one of you.

And finally, to YOU, the reader – if you've read this far, all the way into the acknowledgements? Kudos, babe. And I just want you to know that none of this would be possible without you. There isn't a day that goes by that I take any of this for granted, that I don't pinch myself and send gratitude bombs into the universe. Thank you for reading my books, for posting about them on social media, for leaving reviews, and for reading indie, period. You are the wind beneath my wings, and I appreciate you more than I could ever convey.

ABOUT THE AUTHOR

KANDI STEINER is a #1 Amazon Bestselling Author. Best known for writing "emotional rollercoaster" stories, she loves bringing flawed characters to life and writing about real, raw romance — in all its forms. No two Kandi Steiner books are the same, and if you're a lover of angsty, emotional, and inspirational reads, she's your gal.

An alumna of the University of Central Florida, Kandi graduated with a double major in Creative Writing and Advertising/PR with a minor in Women's Studies. Her love for writing started at the ripe age of 10, and in 6th grade, she wrote and edited her own newspaper and distributed to her classmates. Eventually, the principal caught on and the newspaper was quickly halted, though Kandi tried fighting for her "freedom of press."

She took particular interest in writing romance after college, as she has always been a die hard hopeless romantic, and likes to highlight all the challenges of love as well as the triumphs.

When Kandi isn't writing, you can find her reading books of all kinds, planning her next adventure, or pole dancing (yes, you read that right). She enjoys live music, traveling, hiking, yoga, playing with her fur babies and soaking up the sweetness of life.

CONNECT WITH KANDI:

NEWSLETTER: kandisteiner.com/newsletter
FACEBOOK: facebook.com/kandisteiner
FACEBOOK READER GROUP (Kandiland):
facebook.com/groups/kandilandks
INSTAGRAM: Instagram.com/kandisteiner
TIKTOK: tiktok.com/@authorkandisteiner
TWITTER: twitter.com/kandisteiner
PINTEREST: pinterest.com/authorkandisteiner
WEBSITE: www.kandisteiner.com
Kandi Steiner may be coming to a city near you! C
heck out her "events" tab to see all the signings
she's attending in the near future:
www.kandisteiner.com/events

9 781960 649195